Abattoir of Dreams

Mark Tilbury

The Abattoir of Dreams
Mark Tilbury 2020
Cover Art by Emmy Ellis @ studioenp.com © 2020

Second Edition Published by Red Dragon Publishing 2022
ISBN; 978-1-7397319-3-9

Praise for The Abattoir of Dreams

"The Abattoir of Dreams is darkly impressive the tension and sense of foreboding that radiated from each page made this a hard book to put down..." Lorraine Rugman - The Book Review Café

"Dark and cruel but incredibly compelling. I can see this one ending up in my top 10 books of the year and it will probably haunt me for a while yet." Eva Merckx - Novel Deelights

"This is a masterpiece of writing with nothing like it around. Very violent and descriptive and extremely addictive." Susan Hampson - Books From Dusk Till Dawn

CHAPTER 1

Nurse Emily Dixon fussed with my bedsheet and fixed me with a smile that seemed more professional than friendly. 'There's someone here to see you, Michael.'

'Who?'

'Detective Inspector Carver. Thames Valley police.'

'Has he found my memory?'

'I think it's more serious than that.' She left, replaced by a tall, slim man in a charcoal suit.

'Hello, Mr. Tate.'

There was something about his lopsided grin I didn't like. Half-sincere, perhaps? 'Hello.'

'I see they've given you your own room.'

Wasn't I the lucky one.

He sat on a chair next to the bed. 'Do you know why I'm here?'

'No.' I wiped sweat off my forehead with the back of my hand. There was a fan on top of a five-drawer unit by the window; its blades didn't so much as spin but lurch, like a buckled wheel. Next to the unit, a wheelchair, my only mode of transport in this brave, new, paralysed world. If anyone ever bothered to hoist me out of the bed, that was.

'Look at me when I'm speaking to you, Michael. Didn't your mother teach you any manners?'

This sudden change of tone sent a shiver through my body. I didn't have a clue whether my mother had taught me anything; I didn't even remember her. I looked into his pale blue eyes; they seemed to glisten in the afternoon sunlight pouring through a small window behind the bed.

'That's better,' he crooned. 'You can tell a lot from a man's eyes.'

The room didn't seem to have enough air. I wanted to run to the window. Dive through it. Put an end to this eternal nightmare of paralysis and amnesia.

'You look better than the last time I last saw you.'

'Last time?'

'I've been to see you three times, Michael. First time, you had tubes sticking out of everywhere. Second time, you were still in a coma. Not very chatty.' He grinned, seemingly pleased with his own lame joke. 'But, today, hey presto, the wanderer returns.'

'Why are you here?'

He ignored my question. 'Funny things, comas; neither dead nor alive. Strange sort of limbo.'

'If you say so.'

'Have you remembered anything yet? Doctor claims you're suffering from amnesia.'

'I don't remember a thing.' The truth.

'If I was to be cynical, Michael, I might think your memory loss was a tad convenient. But, just for the record, let me help you with the events of Monday, June twenty-first; the night you walked to the top of Evenlode flats and tried your hand at flying. A witness said you came home from work at nine-fifteen. She remembered you because you always dragged your work bag up the metal handrail and pissed her off.'

'Work?'

'The George Hotel in Feelham. You were a washer-upper. A dish-jockey. But, that's not relevant, Michael. Suffice to say, you left work at eight forty-five, and clunked your way upstairs at nine-fifteen. Our witness says she heard a lot of banging and thudding coming from your flat, but she just assumed you were having sex. Then, at ten thirty-five, according to two eyewitnesses, you jumped off the roof. So, that just leaves the missing hour and twenty minutes when you stabbed your girlfriend to death with a kitchen knife.'

My heart stopped. 'What?'

'Murdered her in cold blood, Michael.' He spoke the way some adults speak to old people as if they're all deaf and daft. 'Stabbed her twenty-one times.'

'My girlfriend?'

'Becky Marie Coombs. Name ring a bell?'

It didn't. How was I supposed to react to the news I'd killed my girlfriend if I didn't even remember her? It felt as if Carver was describing a nightmare which had happened to someone else.

'Did you let yourself into your flat, or did Becky let you in?'

'I don't remember.'

'Course. I forgot. All Dumbo's memories fell out of his ears when he hit that builder's van. Let me help you. Tell you what I think happened. You got home after working your bollocks off in that hotel kitchen. Only thing you're bothered about is a drink to unwind and hitting the sack, right?'

'If you say so.'

'You like a drink, don't you, Michael?'

'I don't know.'

'You do. Becky's mum called you a piss-head, but that's neither here nor there. So, you let yourself in, and then you realise your worst nightmare. Becky's in bed with another man.'

'I don't—'

'I'll tell you this for nothing, son: I would have been bloody furious as well. How dare some dirty dog get into your bed and soil your sheets?'

The room was stifling. Suffocating. There was an oxygen cylinder by the door. I almost called out for a nurse to come and connect me up to it.

'Let's face it, Michael, you've not got much going for you, have you? A shitty job in a shitty hotel. Crap pay. Crap hours. A drink problem. A face like a smacked arse. If life was a pair of underpants, you'd be a skid mark, right?'

'Could you open the window?'

He didn't seem to hear me. 'Do you know how I do my job, Michael?'

'No.'

'I imagine myself in the same situation as the criminal. Ask myself what would I do if I came home knackered from work and found my bird in bed with a stranger. A fucking freeloader. And here's the truth: I'd want blood, too. Not the man's. No way. Uh-uh. That slimy twat has no contract with me. No promises to stay faithful. No declarations of undying love. Just a dirty little opportunist. But, Mrs. Carver, bless her, well, she swore to be mine and mine alone. Not get in the sack with someone else as soon as my back's turned. Open her legs to the first dirty bastard who paid her a compliment. Are we thinking the same thoughts, Michael?'

'I—'

'Of course we are. It's a universal truth no man is willing to share. What's his is his. So, I'd throw out the imposter. Naked if need be. Then I'd do the same as you Michael. I'd stab the bitch to death in a jealous rage.'

I focussed my attention on the knackered fan. It looked the way I felt.

'Twenty-one stab wounds, Michael. And you expect me to believe you don't remember a single one of them?'

'I don't.'

'What about the one in her neck?'

'I need water.'

'Or the ten in her left breast?'

'Please. I don't—'

'Was the breast significant, Michael? Maybe the bloke was sucking her tit when you caught them at it?'

My chest felt as if a boa constrictor had coiled itself around me and was squeezing for all it was worth.

'You stabbed her in the eye, Michael. Was that symbolic?'

I shook my head. What did he want me to say? Oh, yes, come to think of it, I did mutilate her. It must have slipped my mind.

Carver took a picture from the breast pocket of his suit. He handed it to me. 'This is what you did, Michael. Take a good look. See if it jogs your memory.'

I gawped at the mutilated corpse of a naked young girl lying on a blood-soaked double bed. Her hands were bound to the brass headboard with a scarf. Blood covered her upper body, and her long, blonde hair was streaked a murderous shade of red. One eye stared at the ceiling, as if searching for salvation, the other, a bloody unrecognisable pulp, bore no relation to its sightless counterpart.

'Becky Marie Coombs. Twenty-one years of age. Do you recognise her, Michael?'

Of course I fucking well don't. How many more times? 'No.'

'Her mother says you were with Becky for three years.'

Three years, three minutes, it made no difference to my blank memory.

'That's a long time, Michael. You must have been in love.'

I agreed, tired of telling him I didn't remember.

'Must have been a hell of a shock?'

'What?'

'Seeing her in bed with another man. At her, like a stray dog on heat. Fucking her. Touching her. Handling stolen goods.'

I put the picture on the bed. Face down. A nasty, queasy feeling in my stomach.

'Come on, Michael. You can tell me. I get it.'

'I can't tell you anything.'

He picked up the picture and looked at it. 'Pretty girl, I should imagine. Long, blonde hair. I can't quite make out the colour of her eyes.'

'Can you ask the nurse to get me a glass of water?'

Carver continued to study the picture. 'They look grey to me. Well, the one you didn't butcher does.'

5

Why couldn't I be in a shared ward?

'Nice lips, too,' Carver went on. 'What you might call cock-sucking lips.'

Shut up. Shut the fuck up. Leave me alone.

'Was she giving him a blow job, Michael?'

'I don't—'

'Or on top of him? In the saddle, so-to-speak?'

'Nurse?'

Carver put the picture back in his jacket pocket. 'We will find out, Michael. It'll be much better for you, if you cooperate. You understand that, don't you?'

'How can I when I don't remember?'

'I don't believe you. You're concocting this memory loss nonsense. The way some murderers claim they've heard voices telling them to kill. What a load of bollocks that is. How come no one else can hear these voices?'

'How should I know?' My head felt as if it was filled with thick fog.

'You'll get life for this, Michael. That's a fact. If you had one ounce of decency, you'd say what happened. Not for my sake. I'll still go home to Angie tonight, eat a nice steak dinner and watch TV. Get in my comfy bed and sleep peacefully. Do it for Becky's mother. She's the one suffering. You've robbed her of the chance to watch her only daughter get married and have children. All because you couldn't control your emotions. How does that make you feel?'

Like he was talking to someone else. Someone I was vaguely related to.

'I think you're a lying little shit.'

Something collapsed in my stomach. Well, the part of it I could still feel. I was paralysed from the waist down. 'I'm not.'

'Let me tell you this for free, Mr. Tate: you can't kid a kidder.'

'I'm not trying to kid any—'

'They say you'll have to piss into a bag for the rest of your life. Do you think that's fair recompense for what you've done?'

6

'No.'

'Damned right it isn't. So, tell me, can you still feel your balls?'

I shook my head.

He pulled aside the thin sheet covering my legs and sucked in a breath through clenched teeth. 'Looks like your football days are over.'

I called for the nurse.

Carver put a finger to his lips. 'No one can hear you, Michael. Between me and you, the hospital staff can't wait to get rid of you. They have a duty of care, but no one likes a murderer.'

'Look, if I knew anything, I'd tell you.'

'The detective inspector in me thinks different. The detective inspector in me reckons you're putting on an act.'

I watched in horror as his hand slid up my leg and rested on my thigh. 'What do you think you're doing?'

He pursed his lips. 'Me? Questioning a Prime Suspect about the murder of his girlfriend.'

I looked at his hand. 'I mean—'

'What?'

I pushed myself back against my pillows, trying to move away from him.

Carver moved up to my crotch. In an instant, he grabbed my balls. Like a snake striking. 'How does that feel?'

I couldn't feel a thing. Thank heavens for small mercies. 'Get off me!'

'You could say I've got you by the balls. How would you like me to give them a little squeeze?'

'Nurse.'

'Or how about I cut them out of the sac and take them home for my dog's dinner?'

'You can't talk to me like this.'

'I can talk to you any way I please, Michael. Becky's mother said there was always something she didn't like about you. Something sinister. Like you were hiding something. What were you hiding, Michael?'

'I don't know.'

'Did you fantasise about killing Becky?'

'I—'

'Did you plan it?'

'I thought you said I found her in bed with a—'

'Just a theory, Mikey. Here's another: you're a sexual sadist.'

Why was he calling me Mikey? 'A what?'

'Someone who likes torturing women. Gets off on pain. Perhaps you tied her to the bed and tortured her with that knife. Put her through hell until you finally lost it in a frenzy of lust. Is that right, Mikey?'

My breath froze as I watched his hand manipulate my private parts.

'Are we in the right ballpark, Michael?'

'I—'

'How old was Becky?'

'I don't know.'

'Let me help you. Twenty-one. In the prime of her life. No age to die, right? Twenty-one stab wounds. Do you see a link, Michael? One for every year that poor girl was alive. So much hate. So much rage. You fucking sadistic, little twat.'

I looked away.

Carver retracted his hand and smelled his fingers. 'You need a bed-bath, son. You stink.'

I relaxed my grip on the edge of the mattress. I tried to take slow, even breaths. My heart thudded in my chest.

He took a knife out of his jacket pocket. A penknife with a foldaway blade. 'You know what this is, Mikey?'

I watched him unfold the blade and run it across the tip of his index finger, drawing blood. 'Good and sharp. Just as you like it. Cutting is good for the soul, isn't it, Mikey?'

I wanted to tell him my name was Michael, not Mikey. Why was he calling me that? But, my tongue felt as useless as my legs.

'I reckon it might be a good idea to cut your balls out. I reckon they'd taste sweet on toast.'

I willed my useless legs to kick out. Protect me from this madman. Unfortunately, their kicking days were well and truly over.

'Or perhaps you'd prefer I gut you like a fish?'

'Nurse.'

'The nurses can't help you, Mikey. They're busy looking after sick people.'

I called out again. The word echoed around my head.

'You're never going fishing with that tackle again.' He moved the blade close to my penis.

'Please.'

'I ought to castrate you, you filthy little pervert.'

At least I wouldn't feel it. I could just bleed out and be done with it. Endless black death.

Carver shook his head and withdrew the knife. He folded the blade and put it back in his pocket. 'You deserve to suffer. The consultant tells me you've fractured two vertebrae. I dread to think what will happen to you in prison, with all those horny bastards waiting to get their grubby mitts on you.'

'Why are you doing this?'

Carver sighed. 'I'm just calling it like it is, Michael. I don't want you to be under any illusion. It's a blessing you can't feel your arse.'

I looked away from his smug chops and stared at the peeling yellow paint on the wall.

'If you tell me the truth, tell me what really happened the night you murdered Becky Coombs, I might put in a good word for you. See if the screws can't keep an eye out for you.'

'If I killed this girl, I deserve all I get.'

'There's no "if" about it, son. You killed her. That's what we call a stone-cold fact. Stabbed her with a kitchen knife. Cut and dried case, you might say.'

'I don't know what you want me to say.'

'I want you to tell the truth.'

9

'I don't remember.'

'Do you seriously expect a court to believe you have no recollection of your despicable crime?'

I didn't.

'Next time I visit you, we can go for a little walk in the garden. It's lovely this time of year. Lots of pretty flowers. Do you like flowers?' He didn't wait for an answer. 'Becky's mother puts fresh flowers on her daughter's grave every Sunday, without fail. Said she goes there every day to talk to her. Terrible thing for a mother to have to do.'

'I know.'

'You know jack shit, Tate. Have you ever had to put flowers on your daughter's grave?'

'I haven't got a daughter... have I?'

Carver grinned and touched the tip of his nose with his index finger. 'That's for me to know.'

I tried to shut my mind off. Tell myself he was just messing with my head. But, now he'd planted the seed, I was powerless to stop it growing.

'So, what do you say, Michael? Want to go for a walk next time?'

'I can't walk.'

Carver nodded towards the wheelchair sitting idle against the wall. 'Don't be so pedantic. I meant in the wheelchair. I don't mind pushing. My treat.'

'I don't want to go outside.'

'Fresh air might do you good. Help to jog that memory of yours.'

'I doubt it.'

'Never try, never know. That's what my mother used to say to my old man. Lazy bastard never listened. Conducted most of his life from an armchair unless he went to the boozer to warm up his fists. I'd call that a waste of life, wouldn't you?'

'If you say so.'

'We'll go for a nice walk amongst the rhododendrons.'

'I—'

'Michael William Tate, I'm placing you under arrest on suspicion of

the murder of Becky Marie Coombs You do not have to say anything, but anything

you do say will be taken down and may be given in evidence. Do you understand the charge?'

'Yes.'

'Good. I'll be back to see you soon.'

I watched him leave the room, my upper body alive with goosebumps.

CHAPTER 2

I pinched the skin on my forearm hard enough to draw blood. This had to be a dream, right? People like Carver didn't exist in the real world. He had to be a figment of my imagination. I tried to process his words, but it was like trying to fashion a cow from minced beef.

'Twenty-one stab wounds. Do you see a link, Michael? One for every year that poor girl was alive. So much hate. So much rage. You fucking, sadistic, little twat.'

I shivered, in spite of the stifling room. I tried to swallow. My throat felt as dry as burnt toast. Had Carver really put his hand on my leg? Slid it up towards my groin? Touched my testicles?

'Becky.' I spoke the name aloud, hoping it might jog a memory. Perhaps one that wasn't covered in blood. It didn't. It just brought to mind an image of that awful photograph in all its gory detail. Red-streaked hair fanning out, one sightless eye staring at the ceiling.

I wanted to convince myself I wasn't capable of such an atrocity, but the truth was simple: I didn't know who I was, much less what I was capable of. I closed my eyes and begged my mind to remember something.

Blank. And then a flash. Scattered beer cans. A man's giant hand crushing one and tossing it onto an old pine table. An overflowing ashtray. A moustache. A strong chin, peppered with dark stubble. Then, it was gone as suddenly as it had appeared. I tried to rewind, capture the image again, but it was lost.

'Shit.' I opened my eyes. A name flashed across my mind. Billy? Perhaps. I wasn't sure. I wanted my mum. Wanted her so badly. Which was strange, considering I didn't have the faintest idea who she was. I smelled a faint whiff of perfume.

Did I even have any family? I'd been awake for three days now, and Carver had been my only visitor. One doctor had told me my memory might come back in time, but not to expect anything. Expectation led to disappointment, or words to that effect. I should be grateful I could still form 'new' memories.

Like Carver's visit.

The doctor had asked me a lot of questions. Who was the Prime Minister? What was the capital of England? Stuff like that. I didn't have a clue until he told me. I wasn't even aware I was in England. The John Radcliffe Hospital, Oxford, to be precise.

I was also informed it was 1976, England was experiencing one of the worst droughts on record, and I would probably spend the rest of my life pissing into a bag. Just when I didn't think things could get any worse, Detective Inspector Carver had turned up with his sickening revelations.

I stared at the wall. At the wheelchair pushed against it.

Your chariot awaits.

I had a sudden longing to walk on grass. Barefoot. Dew beneath my feet. Something real. But, that was now impossible.

No more than you deserve.

I had no argument with that. Anyone who murdered their girlfriend with a kitchen knife deserved all they got. And more. But Carver? It was as if he got some kind of sick pleasure out of touching me. Mocking me. A detective inspector. A representative of the law. Not a...

Pervert?

I closed my eyes and relived the moment when he'd touched me. That lopsided grin. The glistening eyes. The eyes of an animal. Predatory, alert, mocking.

After a while, I drifted off into a restless sleep. I dreamed about Carver, only he was a surgeon, standing over me in an operating theatre. I kept trying to tell him I was still awake, but he just grinned at me, scalpel gleaming under the arc lamps.

'We need to cut away the dead wood, Mikey.'

'Nurse.' The word had all the strength and conviction of a soap bubble.

I called out again. Louder.

Carver kissed the blade of the scalpel which was now the exact shape of his mouth.

This time I screamed for all I was worth.

And then I heard a woman's voice, firm and efficient. 'Michael?'

I opened my eyes to see Nurse Emily frowning at me. 'Huh?'

'You were yelling at the top of your lungs.'

'Carver?'

'What about him?'

'Is he here?'

'No.'

'But I…'

'Had a dream?'

I let out a deep sigh and nodded. 'Something like that.'

'It's probably the morphine. You'll settle down as soon as you come off it. I'll fetch you a fresh jug of water.'

Would that be the same morphine which had caused the real Carver to grab my balls and threaten to castrate me? Perhaps the brain injury was also affecting my sanity.

Emily returned a few minutes later with fresh water. She poured some into a glass and handed it to me. 'I'll be back in ten minutes to change your catheter.'

I gulped the water without pausing for breath. I put down the glass and leaned back against my pillows. Just a stupid dream.

A nightmare to end all nightmares, more like.

I stared at the wall. It looked different somehow. And then I realised. There was an emergency door with a silver release bar. The words, Emergency – Push to Open, written in faint, red lettering above the bar.

Was I dreaming again? I looked around the room. Everything else was as it should be. The wheelchair, the oxygen cylinder, the bed sheet, the knackered fan, the jug and glass on the bedside locker.

I told myself not to be dumb. The door couldn't be there. It was my mind playing tricks, making stuff up. I caught a whiff of perfume, faint and lingering, which triggered a memory: a coarse, black and white checked skirt, its rough fabric rubbing against my cheek. Abrasive, yet reassuring.

The word "Emergency" appeared to be dripping.

Like blood?

I looked at the ceiling, then back at the door. Still there.

I'll take the boy tonight.

A voice I thought I recognised. A woman's. Rasping, as if she had a bad cold. My attention was suddenly abducted by the bolt on the door as it slid open, crunching inside its rusty barrel.

'Can't be happening,' I told myself. 'It's just the morphine.'

Lock the bastard out. The woman's voice again. Harsh and abrupt. It can't be good for the boy, seeing all that stuff.

The bolt stopped moving. I waited for the door to open. For the Devil himself to step into the room and claim me for his own. Take me straight to hell.

I caught another whiff of perfume. Sweet and sickly.

Sometimes it's better when Mikey's with me.

Another woman's voice, softer, which seemed to wrap itself around my heart and squeeze.

Emily came back into the room. 'What's wrong, Michael? You look like you've seen a ghost.'

I looked from Emily to the door and then back again. 'I—'

'Why are you sucking your thumb?'

'Huh?' I looked down and noticed my thumb was indeed plugged into my mouth. I yanked it out.

She changed my catheter. 'My mother reckons it pulls your teeth out of line.'

'What does?'

'Sucking your thumb.'

I sniffed the air, trying to detect if Emily was wearing perfume. Nothing. Just a faint odour of disinfectant. 'Do you know what I'm supposed to have done?'

Emily looked away. 'It's none of my business.'

'You know I can't remember a thing?'

'I'm not here to talk about that, Michael. I'm here to care for you. For what it's worth, I believe someone is innocent until they're proven guilty in a court of law.'

'Thanks.'

She fitted a fresh bag. 'Just stating a fact.'

I looked at the newly formed emergency door. 'Can morphine give me hallucinations?'

'Yes.'

I pointed at the door. 'I'm not really seeing that, right?'

'What?'

'There's a door there. An emergency door. It's got red writing on it.'

She looked at the wall. 'There's no door there, Michael.'

'But, I can see it as clearly as I can see you.'

Emily straightened up and walked over to the door. 'Where?'

'Right next to the wheelchair.'

'There's nothing here.'

'But, how come I can see it?'

She shook her head and then ran her hand over the door. Over the metal bar. The rusty bolt. 'There's nothing here.'

I sank back against my pillows and closed my eyes. 'Okay.'

'Michael?'

'What?'

'You're sucking your thumb again.'

CHAPTER 3

I slept for the rest of the day, occasionally waking up to rummage through the debris of my dreams for clues to my previous existence. Nothing. I now had a new nurse. Sharon. Not as nice as Emily. Maybe because she was on the graveyard shift, or just because she wasn't as good as Emily at hiding her true feelings. I didn't blame her either way; I was hardly going to elicit sympathy after what I'd done.

The emergency door had still been there when I'd eaten my hearty supper of dried-up fish, lumpy mash and peas. Still there when Sharon had given me my evening medication. And still there now. The lights had been turned off at ten, leaving a small shaft of light from the corridor to encroach on the darkened room. I could make out the edges of the door, along with the metal bar. But how?

I wished with all my heart I could get up off that bed and touch it for myself. Run my hands over the wall. Whoever said seeing was believing hadn't spent a day in this bloody room at the mercy of a deranged detective and an imaginary door.

It would be a long night. Apart from sleeping for most of the day, my mind was whirring like a child's spinning top. I could hear the distant chatter of the nurses at the night station. I imagined they were talking about me, condemning me, and hoping I rotted in hell for what I'd done. Perhaps even harbouring a secret wish to spike my medication and kill me.

I twisted my neck to one side and felt a satisfactory crack. My back was as stiff as a board. Emily had told me they would hoist me out of bed soon and put me in the wheelchair. Take me for a walk in the garden. I couldn't wait. A change of scene would be wonderful. So long as Carver wasn't escorting me.

Mikey?

My heart stopped. I held my breath and listened. Nothing. Just my heart thumping in my ears. And then, a loud click, followed by a creak.

'Who's there?'

What happened next shattered all rational thought. The wheelchair crept across the room towards the bed. The rubber tyres screeched on the tiled floor. I watched in disbelief as it moved alongside the bed. I heard the click of the brake being applied.

Oh, Christ, this couldn't be happening. 'Who is this?'

I reached out and touched the arm of the wheelchair. Real. I raised my hand to my mouth and bit down. Hard. I looked at the emergency door, in case someone (Carver) had sneaked inside.

Through a door that isn't even there?

Shit, shit, shit.

No answer. The bed sheet moved to one side, revealing my useless legs, and the catheter strapped to my right thigh. I lashed out and hit thin air. I tried to call out, but the words stuck in my throat. A hand grabbed mine. I tried to wrestle it back, but even though the hand was small, the grip was too powerful. Sweat dribbled into my eyes. I was lifted into a sitting position. I felt hands underneath my armpits, helping me off the bed, and into the wheelchair, effortless, as if there was no gravity. I watched my feet being lifted onto the footrests. Then, the wheelchair moved slowly across the room towards the emergency door.

The brake was applied. The bar securing the emergency door was pressed down. I held my breath as the door creaked open. I waited for a sudden rush of fresh air, but there was no change in the atmosphere. It was actually quieter, if that was at all possible.

I was wheeled through the door into suffocating blackness. 'Where are you taking me?'

No answer. I heard the emergency door close. We walked, wheeled, floated, or whatever the hell it was, for ages, on and on through the rolling darkness. I had no perception of time or distance in this unending blackness; just a cold creeping certainty I was heading somewhere, and that somewhere was going to eat me alive.

The dark seemed to leak into my brain. Something brushed against my face. I imagined a spider, huge and hairy, teeth dripping venom. It was as if my eyes had been plucked from their sockets. The air felt thicker, colder, almost tangible.

Stand up straight, you shitty little runt. A man's voice, somewhere to my left. I tried to look beyond the darkness, but it was impossible.

Do you think anyone gives a shit about you?

Perhaps I was dead. Hadn't survived jumping off the flats at all. This was my final journey. Those destined for heaven went through a tunnel of light to meet Jesus; those bound for hell went through a pitch-black tunnel in a wheelchair to meet the Devil.

I want every inch of that floor licked clean with your tongue.

The wheelchair stopped. It spun left and continued on its journey. This had to be a dream. A sick fantasy conjured up by my overwrought mind. Up in the distance, I saw a pinprick of light. As we (whoever we were) drew closer to the source of the light, the wheelchair stopped. A hand took mine again. Small and warm.

A surge of energy passed through me, calming my breathing. 'Where are we?'

Come on, Mikey. Get the coal in before he gets home. A woman's voice, soft and reassuring, but laced with panic.

I caught a sudden whiff of fried onions. Sizzling in the pan with chopped liver. The thought of it made me salivate. A woman's hand flashed in front of my eyes, chipped red nail polish and a plain wedding band.

There's a shilling for the fair, if you're a good boy. You can go to Aunt Jean's after school.

I liked the idea of that. Hot dogs, with tomato ketchup and mustard. Toffee apples waiting to destroy fillings. Helter-skelter rides and the dodgems. The Ghost Train. Hook-a-duck. Cool stuff. A kids' paradise. But, I wasn't a kid, I was a grown man – murderer – on the scariest ride of his life. This beat the ghost train hands down.

The brake released, and we moved forward again. On and on through the rolling darkness towards that tiny speck of light. By the time we emerged onto a dimly lit street of terraced houses, I was convinced I was dead. Had to be. It would explain everything. Carver, the emergency door, the invisible pusher.

Rain swirled in the streetlights. Odd, considering not one drop fell onto me. No wind on my face either. I sat in the street, facing a house with a number "19" hand-painted on the bare wooden door. Three stone steps with a black handrail led up to the front door. The garden was overgrown with weeds. A small brick wall stopped the jungle from spilling out onto the street.

'Where is this?'

As usual, my question went unanswered. A curtain moved to one side in the front room window. I saw the shadowy shape of someone looking along the street. The curtain dropped back into place and the shape vanished from view.

Something crashed. A metal dustbin lid. A man's voice. Singing. Sort of. Danny Boy, the words slurred and mashed together. I watched him lurch along the street. A big man, over six feet tall, broad, shoulder-length brown hair pasted to his face by the rain. The same rain which wasn't even touching me.

As he staggered closer, I realised he was heading straight for me. He would walk right into me. He stopped a few yards away and leaned against a wall. Danny Boy petered out into a few dry croaks as he fumbled in his denim jacket and pulled out a packet of cigarettes. He took a few attempts to get one lit. Then, he lurched towards me.

I closed my eyes and braced myself for the inevitable collision. But, it didn't happen. He walked straight through me. Like a ghost, you might say. Or, perhaps, I was the ghost. Either way, I didn't feel a thing.

He staggered up the steps and hammered on the door.

No answer. He kicked the door twice and almost toppled backwards down the steps. The handrail saved him. 'Sarah? Open this fucking door.'

The bedroom window opened. A woman leaned out, her dark hair tumbling in front of her eyes. 'Where's your key?'

'I forgot it. Lemme in.' He turned around and flicked his cigarette butt in my direction. It landed in a puddle and made a little ksss sound as it went out.

'I don't want you starting on me. I'm tired.'

'Hurry up! I'm fucking soaked.' He muttered something under his breath as she closed the window.

Who the hell were these people?

As the woman opened the door, the man grabbed her by the hair and head-butted her. 'Don't you tell me what to do, you fucking bitch.'

'Get off me. I'll call the pol—'

'See what happens, if you do.' With that, he pulled her out of the house by the hair and shoved her down the steps. She landed on her back, her head smashing against the concrete path.

'You can spend the night out there.'

I tried to get out of the wheelchair, and go to her assistance, but I couldn't move. I thought she was dead. Her head was at a weird angle. Blood mingled with the rain.

'Call an ambulance,' I shouted. 'Someone call an ambulance.'

The street remained eerily silent, save for the rain.

'For God's sake, someone help her.'

The bedroom window opened, and the man leaned out. 'Sweet dreams, you filthy whore.'

The woman stirred. Her hand flopped onto her chest. Blood ran from the corner of her mouth.

He banged the window shut. There was something familiar about him. I searched my elusive memory. Blank.

21

The rain came down hard now, bouncing off the pavement and torpedoing the puddles. I reached up and touched my hair. Dry. My pyjamas, too. It was as if I had an invisible umbrella protecting me.

After a while, the woman sat up. Even though her face was covered in blood, and her hair was sodden and matted, I could still tell she was a pretty woman. No, pretty wasn't quite the right word. Handsome?

She touched her nose with a shaking hand. 'Shit.'

'Are you all right?' I called. The words seemed both inadequate and pointless, considering no one could actually see me or hear me.

'I'm leaving him,' the woman promised herself. 'That's the last time he ever hits me.'

'Hello?' I shouted.

The woman hauled herself up, holding onto the handrail for support. She hobbled out of the front garden and into the street, one hand clutching her injured face, as if trying to hold it in place. She came close enough to make contact, but passed right through me. I hate him. I hate him. I hate him.

I felt a sudden surge of pain spreading out from the bridge of my nose. Her words chanted inside my head like a mantra. I smelled a faint whiff of perfume, and the warmth of her body lingering on my skin.

I watched her hobble up the street to a house about five or six doors away. She banged on the door. She turned and looked right at me. You're my little love-bug, Mikey. And then she was gone, whisked inside the house by another woman.

I wanted to fall to my knees and sob forever. Without warning, I was wheeled away from the street and back into the tunnel. On and on, a thousand questions burning my mind.

As the wheelchair butted open the emergency door, I didn't know whether to laugh or cry. All I could think of, as those invisible hands helped me back into that hospital bed, were the words the woman had spoken, You're my little love-bug, Mikey.

I watched the wheelchair roll back to its place by the wall. The emergency door closed, and the rusty bolt slid along its shaft. A few minutes later, I fell into the deepest dreamless sleep I'd ever had in my life.

CHAPTER 4

Emily woke me up mid-afternoon the following day. 'You've been out for the count.'

My mind felt like sludge. 'What time is it?'

'Half two.'

'Jesus. I...'

'What is it?'

I stared at the emergency door. Still there. Only now, written on the main body of the door in spidery red paint, were the words my little love-bug.

'Michael?'

Maybe I was still asleep. Emily was just another part of the dream. I shook my head and averted my eyes.

'What's wrong?'

'It's nothing.' I looked again. The message was still there. I wanted to ask Emily if I could touch her, just to make sure she was real.

'How's your pain?'

My head felt fit to burst. Or, more precisely, my nose did. 'Can I ask you something?'

'Okay.'

'Is it possible to have a dream while you're still awake?'

She fussed with the bedsheet. 'Some people reckon there's a twilight world where you're neither asleep nor awake. I'm not so sure. The mind's a funny thing. Can you still see the door?'

'No,' I lied. 'I just wondered.'

'You've had a traumatic head injury, Michael. It's bound to affect you. Anyway, there's someone here to see you.'

Please don't let it be Carver. 'Who?'

'His name's Jimmy. Jimmy Pearce.'

I didn't recognise the name. At least it wasn't Carver. I thanked heaven for small mercies.

'Says he's a friend. Worked with you at the hotel.'

'I don't remember.'

'Do you want to see him?'

I hesitated. What if Jimmy was the man from the street? The bastard who'd set about the woman and threw her down the steps. 'What does he look like?'

'Short and bald.'

Good enough. 'Okay. I'll see him.'

Emily's description was pretty accurate. He ambled into the room and smiled at me. A nervous grin that revealed two chipped front teeth. 'Hello, Michael.'

I tried to return the smile. My mouth refused to cooperate. 'I'm sorry. I don't remember you. Don't take it personally; I don't remember anything.'

He sat down. 'You don't remember the George?'

Only what Carver had told me. 'No.'

'You were the fastest washer-up in the West.'

'Did I get a prize?'

Jimmy laughed. 'Yeah, another pile of pots.'

'How long did I work there for?'

'Three years. Almost to the day before you—'

'Went home and murdered my girlfriend?'

'I don't believe you did it. I really don't.'

I looked at the emergency door. 'I don't know what to think, anymore. I don't remember a single thing. It's as if I've just read about it in the newspapers or something. Like it happened to someone else.'

'It's a bloody miracle you're still alive.'

'I wish I wasn't.'

He looked away.

'What do you do at the hotel?'

'I'm a chef.'

'How long have we been friends?'

'Ever since you started working there.'

'What did I do before that?'

Jimmy shrugged. 'Don't know. You never talked about your past. Said you didn't want to go raking through shit. I respected that. Took you for what you were: an honest, hard-working guy who liked a laugh and a beer.'

'And my girlfriend?'

'Becky?'

'How well did you know her?'

'Pretty well. Me and Lucy used to come around the flat sometimes. Nice girl. Easy going. No airs and graces.'

'Lucy?'

'My girlfriend.'

I remembered Carver suggesting I'd found Becky in bed with another man. Could it have been Jimmy? 'When did you last see me?'

'Monday at work.'

'The day of the murder?'

Jimmy nodded. 'You were acting a bit strange, you know, like your head was somewhere else. But, that's nothing new.'

'Carver reckons I caught Becky in bed with another man.'

'As in Detective Inspector Carver?'

'You've met him?'

'Worse luck. For what it's worth, I don't reckon there's any way on earth Becky would have slept with another man.'

I didn't know whether I was pleased by that, or confused.

'She loved you, mate. Really loved you.'

'I still killed her.'

'Like I said, I don't believe it.'

'But, what other explanation is there? She's dead. Stabbed to death. Carver even showed me a picture.'

'I reckon you've been stitched up.'

'By who?'

Jimmy shrugged. 'It wouldn't be the first time someone's took the blame for something they didn't do.'

'But, why would anyone set me up?'

'I don't know. But I do know you're not capable of killing anyone.'

I wanted to thank Jimmy for his kind words, but the truth was inescapable: my girlfriend was dead, and I had probably killed her. 'What did Carver say to you?'

Jimmy sighed. 'He kept trying to put words in my mouth. Told me I must have known how dangerous you were. Working with you. Friends with you. Then, he asked if—'

'What?'

'Don't take this the wrong way. As far as I'm concerned, Carver's full of shit.'

'What did he ask, Jimmy?'

'If Becky put it about... but I put him straight. Becky wasn't like that at all.'

He looked uncomfortable. I changed the subject. 'Have I got any family?'

'You never said. Just Becky.'

'So why the fuck would I kill her?'

Jimmy shook his head. 'You seemed fine when we went to Brighton a few weeks back. Lucy was cribbing on about being pregnant, and you joked she could give birth in the sea. Like a water baby.'

'Lucy's pregnant?'

Jimmy looked down. 'She lost it.'

'I'm so sorry. I didn't—'

'She's miscarried twice before. We'll try again.'

I wondered if Becky's murder had contributed to the miscarriage. I changed the subject. 'What else did Carver say?'

'Nothing much. He kept putting you down. Over and over. Called you a low-life scum. Asked me to imagine how Becky's mother must feel, losing her only daughter. It was as if he was trying to convince me you were guilty by playing on her grief.'

I wouldn't have put anything past Carver. 'Can I tell you something?'

'What?'

'It will sound stupid.'

He looked less certain. 'Fire away.'

'Carver threatened me.'

'How?'

'He grabbed hold of my balls and threatened to cut them off.'

'Jesus Christ. What sort of fucking sicko is he?'

'I didn't feel anything. I'm dead from the waist down. But, well, it's not the point.'

'You should report him.'

I laughed. 'Who will believe me? They'll probably give him a pat on the back.'

'The bastard.'

'Do you believe me?'

'Yes.'

'But, why would he do that? He's got enough on me to charge me with murder. It's not as if he's trying to get a confession out of me, is it? I don't get it. It's as if he's playing games with me.'

Jimmy shook his head slowly.

I thought about telling him about my trip in the wheelchair. The invisible pusher. The man head-butting the woman. But it all seemed far too crazy to talk about. I didn't want to scare off my only potential ally.

'You've got to try to stay positive.'

'How am I supposed to do that? I did it.'

'But, it's completely out of character.'

28

'Does anyone really know anyone?'

'I know you saved my life once.'

'Saved your life? When?'

'Couple of years back. We'd been to the pub. We were on our way home. We split at Shaftsbury Avenue. I don't suppose you remember Shaftsbury Avenue?'

I didn't.

'That's where you lived. In the Evenlode flats. I lived a few streets away. Anyway, we were both pissed. Not staggering, but singing and larking about. I got about a hundred yards up the road when a guy jumped me. Came out of nowhere, like a fucking alley cat. He had a knife. Wanted my wallet. I sobered up in five seconds flat. I thought about how hard I'd worked for the money in that wallet. How many hours I'd toiled in that hotel kitchen to get a few bob in my pocket....' Jimmy paused, looking at his hands.

'What did you do?'

'I told him to fuck off and get a job. That's when he stabbed me. At first, I didn't realise what had happened. I didn't even feel the blade go in, just something warm running down my stomach after he pulled the knife out. I'll never forget the look in his eyes; like he was a fucking zombie.'

'Jesus.'

'He stabbed me again. In the top of my left thigh. That's when you appeared. Not to put too fine a point on it, mate, you beat the crap out of him. Some old guy in the house opposite saw the whole thing and called the cops. You ripped off your shirt, tore it into strips, and bandaged the wounds as best you could until the ambulance arrived.'

I recalled none of this. It was as if Jimmy was describing someone else. Someone in a novel or a film.

'You risked your neck for me, Michael. I owe you big time.'

'I don't know what to say.'

Jimmy shrugged. 'You always were a modest bugger. I spent a week in hospital. Lost about five pints of blood. You visited me three times a day, without fail. Lucy joked that me and you were having an affair.'

'I was just doing what mates do,' I said, not relating to my words.

'Above and beyond.'

We fell silent again as I tried to imagine tackling a knife-wielding thug; it was beyond my comprehension.

'I was off work for a month. On sick pay. You could say the bastard robbed me, anyway.'

'What happened to the mugger?'

'Got six months and a fine. Heroin addict. As if that makes it all right. But, you and Becky were great. Helped out with the rent when we fell short. Ran errands for me when Lucy was at work.'

'What does Lucy think about all this?'

Jimmy looked away. 'She's in shock.'

'Does she think I did it?'

'She only knows what people are saying. She doesn't want to believe it.'

'Don't let it drive a wedge between you.'

'It won't.' His eyes contradicted his words.

'If I was looking at this from the outside, I'd be certain I was guilty. My flat, my girlfriend, my kitchen knife, my attempted suicide.'

Jimmy seemed thoughtful for a while. When he spoke, his words were measured, 'So would I. But, I'm not looking at it from the outside. I'm looking at it from the point of view of someone who knows you. Knows the real Michael Tate. The guy who would give you his last penny. Put his life on the line for you.'

'People snap.'

'When they're at breaking point. But, you were talking about getting married at Christmas. This whole thing just stinks.'

'Doesn't it just.'

'Things have a habit of working out, Michael. You've got to keep believing that.'

I wanted to. Wanted to with all my heart. But, I still couldn't see past Carver reading me my rights, and telling me he'd be back. Smiling that lopsided grin, like a broken puppet.

Jimmy stood up. 'I've got to go. I'm working four 'til midnight. I'll come back in the morning.'

'You don't need to—'

'I want to.' With that, he walked out of the room and left me with tears stinging the backs of my eyes.

CHAPTER 5

I'd spent a reasonably sane night. No trips out in the wheelchair. The emergency door was still there, along with the strange, spidery writing, but at least it had remained closed and locked.

Emily changed my catheter. 'You look brighter today, Michael.'

Relieved, more like. 'I slept better.'

'How's the pain?'

My neck, shoulders and head all screamed for attention. 'Not too bad,' I lied. In truth, I wanted to come off the morphine. Especially if it was responsible for the emergency door and the amazing self-propelled wheelchair.

'I've spoken to the doctor. He says we could take you off the morphine and try you with aspirin. See how it goes.'

Good old, common as muck aspirin. Pain relief without the trips – literally. 'Okay.'

'Your friend seems nice.'

'He is. Shame I can't remember him.'

'It's early days.'

'Will my memory ever come back?'

Emily straightened up and took the empty water jug off the bedside locker. 'It might. It's a good sign you're forming new memories. At least you've got a certain amount of function going on in there.'

More than I cared to admit. 'Is there anything I can do to help it?'

'I don't follow?'

'Like mental exercises.'

'You'll just have to be patient. I'll have a word with the doctor.'

'What about old newspapers? Could I have some? See if I can recognise anything?'

'I'll ask. Is your friend coming back to see you today?'

'He said he would.'

'There you go. A fresh memory.'

I didn't want fresh memories. I wanted old memories. Ones which would tell me what I had done in the hours leading up to my attempted suicide.

A head peered around the door – Carver's unmistakable, leering face. 'Am I interrupting?'

Emily's lips pressed into a thin line. 'Not really. But I don't want you upsetting the patient. He needs to rest as much as possible.'

Carver walked into the room. 'He'll have plenty of time to rest, once the courts have decided what to do with him.'

'He's in the hospital now, so we'll decide on what's best for Mr. Tate.' She walked out, leaving the door wide open.

Carver closed it. 'Hello, Michael. How are you bearing up?'

I ignored him and focussed on the emergency door. The red lettering.

'I didn't tell you where we found the knife, did I?'

'What knife?'

Carver sat on the edge of the bed. 'Don't play games with me. You know full well what knife. The one you butchered your girlfriend with. It was hidden up in the guttering. What were you trying to do, Michael, play a game of hide-and-seek?'

'I don't remember.'

'Of course you don't. Your memory's taken a rather convenient hike in the hills. But, it does seem odd you tried to hide it before leaping to your death. I mean, why bother? You know what this tells me?'

I didn't.

'Tells me you were in complete control of your mind. Which is a good thing because no doubt your brief will claim you didn't have a clue what you were doing. Diminished responsibility and all that bollocks. But, hiding that knife in the guttering proves, beyond a reasonable doubt, you were fully aware of what you were up to. Am I right, Michael?'

I stared at the emergency door. Tried to focus my mind on anything but Carver.

He reached into the inside pocket of his jacket. 'I thought you might like to see this.'

I looked, in spite of alarm bells clanging in my head. Poking out the top of his pocket, a knife handle, silver and gleaming.

'Do you recognise it, Michael?'

'No.'

'It's from your kitchen.'

'I still don't recognise it.'

Emily breezed back into the room with a fresh jug of water. Carver let his jacket fall back into place, hiding the knife.

'Are you all right, Michael?'

I wanted to tell her what Carver had in his pocket, but the words stuck in my throat. 'Yeah. Just tired.'

She looked at Carver. 'Ten more minutes. He needs to rest.'

Carver smiled. 'Whatever you say, Nurse.'

She walked away. Carver closed the door. 'She's a little cracker, isn't she?'

'If you say so.'

'Bet you'd like to fuck her, right?'

'No.'

'Bend her over the bed in that little nurse's uniform and have your wicked way with her?'

'No.' The truth. His words sickened me more than the knife in his pocket.

He sat back down on the bed. 'She could take my temperature any time. Anyway, we haven't got long. Better not get bogged down in your deviant fantasies.'

He pulled the knife out of his pocket. The blade was about six inches long. 'Sharp enough to cut stone, I'd say. What did it feel like to plunge this knife into your girlfriend's body over and over again?' He grinned, the grotesque image reflected in the blade.

'I don't know.'

'You expect me to believe that?'

I shook my head.

'You know what they say about liars, don't you?'

'No.'

'They need good memories. Which is a shame, considering you don't have one at all.'

'I don't know what you want me to say.'

'I want you to tell me what happened.'

'I—'

'Can't remember? Yeah, I remember.' He held the knife in front of his face, inspecting the blade. 'How did it feel when you plunged the knife into Becky's eye? Did it pop?'

I tried to imagine holding the knife. Committing the terrible crime of which I'd been accused. Remember something. Anything. A tiny fragment of truth. Was that too much to ask?

Carver pulled the sheet off me.

'What are you doing?'

He placed the tip of the blade against his lips. 'Hush little baby. I'm going to ask you some questions. Depending on your answers, we'll see how we get on. Now, I want you to understand this: if you lie, there will be a consequence. Can you remember that?'

I nodded.

'Let's start with something simple. Get you into the swing of things. Are you Michael William Tate?'

'Yes.'

'Previously resident at number twenty-five, Evenlode flats, Feelham?'

I shrugged.

He moved the blade close to my right foot. 'You can do better than that.'

'Yes. Yes, all right.'

'Was Becky Marie Coombs your girlfriend?'

'Yes.'

Carver smiled. 'See how easy it is?'

'Yes.'

'Now, I want you to listen carefully to the next question, Michael. It's a big one. The sixty-four-million-dollar question, as they say. Did you kill Becky Marie Coombs?'

'I don't know.'

He pressed the tip of the knife into my foot. 'How does that feel, Michael?'

'I can't—'

'Oops, silly me. You're dead from the waist down, I forgot. No good bringing you any porn, then?'

'Apparently not.'

'Did you kill her?'

'I don't... yes... I must have.'

'Correct answer. And did you use this knife to commit the crime?'

Fuck it. Carver wasn't interested in the truth. 'Yes.'

'Is that a confession, Michael?'

'Yes.'

'But, how can I trust a word you say? It was only two minutes ago you were telling me you have no memory. Now you're telling me you used this knife.'

I shook my head.

'For the tape, the accused is shaking his head in a manner suggesting denial.'

'Tape?'

'The one in my pocket, Michael. Right, you might feel a little prick.' He jabbed the blade into the sole of my foot.

I didn't feel a thing.

'All done.' He took a cotton handkerchief out of his pocket and wiped the tip of the blade. 'We need a blood sample to match up with our records.'

'What records?'

He ignored my question. 'Wasn't so bad, was it? Just a little prick. You don't mind a little prick, do you, Michael? Or do you prefer a nice, big fat one? I don't buy that bollocks about size doesn't matter. That's to make inadequate fools feel better about themselves. Now, I want you to hold still while I take a hair sample. One false move and you might not have a dick left to reminisce about.'

I watched in horror as he cut a chunk of pubic hair from my crotch. He put the knife back in his pocket, along with the handkerchief and the hair. He covered my body with the sheet. 'I expect you're wondering why I need a sample of your pubic hair.'

I wanted to say I was past caring, but I wasn't. A strange mixture of shame and fear sloshed around inside my head.

'Are you aware of the practice of planting evidence?'

'No.'

'How pure you are. That's almost admirable. Well, here's what we do when the evidence runs thin on the ground, so-to-speak. We get some of our own. Do you follow me, Michael?'

I didn't. But, what did it matter? I was in hell. All the rules had changed. The Devil was in charge, and Carver was just part of the plan.

'Here's the way it works, Mikey. We've got to kill a young boy. Don't ask me why. Suffice to say, he's served his purpose. Now he has to die because we don't want him telling tales out of class. Do you follow?'

Unfortunately, I was starting to.

'We thought it might be a nice idea to put your blood and pubes on the body.'

'You're sick.'

'Not as sick as you, you filthy little pervert. Not even close. Oh, and for the record,' he patted his suit pocket, 'this isn't the knife you murdered Becky with. Just one like it. The real one's still at the lab. Bagged and tagged. But don't worry, you'll get to see the real thing in court.'

The door opened and Emily breezed in. 'That's enough. Michael needs to rest.'

Carver stood up. 'Of course, Nurse. I'll see myself out.' Smooth and sickly.

'Are you all right, Michael? You're as white as a sheet.'

What could I say? Carver stabbed me and took some of my pubic hair to fit me up with another crime? It sounded almost as absurd as the invisible emergency door and the self-propelled wheelchair. Absurd, and yet so damned real.

CHAPTER 6

Jimmy came, as promised, around midday. He was carrying a bunch of bananas and a magazine. 'How are you?'

I wanted to grab hold of him, beg and plead with him to get me out of there. 'Not so good.'

He plonked himself down in the chair. 'Do you like bananas?'

'I'm not hungry.' I doubted if I'd ever have an appetite again.

He put the bananas next to the water jug. 'I got you a car magazine.'

I tried to be grateful. 'Thanks.'

'You used to like cars, but I doubt you remember that, do you? I thought it might help to jog your memory.'

'Thanks.'

'Carver came to see me at work last night.'

'Why?'

'He was just sniffing around. He knows I came to see you yesterday. Asked what we talked about.'

'What did you tell him?'

'I told him the truth. Said you can't remember anything. He suggested you were having us all on. Asked if you were always a joker. A bluffer. I told him you were a good friend, end of. He warned me about perjury.'

'Perjury? Why?'

'Who knows? It's not like I'm a witness or anything. He kept blowing hot and cold. One minute, he was trying to be my best mate, the next, a playground bully. Anyway, he got nothing out of me.'

I told him about Carver's earlier visit.

'He stabbed you?'

'In the bottom of my foot.'

'Can I see?'

'Be my guest.'

He went to the bottom of the bed and lifted the sheet. 'It's left a mark. We ought to report him.'

'No.' Louder and more abrupt than I'd intended.

'But, we can't let the bastard get away with this. What sort of copper stabs a suspect in the bottom of the foot?'

'Won't do any good reporting him. He'll just deny it. Say I'm making up stuff to stall the investigation, or something. He's pure evil.'

'But, he'll have a boss,' Jimmy insisted. 'I don't mind going down the nick and trying to talk to him.'

'Who's to say his boss isn't aware of what he's up to?'

'But, why your pubes?'

'Oh, you'll love this. He reckons they're going to kill a kid, and plant my pubes and blood at the scene.'

'Kill a kid? Jesus Christ.'

'I think he's bluffing. Trying to scare me. Messing with my head.'

'This is like some fucking horror story.'

I looked at the emergency door. It gets better, I thought. Boy, does it get better.

Jimmy sat back down in the chair. 'This whole thing stinks.'

I had no argument with that. 'Whatever his game is, I'm going down for life. Even if I am innocent, I can't remember a thing and I can't walk. How do I even begin to prove my innocence?'

'I'll be your memory,' Jimmy promised. 'I'll be your legs.'

I forced a weak smile. 'Thanks.'

'Carver visited Lucy last night as well. Kept asking the same questions he asked me. She reckoned his eyes were roaming all over her body. But, he said something odd. It wasn't threatening. Not directly. But, she said it seemed to have a hidden meaning. Or a double meaning if you like.'

'What was it?'

'He said, "It's a crying shame what happens to people when they least expect it".'

'Maybe he was referring to Becky.'

Jimmy didn't look so sure. 'Maybe. But, he said, people.'

In light of what I knew about Carver, Jimmy had a point. However, it wasn't anything substantial. It couldn't be proved, threat or no threat. I took the plunge and told him about the emergency door.

He looked around the room. 'Where is it?'

'Next to the wheelchair.'

'I can't see anything.'

I laughed. 'That's what Emily said. So, it can't be there, right?'

He shrugged.

'Emily thinks it might be the morphine messing with my head.'

Jimmy looked pleased to have an explanation. 'Maybe.'

'There's also writing on the door. It looks like dripping blood.'

Jimmy squinted at the wall. 'What does it say?'

'One bit says Emergency – Push to open. The other bit says my little love-bug.'

'Love-bug? What's that supposed to mean?'

If only I knew. I then told him about my journey in the wheelchair. Along the pitch-black tunnel. The street. The terraced house. Number "19" handwritten in the same way as the writing on the emergency door. The man walking along the street, pissed, singing, smoking. How I'd seen everything in absolute clarity, in spite of the dimly lit street and the rain lashing down. The man banging on the front door. The man headbutting her and throwing her down the concrete steps. Opening the bedroom window a few minutes later and flicking a cigarette butt at the woman. Saying, sweet dreams, you filthy whore.

'Bloody hell.'

'She managed to get up and stagger out of the garden. Here's the thing, Jimmy: she passed right through me, like a ghost. I could smell her perfume. Feel her pain. Then, she went along the street, and banged on someone's door. Before she went inside, she looked right at me and said, "you're my little love-bug, Mikey."'

'Like what's written on the door?'

'Sounds crazy, doesn't it?'

'Did you recognise the woman?'

'No.'

'Can you describe her?'

'Quite young. Pretty. Dark hair. The bloke bust her nose. There was blood all over her face.'

'What about him? Jog any memories?'

'No. He was big. Broad. Shoulder-length, dark hair. Nasty eyes.'

Jimmy stood up and walked over to the wall next to the wheelchair. 'And you reckon the door's here?'

'Yeah.'

He put the flat of his hand against the wall. 'Whereabouts is the writing?'

At least he wasn't trying to tell me the bloody thing wasn't there. I verbally guided his hand, so it was right over the word love-bug. 'Crazy shit, right?'

'Not if it's real to you, Michael, no.'

'Can you feel anything?'

'Not really.'

'What does it look like to you?'

He hesitated, and then said, 'Just a wall.'

'If you move your hand up about two feet, there's a bolt. It's covered in rust.'

He looked unsure, but did it anyway. 'Nothing. Sorry.'

I was about to ask him to try the silver release bar, but what was the point? It was about as real as the Tooth Fairy. 'Thanks for trying.'

He stared at the wall for some time before returning to his chair. 'How long have you been seeing this door?'

'Since yesterday.'

Then, Jimmy said, 'You can go to Aunt Jean's after school.'

I jumped at the sound of a woman's voice coming from this man's mouth. 'What?'

He looked confused. As if he didn't quite comprehend where he was. 'I've got to go, Mikey. Get ready for work. There's some photos inside the magazine from our trip down to Brighton. Might help to jog your memory.'

I thanked him, in spite of my racing heart.

He smiled. 'There's a shilling for the fair, if you're a good boy.'

CHAPTER 7

Carver didn't show up that day. In some strange way, I almost wished he would. At least he was real. Tangible. Even if it was in the most dreadful way possible. I tried to make sense of what had happened with Jimmy. The way he'd spoken in that woman's voice. The only logical explanation I could think of was I'd imagined it.

Like the door?

Exactly like the door.

I picked up the car magazine. Custom Car. A semi-naked woman sitting on the bonnet of a silver car, licking her lips, a cane held provocatively in her right hand, boobs blocked out by a box proclaiming Limited Edition. Tacky. I opened the front cover. A dozen or so photographs fell out. Two of them dropped onto the floor. The others were scattered on the bed.

I put the magazine on the bedside locker and picked up one of the pictures. Two guys grinning at the camera. Me and Jimmy. A pier vanishing into the sea behind us. I had my trousers rolled up to my knees, and Jimmy was dressed in khaki shorts and a white baggy T-shirt. I had no recollection of the moment. I only knew it was me because I saw myself in the mirror every morning when the nurses shaved me. No mistaking my long nose and thatch of blond hair.

The next picture was one of Jimmy and his girlfriend, Lucy. She had short, spiky hair, and was wearing a bright yellow top. They were both pulling silly faces at the camera. Two more of me and Jimmy. Three of Lucy on her own. Two of Jimmy on his own. One of me and

Lucy. None of them sparked a single flicker of recognition. But, what had I expected?

Not a single one of Becky.

I leaned over the edge of the bed. The photos on the floor lay face down. Shit. I straightened up and tucked the other pictures back inside the magazine. I was about to put it back on the locker when the cover girl winked at me. I jumped and almost dropped it on the floor.

Not real. I rang the bell for help.

A few moments later, Emily walked into the room. 'What is it, Michael?'

'Sorry to be a pain. I dropped a couple of pictures on the floor. I wonder if you could get them for me?'

'No problem.' She retrieved them and handed them to me. 'How was your visit?'

'Fine,' I lied. If you don't mind a grown man speaking in a woman's voice.

'Jimmy seems a nice guy.'

'Yeah.'

'Did he bring these?'

I nodded.

'I'll leave you to it. I'll be back in about half an hour with your tea.'

I waited for her to close the door before looking at the pictures. They both featured Becky. One on her own, the other with me. I had my arm around her shoulder. She was wearing a pair of white trousers, with a matching white blouse. She was grinning at the camera, her blonde hair fastened back with a bright red headband. The sun sparkled on the sea behind us.

I heard something, faint at first, then more defined. The sound of rushing water. I watched in utter disbelief as the sea in the photograph moved and lapped against the pebbled beach. A boat in the distance bobbed on the water.

And then, I heard Jimmy's voice: 'Say cheese.'

Becky turned to face me. 'I hope your hands are clean. This is my best blouse.'

'I thought you preferred dirty hands.' Me this time. Running my other hand through my hair.

'Michael Tate, wash your mouth out with soap.'

'Hold still,' Jimmy said.

'Get one of us kissing,' Becky said.

Jimmy laughed. 'No tongues.'

'Jimmy!' A woman's voice to his left. Out of the picture. Lucy?

'Okay. That's it. There's only so much you can do with a face like Michael's.'

'Ha, ha. You're a fucking scream, Jimmy-boy.'

Lucy wandered into shot. 'What are we going to do tonight?'

'I fancy sleeping on the beach,' I said. 'Under the stars.'

Becky shook her head. 'If you think I'm sleeping out here all night, you've got another think coming. It gets bloody freezing at night.'

I didn't seem deterred. 'I'll keep you warm.'

'What? By slobbering all over me?'

Everyone laughed.

'You can call it slobbering, if you like,' I said. 'I prefer to call it making love.'

Becky adjusted her headband. 'You can forget that. I'm not doing it outside.'

'I remember Charlie Dalton telling me he did it outside once,' Jimmy said. 'In a farmer's field. A horse bit his arse. Put him off sex for ages.'

Lucy turned to Jimmy. 'Sounds like horseshit to me.'

'Very funny.'

'Remember when you thought it was romantic to put those candles around the bed?'

'How could I ever forget?'

Lucy grinned. 'He starts doing it, then goes all frantic, bucking and jerking like a madman. Tell them what happened, Jimmy.'

Jimmy hesitated, and then said, 'Burnt my fucking toe on a candle.'

Everyone fell about laughing. And then, they were all abruptly still again. The picture returned to normal. Just a simple snap of me and Becky, posing for the camera. I turned it over. I don't know what I was expecting. Some mechanism which turned it into a 3D moving picture? The four of us hiding on the back? Ha, ha, fooled ya!

I realised I was holding my breath. I let it out and gasped for air. I put the photo on the bed and leaned back against the pillows. I wondered if I'd been transported back in time. Back to that moment on the beach. It was no dumber than being wheeled through an imaginary door to a rain-swept street, was it?

When my breathing had settled down, I looked at the other photo. The one with Becky on her own. She was sitting on a wooden bench on the pier. The sea shimmered in sunlight. A seagull pecked at a chip on the floor. Becky still wore the same clothes, but the headband was no longer in her hair. She smiled, but the smile looked forced.

She moved along the bench. 'Where's Jimmy and Lucy?'

I sat down next to her. 'Gone to have a look around town.'

'Why did you walk off like that?'

I shrugged. 'I don't know'

'I thought you were enjoying yourself.'

I turned to face her. 'I am. It's just…'

'The other stuff?'

'Yeah. I keep thinking it will be all right, and then I think about it, and I'm not so sure. I can't seem to get my head around it.'

'Me, too. Perhaps we ought to go to a lawyer, or something.'

I laughed. 'What lawyer's going to listen to someone like me?'

'You don't know until you try.'

I shook my head. 'I ain't talking to no lawyers. I don't trust them.'

'Then go to the police.'

I gazed out to sea for a while, gnawing on my index finger. The seagull plucked the chip off the wooden boards and flew off. I envied his freedom. I wanted to fly away, too. Somewhere. Anywhere. 'I don't trust coppers; they're all bent.'

'Not all of them, Michael.'

'Most of them.'

'But, we don't have much choice, though, do we?'

'We could just forget about it.'

'And let them win? I love you too much to let that happen. We have to be strong.'

The photograph suddenly stopped moving. I vanished from the picture. The ocean stilled. Back to the original picture of Becky, with that troubled look on her face.

Emily walked back into the room, carrying a tray. 'Hey, what's up?'

I put the photo down. 'Huh?'

'You've been crying.'

I reached up and touched my cheeks. Soaked with tears. 'I...'

'Did you remember something?'

'I don't know. Maybe.'

'It might help you come to terms with—'

'Murdering my girlfriend?'

She put the tray down on the over-bed trolley. 'I didn't mean that. I just meant... with your situation.'

'I'm not hungry.'

'You need to eat something.'

'Do you really think I care about food?'

'It's shepherd's pie.'

I was about to say I didn't care if it was humble pie, but I didn't want to get mad with Emily, one of the few people willing to treat me like a human being. 'Okay. I'll try it.'

She smiled. 'That's better. You might want to take your thumb out of your mouth first.'

I unplugged my thumb and watched her walk out of the room. I played Becky's words over and over in my head. I could even smell salt in the air. What the hell was this? I looked around the room, half-expecting to see Becky standing in the corner, covered in blood, her sightless eye staring at me. Accusing. Thankfully, she wasn't.

But, scrawled on the door, in fresh red lettering, were the words: we have to be strong.

CHAPTER 8

Sharon, and another nurse I'd never met before, hoisted me out of bed and into the wheelchair the following morning. Apart from the fresh writing, the night had passed without incident. I'd slept fitfully, unable to shut out the impossible moving images displayed on the two photographs.

Just being upright felt better. I tried not to think about the journey along the pitch-black tunnel a couple of nights ago. The invisible pusher propelling me towards that terraced house. It was even possible to convince myself I'd dreamed the whole thing, until I looked at the emergency door and its secret messages scrawled in red.

The other nurse, Tina, put my feet on the footrest, and then crammed my feet into bright green slippers which looked as if they might glow in the dark.

'Where are we going?' I asked.

Sharon gawped at me as if I'd just propositioned her. 'We aren't going anywhere. You've got a visitor who wants to take you for a walk in the garden.'

'Jimmy?'

'Since when have you been on first-name terms with the police?'

'Carver?'

'Detective Inspector Carver to you.'

'I'm not going anywhere with him.'

Sharon didn't look at all bothered. 'It's not your choice. You're a murderer. Murderers don't get to pick and choose who they see.'

'Where's Emily?' A dumb question. Desperate.

'Emily's off for two days. You've got me and Tina. I'll personally be glad to see the back of you. People on the ward are talking about you as if you're some sort of celebrity. But, we all know what you are, don't we? A nasty, vicious killer.'

'I don't feel well.'

'Then, it's a good job you're in hospital,' Tina said. 'For now.'

Carver walked into the room. His pale blue eyes flashed. He treated me to that awful lopsided grin. 'Nice to see you vertical, Michael.'

I looked at the door. At the words, we have to be strong. Becky's words, before I'd taken a knife to her and silenced her forever.

'It's a beautiful day outside, Michael. I thought we might take a little walk in the garden.'

'I don't want to.'

'Really? A little dicky bird tells me you need some fresh air. Isn't that right, Nurse?'

Sharon nodded. 'Might put a bit of colour in his cheeks.'

'I need my painkillers.'

'Stop being a baby, Michael. These girls don't care about your headaches.'

I almost reminded him I'd suffered a fractured skull in the fall, but I knew it wouldn't make a scrap of difference. He was enjoying this. My pain was just a bonus.

'What a wimp,' Sharon said.

'Haven't you got any pride, Michael? Making yourself look like a big baby in front of these two lovely nurses.'

Tina and Sharon walked out of the room, whispering among themselves.

Carver shook his head. 'What are you like?'

'I can't think straight.'

He put his face close to mine. 'Do you think I care about that?' Saliva flew from his mouth as he spoke. 'You sick fuckers are all the same; willing to dish it out, but when it comes to taking a bit back, that's a different matter altogether, isn't it?'

I wiped his spit from my face.

'I don't suppose you offered poor Becky some aspirin after you plunged that knife into her eye, did you?'

'I don't—'

'Remember? So you keep saying. But, I don't believe you. That's why we're going somewhere quiet. Have a little chat about that.'

On the way through the main ward, I almost called out and asked someone to help me. But, what could I say? Help, call the cops? By the time we reached the garden, I felt nauseated. He parked the wheelchair next to a wooden bench with In Memory of Joan Hurst inscribed on a brass plaque. The garden looked colourful, alive, with flowers and shrubs in a variety of stone pots and troughs.

Carver sat down on the bench. 'I love the peace and tranquillity of gardens, don't you, Michael?'

I focussed on a large bush, with blood-red flowers.

'So symbolic of life and death, flowers, don't you think?'

'If you say so.' I studied that bush for all I was worth. I played the words, we have to be strong, over and over in my head.

'You'll be pleased to know your pubic hairs are currently residing on the semi-naked body of a young boy called Thomas Wakeman. He's buried in Bluebell Woods. I doubt anyone's going to find him, but just in case they do, you'll be the prime suspect.'

We have to be strong.

'There's no end to your depravity, is there, Michael? It's a damn good job you landed on that builder's van, else Becky's mother might never have seen justice done for her daughter. Your lot always try to take the easy way out, don't you? Fucking cowards, the lot of you.'

'Says the man who's trying to stitch me up with some boy's murder.'

Carver laughed. It sounded like smashed glass. 'Wash your mouth out with soap. No one's trying to stitch you up. Your pubes are simply an insurance policy.'

'For what?'

'Don't worry your pretty head about that. Suffice to say, everyone thinks the world spins clockwise. But, it doesn't. Not on your nelly. It turns anticlockwise.'

I didn't have a clue what he was babbling on about.

'You're going down for life, Michael.'

Back to more familiar territory.

'You like going down, don't you?'

'Why are you even bothering to talk to me?'

'Because my boss says I need to nail your arse to the mast. Leave no stone unturned. And we all have to do what our bosses tell us, don't we? That's how come the world keeps spinning anticlockwise.'

'You've got the knife. You've got the evidence. I don't understand why—'

'Yours is not to reason why, Michael William Tate. Yours is but to do or die.' He pulled a long, thick needle from his pocket and stood up.

I gripped the arms of the wheelchair. I thought about trying to wheel myself away from him. Back into the ward, call for help, but, thoughts and actions were only distant cousins. He pulled my dressing gown aside, and thrust the needle into my leg, just above my right knee.

I cried out, even though I couldn't feel a thing. He left the thing embedded about half an inch deep. 'How does that feel?'

What was I supposed to say? Wonderful, Detective Inspector. Just what the doctor ordered. A fresh approach to the healing process.

'That's Mrs. Carver's best darning needle. She's a stickler for mending things. I couldn't tell you how many pairs of socks she's mended with that darned thing. Darned thing, get it?'

He pushed it in further. About an inch now. 'Women, eh? Can't live with 'em, can't live without 'em. But, I'll tell you this for nothing; I wouldn't be without my Angie. She's my rock. My calm water. My clockwise in this anticlockwise world. Just like Becky was, right?'

I closed my eyes as he pulled the needle out. He put it to his lips and licked the blood off the shaft. Slowly and deliberately as if relishing the taste. 'I always like to lick it clean.'

I watched a blob of dark red blood bloom on my leg.

'How about I thrust this needle into your eye, Mikey?'

Why was he calling me Mikey again? 'Please...'

He held the needle up to my face. 'How would you like that?'

I tried to edge away from him, but there was nowhere to go. The needle glinted in the sun.

'I want you to tell me, in your own words, why you killed Becky Coombs.'

'I don't know.'

He suddenly changed tack. 'Who's the Queen of England?'

'I don't—'

'Queen Elizabeth or Mary Queen of Scots?'

'I've no idea.'

'The Prime Minister?'

'I—'

'Wilson or Callaghan?'

I didn't recognise either name.

He held the needle in front of my eyes. 'See no evil, Mikey.'

What happened next defied logic. The wheelchair lurched forward and banged into his legs. He dropped the needle on the floor and staggered backwards. He gawped at me, grin slipping from his chops. 'What the hell...?'

I felt a slight rock as the wheelchair settled. The brake was applied. No one anywhere near it.

Carver rubbed his shin. 'What the fuck?'

I felt hysteria bubbling up inside me, like a volcano about to erupt. I pulled the dressing gown around me and tightened the cord.

'There you are.' Jimmy. Thank Christ.

'What are you doing here?' Carver asked.

Jimmy ignored him. 'Has he been harassing you again?'

'I'd watch your mouth, if I were you, Mr. Pearce.'

54

'Is that right? And why would that be?'

'You know full well why. You're a direct associate of the accused.'

'Has he been doing anything to you?' Jimmy asked me.

'No.'

'If he—'

'Don't let that mouth of yours run away with itself,' Carver said. 'You never know where it might lead you.' He bent over and picked up the needle. 'I've got better things to do than shoot the breeze with a pair of losers like you. But, before I go, I want you to remember one thing. This is a cut and dried case. If you think you can worm your way out of anything by cooking up some half-baked plot – don't bother. That applies to you more than him, Mr. Pearce. Do you see the colour of my ink?'

Jimmy ignored him and rolled a cigarette. When Carver was gone, he sat down on the bench. 'Twat.' He lit his cigarette, took a couple of deep drags, and picked a flake of tobacco off his top lip. 'What did Carver want?'

'The usual shit. He likes playing games. Before you turned up, he stabbed me in the leg with a needle.'

Jimmy's jaw dropped. 'What?'

I lifted my dressing gown and showed him.

'He can't fucking do that.'

'He can do whatever he likes.'

'No, Michael, he thinks he can. There's a difference.'

I didn't agree. From where I was sitting, Carver could do exactly as he pleased. I changed the subject. 'I've had a look at the photos.'

'And?'

'How well do you remember the day they were taken?'

'Pretty good. Why?'

'Do you remember telling us a story about Charlie Dalton having sex in a field?'

Jimmy grinned. 'Yeah. He got his arse bitten by a horse. You remember that?'

'Not exactly. Not in the way you might think.' I told him about the photos coming to life. How me and Becky were talking about going to the police. 'I could actually hear the ocean. It was so real, Jimmy. Did I ever say anything to you about going to the cops?'

Jimmy shook his head. 'No.'

'Did I have any enemies?'

'Not that I know of. Except that guy you beat the crap out of when he stabbed me.'

'What about at work? Did I fall out with anyone there?'

'No. You just did your job and went home most nights.'

'So, what the hell does all this shit mean?'

Jimmy dropped his cigarette on the ground and stamped it out. 'Seems as if someone – something – is trying to help you.'

'By making photos come to life?'

'The story about Charlie Dalton is true. That's something solid.'

It didn't alter the fact I felt like a drowning man clinging to a piece of driftwood, did it? 'That's not all. There's more writing on the door.'

'What does it say?'

'We have to be strong.'

We sat in silence for a minute or so. Then, I told Jimmy about the wheelchair lurching forward and hitting Carver in the leg.

'That sounds like something Becky would do.'

I wanted to believe that, but it was hard to have faith in something which defied logic. I wasn't even sure if Jimmy was real, for Christ's sake. 'Can you take me back inside now? I need a rest.'

CHAPTER 9

After Jimmy left, I dozed for most of the day. Before lights out, I looked at the photographs again. This time the images stayed still. I studied the one of Becky sitting on the bench, willing it to come to life again, talk to me, tell me why we'd spoken about going to the cops. Nothing. Not even a flicker. The seagull remained in situ, the chip waiting to be plucked from the wooden boards.

I looked at the wheelchair, dormant against the wall. Had it really reared up and banged into Carver's leg? I mean, obviously, that was impossible, unless someone had physically pushed it. I didn't know whether the thought of an unknown entity taking my side and attacking Carver was comforting or terrifying. The same entity which had helped me into the wheelchair two nights back and had taken me on a journey to the rain-swept terraced street.

But, this still didn't alter the fact Carver had me by the balls. I wasn't going to be saved by a ghost, was I? Perhaps my memory had been replaced by a bloody good imagination. What next? Flying around the hospital? Underwater adventures? Visits by angels?

Or devils.

I shuddered. Not only was I at the mercy of Carver, I was also at the mercy of a mind teetering on the edge of insanity. I took several deep breaths and tried to calm down. At least Jimmy was real. Tangible. Willing to help.

A little too readily?

Maybe. But, he was all I had.

Apart from the wheelchair pusher.

None of this altered the fact I was going down for Becky's murder, and quite possibly the murder of some poor lad buried in the woods. There was nothing Jimmy and the wheelchair pusher could do about that. My best bet was to save up my painkillers and take the lot in one go. Get out of it. Be free of Carver. Free of his persecution. Free of my useless body. Becky's mother would even get some sort of justice for her daughter.

I couldn't spend my whole life in jail, being dependent on others. Carver would have influence over the guards, make my life a living hell. I might get out in twenty years, perhaps less, if I behaved myself, but there would be nothing left of me. And that wasn't even taking into account doing time for the poor kid who was buried in the woods.

Part of me wanted to believe Carver was bluffing, playing stupid mind games, but, I knew he wasn't. Either he'd killed the kid himself, or some sicko friend of his had done it.

Everyone thinks the world spins clockwise, but it doesn't. Not on your nelly. It turns anticlockwise.

Two nights had passed since the 'trip' into the tunnel. The enormity of what had occurred was fading, like steam from a window. Part of me knew it couldn't have happened, but why was the emergency door still there? The writing still there? Becky's words?

Questions, questions, questions, and not one fucking answer.

The wheelchair moved. I heard the click of the brake, and the faint screech of the tyres on the polished floor. And then, it rolled towards the bed.

I bit down on my lip hard enough to draw blood.

It manoeuvred itself alongside the bed. The brake was applied. The bedsheet slipped to one side, and invisible hands pulled me up into a sitting position. I tried to call out, but my throat was frozen. My breath came in jagged gasps. My legs were pulled sideways, and then, those gentle hands were once again under my armpits. Small, perhaps a woman's?

'Becky?' I whispered.

No answer. I was helped into the wheelchair, and my feet were lifted onto the footrests.

'Becky? Is that you?'

If it was, she wasn't saying. I was wheeled slowly across the room towards the emergency door. The bolt slid open and then the release bar was pushed down. The door swung open. There was a loud screech as the rusty hinges protested. Surely someone at the nurses' station would hear that?

'Please... who are you?'

We entered the black abyss of the tunnel in silence. The door closed behind us as a jail cell door might close on a prisoner. On and on, through the darkness. Back to the terraced street. Back to that house with the number "19" painted on the door.

'Why do you keep taking me here?'

No answer. Just the rain splashing into the puddles. I looked along the street, expecting the abusive man to come staggering towards me again. Nothing. Just a car reversing into a parking bay, and a dog relieving itself against a garden gate. A tatty looking mutt, soaked and bedraggled. It sniffed at something on the pavement and then trotted towards me. Something stirred in my mind, as I watched the dog weaving in and out of gardens, sniffing dustbins and mooching.

The dog stopped near the wheelchair. It sat on the wet ground, and looked up at me with doleful, brown eyes.

'Do I know you?'

The dog wagged its tail. Once. As if sweeping rain from the pavement. It was a black and tan mongrel. Medium build. Not too threatening, but I didn't fancy putting its teeth to the test. It cocked its head to one side.

'If you're looking for food, I haven't got any. I haven't even got any...' I suddenly noticed my dressing gown had been replaced by a red T-shirt and grey baggy shorts. My legs poked out the bottom of the shorts like matchsticks. Only these legs were no longer my legs. They belonged to a child. My feet were bare. Small. Size five or six.

The dog edged towards me and licked my child's hand. He barked once; the sound boomed along the street like a pistol shot.

'What is it?' I said, in a child's voice. 'What is it, Oxo?'

Oxo barked again. More of a yip this time. An acknowledgement, perhaps? And then, something miraculous happened. I climbed out of the wheelchair and stood beside him. He licked my hand.

'Where have you been, boy?'

Oxo wasn't saying. He scratched his nose with a paw, as if to say, mind your own business.

The front door opened, revealing the same battered woman from my previous trip. Face swollen. One eye closed to a slit.

'Come on in, Mikey. You'll catch your death out there.'

Her voice sounded as if she had a bad cold, but I knew, as sure as I knew my name was Mikey Tate, that it was because my dad had beaten the crap out of her again. 'Are you okay, Mum?'

She nodded.

I walked up the steps, Oxo tagging along right behind me. 'What happened to your face?'

She touched her nose. 'Nothing. I banged into a door.'

A blatant lie. Her eyes told me that much.

'Wait there. I'll fetch a towel for Oxo.'

We stood under the shelter of the front porch and waited for mum to bring Oxo's towel. She handed it to me. I loved the smell of that towel. Oxo's special smell. My best pal in the whole world. He slept on my bed at night. I didn't need an alarm clock to get up for school; I had a ready-made one in Oxo's tongue. I also got to walk him most mornings before school.

Speaking of school, I was about to move up to secondary school after the summer. Hitting the big time. Twelve in October. One year away from the dizzy heights of being a teenager. The land of deep voices and girls. I wasn't too sure about girls; they looked dangerous to me. All boobs and giggles, like they knew something important I didn't. I was happy to just practice kissing in the mirror for now, or smooching with my pillow. I drew the line at practicing on Oxo.

We followed Mum into the kitchen. My stomach growled. 'What's for tea?'

'Liver and onions.' This came out as Libber an odions.

I saw a purple bruise extending down her face, almost touching her top lip. Some wardrobe door.

'Did you have a nice time at the fair?'

'Yes.' A lie. I'd not been to the fair. I'd bought a pack of cigarettes, and gone up the Bunky Line with my mate, Robert Harkness. It was safer to have a smoke when I was staying at Aunt Jean's. She clanged them off one after the other. Woodbines. Unlike my mother, who didn't smoke, Aunt Jean could never smell it on me.

The Bunky Line was a great place to escape to. An old train line which transported goods from the malt factory to the main railway station. I didn't know what its proper name was, we just called it the Bunky Line because we bunked off school there. There were several old air raid shelters dotted along the track, about a mile apart. We'd pretend to be soldiers, jumping into the tall grass, parachuting into German territory. One of my mates, Steve Wilson, had a gun. I don't know if it was real or not, we never got to fire it, but he reckoned his old man was in the SAS, and used to teach him survival stuff.

Sometimes, we'd stake out the malt factory, a top-secret German ammunition dump. Moving through the grass, getting ready to take out the German sentries protecting the imaginary barbed wire fence. Fine, until one night, I saw a rat making its way towards me. The bloody thing was huge. The size of a small cat. Bugger being a soldier, I ran for all I was worth, squealing like a big girl's blouse.

Mum asked, 'Did you go on many rides?'

'The dodgems,' I lied. 'And I bought a toffee apple.'

Mum smiled. This seemed to hurt her. 'I hope you've still got all your fillings.'

I returned the smile. It hurt me as well, but for different reasons. 'Yeah.'

'How's Aunt Jean?'

'I didn't see her.'

'I thought—'

'Not with all that fag smoke.'

Mum laughed and held the side of her face. 'You cheeky young bugger. Go wash your hands and get ready for tea.'

I scampered up the stairs. Oxo did his best to trip me up and beat me to my bedroom. Well, I say bedroom, it was little more than a broom cupboard, with a single bed and a wardrobe somehow squeezed into it. But, it was my broom cupboard. My private space. Somewhere I could imagine being anything I wanted to. A spaceman. A footballer. An astronaut. Owner of a dog who didn't smell like the river.

But, right now, I only had one thing on my mind; it was Friday, Dad's payday. The worst day of the week. Big Billy Tate. No one ever dared to say a wrong word to him. The bailiff had come to take away our TV once. Big man, with a crewcut. The only thing he'd left with was a black eye and a missing front tooth. The police hadn't been quite so willing to accept defeat; three of them had set about Dad with truncheons, slapped him in handcuffs, and carted him away. It had given the neighbours enough gossip to last all winter.

Steve Wilson had thought my dad was some sort of hero for that, but I knew different, knew what a coward he was. How he beat up my mum. How he threw his dinner across the kitchen for no reason. How my mum walked around for days, making excuses for him. Blaming wardrobe doors. Blaming herself. It was a wonder poor Oxo didn't get the blame sometimes.

Mum had a friend, Rachel, a kind woman who would sit at the kitchen table sometimes, drinking coffee, and listening to my mum talk about her latest incident with a fist-shaped wall or door. It was funny how adults didn't think you were paying attention just because you were a kid.

Mum called us – yes, Oxo was invited, too – down to dinner. We ran down the stairs, Oxo scooting between my legs and finding his spot beneath the table.

'You washed your hands, Mikey?'

'Yes.' A lie. I couldn't see the point in washing hands.

She walked over to the table. 'Let me see.'

I showed her my palms, confident.

'Don't fib.'

'I'm not fibbing.'

'There's a grass stain on your right hand. What did you wash them with? Mud?'

'No. I—'

'Kitchen sink. It's bad manners to eat with dirty hands.'

I did as she asked. My tummy was rumbling too much to protest. By the time dinner was served, I was almost hungry enough to eat Oxo. Only kidding. Too hairy. Although me and mum sometimes joked we could put his tail in a bowl and call it oxtail soup.

I wolfed down half of my meal without pause. I dared a proper look at my mum's face. The top half was the colour of a plum. Her closed eye seemed fixed in a permanent wink as if sharing some sort of sick joke. Her right ear was cut. Her lower lip split.

'You all right, love-bug?'

I nodded. As all right as I could be on Billy the Bully's payday. I mopped up gravy with a hunk of bread and wished with all my heart I was older. Bigger. Stronger. That I could grow bionic arms, pick my dad up, and throw him out the window. Or rush downstairs when I heard the first glass or plate smash, stand in front of my mum, and tell that bastard to pick on someone his own size. But, I was just little Mikey Tate, knee-high to a grasshopper, as Aunt Jean called me.

'Can I ask you something, Mum?'

'Course.'

I'd thought about this long and hard all night, while I'd been trying to sleep on Aunt Jean's lumpy mattress. Playing it over and over in my mind. 'Why do you stay with him?'

She looked down at her barely touched meal as if the answer lay in the lumpy mashed potatoes. 'What sort of question is that, Mikey?'

I felt Oxo wriggle closer, reminding me of his entitlement to scraps. Oxo didn't seem too bothered about my violent, bullying dad, so long as he got fed, and let loose sometimes to roam in Baker's field. 'Just wondering.'

'Wondering is dangerous, Mikey.'

So was living with that madman. 'We could find somewhere else to live. He wouldn't even know.'

She laughed. 'He's a lot of things, Mikey, but he's not that dumb.'

'I mean, he wouldn't realise until we'd gone.'

'And where are we supposed to go?'

I shrugged. I'd fallen asleep before I'd figured that one out. 'Does it matter? Just so long as he doesn't hurt you anymore.'

She put her knife and fork on her plate and pushed it away. 'You don't understand.'

But, I did. He beat the shit out of her, and she kept on crawling back for more. Even Oxo wouldn't have stood for that, and he was only a dumb mutt. 'Then explain, Mum.'

'It's not that simple. For starters, we've got nowhere to go.'

'Can't we go to Aunt Jean's?'

'Don't you think your father would come looking for us there?'

True. Aunt Jean was Dad's sister. The first place he would probably look. Apart from Rachel, who lived a few doors along the street, Mum didn't really have anyone else to call on. 'But, there must be somewhere we can go.'

'There isn't,' she snapped. 'So we'll just have to stay here.'

'And wait until he kills you?'

'He's not going to kill me.'

Her face told a different story. Sometimes, in the mornings, before she'd put on her makeup, you could see tiny scars littered all over her face. Battle scars, from the most one-sided war ever. Suddenly, I wasn't hungry anymore. I took my plate to Oxo's bowl and scraped the leftovers on top of some dried Bonio biscuits. Oxo tucked in, snout down, backside in the air.

I took Mum's plate to the sink and put it on the side.

'He's not all bad, Mikey.'

I almost laughed. 'Really?'

'You don't see the other side of him.'

'I'm not sure I want to.'

'He can be quite loving, sometimes.'

Oh, yes, I'd forgotten all about that. The same Billy Tate who sometimes cried and told Mum how sorry he was after his latest drunken outburst. Who swore blind he would change. Stay out of the pub. Keep away from his precious mates. Go for counselling. Get a better job. Try not to step on the cracks in the pavement.

Oxo finished his meal and slurped water. Schlupp, schlupp, schlupp. Good clean water that didn't turn your brain to mush and your fists into weapons, like booze did. My dad could learn a lot from Oxo.

I'd thought about talking to a teacher. There were a couple of decent ones who didn't bawl at you for no reason. Mr. Griggs seemed like someone who might listen to a boy who feared his mother would get hurt bad enough to put her into a grave.

'Go on up to your room, Mikey. See if you can get to sleep before he comes home.'

That gave me until about midnight. Plenty of time under normal circumstances. But, these were not normal circumstances. I would be awake until that bastard had done his worst. Probably all night.

CHAPTER 10

I lay on my bed, Oxo curled up at my feet; impressive, considering those feet hadn't seen a bath all week. I tried to imagine a world without my dad, Billy the Bully. Billy the Drunk. Billy the Bastard. Why was I such a puny kid? Billy the Bully could probably flick me over with his little finger.

In my head, I was Superman, flying through the air, wind beneath my cape, fist held out in front of me. Invincible. Untouchable. The ability to fly through solid brick walls. I'd been sent to Earth to beat up Billy the Bully and save the world from his sledgehammer fists.

Oxo farted and spoiled the moment. Liver and onions, with a dash of sewer. I held my nose. 'You stink.'

Oxo looked sheepish, if that was at all possible for a dog. He grinned at me in that odd way he had. As if baring his teeth to attack, but really showing love.

'You're sticking to your own food in future, if you keep stinking out my room like that.'

He rested his head on his paws and fixed me with a doleful look. Apart from my mum, I loved that dog the most. He was my best friend. I could chat away to him for ages, moaning and pouring out all my secrets, and he never once seemed to get bored. He would watch me, in that strange knowing sort of way, as if taking it all in. And the best thing about it? He wouldn't tell anyone. From my hatred of my dad, to my secret crush on Karen Bridges, it all stayed locked in his head.

At least there was no school in the morning. Even if I didn't get any sleep, I didn't have to force myself to stay awake through a load of boring lessons. Just stay in bed until the afternoon, and then take Oxo along the Bunky Line, meet up with one of my mates, and doss around. There was a fizzy drinks factory nearby. The Creamery. God alone knew why it was called that, but they made the best fizzy drinks ever. Cream Soda, lemonade, orangeade, limeade, and dandelion and burdock. And here was the best bit: they used to leave the storeroom window ajar. If you got a long enough stick and hooked it through the gap, you could flip the latch and open the window right up. We'd often pinch a few bottles, and disappear up the Bunky Line, as if we were the smartest kids on the planet and adults were too dumb to mention.

We would throw the empty bottles against the air raid shelters, pretending they were hand grenades, watching them explode in showers of glass. My childhood was all right in some ways. I had good mates, the Bunky Line, Oxo, and my mum. The only thing spoiling it, putting a great big skid mark on it, was my dad. That man-mountain, with the angry eyes. Even his fucking moustache scared me, crawling across his top lip like a caterpillar from hell.

I looked at Oxo and wished with all my heart I could train him to tear the bastard to shreds. Unfortunately, Oxo didn't look capable of tearing a fly to shreds. His teeth were more for noshing than gnashing.

The silver alarm clock on the bedside table told me it was just gone six-thirty. Five more hours before Billy the Bully came home and started World War Three. Why couldn't he just die of a heart attack or something? One of our teachers, Mr. Warwick, had gone on holiday last summer and never returned. He'd had a heart attack in France and died. A nice bloke. Still young. If God could kill someone like Mr. Warwick, then why couldn't He do the right thing and kill my dad? It didn't seem fair.

I tried to remember when I was little, if my dad had always been such a monster. It was quite sketchy, but I recalled him taking me to school once when I was about six. He'd perched me on top of his shoulders and made me feel about ten feet tall. I also remembered him taking me fishing once, but I hated it. Maggots. Ugh! Disgusting things, wriggling around in a plastic tub. Putting a fishhook between their eyes. How shit is that? And here was the thing that made me really want to puke: he put some in his mouth to keep them warm. I kept imagining them slipping down his throat and wriggling about in his stomach.

When I thought back to those days, I couldn't remember him drinking. Maybe he did; I was probably too young to notice. I didn't recall fights either, but that didn't mean there weren't any. In those days, I used to go to bed and fall asleep before my head hit the pillow. I had no worries. I was happy. I thought my mum and dad were happy, too. That they would always be together and always love each other.

The first time I actually remember them rowing was a few nights after my ninth birthday, over a pair of school trousers my mother had bought for me. I was up in my room, getting ready for bed, when it started. I heard them clearly because the stairs led directly down into the front room. He kept going on and on about wasting five pounds on them. My mother had tried to reason with him at first. Told him I needed them. But, he wasn't having any of it. He told her to take them back and go to the jumble sale instead.

One-nil to Dad.

Mum told him if he spent less time in the pub, she wouldn't have to resort to scratching around at jumble sales.

Great equaliser!

'I work my bollocks off all week in that factory. I'm entitled to a drink.'

Two-one.

'A drink, yes. But, you're in the pub most nights.'

Good point, but, the goal was ruled offside. 'Most nights, my arse. Thursday and Friday. End of.'

'So where were you on Tuesday?'

'Clem's birthday?'

'And Clem's more important than your own son?'

'What's that supposed to mean?'

A short silence. I pushed open my bedroom door, and stood just inside my room, waiting for mum to say something. Score a goal. Win the match.

I heard a katush sound. A can opening. No prizes for guessing it wasn't fizzy pop.

'You think everything revolves around you. You and that bloody kid.'

My mum made a strange snorting sound. 'That's a nice way to speak about your own son.'

'Who earns all the money in this house?'

'I want to work. It's you who keeps saying I have to stay at home and take care of the house. I'm more than happy to get a job, now Mikey's older.'

My mum was definitely winning now. Game over.

'Will you stop calling him Mikey? His name's Michael. It's the same as that "love-bug" nonsense. You'll turn him into a queer.'

'Don't be so bloody ridiculous.'

'I'm not. Next thing you'll be dressing him up in a frock and high-heeled shoes.'

'I'd like to know how, when I can't even buy him a pair of bloody school trousers.'

My mum was good. She ought to get a job at the school. No one would ever get one over on her.

'I didn't say you couldn't buy him school trousers. I just said—'

'Go to the jumble. I know. I heard you the first time.'

'Don't get smart with me.'

Another long silence. I knew I should go to bed. Shut the door. It was wrong to listen. But, the argument had sucked me in.

'Don't look at me like that.'

'I'm tired, Billy. I'm tired of rowing. Tired of having no money.'

'You're all the same. Fucking women. Moan, moan, moan. What do you do all day?'

'Cook your meals. Clean the house. Washing. Ironing.'

'Coulda fooled me.' His voice had taken on a nasty tone, like kids when they taunt one another in the playground. 'House looks like a shit-tip.'

'If you're referring to the ironing pile, pardon me for not getting it all put away.'

A chair scraped back. 'Lazy bitch.'

'You can talk.'

There was a loud crack, followed by a scream. I'd never heard my mum make a noise like that before. It sounded so full of hurt, like a wounded animal caught in a trap. I wanted to run down the stairs and protect her, save her from the evil monster who used to be my dad, but I had only just turned nine. A puny nine, at that. I had about as much chance of standing up to my dad as I did of flying to the moon.

The scream was followed by a creepy silence. I closed the door and tiptoed over to my bed. I threw myself on top of it and spent half the night trying to convince myself I'd made a mistake. Imagined it. Got it all wrong.

By the time I went down for breakfast the following morning, I was convinced I must have dreamed the whole thing. My mum didn't scream like that. My dad wouldn't hurt her. He might not be the friendliest bloke in the world, he might even keep maggots in his mouth when he went fishing, but he wouldn't—

'Morning, love-bug.'

My jaw dropped. There was a huge bruise underneath her left eye. Some of the skin was broken. She'd tried to put makeup over the wound, but it made it look even worse.

I had a nasty queasy feeling in my tummy, like when I had to go somewhere on a bus. 'What's up with your eye?'

She smiled. Not her usual smile; the one which made me feel warm inside. 'I banged it on the door.'

I wanted to ask her if she'd been arguing with Dad. If he'd hit her. But, I somehow knew this would only hurt her more than she already was. 'Oh.'

'You want me to walk you to school?'

I shook my head. No way. I was nine, not four. Black eye or no black eye, I'd never live it down.

In the three years following the row over my school trousers, I lost count of how many times my dad had beat up my mum. If I said once a month, I'd be close. Sometimes, it was more, sometimes less.

There was only one thing worse than listening to the beatings, and that was hearing him crying and apologising to her, promising to change and get help. Telling her she meant everything to him. How sick was that? Did he really think apologising made any difference? Healed my mum's face? Mended her broken ribs? The bastard was evil, fake tears or not.

I didn't understand why she stayed with him. I mean, I knew what she told me about having nowhere to go, but surely anywhere was better than this? I'd have lived in the park in a tent, if it meant she didn't have to suffer. Or live in one of the air raid shelters along the Bunky Line. Anywhere away from his stinking breath and piles of beer cans.

I looked at Oxo. 'I bet you hate him, too?'

Oxo licked the tip of his nose. He didn't look like he could hate anyone. Not even the farmer who'd kept him tied up at Finley's Farm. Me and Tommy Preston used to go down there and steal chicken eggs from the battery houses. A dozen at a time. Brilliant for whizzing at windows. A great pastime for two eleven-year-old losers. Oxo had looked about as sorry as it was possible for a dog to look. For quite a while, we mistook that grinning mutt for being vicious.

'But, why's he wagging his tail?' Tommy had asked one day. 'He looks all right to me.'

'He's just trying to trick us into thinking he's friendly.'

'Nah. He's just a mongrel. I'm gonna stroke him.'

I kept my distance. Any minute now, Old Man Finley would come plodding though the farmyard in his big green Wellington boots, and blast us with his shotgun for trespassing on his land.

'Come on, Tommy, leave it. Let's just get the eggs.'

Tommy didn't seem to hear me. 'Hey, you're all right, aren't you, boy?'

'Like he's going to answer you.'

The dog's tail whirred behind him like a helicopter blade.

Tommy got to within two feet of the dog, and held out his hand, palm down. 'Hey, that a boy.'

The dog licked Tommy's hand for all it was worth. Turbo-tongue and turbo-tail.

Tommy turned to me. 'See. He's really friendly.'

Reluctantly, I ambled over, keeping half an eye on the farmhouse. 'I wonder what his name is?'

Tommy grinned. 'Slobber.'

I crouched down beside Tommy and stroked the dog's back. He was a lovely colour. Black and tan. Long haired. The best eyes ever. They weren't so much as looking, but bubbling in their sockets.

'I wonder why he's tied up?' I said. 'He's about as vicious as a butterfly.'

Tommy looked at me as if I was the dumbest person alive. 'How should I know?'

'It's cruel. He hasn't even got a kennel.'

'Maybe Finley takes him indoors at night.'

'What if he doesn't?'

Tommy shrugged. 'Not much we can do about that, is there?'

'We could tell the cops.'

'And say what? A farmer keeps his mutt tied up in the farmyard? They're hardly going to give a damn about that, are they?'

'Maybe we ought to come back tonight.'

Tommy looked as if I'd just suggested burning the farm down. 'What for?'

'See if Finley's taken him indoors.'

'I'm not allowed out past eight o'clock.'

'I'll tell my mum I'm going to my Aunt Jean's. You can tell your mum you're going to my house. That way, it doesn't matter.'

He considered this for a while, and then said, 'I'll try.'

'Do you reckon you could get a knife?'

'What the fuck for?'

'To cut him free.'

'We can't just set him loose. He won't have anywhere to go.'

'I'll take him home.'

'And what if your old man tells you to get rid of him?'

'He won't.' A lie. I hadn't even thought of that.

'I ain't nicking no knives from home. My mum would slit my throat with one if she caught me. But, I've got a good blade on my Swiss Army Knife.'

And so it was agreed. We met down near the entrance to Finley's Farm. November ninth. The day I rescued my best friend from that muddy farmyard. Tommy was ten minutes late. I was about to give up and go home when he lumbered around the corner.

'I didn't think you were coming,' I said.

'My old lady wasn't going to let me. I ended up telling her it was important stuff for a science project. That just about swung it, so you make sure you tell her the same if she ever asks you, right?'

I nodded. 'You got your knife?'

He patted his jeans' pocket. 'Yeah.'

By the time we reached the farmyard, my belly felt as if a load of bees were buzzing around inside it. At least the place was well lit. The dog was still there, but he'd moved close to one of the barns surrounding the yard. As soon as he saw us, his tail sprang into action.

Stupidly, I put a finger to my lips to shush him.

'What are we gonna do if Finley comes?' Tommy asked.

'He won't. Not if we're quick.' As if that would make any difference. By the time we reached the dog, my hands were shaking so badly I could barely stroke him. 'Quick, Tommy. Cut the rope.'

He pulled out his Swiss Army Knife and selected a blade. 'This ought to do it.'

The rope was about half an inch thick. It took Tommy an age to get through it. 'I thought these Swiss knives were meant to be good.'

'Nearly—'

'You boys! What are you doing?'

Shit. Finley. About a hundred yards away. 'Have you cut the fucking thing yet?'

'Stay right where you are. Don't move,' Finley shouted. He was carrying a large stick, and a lot of weight. As tall as my old man, but twice as round. We wouldn't have any trouble outrunning him, but I wanted that dog first. I wanted him so bad I almost peed my pants as Finley drew closer.

Tommy shoved the knife back in his pocket. 'It's through.'

The best words I'd ever heard in my life. Tommy held the free end of the rope and walked the dog out of the farmyard.

'Bring that dog back!'

I turned around. 'Or what?'

'The rope's too short to walk with him properly,' Tommy said, as we neared the cinder track leading away from the farm.

'I'll have the police on you.'

'And I'll have the police on you for being cruel to animals,' I shouted back.

Finley moved quite fast for a man of his size. We hurried away, but the short length of rope was holding us back. Tommy looked at me. 'I've got to let it go.'

Finley was closing in. Tommy let go of the rope, and we sprinted along the cinder path towards the main road. I didn't once look back. We'd let the poor dog down. Failed. A pair of cowards.

We reached the road. 'Fuck, that was close,' Tommy said.

I bent over, resting my hands on my knees. I had a terrible stitch, and my lungs were burning. 'Why'd Finley have to come into the—' The words caught in my throat, as I saw the dog trotting towards us.

'Slobber,' Tommy shouted. 'Hey, boy, you made it.'

I didn't like the name Slobber. It didn't suit him. I patted my knees and called him. He trotted up to me and sat down, tail sweeping the dirt, grinning in that crazy way he had.

'I've got to go,' Tommy said. 'I told my mum I'd only be an hour, tops. What are you gonna do with him if your dad won't let him stay?'

'I don't know. He'll be at the pub until closing time.'

By the time I reached home, I'd rehearsed my lie about just finding him enough times to believe it myself.

'But, you can't keep him here. Your dad won't have a dog in the house.'

I tried to impersonate the dog's pleading eyes. 'Please, Mum. He hasn't got nowhere to go.'

'You'll have to take him somewhere else.'

After a good ten minutes bargaining, I persuaded her to let the dog stay for one night. 'You keep him in your bedroom. But, I'm warning you, if your father hears him, he'll go mad.'

I left him in my room the following morning while I ate breakfast. Told him to be quiet; about as much use as telling a kid to be careful. Dad was buttering a slice of toast when the dog barked. A single yap.

Dad froze, the butter knife hovering above his plate. 'What was that?'

Mum looked at me as if I'd just let one go at the dining table. 'Probably kids mucking about outside.'

He shook his head. 'It was a dog.'

I studied my toast. I could feel my cheeks burning. I prayed to a God I didn't really believe in to keep the dog quiet and make my dad think he was imagining things.

Mum poured tea into my dad's cup. I could see the teapot juddering in her hand. Oxo yapped again. No mistaking that noise, or where it was coming from.

Dad looked at me through red-rimmed eyes. 'You got a dog in your room?'

'I found him. He was wandering about in the street.'

'So, you just thought you'd bring him home?'

I needed to pee. 'Sorry, I—'

'What do you think this is, boy, Battersea Dogs' Home?'

Mum tried to help. 'It was only for one night.'

'So, you knew about this?'

'He's going to take the dog back to where he found him on the way to school, aren't you, Mikey?'

'But, he's got nowhere to go,' I protested. 'It's not like he's any bother. He's really friendly. I'll take him for walks. I'll brush him. I'll do everything for him. You won't even know he's here.'

He shook his head. 'Dogs cost too much. They need feeding. Collars and leads. Baskets.'

What about all the money you spend in the pub, I thought. 'Please.'

'And what about if he gets sick? Who's going to pay for the vets?'

'I will.'

'Oh, you will, will you? And where are you going to get the money from?'

'I'll do jobs.'

'Not around here you won't. I'm not paying you to do chores for your mother.'

'I'll get a job.'

'You're nine years old. Where are you going to get a job? In the factory with me?'

'I'll get a paper round.'

'The answer's still no.'

'Please. I promise.'

He slurped some tea. 'You can barely get yourself out of bed for school in the morning. How the hell are you going to manage a paper round?'

'I'll take him with me. I can walk him at the same time before school.'

'And what if it's pissing down with rain?'

'I'll wear a coat.' Smart answer. Perhaps a little too smart, judging by the look in his eyes.

'I don't know. We've got enough problems as it is, without adding a bloody dog to them.'

'I'll make sure Mikey gets up in the morning,' Mum offered.

Mum elevated herself to hero status. 'See. Mum will help.'

'She's got enough to do.'

'I don't mind,' Mum said.

He banged his cup down on the table. 'Bugger it. Keep the damn thing. But, the first sign of trouble, and that dog's out of here, do you understand?'

For the first and last time in my life, I wanted to run up to him and throw my arms around him. But, I simply nodded. All my love for him had long since turned to ice.

He stood up and left for work. 'And make sure you keep the bloody thing out of my way.'

'Okay.'

And so, Oxo was welcomed into the family. That broken, messed up family.

If you were wondering how he got his name, I used to love Oxo cubes. Mum would sometimes let me have one when she was making gravy. Oxo used to lick my fingers for all he was worth.

Sometimes, because he was my best friend, I'd pinch one, and share it with him.

Along with my secrets, and just about anything it was possible for a boy to share with a dog.

CHAPTER 11

fell asleep and woke up at just past eleven. Oxo was asleep, his backside a foot from my face. I didn't want to think about what he might have treated my nose to in my sleep. I clambered off the bed and went to the bedroom window. Rain lashed down, bouncing off the street. Even though it felt bad to even think it, I wished Billy the Bully would stagger into the road on his way home, and get hit by a truck. Splat! Me, Mum, and Oxo left in peace to get on with our lives. No more bruises, broken noses, fucked up weekends.

I looked along the street, waiting for him to stagger around the corner, and weave his way towards the house. Do his usual trick of falling over a dustbin and making enough racket to wake up the whole street. I'd once seen him squaring up to an overhanging bush in a nearby garden. God alone knew what he thought it was. An alien, perhaps?

Oxo rolled onto his back. An invitation for me to rub his tummy. I stroked him for a while. His belly was like a little hot water bottle. The minutes dripped by, like sand in an egg timer when you're starving hungry.

The chain flushed downstairs. I heard my mother sweeping up the ashes in the grate, every sound amplified in the silence. Because the stairs ran from the front room up to the landing, you could even hear her picking up the cups and plates, and carrying them through to the kitchen.

Oxo whined. A sign Dad was on his way. He rolled off his back and jumped onto the floor, claws ticking on the bare wooden boards.

Maybe he won't start on her tonight, I thought, hanging onto hope for all I was worth. He might go straight to bed, or pass out on the sofa. My reasoning was based on the fact he'd already beaten the crap out of her last night. Surely, he wouldn't strike twice in one week.

I watched him stagger up the road. He had his arm around his mate, Tony Higgins. Big Tone, Dad called him. Big Wanker, more like. He owned the local chip shop. Ate most of the chips as well, judging by the size of him. The only advantage of knowing Higgins was he would sometimes let me and my mates have a free bag of chips, on account of he was mates with good old Billy the Bully.

I opened my window an inch to see if I could figure out his mood before he got through the front door. Not that it would make a scrap of difference. I mean, what was I going to do? Make preparations? Warn my mum? Get a kitchen knife and stab the bastard through the heart the minute he walked through the front door?

Big Tone untangled himself from my dad and danced with a lamppost a few doors away. His bald head gleamed in the yellow light.

'C'mon, Tone, less get in. I got a cold one with my name on it in the fridge.'

Higgins stopped prancing about in front of the lamppost. He wiped rain off the top of his head with an exaggerated sweep of his hand. 'We don't want a "cold one" on a night like this, Billy-boy, we want a hot one.'

'Like that bird behind the bar?'

Higgins laughed. 'Now you're talking.'

'I know I am. She takes it up the arse.'

Higgins looked impressed with this piece of information. and then frowned. 'How'd you know?'

My dad tried to tap the side of his nose, missed, and poked himself in the eye. 'Fuck.'

Higgins left his date with the lamppost and went to console Billy the Bully who was acting like he'd been shot in the face. He flailed a hand at an imaginary assailant.

'Come on, Billy. Let's go crack open a bottle.'

They took a good ten minutes to reach the front door. By that time, Billy the Bully kept asking who had punched him in the eye.

'No one's hit you, Billy.'

'Why's my eye throbbing like a bastard?' He banged on the door with his fist, again and again, until my mother opened it, and let them in.

'Bout fucking time,' Billy the Bully said. 'Where you been?'

'Clearing up.'

'Good. Cos it's party time.'

I shut my window and looked at Oxo. 'At least he's got Higgins with him. I don't reckon he'll start anything with him here.'

Oxo scratched his ear. He looked sad, almost as if he was aware something bad would happen. I heard voices downstairs. Loud. Slurred. Then music. My old man, the world's worst DJ, sabotaging his record collection by scratching the needle across the vinyl. The Beatles. Sergeant Pepper's Lonely Hearts Club Band. I hated that damn record. It was all he would ever play when he was pissed. There was someone called Billy on the record. Billy Shears. Dad always thought they were singing about him, the fucking moron.

I heard my mum go to bed about half an hour after Billy the Bully and Higgins came in. So far so good. At least he hadn't been nasty to her. Oxo was lying by the door, nose plugged into the small gap beneath, which was odd because he usually settled on the bed.

'You don't need to go out, do you?'

Oxo ignored me.

'I ain't taking you into the garden while they're still down there.' I sat on the edge of my bed. 'Come on boy, let's go to sleep. I don't reckon he's—'

The words froze in my throat as something smashed downstairs. The music screeched to a stop halfway through Fixing a Hole.

'Don't be fucking stupid, Billy. You're not thinking straight.' Big Tone, sounding more like Pipsqueak Tone, as his voice rose several octaves.

'I ain't being stupid. Don't fucking tell me what I am or I ain't.'

'I'm not—'

'Don't you dare sit there drinking my whiskey telling me shit, Tone. You're supposed to be a mate.'

'I ain't telling you shit, Billy. I wasn't looking at her.'

'I seen you with my own fucking eyes. You were looking. And she was looking at you.'

'I wouldn't look at your missus. Not like that.'

A long silence, followed by, 'Get out of my house.'

'But, I ain't—'

'You want me to smash your face through that telly?'

Big Tone didn't. 'All right, all right, I'm going, but I wasn't looking at her. I swear on Daisy's life.'

I didn't have a clue who Daisy was. Higgins wasn't married. Maybe it was that mangy old black and white moggy who always slept on the window ledge in the chippy. Footsteps retreated into the hall, then the front door opened and banged shut. I peered out my window, and watched Tony Higgins lumbering up the road, looking a lot soberer than when he'd arrived.

I prayed that Billy the Bully would fall into a drunken stupor and leave my mother alone.

My prayers went unanswered. I heard him babbling on about something downstairs. I couldn't quite make out what it was, but it sounded threatening and menacing. Something crashed. It sounded like the dining table had been tipped over. Then, he clomped up the stairs, boots echoing on the bare boards.

Oxo sat by the door, alert, head tipped to one side. I tried not to panic. I wanted to run into Mum's room and stand in Billy the Bully's way. Save her. Just like Superman.

'I know what you're up to.' His voice was low. Almost a growl.

'What the hell are you talking about?'

'You think I'm stupid?'

'No. Don't be ridicu—'

'Are you fucking him?'

'Who?'

'You know fucking well who. Tony Baloney Higgins.'

'Don't be stupid.'

'I saw the way you looked at him.'

'For God's sake, Billy, why would I look at him?'

'Don't get smart with me, you cheating bitch.'

'I'm not—'

'When did we last do it?'

A lengthy silence. I picked up my pillow and hugged it. Oxo whined. Thunder rolled across the sky; God moving his furniture as my mum called it. My heart was pounding so hard in my chest it felt as if it would bounce right up into my mouth.

'Admit it. You've got the hots for him.'

'Now you're being stupid.'

Another slight pause, and then all hell broke loose. I heard my mother scream. Several thumps and crashes. More screams. I threw myself on the bed and covered my head with the pillow. 'Please, God, make him go away. Make him leave my mum alone. I'll do anything. I'll be good. I'll never throw eggs at anyone's window again. I'll take Oxo for a walk every night, instead of letting him loose. I'll brush him every day. I'll help with the washing up. I'll clean my teeth every morning after breakfast, and wash my hands before dinner, instead of just pretending to. I'll never mess about in class again. Do all my homework. Never lie again. Not even when I'm in trouble. Please, God, just make him stop beating my mum up.'

A miracle. The noise stopped. Perhaps God was listening after all. I thought about pushing my luck and asking Him to give my dad a heart attack while He was about it. I took the pillow off my head and sat up. Oxo remained by the door, alert.

My thin sliver of hope was shattered. I heard the sound of shuffling feet, and then my dad spoke, his voice unsure, 'Sarah?'

No answer.

'Get up.'

Oxo whined, snorkelling air through the gap beneath the door.

'Leave me alone.' My mother's voice. All slurry. Something heavy was dragged across the floor. My dad was grunting. Their bedroom door banged against the wall.

'Please, Billy, my head's all—'

A loud thud silenced her. I squeezed my eyes shut, and tried not to think about what had made that awful, hollow noise, but my imagination, as always, filled in the blanks. Treated me to an image of my mum's head being slammed against the wall.

'You can go and live with him, you fucking whore.'

Oxo barked and scratched at the door.

Do something.

I walked to the door, legs shaking, heart racing. But what could I do?

Oxo scrabbled at the door. I stood behind him, my mind in a thousand places at once. Shit, shit, shit. Maybe I ought to open the bedroom window and shimmy down the drainpipe. Run up the road to Mum's friend, Rachel, and get her to call the cops.

I stood rooted to the spot as Billy the Bully threw my mother down the stairs. Thump, thump, thump. All the way down the wooden hill as she used to call it. My beautiful, kind mum, tossed down the stairs like a rag doll.

Oxo howled. I'd never seen him react like this before. Not in all the time since me and Tommy had rescued him from Finley's Farm.

'Shut up, boy. Be quiet.' I tried to shout and whisper at the same time.

He stopped howling, but stood in front of the door, hackles up. I could hear my dad thumping about in his bedroom. Then, the creak of bedsprings followed by silence. I decided to give it ten minutes and then see what I could do to help Mum. Perhaps make her up a bed on the sofa.

At least he hasn't thrown her down the steps outside, I thought. At least she's dry in here.

It's funny what we cling to when we're desperate.

Chapter 12

I don't know how long I waited before I plucked up the courage to open my bedroom door; it might have been ten minutes, it might have been half an hour. By then, Oxo was quiet and still.

Mum was lying at the bottom of the stairs, still as a shop dummy. Her head was at a weird angle as if looking at something behind her. One of her legs was twisted. I didn't need a doctor to tell me it was broken. I'd seen a kid fall out of a tree once, and his leg had been all messed up like that.

Oxo bounded down the stairs, and stood over her, sniffing her face. By the time I reached her, I knew something was seriously wrong. Her mouth hung open, limp and detached.

'Mum?'

She didn't respond. One of her earrings was lying on the stairs. A small gold stud. I picked it up and closed my hand around it. I knelt down and touched her hand. Cold as ice. Her lips had turned blue. My stomach flipped over. I squeezed her hand. 'Mum?'

Oxo stopped sniffing her and walked to the front door. He sat on the mat, looking up at the letter box.

'You're not going out now.'

He made a noise, somewhere between a whine and a bark.

'Mum? Wake up.'

I've no idea how long I knelt beside her, holding her hand, and trying to get her to answer me, before I realised she was dead. It came in a series of clues. The way she lay. The angle of her head. The slight parting of her lips. One eye not quite closed. Her leg at that crazy angle. Cold clammy hand.

It's hard to describe the feeling erupting inside me when I realised she was dead. It started in the pit of my stomach, and rose into my throat, like a waterfall running backwards. I let go of her hand as if it had given me an electric shock. I saw Oxo scrabbling at the front door.

My mummy's dead. This can't be happening. She can't be dead.

Dead. Like the fish on Grudgington's slab. Sightless eyes staring straight ahead. Dead. Like the rabbits hanging outside the butcher's shop. Flies buzzing around them, waiting to lay their disgusting eggs.

My mummy's dead. Over and over in my head.

I felt as if I was four years old again, waiting in the playground one afternoon for her to pick me up. Only she was late. The other parents had picked up their kids ages ago. Ten minutes passed. Fifteen. Twenty. Why wasn't she here? She always picked me up, even in the rain and the snow. With that great big smile, the one that made me imagine rainbows. And then she arrived. Like magic. Out of breath and apologising. She'd stopped to help an old man who'd fallen over in the street. The teacher telling her not to worry.

Where was that teacher now? I needed her to tell me not to worry. My mum would be back from the dead any minute now to give me a cuddle and take me away from this terrible place. Another country, perhaps. Somewhere they appreciated rainbow smiles. Somewhere my dad would never find us. Never be able to use his fists on her ever again.

A sudden thought. One linked right up to my mummy's dead. Even more chilling. My daddy's a murderer. He'll go to jail for the rest of his life. I imagined him standing in a prison cell, holding onto the bars with his big murderer's hands. The hands which had pummelled my mummy's face too many times to keep a count. I wished with all my heart they still hanged people. If anyone deserved to get his neck put in a noose, it was him.

My only real idea of hanging came from the Westerns I sometimes watched on telly. John Wayne riding into town on his horse, shotgun spinning in his hand, sheriff's badge glinting in the sun, ready to round up the baddies. How I wished I was John Wayne. Fearless. Fire in my belly. But, I was just stupid Michael Tate. Mikey, to his dead mummy. Her little love-bug. Her toasted soldier.

Her gutless wonder, more like. Too chicken to shout out when he beat the shit out of her. Too chicken to go onto the landing and stop him throwing her down the stairs. Another thought: Who was going to take care of me? I couldn't stay here on my own. I had no money for starters. Apart from my paper round money, which I needed to buy Oxo's food wi—

My heart stopped. Oxo. What was going to happen to him? There was no way on Earth I was going to let him get carted off to Battersea Dogs' Home. I'd rather die.

Instant relief. Aunt Jean would take care of me and Oxo. I didn't get on too well with my cousin, David. My mum called him a spoiled brat. Not to mention his two sisters, Katie and Christine. Probably because we didn't have as much money as them, or because we lived in a smaller house.

My mummy's dead.

I snatched one last look at my poor, battered mum. Her face looked like wax. I would always remember her this way. I stood up and wrenched open the front door. I don't remember if I closed it behind me. Me and Oxo bolted along the road to Rachel's house. I burst through the front gate and hammered on her door as hard as I could.

Rachel answered as my fists turned to pulp. 'Mikey? What is it? What the hell's happened?'

'My dad.'

'What about him?'

'My dad did it.'

'Did what?' She pulled me inside the house. Oxo scooted in between my legs. 'What did your dad do.'

And then something weird happened. I forgot why I was there. Rain dripped down the back of my pyjama top, cold and slippery, like little wet slugs.

'Mikey?'

I started to cry.

A man's voice. For one mad moment, I thought it was my dad, but it was Rachel's husband. He looked half asleep. 'Whassamatter?'

Rachel crouched down so as she was at eye-level. 'Mikey? Come on, what's happened?'

'Billy Tate been getting handy with his fists a—'

'Shut up, Don. Make the lad a cup of sweet tea.' And then to me, 'What's happened, lad?'

'My mummy's dead.' It felt as if someone else had spoken the words. Taken over my mouth.

Something seemed to squeeze Rachel's face. 'You sure she's not just hurt?'

'Dad threw her down the stairs. She's not breathing.'

'Where's your dad now?'

'In the house.' Where else would he be? On the roof?

'Oh my God. Call the police, Don.'

Don didn't argue. He rushed into the living room, no longer looking half asleep.

Rachel wrapped her arms around me and pulled me close. I smelled talcum powder and TCP, felt the warmth of her body, the touch of her hand on the top of my back, rubbing me in small circular movements. I bit down hard on my lip, trying to stop the tears.

So much for that. The floodgates opened. My knees buckled. My grief spilled out in great big racking sobs. Snot ran into my mouth.

Rachel pulled me close. Took the weight of my body. Tried her best to soothe me, tell me that things would be all right. But, how could they be? My mummy was dead. My daddy had killed her. I was being punished for all the bad things I'd done. Nicking chicken eggs. Lying. Flicking paper at Tina Eaton in class. Stamping in a puddle and getting muddy water up the backs of her tights. Telling the class idiot, Bobby King, that Tina fancied him. Writing made-up love notes to the pair of them. What had Tina ever done to me? Nothing. Tina Eaton would laugh her head off if she could see me now.

By the time I'd finished crying, my whole body felt empty and hollow. Rachel's husband told her the police were on their way. 'Get the boy in the front room and sit him on the sofa.' And then, quieter, 'What a mess.'

I sat down on a massive green sofa. So soft. So comfortable. Not like the rock-hard threadbare thing in our house. Oxo sat by my feet, head resting on my knee.

Rachel sat next to me and encouraged me to drink my tea. Told me I needed to keep my strength up. It would be a long night. She asked if I wanted a biscuit.

'I want my mum back.'

'I know you do, lovey.'

'What's going to happen to me?'

'Let's see what the police say.'

'But she's dead.'

Rachel shook her head. 'Let's wait and see.'

'But, what will happen to me?'

She patted my knee. What sort of answer was that? A secret sign language for kids who no longer had parents.

'What's going to happen to Oxo?'

'He can stay here for now.'

'Really?'

'Yes.'

'You promise?'

Rachel did.

We sat in silence until the police arrived. I prayed with all my heart I'd somehow got it all wrong; that my mum was just unconscious, like she'd been so many times before. The police would tell me to go back home. Mum would be fine. Nothing a few days' rest wouldn't cure. Everything would be back to normal in a day or two.

Whatever normal was.

Maybe this time Dad would realise he couldn't keep beating her up. He would stop drinking, get help, see a doctor or something. Things would be different. But, this wasn't a film or a soap opera on the telly. This was Michael Tate's life, and good things never happened to liars and cowards, who splashed water up Tina Eaton's tights, or hid in their bedroom whilst their dad beat their mum to death, and threw her down the stairs.

The police took me out of the house. Oxo followed me to the front door. I clutched my mother's earring in my right hand. My only source of strength.

Rachel held Oxo by the collar. 'It'll be all right, Mikey.'

It wouldn't. 'Please take care of him.'

'Of course I will, lovey.'

I would never see Oxo again. This wasn't a thought. Not even a feeling. Just an awful pressure squeezing my heart as I looked into his eyes. The most honest eyes I'd ever seen in my life.

They said, Hey, I'm your best pal. Don't you forget it.

And I never did.

I'd trust a dog over a human any day of the week.

CHAPTER 13

The blue flashing light of the police car vanished. Rachel and Oxo, as well. I was back outside the closed door of number "19" again, in the wheelchair, trapped once again inside my useless adult body. The wheelchair turned itself around and headed back towards the darkness of the tunnel.

I tried to process what had just happened. How I'd stepped into a child's world. So real. So terrifying. We rolled along in the darkness. Me and the invisible pusher. The wheels squeaking rhythmically.

Perhaps it was my mother pushing me. Come back from wherever dead people go to show me what had happened to her. But, why? And what did it have to do with me killing Becky?

Maybe she's showing you that you turned out to be just like your dad. Showing you how history repeats itself. Only you outdid Billy the Bully by twenty-one stab wounds. No beating about the bush, so-to-speak, for this second-generation killer, Mikey the Murderer.

After a while, maybe ten minutes, maybe ten hours, the wheelchair veered left, and headed towards the light again. 'Where are you taking me?'

The pusher wasn't saying. I could just make out a large building in the distance. I thought I could hear Oxo whining; a pitiful sound which spoke of sorrow and abandonment.

As my eyes grew accustomed to these new surroundings, I noticed the brick building was a huge, detached place, with a large, central area rising on two levels. It spread out about fifty or sixty feet either side of the central structure. Five windows in each section suggested five separate rooms. A gateway, flanked by two grey, stone pillars, led to a large gravel turnaround area. Grass, with ugly, large, stone ornaments, completed the front of the building.

I half-expected my old man to come lurching across the grass, one fist swinging by his side like a bastard's promise, the other clutching a beer can. A sudden thought, clear and certain: this was a prison. Either where I was heading, or where my dad was serving his sentence.

An ambulance was parked near the front of the building. Its light revolved, slashing the grass with blue blades of light. A kid was carried out of the central building on a stretcher, young, maybe only nine or ten. Blond hair matted with blood.

A short, fat man in a dark blue suit waddled out of the building, and stood by the rear doors of the ambulance. Two men in dark blue uniforms loaded the kid inside.

One of them slammed the doors shut. 'What happened to him?'

Fat Man shook his head. 'I tell them not to run in the corridors. The floors are wet. Do they listen?' He didn't wait for an answer. 'Do they hell as like. Young fool slipped and went headfirst into the wall.'

The ambulance man gave a knowing nod. 'Kids don't have ears for good sense.'

Fat Man mopped sweat from his forehead with a cotton handkerchief. 'I do my best. But....'

I watched the ambulance pull out of the gravel drive and turn right. It vanished from sight. Fat Man walked towards me. He stopped near the gate and rested a hand on one of the stone pillars. He looked at me. Beads of sweat glistened on his forehead. His dark, curly hair looked either greased or wet. Perhaps both. His blue eyes glinted.

My chest tightened. Who was he? Why did my head feel like it was melting?

He grinned at me. 'Hello, Michael.'

I tried to look away from those mesmerising eyes, but I couldn't.

He shook his head. 'Kids, eh?'

I looked down at my useless legs, and willed them to work. Get me out of that wheelchair.

'Whatever is the world coming to? Everyone thinks it's spinning clockwise, but you know as well as I do it spins anti-clockwise.' As he spoke, he made a circular movement with his index finger, indicating a clock ticking backwards. I'd heard the words before, but couldn't quite remember where from.

'Who are you?'

He ignored me. 'Tick-tock, tick-tock, tick-tock. Funny how time grows wings, and flies away when you're having fun, eh, Michael?'

I couldn't see anything funny about it.

'Which way does your wheel spin, Michael Tate?'

'I don't—'

'Backwards or forwards? Or is it a job to say when it's buckled?'

I looked to my left and right. Nothing but black empty walls.

'I've lost count of the kids I've seen trying to ride along the road with tyres as flat as pancakes. Do you understand what I'm saying?'

I didn't.

'Are you a mummy's boy, Michael?'

I wanted to shout at him, scream at him, tell him my mummy was dead, but he already knew that; it was written in those twinkling blue eyes.

'Or are you a chip off the old man's block, Michael? A splinter, perhaps?'

I'm nothing like that bastard. Firm and definite. But, only in my mind. Why was I such a fucking scaredy-cat?

'You look like you might be trouble, Michael. Trouble with a capital T. So peg back your ears, and listen to what we call a home truth – no one wants you, boy. You're an outcast. Do you know what an outcast is?'

I did. Only too well. But, I wasn't a boy anymore.

Fat Man licked his lips. 'I can't understand why society would want to waste money on a little runt like you. Perhaps you could enlighten me?'

'I don't know wh—' The wheelchair suddenly jerked and turned around. It headed back into the tunnel, wheels squeaking, picking up speed. Ark, ark, ark, like a demented bird. Laughter echoed around the walls. Evil laughter. Taking pleasure from someone else's suffering. Mine? Probably. Fat Man licked his lips in my mind's eye. Licked his lips and scolded me with those sharp blue eyes.

We burst into the hospital room. The door slammed back against the wall, loud enough to alert someone at the other end of the hospital, never mind the nurses' station. I heard the hiss-koosh of a machine. Or was it my breathing? Or my heart? Or both? The wheelchair ground to a halt alongside the bed. The footbrake snapped into place. Those gentle hands helped me out of the chair and back onto the bed.

I watched the wheelchair move back alongside the wall. Brake applied. Seat creaking, as the leather settled. I took several deep breaths and leaned back against my pillows. I tried to make sense of what had just happened. Had I glimpsed my past? Witnessed the murder of my mother? And who was the Fat Man standing at the gates of that big ugly building?

Even in the dim light cast from the corridor, I could still see the emergency door and the red lettering. There was now a new message nestled between My little love-bug and We have to be strong. No one wants you, boy.

I expected the door to burst open any minute and reveal the Fat Man, blue eyes glinting. Thankfully, the door remained closed and bolted, for now. I looked at my hands. The same hands which had touched my mother's dead body. Held her cold, clammy hand. But, how was that possible? Invisible people didn't visit you in hospital at night and take you for walks in wheelchairs.

Photographs don't come to life, either.

I looked at the magazine lying on my locker and resisted an urge to check if the photos were still inside. I didn't think I'd be able to cope if the bloody things started moving again. I'd had enough drama, real or imagined, for one night. I just wanted to go to sleep and get relief from this waking nightmare.

My right hand was balled into a fist, knuckles gleaming white in the shadowy darkness. I relaxed and uncurled my fingers. At first, I thought I was imagining things.

Sitting in my sweating palm, was my mother's gold stud earring.

Chapter 14

So hot. Burning. Shaking. Can't feel my legs. A crowd of people around the bed. Voices. One booming above the others, calling my name. 'Michael? Can you hear me?'

A thought. Loud and clear. Of course I can hear you, you idiot. You're shouting loud enough to burst my eardrums.

'Do you know where you are, Michael?'

That one was easy. Hell. Where else? I tried to answer, but my tongue felt as if it was wrapped around a tree. No, that wasn't right. Not a tree. Only Oxo's lead could be wrapped around a tree.

'Michael?'

I now realised the booming voice belonged to the Fat Man in the dark blue suit. The one standing at the gates of hell. And then darkness engulfed me. Sweet and black and as quiet as death.

A rude intrusion. Light shining in my eyes. Someone slapping my cheek. Soft at first, and then harder. 'Michael? Can you hear me?'

The words screeched through my head, like fingernails down a blackboard. I tried to open my eyes, but the lids were glued shut.

'Fetch him some water. He's coming round.'

The mention of water made my throat spasm. I wanted to go back into the darkness, to the comfort of nothingness.

'Michael?' A softer voice. A woman's gentler tone.

I opened one eye and gawked into the distorted face of Emily. It floated above me like a child's balloon. 'Where am I?'

She poked a drinking straw between my lips. 'You're in hospital. Have a few sips.'

The water tasted good, as sweet as honey. I sucked for all I was worth.

Emily pulled the straw away. 'Steady. You don't want to gulp it, you'll get stomach cramps.'

My eyes slowly adjusted to my new surroundings. I saw three other beds on the ward. The one next to me and the one opposite were both occupied. The one near the window was empty. The empty bed made me think of death.

I grappled with reality. Remembered my last trip out in the wheelchair. The murder of my mother. The big building, with Fat Man at the gates. My mother's earring. 'What happened? Why have I been moved here?'

'You were delirious.'

'Come again?'

She smiled. 'Away with the fairies for the best part of two days, Michael.'

'Why?'

Emily shrugged. 'We're not sure. It might have been drug withdrawal; it might have been an infection. Maybe both. Your temperature's much more stable now. You don't seem to be hallucinating anymore.'

'Hallucinating?'

'Don't worry. It's common. You were seeing some pretty weird things.'

'Like what?'

'A fat man in a blue suit.'

My heart stood still. 'What did he look like?'

'I don't know, Michael. It was your hallucination. You kept yelling for someone to stop him. Said he was going to take you into a tunnel. Back to the building with the stone pillars.'

'I don't remember.'

'You said something about a boiler room.'

This threw me completely. I remembered nothing about a boiler room.

'At one point, you thought Dr. Prendergast was your father. Said he was going to take you home to kill your mother. Then, you giggled hysterically, as if he'd just told you the funniest joke ever.'

'Jesus.'

'Oh, and you kept asking for Oxo. Who's Oxo?'

An image of the dog flashed in my mind, head resting on my knee, alert brown eyes watching my every move, tail sweeping the floor like a turbo-charged broom. 'I don't know.'

'You said you missed him.'

'Really?' I didn't want to get drawn into a conversation about what may or may not have happened beyond the emergency door. I'd already got Emily to touch the wall once. Satisfy my curiosity. If I started babbling on about trips along a pitch-dark tunnel to a terraced house and beyond, she would probably mark me down as a total nutter, and recommend they shoot me full of sedative.

'You cried. Sobbed your heart out. Insisted someone had to save him. Are you sure the name means nothing?'

'No.'

'Weird name – Oxo.'

'Maybe I was dreaming about gravy.'

Emily laughed. 'You seemed pretty adamant Oxo needed rescuing.'

I assured her again the name meant nothing.

'You might remember something in time. I reckon you might be experiencing memory flashes.'

'Did I say anything else?'

'Not while I was around. Only gobbledegook. You kept saying my little love-bug, over and over. Mostly, you just drifted in and out of consciousness. Your temperature went through the roof at one point; that's when the doctor moved you here to keep a better eye on you.'

'Will I ever go back to my old room?'

Emily shrugged. 'I don't know.'

'Is something wrong?'

She didn't answer for a moment. When she did, her voice was hesitant. 'Nothing's wrong, Michael. It's just that I overheard Detective Inspector Carver talking to the Doctor. He reckons they're going to transfer you to a remand centre soon.'

Just the mention of Carver's name made my stomach loop-the-loop. 'Did he say when?'

'No. But, I got the impression they want you out of here as soon as possible.'

What could I say to that? I don't want to go? Please save me from the evil policeman?

'Oh, before I forget, I found this on the floor.' She held my mother's gold earring out for inspection. 'Do you recognise it?'

'It belonged to my mother.' And then, hurriedly, 'Jimmy brought it in.' What else could I say? I brought it back with me after witnessing her murder?

She didn't look convinced. 'Oh.'

'Can I have it?'

'Of course.' As she dropped it into my palm, her fingers brushed against my skin. A tiny electric shock passed through me. I watched her go. She didn't so much as walk along the ward as glide.

The thought of being moved to a remand centre filled me with dread. Carver would have free rein to torture me, set people on me, make my life a living hell. As if that wasn't bad enough, I wouldn't have access to the emergency door and the tunnel anymore. I didn't know whether that was a blessing or a curse, but a tiny part of me believed the truth lay beyond that door. If I left the hospital, I would never know.

Perhaps I could feign an illness, buy some time, pretend to hallucinate, and talk rubbish. It might be worth a try. Anything was better than being released into the care of Carver and his cronies.

I looked at the earring – tangible proof I had really gone through that tunnel to Whitehead Street and been transformed into a boy. I pinched it between my thumb and forefinger. As real as the man next to me. The vase of flowers by his bed. The black woman sweeping the floor. The old woman opposite, propped up on her pillows, mouth open, eyes closed.

At least you've got some proper memories now.

My mother's murder? Some fucking memory.

I felt a sudden urge to hold up the earring and shout out it was real. R-E-A-L. Might have even done so if the old woman hadn't spoken to me.

'It's so hot in here. I don't like the heat; it always makes me tired.'

I closed my hand around the earring. 'A fan would be nice.'

'Fans only swirl up the warm air. You need something which will make the air colder.'

The man next to me hacked up something unpleasant, and spat it into a small, silver spittoon.

The old woman looked at me. 'How are you getting on?'

'I'm okay.' Quite possibly the biggest lie I had ever told.

'Try not to worry too much about your legs. As long as you've got your mind.'

How did she know about my legs?

'Hold tight. Keep the faith.'

I forced a smile. 'I'll try to remember that.'

'Folk are always too quick to judge, point the finger, but you know what they're really saying, don't you, Michael?'

How did she know my name? 'No.'

'They're saying, hey, look at me, at least I'm not as bad as him. I don't stab my girlfriend with a kitchen knife and jump off the top of a block of flats. That's what they're really saying, isn't it?'

I could barely breathe as I watched the old woman's features smooth out. The wrinkles blended into one another and then vanished. Her mop of frizzy white hair straightened and grew longer. Darker. Fixed back in a loose ponytail.

'That's the trouble with this world, Mikey. Everyone's too concerned with what's going on in other folks' backyards.'

'I—'

'Until it's their turn to be in the firing line. Then it's a different story. They want justice for others, and compassion for themselves. But you don't need me to tell you that, do you?'

I watched her blue eyes turn brown. A purple bruise form on her rejuvenated cheek. A split on her bottom lip. 'No one wants to know the truth, Mikey. Not the real truth. They don't want to think too hard about their own rubbish lives. That's why they watch the soaps on TV. To watch someone else's suffering.'

I closed my eyes and counted to ten. This had to be another hallucination. It wasn't. She was still there when I opened them again.

She touched the bruise on her cheek. 'If they want the truth, Mikey, then you tell them this is the truth. This is what happens when you turn a blind eye.'

'Who are you?'

She didn't answer. 'Stay close to the truth.'

'Are you my mum?'

She smiled. 'I'm whoever you want me to be, Mikey.'

'But, I don't understand.'

A strand of dark hair fell across her face. She brushed it away. 'You will, as long as you look. As long as you listen.'

'Listen to who?'

'To the truth. Listen to the truth.'

Something glinted in her right ear. A small gold stud. I held up the one in my hand. 'Is this yours?'

'I wondered where that had got to.'

'It was on—'

'The stairs?'

'Yes.'

'It must have fallen out when Billy pushed me. I want you to keep it. Keep it always and forever, Mikey. Can you do that for Mummy?'

Tears spilled onto my cheeks. 'Yes.'

'I want you to promise to be a good boy for Mummy.'

'Yes.'

'Always tell the truth, no matter what. I know it's hard to tell the truth, when you're surrounded by dirty liars, but I want you to try, okay?'

'Yes, Mummy.'

'Remember, Mikey, the truth will always out. What goes around comes around. You just have to be patient.'

I watched her dark hair fade to grey, then white, then back into the old woman's frizzy mop. The bruise on her face vanished. The leathery cracked skin returned. The lips thinned.

'Be true to yourself, love-bug. Stay strong and do what's right.' Her mouth stilled. Her eyes rolled back in their sockets, and her head flopped to one side.

The old woman was dead.

CHAPTER 15

They moved me back to my old room a few hours later. I was grateful to get away from the man in the bed next to me, who kept asking me why I'd been talking to a dead woman. I didn't have an answer for him, or the strength to make one up. There was a new message scrawled in spidery red writing on the emergency door: Be true to yourself, love-bug. I didn't know whether to draw hope from the earring and the conversation with the old woman, or to question my sanity.

Dead women don't strike up conversations, much less turn into dead mothers.

Jimmy walked into the room. A friendly face. A rare thing. 'You look a bit better. How are you feeling?'

'Washed out.' A strange expression. Wrung out was probably a more apt description.

'I came to visit you two nights ago, but you were in a bad way. Kept babbling on about some fat man taking you to a boiler room.'

'Emily said.'

'Does it mean anything to you?'

'Fat Man does. The boiler room doesn't.' I told him about my latest journey into the tunnel, the murder, and the visit to the building, with the Fat Man leaning on the stone pillar.

He sat by the bed, silent, chewing his fingernails. When I was finished, he took a deep breath, and let it out between clenched teeth. 'Jesus, Michael, what the fuck is all this?'

I held out my mother's earring.

'Is that what I think it is?'

'I picked it off the stairs at the house. Brought it back with me. How fucking crazy is that?'

He took it out of my hand and studied it. I told him about the old woman in the bed opposite me.

'How the hell could she turn into your mother?'

I shrugged. 'Scared the shit out of me. Scared the shit out of me even more when it turned out she'd been dead all along.'

Jimmy seemed to mull this over, and then said, 'If I didn't know better, I'd say you dreamed it. Or had another hallucination, or something.'

'She had my mother's face, Jimmy. Her eyes. The bruises. The split lip. The matching earring. Everything. And now it says be true to yourself, love-bug, on the door. What the fuck am I supposed to do?'

'Sit tight and see what else happens.'

'Oh, and Carver wants to put me on remand.'

'Shit.'

'Even if all this stuff with the door and the tunnel is really happening, it's going to stop once they move me out of the hospital, isn't it?'

Jimmy didn't answer that. 'This house where you found the earring?'

'What about it?'

'Do you know the address?'

'It had a number "19" hand-painted on the front door.'

He laughed. 'That narrows it down to most of England.'

'Whitehead Street.'

'Do you know where?'

I didn't. 'Oxford, maybe?'

'I'll have a look on a street map. See if there's a Whitehead Street in Oxford. Go out there.'

'Are you sure?'

'It's the least I can do. You saved my life, remember?'

I couldn't. There was still a huge black hole between my mother's death and winding up in the hospital. 'The woman I went to after the murder lived about five or six doors along. Her name's Rachel.'

'I'll see if I can find her.' He was thoughtful for a moment, and then said, 'It's as if something's giving us a series of clues.'

'Or telling me I'm just like my old man.'

'No, Michael. I know you. And Becky. I've never seen that girl with a mark on her face. I've never heard her say a bad word about you. Ever. Lucy used to hang out with Becky sometimes. Same. Not one bad word. If you'd been anything like your old man, one of us would have known.'

'People hide things, Jimmy.'

'You can't hide the big stuff. The bruises. Depressions. Shit like that.'

'What does Lucy think?'

'She doesn't know what to think. She's only got the official story. What Carver said. You went home and stabbed Becky to death. That's it.'

'But, she must have an opinion?'

'She can't believe you'd do such a thing.'

'Have you told her about the wheelchair? The emergency door?'

Jimmy shook his head. 'I didn't want to risk that, mate. It would only convince her you were...'

'Nuts?'

'I'm certain you never killed Becky.'

'I'm not.'

'Yeah, well, you can't remember the real you, can you? You don't remember the Michael Tate I do.'

'Do you know how much that scares me.'

'I can imagine.'

'What do you think all this stuff means, Jimmy? Really means?'

'If I had to pin my money to a horse, I'd say your memory's coming back, bit by bit.'

'But, what about the earring?'

'For what it's worth, I think you're travelling back into your own past.'

'Really?'

'As mad as that seems, yeah.'

'So, who's the Fat Man at the gates of that building?'

'I don't know... but I reckon you're going to find out.'

I shuddered, as I remembered his glinting blue eyes, sweating face, shock of dark curly hair, finger ticking backwards, telling me the world ran anticlockwise. A sudden thought struck, chilling and realistic: maybe Carver was somehow related to him.

'Are you all right, Michael?'

I jumped back to reality. 'Yeah. Fine.'

He put a hand on my arm. 'It'll be all right. I'm going to get off, see if I can find this Whitehead Street.'

I thanked him and flopped back against the pillows. I felt stronger for having him fight my corner, comforted by the fact I'd rescued him from a knife-wielding thug. At least I wasn't all bad, wasn't a total coward, and possessed a tiny sliver of decency.

Emily came to see me, just before she went off shift. Like Jimmy, she told me I was looking better. I wished to Christ I felt it.

'Do you want anything before I go?'

I want you to stay. 'No.'

'I'll be off until the weekend.'

My heart buckled. 'Doing anything nice?'

'If you call celebrating my divorce nice, then, yes.'

'Sorry, I didn't—'

'It's all right. To be honest, I'm glad it's over. He was a nasty piece of work. If I had a shilling for all the promises he made and broke, I'd be a rich girl by now.'

'I'm sorry to hear that.'

'You've got enough worries of your own. You don't need to listen to me rabbiting on about my problems.'

'I don't mind.' It came out a lot quicker than I'd intended. And then, a little slower, 'You're the only person who hasn't judged me.'

'I'm only showing you a duty of care, Michael. Others might do well to remember their responsibilities.'

'But, you don't have to be nice. Not to someone like me.'

'You're innocent until proven guilty in this country.'

I didn't feel very innocent. 'What does the future hold for you?'

Emily spent the next half an hour talking about everything, from her newfound freedom to her pending promotion to staff nurse.

'That sounds like a good enough reason to celebrate,' I said, as she finished up and straightened a crease in her pale blue uniform.

'Can I say something, Michael?'

'Of course.'

'I like you. You don't seem like you've got a bad bone in your body. For what it's worth, I hope justice is done.'

My mouth hung open. I wanted to thank her. I wanted to tell her not to be stupid, I was guilty as charged. Carver knew it, I knew it, and soon, the rest of the world would know it, too.

She smiled down at me. 'Just stay strong, love-bug. Stay strong, and glue all the pieces together.' And then, she left, gliding out of the room in that odd, majestic manner of hers.

I spent the rest of the day trying to come to terms with the fact my mother had spoken from the lips of an old dead woman, and the lips of a beautiful young nurse.

CHAPTER 16

Jimmy returned the following morning. He looked about ready to explode. He'd barely made it into the room, before he started talking like a man possessed. 'Jesus Christ, man, it's true. It's all true.' He paced around the edge of the room, close enough to the emergency door to bang his hip on the bar which, of course, he didn't. It passed right through him. 'I looked Whitehead Street up on a map of Oxford. It's right before you get to the bridge, just off Dixon Street.'

Dixon Street meant nothing to me.

'Big row of terraced houses, right?'

'Yes.'

'Number 19?'

I nodded.

'Slap bang in the middle of the street?'

'Yeah.'

Jimmy stopped pacing and turned to face me. 'It was all like you said, Michael. Except the number wasn't hand-painted on the door. It had proper brass numbers. But, there were steps leading up to the front door, just like you said.'

I had a sudden flash of my mother being thrown down those steps, lying unconscious in the pouring rain.

'Anyway, I didn't get no answer when I knocked, so I went further along the street to see if I could find Rachel.'

'And?'

'The first door I knocked on said Rachel lived next door. Horrible old bag, who kept asking if I was from the social.'

'But, you found her?'

Jimmy grinned. 'Yep. Said I was a mate of yours passing through. Promised to look her up for you.'

'What did she say?'

'She seemed a bit shocked at first. Asked me how you were. Where you were living. I told her we were flatmates in London.'

'London?'

Jimmy shrugged. 'The best I could do with short notice. Anyway, she finally invited me in, after I mentioned Oxo.'

My heart stalled. 'Is he still there?'

'Yeah. He's old. Poor thing can't walk anymore. But, it was weird, like he knew me, was really pleased to see me.'

I imagined Oxo, with his head resting on my knee, brown eyes ever watchful. 'Maybe he knows.'

Jimmy smiled. 'I reckon he does. I told him you loved him. He looked like he understood, Michael. Really understood.'

I wanted to get out of that hospital bed, go to Whitehead Street, and give my best pal a hug. Tell him how much I loved him, how much I missed him, and how I wished we'd spent the rest of my childhood together.

'He's got a good home with Rachel.'

I wiped a tear from my eye. 'I'm grateful for that.'

'Anyway, she made a pot of tea. I told her we worked in a hotel together in Piccadilly. Close enough to the truth to stop my nose from growing long. She asked me if I knew what had happened with your mum. I made out I didn't. Then, she told me, Michael. Told me everything.'

'What did she say?'

'Same as you. How your dad was a nasty piece of work, and how he'd been beating up your mum for years. How she used to make excuses for him, saying she'd walked into doors and all that stuff and nonsense. Said she was going to get some cleaning jobs while he was out at work, save the money, and get as far away from him as possible.'

'I didn't know that.'

'She probably couldn't risk telling you, in case you got too excited and gave the game away. If you ask me, your mum was a brave woman. She didn't have too many choices. It's easy to say she should have just left him, but most battered women don't have anywhere else to go. They're trapped.'

'I feel so sorry for her, living with that bastard for all that time.'

After a few moments, Jimmy said, 'Do you want me to carry on?'

I nodded. I wanted it all. Every piece of information I could get. Whether it would help me in the long term was another matter altogether.

'It happened on Friday, December fifth, nearly ten years ago. Rachel said it had been pissing down all week. Your old man had already attacked your mum on the Thursday night. You banged on her door at about two in the morning. At first, she thought it was your mum, you know, run away from your dad again, but it was you and your dog, both soaked to the skin. She let you inside and called the cops. Exactly like you said, Michael.'

Thoughts formed in my mind and then popped like soap bubbles.

'Rachel said the whole street lined up for your mum's funeral. All paid their respects. That says a lot about your mum, Michael. A hell of a lot.'

It did. But, it still didn't make the pain any easier.

'Your old man got life. Minimum of twenty years.'

'At least there's some good news.'

'Rachel went to court for the trial. Said he showed no emotion. Just stood there like a lump of rock, staring ahead like a zombie. The judge called him a callous man, and a danger to women.'

'Stating the bleeding obvious.'

'There's something else.'

'What?'

'He hanged himself in jail a few years into his sentence.'

This news should have pleased me. Delighted me. My mother had finally got justice for all the years of abuse she'd suffered. But, it made me feel numb. Random thoughts popped into my mind. Good riddance. How did he hang himself? Now, I'm an orphan. How am I supposed to feel?

'Are you all right, Michael?'

Probably the daftest question I'd ever been asked in my new short-term-memory life. I felt like laughing and crying at the same time. 'So, what happens now? It doesn't alter anything, does it? Maybe I should just take what's coming. Go to prison, do my time, forget all this other stuff.'

'You can't think like that, Michael. Try to stay positive.'

'What for? Becky?'

'She wouldn't want you to give in.'

'Even if I killed her in cold blood?'

'You didn't.'

'But, you don't know that, do you? You just hope I didn't. There's a difference.'

'It's more than that.'

'Based on what?'

'Based on what I know about you.'

'What if you're wrong?'

'I wouldn't be here, if I believed you killed her.'

I wished I shared his optimism.

'Rachel said you were a good kid.'

'Kids grow up, Jimmy.'

He ignored that. 'She said you stayed with her for a few weeks after the murder. You and Oxo seemed to help each other.'

I still felt an invisible bond to that dog, even though my recent experience with him had only been brief. 'Where did I go after Rachel's? Aunt Jean's?'

Jimmy shook his head. 'Your aunt sided with your dad. She wanted nothing more to do with you. The authorities had to take you in.'

'Authorities?'

'The council took you away.'

'Where to?'

'A children's home. Then, to a foster family for about eighteen months. Then, back to the children's home.'

'Where is this home?'

'North Oxford somewhere. Out in the sticks. She came to visit you every Saturday morning the first time you were in there. Second time around, you refused to see her.'

'Why?'

'She doesn't know. The superintendent told her you refused her visiting order.'

'I thought I liked Rachel?'

'You did.'

'I don't get it.'

'I don't know, Michael. Maybe it was just easier if you didn't see her.'

I didn't believe that. Not if she was looking after Oxo. I'd have wanted regular contact, regular updates. 'Maybe the superintendent was lying.'

'Maybe.'

'Did she tell you anything else?'

'Not really. The last time she saw you was May ninth, nineteen sixty-seven.'

I considered asking Jimmy to go back and tell her how grateful I was for what she'd done for me. For looking after Oxo. But, what good would it do?

Jimmy asked, 'What do you want me to do now?'

'I need to think. Get my head around this.'

'Do you want me to leave?'

'If you don't mind. I'm knackered.'

'I'll come again tomorrow.'

I forced a smile. 'Thanks, Jimmy. Thanks for everything.'

He touched two fingers to his forehead. 'No problem.'

I watched him go. Truth be told, I just wanted God to let me die, and take me away from this unending mess.

CHAPTER 17

Carver came to visit later that day. He looked pleased with himself. Smugness seemed a perfect match for his ugly features. 'Hello, Michael. Nice to see you've got over your little bout of delirium. Doctor tells me your temperature soared right up to one hundred and two degrees. Would have been a shame to lose you right on the cusp of justice being served.'

I looked away. 'What do you want?'

He sucked in air through clenched teeth. 'Tch, tch, is that any way to greet the bearer of good news?'

I didn't give him the satisfaction of responding.

He sat down in the chair next to the bed. 'We're moving you out of here, Michael. Monday morning. How does that sound?'

It sounded like the worst thing I'd ever heard. 'Whatever.' I tried to sound nonchalant. I didn't. More like scared and helpless.

'Don't worry, we'll take care of you. See to your every need. Would you like that?'

'No.'

'Look at me, Michael.'

I tried not to, but did so all the same.

'That's better. I like to look into the eyes of criminals. It helps me to understand them better. What makes them tick. You can tell a lot from a man's eyes, don't you think?'

Yes, I can see evil in yours. 'I don't know.'

He smiled. 'You don't know a lot, do you?'

At least we could agree on something. 'No.'

'Convenient lapse of memory. Convenient injuries. If I didn't know you better, Michael, I'd think you were having us on.'

'I'm not.'

He laughed. 'Why don't you repent? Lay your soul bare to Jesus.'

'I don't believe in God.'

'Really? How do you know you don't believe? You said you don't remember anything – remember?'

I didn't respond. I wanted to reach out and touch him, just to make sure he was real. Not another illusion conjured up by my malfunctioning mind. Or, worse, someone who had somehow come from the tunnel. A hideous character from my past, intrinsically linked to the Fat Man.

'What's the matter, Michael? You look as if you've seen a ghost.'

'I'm tired.'

He shook his head and made a strange clucking noise with his tongue. 'I can see why. Keeping up all these lies. Deceiving all these people. It must be draining.'

'I'm not—'

'You can't kid a kidder, Tate. I've been around the block and back more times than I care to remember. I've seen it all. Liars, cheats, rapists, murderers, perverts. Guess what they all have in common, you scabby little shit?'

I swallowed hard and shook my head.

'They all say, without fail, they're innocent. I can guarantee it. You'll find that out when you go to prison. All have been fitted up by the cops. Or can't remember a thing. That's the piss-heads' favourite one. The old blackout clause. But, no one forced a glass to their lips, and poured the stuff down their throat, did they?'

'I suppose not.'

'You suppose right, sunshine. You take that useless idiot who spawned you. Remember him?'

For once, I actually did. 'No.'

'No. Silly me, you can't remember a thing. Okay, let me enlighten you. He beat your mother to a pulp and threw her down the stairs. Ring any bells?'

'No.'

'Claimed he couldn't remember a thing. Not even coming home with that useless tub of lard from the chip shop. Mind was all a blank. Personally, I never met your pop, but some of my colleagues have. Let me tell you, Michael, he was a shit of the highest order. A wife beater. A pisshead. A useless piece of crap.'

I had no arguments there. 'It's a good job I don't remember him, then, isn't it?'

'He hanged himself in prison. Wasn't even man enough to take his punishment. What sort of gutless wonder was he?' He didn't wait for an answer. 'The same sort of spineless coward I'm looking at right now. A chip off the old block. You're certainly a daddy's boy.'

I gripped the edge of the mattress.

'Only you went one better, didn't you? Outdid the old man. He'd be proud of you. Proud you stabbed poor Becky to death with a kitchen knife. Proud you had no intention of taking your punishment like a man. Proud you jumped off that block of flats. What do you reckon, Michael?'

'I don't know.'

'He hanged himself with a bed sheet. Quite a fitting way to go to the Big Sleep, don't you think? Oh, no, silly me, you don't think, do you? But, let me tell you this, Tate. I won't let that happen to you. I don't want you getting any ideas about taking the easy way out. I'll make sure they watch you like a hawk. I want you to serve every minute of your time. I want you to remember serving every minute of your time. Am I setting your alarm clock, Mikey?'

'Why did you call me that?'

'Call you what?'

'Mikey.'

'I didn't.'

'You did.'

He reached out and grabbed my nose. Squeezed it hard enough to bring tears to my eyes. 'Don't try to put words into my mouth, you little shit-popper. I never called you Mikey. Why would I call you Mikey? It sounds like the biggest baby name in the whole world.'

'Okay. Okay,' I squawked.

'Next you'll be accusing me of calling you my little buttercup. Is that what mummy used to call you before she fell down the Wooden Hill to Deadfordshire?'

'I don't know. I—'

'You can't go running to her now. Pissing your pants because the nasty man doesn't want to play your silly games.' He let go of my nose. 'Is that clear, Mikey?'

I nodded and touched my throbbing hooter.

'Good. As long as we understand each other. Where was I? Oh, yes, remand. You'll be taken from here on Monday morning and placed in a cell at the police station. It's just a formality. We'll try to sort you out a proper cell at the remand centre in due course, whilst you await trial.'

'Why can't I stay here?'

'Are you having me on?'

'No.' Desperate now. Almost on the verge of begging.

'You can't stay here. This is a hospital. It's for sick people, not a hotel for murdering bastards like you. Nurses have better things to do than waste time wiping your backside. Much better things to do.'

I thought about Emily. Never seeing her again. Dear sweet Emily. Her smile. Her compassion.

'From what I hear, they'll be glad to see the back of you. Get you out of their bed. I don't suppose you've got any idea how much it costs the taxpayers of this country to keep you in here? Treat you like a king?'

'No.'

'You're a selfish, little sponger, Tate. It will cost a bomb to keep you in prison, too, but that will be money well spent. Make you suffer. It's called getting something back.'

I had four days left in the hospital, then I would be left open to whatever abuse Carver wanted to mete out. I felt as helpless as a fly without wings.

'Ever heard of Johnny Proctor?'

'No.'

'The Butcher of Basildon?'

'No.'

'I'm going to make sure you share a cell with him. You'll like Johnny. I went to visit him last week. Told him he's on a promise with a pretty, blond boy. I know, stretching the truth a bit, but it's amazing what a little time inside does to a man. Some of them go in as straight as a ruler, come out as bent as a clock spring. Couple of years inside, and most of them are about ready to screw a skunk.'

I thought he was bluffing. Trying to wind me up.

'I watched that bulge in his crotch growing stiff just talking about it. He reckons it will be a challenge, you know, what with you being paralysed from the waist down. I take it you can't feel your arse, Mikey?'

I didn't answer him. It was only feeding his perverted mind.

'I'll take that as a no. Good thing really. Doesn't have to worry about you squealing like a girl when he shags you. And you don't have to worry about whether he's hung like a donkey. A match made in heaven. But, I can tell you, Mikey, he's a big boy.' He stretched his arms wide. 'And he likes to use things. Rolling pins, broom handles, bottles. He's very imaginative for someone who killed his whole family with a baseball bat.'

'Leave me alone.'

'As you wish, Mikey. But we still need to go over a few things first. Iron out a few creases, and then I'll leave you to it. Leave you to enjoy the weekend. First up, what is your name?'

'You know what my name is.'

'Just answer the question, or I'll poke you in the eye and see what pops out.'

'Michael.'

'Michael what?'

'Tate.'

'Age?'

'Twenty-one.'

'Why did you kill Becky Marie Coombs?'

'I don't remember.'

'Why did your daddy kill your mummy?'

'I don't—'

'Liar! I told you why. He was a no good, drunken pig, who liked to reshape your mummy's face with his fists.'

'I—'

'Why did you kill that poor boy buried in Bluebell Woods?'

'I didn't.'

He thumped my leg with his fist. 'Don't play games with me, Tate. You killed the boy. You sexually abused him and then strangled him with a pair of tights.'

'I—'

'Do you get off on throttling fifteen-year-old boys with girls' tights?'

'No.'

'Do you like the feel of tights?'

'No.'

'Dressing up in women's clothes?'

'No.'

'Are you a transvestite?'

'I don't—'

'Remember? No, of course you don't. You'll get on famously in prison, if you put a frock on, Mikey. Maybe some pretty, French knickers. Eye shadow and lipstick. You'll be the belle of the ball.'

I gave up trying to answer.

Carver was quiet for a moment as if weighing up something important. 'If I find out you've been lying, I'll make you suffer like no one's ever suffered before. If you get in that court room, and blather on about how you suddenly remember everything, claim Jesus has gifted you a miracle, I'll make you wish your mummy was already dead the night your old man got her knocked up. Do you understand, Mikey?'

I did. Only too well.

He stood up and left without another word.

CHAPTER 18

By lights out, I was contemplating suicide again. Saving up my painkillers and ending it all. The only thing holding me back was the fear of it going wrong, not using enough pills to do the job properly, and ending up in a worse state than I already was. If that was at all possible.

As my mind hopped from one decision to another, like a bird searching for worms, the bolt on the emergency door slid open, screeching in its rusty sheath. The locking bar moved down, and the door swung open to reveal the waiting darkness. The brake released, and the wheelchair moved across the room. It pulled alongside the bed. Again, those invisible hands helped me into the chair.

For one terrible moment, I thought the pusher might be my father, come back from the dead to take me to hell. 'Who are you?'

No answer.

Goosebumps hatched on my arms as we moved across the room and through the open doorway. The unoiled wheel screeched like a gull. The door closed, and I was swallowed up by the darkness. The wheelchair rolled on and on through the pitch black. Somewhere in the distance, I thought I heard a dog barking. Or was it just my imagination playing tricks?

You'd better not tell, boy.

The words came from somewhere above me. Whispered, yet clear.

You'd better not scream.

'Who's there?' I shouted.

No one can hear you.

'What do you want with me?' The words bounced off the tunnel walls. 'What the fuck do you want with me?'

In the abattoir of dreams.

I felt wetness on my cheeks. A terrible emptiness squeezed my heart. A longing, undefined and intangible, as if my heart held a long-forgotten memory.

I heard sobbing, a child's. The sound poured from the very fabric of the tunnel. Oozed from the foundations, like a deep well of grief. And then it vanished, replaced by a man's voice, cracked and dusty with age. The road to salvation is long. Many seek it, few find it, fewer endure it.

What the hell did that mean?

Many look, but do not see. Many touch, but do not feel. Many hear, but do not listen.

The wheelchair rolled on, deeper and deeper into the dark. I was again reminded of death. Oblivion. Nothingness.

Don't let them win, Mikey. Don't let the fuckers win. A boy's adolescent voice. I'll never cry. Never. Not in front of them. I wouldn't give them the satisfaction.

'Who are you?' I called again. No answer, just the swish-squeak of the tyres. The wheelchair veered right and headed towards a rectangle of light. As I drew closer, I realised it wasn't Whitehead Street; it was the building I'd seen on the way back from Whitehead Street. The one with the Fat Man leaning against the stone pillar. I remembered the kid being loaded into the ambulance, blond hair matted with blood.

The wheelchair stopped close to the entrance. I heard the click of the brake. Wind whipped against my face, cold and icy as death, kissing my bones. I suddenly realised I was once again a child, dressed in a pair of dirty grey trousers and a matching grey jumper. On my feet, a pair of scuffed black shoes. My teeth rattled in my head. Snot leaked onto my top lip.

I got out of the wheelchair, no longer burdened by my injuries. I stood facing the gate. A crisp packet blew along the street, brought to life by the wind, tumbling over and over, performing roly-polies, as my mother might say before Daddy threw her down the stairs and shut her up forever.

I saw Fat Man in the blue suit walk out of the central building. My heart froze. He waddled towards me, arms pumping, a nasty sneer on his face. As he drew closer, I could see beads of sweat on his forehead. How could that be? It was cold enough to kill. And then, I remembered him. Kalvin Kraft. The Superintendent at Woodside Children's Home. The man who had welcomed me with a punch in the stomach a few weeks after my mother's death. The man who had made my life hell for six months before shipping me off into the care of Mr. and Mrs. Davies.

He got to within about fifty feet of me. 'What are you standing there for, you gormless idiot?'

'I—'

'Where's Mr. Davies?'

'I don't know.'

'What do you mean, you don't know?'

'I don't know where he is.'

He stopped a few feet away, breath rasping in his throat. 'If you continue to stand there, like a dumb mutt who's lost its tail, I'll knock the stuffing out of you, sunshine. Is that clear?'

It was. I knew all about having the stuffing knocked out of me. 'Yes.'

'Yes, what?'

'It's clear.'

I didn't see his fist coming. It seemed to just materialise out of nowhere and hit me square on my right ear. The blow made me bite my tongue. A stinging pain erupted in my mouth.

'You call me sir, you useless waste of God's air. Is that clear?'

Crystal. 'Yes, sir.'

'I'll ask you one more time. Where's Mr. Davies?'

Hopefully, his car's been hit by a truck, I thought. 'He dropped me off here.'

'Why?'

Because I tried to bite his dick off. 'I don't know.'

Another whack. This time a slap around my cheek. It throbbed like a dozen bee stings. 'What did I say to you?'

For half a second, I was tempted to tell him to jump off a cliff. Turn around and run for my life. But, it was too cold. I'd probably only survive for a few hours out here wearing nothing but my flimsy jumper and threadbare trousers. 'Sir?'

'Yes, sunshine, sir, and don't you forget it.'

I made a mental vow not to. Mistakes bloody well hurt. 'No, sir.'

'Where's your stuff?'

'My stuff?'

'Are you an imbecile? Has your eighteen months with the Davieses addled your brain?'

'No, sir.' My eighteen months with the Davieses had done far worse than just addle my brain.

'Then why do you seem so confused by the simplest of questions? How old are you, boy?'

'Fourteen, sir.' It was hard to be sure; I hadn't had a proper birthday since my mother had died.

'So why are you acting like a snot-rag, who doesn't even know his times table yet?'

Because you scare the shit out of me. 'Sorry, sir.' By now, my teeth were rattling hard enough to break fillings.

'Where are your belongings?'

'I don't have any, sir.'

'What do you mean?'

Now who was a dumb fuck? 'I've only got these clothes, sir.'

'You expect me to believe that?'

I didn't. 'It's true, sir.'

He pulled the end of his nose as if trying to stretch it. His eyes seemed lost in the folds of flesh beneath them. 'I've had reports of your insolence, sunshine. The way you can lie at the drop of a hat. The way that you steal.'

I almost blurted out I only stole food because they sometimes refused to feed me when I wouldn't do as Mr. Davies asked. Something in Fat Man's eyes stopped me. A storm about to brew. 'Yes, sir.'

'You ought to think yourself lucky you don't live in Victorian times, Tate. They had the right idea, chopping off the hands of thieves.'

'Yes, sir.'

'Bastards like you would have been working in the mills and shimmying up chimneys in that Golden Age. You don't know how lucky you are, much less appreciate it.'

I wanted to go inside. Get out of the freezing cold weather. It felt more like the North Pole than North Oxford. 'Yes, s-sir.'

'Have you had a shower?'

I shook my head. The Davieses didn't have a shower. Just a bath. The only time I'd been allowed anywhere near it recently was to clean it in return for scraps of food. I'd never forget fishing their disgusting pubic hair out of the plughole and scrubbing the inside of the bath with Vim to get rid of black tide marks.

'Have you got lice?'

'I don't know.'

'You don't know much, do you?'

'No, sir.'

'Here's the problem we've got, sunshine. We can't let you go inside when you might be infested. You do know what infested means?'

I nodded.

'We don't want you giving lice to the other boys, do we?'

I imagined a nice hot shower, water cascading over my battered body, soothing my aching muscles, maybe some soap to cut through the scum on my skin. 'No, sir.'

'Good. Follow me. And look smart about it.'

I followed him along the front of the red brick building, past huge glass windows in chipped and peeling frames. It must have stretched for about fifty feet either side of the central structure. And now, I remembered what horrors lie behind those windows. The senior block, home to kids aged between eleven and eighteen. The toilets and showers block – possibly the most dangerous place on Earth. Junior block. Kalvin Kraft's office and study – the second most dangerous place on Earth. Boiler room and boot room. Unwanted memories invaded my brain. Some of them made Mr. Davies seem like a kind and generous man.

We turned around the corner of the building, past the huge brick-built coal shed, the bright yellow salt locker for de-icing the pathways, and to the huge playing field which stretched out to Bluebell Woods and beyond.

Kraft stood on the path, and sniffed the air, like a fox sensing prey. I stopped a few feet away from him. I was now shaking all over; part fear, part weather.

'I like the fresh air. Do you like the fresh air, Tate?'

Best to just agree. 'Yes, sir.'

'A good winter kills all the bugs. Gets rid of all those nasty diseases.'

'Yes, sir.'

He looked at me as if inspecting a turd. 'Are you all right?'

'I'm cold.' A lie. I was frozen to the bone.

He grinned, exposing two large yellow front teeth. 'Cold?'

I nodded and tried to lock my jaw to stop my teeth rattling.

'Don't you worry about that. You'll soon warm up.'

Again, I imagined a nice hot shower. 'Th-thanks.'

'You're welcome, Tate. Now, strip.'

At first I thought I'd misheard him. 'Sorry, sir?'

'Deaf as well as dumb?'

'No, sir.'

'Then get to it. Take off all your clothes and leave them in a pile on the path. I'll get Hodges to burn them.'

I studied his eyes for signs of teasing. They remained hard and cruel. Slits sleeping in folds of flesh. 'But—'

'But, nothing, you little shit-pike. Get out of those filthy clothes and drop them on the path. And that includes underwear.'

'But, why?'

A mistake. He stepped forward. Reached me in two strides and punched me in the stomach. A ball of flame erupted in my belly. I bent double, holding my stomach, head almost touching my knees. Tears blurred my vision.

'Stand up straight.'

I summonsed every ounce of strength I possessed to do as he asked. I could now see two of him. Twin evil. I wanted to puke. I wanted to cry. I wanted to scream in his face he was the world's biggest cunt, that he made my dad seem like a saint, but, I didn't dare to do any of those things. I was only brave in my head.

'You were only here for five months before Mr. Davies and his wife were kind enough to take you in, weren't you?'

How could I ever forget? 'Yes, sir.'

'You were a runty little shit then, and you're a runty little shit now, aren't you?'

'Yes, sir.'

'There are three types of people in this world, Tate. Firstly, we have good honest hard-working people, who dedicate their lives to serving their country. Those who work for the greater good. You do know what the greater good is, don't you?'

I didn't, but I didn't want to give him another reason to belt me. 'Yes, sir.'

'But, scum like you don't appreciate such people, do you?'

'Yes, sir.'

Wrong answer. I was treated to a flat-handed slap to the side of my head. My brain lurched to one side of my skull and back again. 'Don't lie, you little shit-pike. You don't appreciate anything. You've proved that much with your lack of respect for Mr. and Mrs. Davies.'

Respect, my mind screamed. Respect for those evil bastards? 'I'm sorry, sir.'

'You will be. By God, you will.' He seemed lost for a moment, and then said, 'Which brings me onto the second type of person. Those who see the error of their ways, get their act together, and put themselves on the straight and narrow. Tainted, but nonetheless worthy of praise. God likes a trier, Tate.'

As far as I was concerned, God also seemed to like a psychopath. Other than my mother, Rachel, and Aunt Jean, all women, incidentally, everyone else seemed like they'd come straight from hell.

'And then, there's the likes of you, Tate. The low-life and the scum. The worthless shits of the world. The ones all the good people have to take care of because they're too useless to take care of themselves. Breeding like rabbits in their dirty little hutches and expecting the state to wipe their backsides when it all goes wrong. The drinkers. The gamblers. The murderers. The philanderers. Ring any bells?'

It did. My father. I opted for silence. I was too cold and hurt to make any more mistakes. At least that's what I thought, before Kraft cranked his evil ways up a notch.

'Yes, Tate, you might well look at the floor in shame. You recognise your own worthless father in that lot, don't you?'

'Yes, sir.'

'Look at me when I talk to you.'

I peered up into that twisted sneering face.

'This world would be a much better place, if runts like you were wiped off the face of the Earth. Stop the cycle. Sterilise the women at birth and stop them breeding like whores.'

'Yes, sir.'

'But, until the state comes to its senses, we have to take care of you. Does that sound fair to you, Tate?'

'No, sir.'

'Bloody well right it isn't. But, here we are. All I can do is serve my country and make the best of a bad lot. So, you strip out of those clothes and put them on the path like I asked you. Now!'

I peeled off my jumper and the thin vest and dropped them onto the ground.

'I've seen more backbone on a snake.'

I no longer cared what he was saying. I was too cold to think. The wind whipped around my skeletal body as if sensing premature death. I kicked off my shoes and stepped out of the trousers. I watched his eyes roam all over my naked body as I stood shivering in my baggy white underpants.

'There's no hope for you, is there?'

'No, s-s-sir.'

'Do you think it's acceptable to be a liar?'

'N-n-no, s-s-sir.'

'A despicable little thief.'

I shook my head and wrapped my arms around my chest.

'I can't hear you, Tate.'

'No, s-s-sir.'

'You're damn lucky you're not in borstal after what you did. We've got your cards marked.'

'Y-y-yes, sir.'

'Now, get out of those underpants. What part of strip don't you understand?'

'It's f-f-f-freezing.'

'It's a good job it is. Kill all your disgusting germs. Unless you think infecting the other children is a good idea, do you?'

'N-no.'

'You'll soon warm up.'

Again, I imagined a lovely hot shower.

'This field is the best part of three quarters of a mile around the perimeter, Tate. I'm going to give you a little sum to do. I want you to tell me how many times you would have to run around the field to complete three miles?'

I tried as hard as I'd ever tried in my life, but my brain refused to play any more games. It had, quite literally, frozen. 'I d-d-don't know, s-sir.'

Kraft shook his head. 'Fourteen years of age, and you can't even do a simple sum? Is that what you're telling me?'

Unfortunately, it was.

He reached down and grabbed my balls. Squeezed them hard and twisted. Pain erupted in my groin and spread like wildfire into my stomach. I stood panting like a steam train.

'Try again.'

'I... d-don't... know.'

He let go of my balls, and wiped his hand down the front of his neatly pressed, blue trousers. 'You disgust me.'

I didn't care. Hopefully, I disgusted him enough to let me crawl off somewhere and die.

'The answer is four. Four times three quarters equals three.'

I threw up. Nothing substantial. I'd eaten virtually nothing for two days. Bile scorched the back of my throat.

'Off you go.'

'What?'

'Four laps of the field, you stupid little retard. And I don't mean dawdle, like you're out for a nice country walk, I mean run. You do know what run means?'

'Yes, s-sir.'

'Then, get to it.'

I set off. I tried to tell myself at least I might warm up a bit, stand a chance of surviving if I could move fast enough. I knew Kalvin Kraft would have been more than happy to watch me die. In fact, I'm sure he would have got some sort of sick pleasure out of it. I remembered him almost killing me once before. Choking me until I passed out. Coming around to find him doing stuff that had made me wish I was dead.

I reached the bottom of the field. There was a six-foot steel fence separating the field from the surrounding woods, and a locked gate barring access. I wondered if I could climb over the gate and disappear into the woods.

Great idea, Mikey. And then what? Make a nice bed out of leaves and settle down for the night under the stars. You'll be dead before you can say Jack Frost.

Maybe dead was better than this. At least I'd no longer feel the cold. Or my aching battered body. I ran past the gate and started back up the other side. There was a terrible dull ache in my balls. My lungs burned. My eyes blurred. Tears froze on my cheeks.

The field was quite a steep climb on the way back to the top. I thought I was going to throw up again. I was running on empty.

He clapped his hands together. 'Come on, Tate. Put some effort into it.'

I wanted to run up to him, and put my hands around his throat, squeeze the fucking life out of him. Spit on his corpse. But, power was everything, and they had all the power. Power thrived on helplessness, and we were certainly helpless. Just kids, with nowhere to go, and no one to love us. A perfect match, you might say.

I made it around that field three times before I finally collapsed. Kraft kicked my naked body several times. Threatened punishment, if I didn't get up off my lazy arse and start running again. At one point, he stood on the back of my neck, and pushed my chin into the frozen earth.

I didn't care anymore. I was convinced I was going to die. Get a ticket out of there. See my mum again. Feel her warm arms around me. Snuggle up. Mummy and her little love-bug.

No Billy the Bully.

No Mr Davies.

And no Kalvin Kraft to ever hurt us again.

And then, I slipped into unconsciousness.

Thick, black, and comforting.

CHAPTER 19

I woke up to find myself in a soft warm bed, with a tall thin woman standing over me, hair scraped back from her face, and fixed in a bun on top of her head. She looked like a bird of prey. God on Earth, where was I now? I closed my eyes and then opened them again. Still there.

'How are you, Michael?'

I licked my lips; scaly as a lizard. 'Where am I?'

She smiled. The smile never reached her eyes. 'In the sick bay. You caught a chill. You've been in bed for the last three days.'

My throat felt as if it was lined with sandpaper. And then, a nasty realisation crept in, as I remembered Kraft making me run naked around the field. 'Who are you?'

She smiled again. Those beady eyes ever watchful. 'I'm Aunt Mary.'

'I don't remember you.'

'I've only been here a year. Superintendent tells me you were here eighteen months ago.'

I nodded. Now fully aware. Did he also tell you he's a cruel and sadistic bastard, who gets off on watching young boys suffer? 'Are you a nurse?'

This time she laughed. She clapped a hand over her mouth as if trying to stop the sound escaping. 'Me? A nurse? Cripes, no. I'm a seamstress.'

'What's that?'

'You don't know?'

I shook my head.

'I sew things. Mend things. All the uniforms. The bedding. If it's got a stitch, I'm in charge.' Another tiny laugh. More of a nervous giggle. 'But, I also help with the sick bay.'

'I don't remember a sick bay last time I was here.'

'It's not a proper one. It's just a bed out the back of the clothing store for minor stuff. Anyone who gets really sick has to go to the hospital.'

'Like Davy?'

'Who's Davy?'

I almost told her how Thomas Reader, the deputy supervisor, had hit him over the head with a poker one morning in assembly. His only crime? Not reciting the Lord's Prayer properly. Davy was only nine. A good kid from the junior block. We never saw him again after the ambulance took him away. I'll never forget the blood staining his dirty blond hair crimson. The way his eyes had rolled back in their sockets. The way he'd slumped to the floor. The awful silence hanging in the air, thick and suffocating.

'Michael?'

'Just some kid. No one important.' An understatement in this place.

'I've brought you some aspirin. Sit up, we don't want you to spill.'

I forced myself to do as she asked. Even though I was suspicious of all adults, Aunt Mary didn't seem as bad as some of the others. I forced down the tablets and finished the glass of water. Some of it dribbled down my chin. I wiped it away with the back of my hand.

'I reckon you'll be all right to go back to the senior block this afternoon.'

I didn't want to. I wanted to stay here, out of the way, safe and warm, under the watchful eye of this strange, but seemingly decent woman, with her starched face and scraped back hair. 'I feel like death.'

'It'll do you good to get up. Get your muscles working again, and the blood pumping around your body.'

'I don't want to.'

'Don't be silly. Would you like soup for lunch?'

My stomach roared to life. 'Yes.'

'Yes, what, young man?'

'Please.'

'That's better. There isn't much free in this life, but manners and the air you breathe are. You'd do well to remember that.'

I watched her walk away, her back ramrod straight, her starched black dress sweeping the floor as she went. She reminded me of a Victorian woman in the history books at school. I wondered if she was wearing one of those corset things, which had to be laced up the back and pulled tight enough to crush rocks. I also wondered if she had any idea what really went on at Woodside. The way the kids were treated. If she did, she was doing a good job of hiding it. Perhaps she had it tucked away in that neat bun of hers, locked up tight and fixed in place with bobby pins.

My first spell at Woodside was hazy, dimmed by my eighteen months with the Davieses. It had lasted about five months, until May fifth, nineteen sixty-seven. I'd arrived straight from Rachel's, about two weeks after my mother's death. December nineteenth. Pissing down with rain. A large green car had pulled up. A man had come to the door wearing a bowler hat and a black suit. He had a short, trimmed moustache and cold grey eyes. I remember thinking how much this man seemed to match the weather.

'This is Mr. Bloomsbury,' Rachel had said, as she'd showed him into the living room.

I didn't greet him. I wondered if he was an undertaker come to talk about my mother's funeral. I focussed all my attention on Oxo, who was curled up on my lap.

'Hello, Michael.' He removed his hat and stood in front of me.

'Mr. Bloomsbury is from Social Services, Michael.'

I studied Oxo's back, making patterns in his fur with my fingers. 'So?'

He shifted his weight from one foot to the other. 'How are you, lad?'

'I'm all right.' A lie. My heart felt like a lump of coal. The image of my dead mother lying at the bottom of the stairs, body twisted, one eye half-open, as if refusing to die, haunted every waking hour.

He lowered his bowler hat and held it in front of his crotch. 'Has Mrs. Cougan talked to you?'

'About what?'

He looked uneasy. 'About how you can't stay here, lad?'

I switched my attention to Rachel. 'Why can't I?'

'It's not because I don't want to look after you, Mikey. I want you to know that. It's just that there's not room.'

'But, I don't mind sleeping on the sofa.'

'I know. But, once the baby's born, Tommy will have to sleep in the front room. We're cramped as it is.'

'What baby?'

She looked hesitant. 'I'm pregnant.'

Why did she want another kid if the place was cramped already? I didn't understand.

Bloomsbury said, 'You'll have your own bed at Woodside, Michael. No more kipping on the sofa.'

I looked into that wintery face. 'Woodside?'

He nodded. 'Woodside Children's Home. It's a special place for children like you.'

'I don't want to go.'

'I'm afraid you don't—'

Rachel cut him off. 'Just give it a go, Mikey. Like Mr. Bloomsbury says, you'll have your own bed. Meet other boys your age. It'll be more like an adventure.'

'It won't. I'm not going.'

'And you get the chance to earn money each week,' Bloomsbury offered.

I didn't want money. I didn't want my own bed, or to meet other boys. 'I don't care if it's the Queen's palace. I'm not going.'

Bloomsbury pulled a piece of paper out of his jacket pocket. He unfolded it and held it out before him like a declaration of war. 'Do you know what this is, Michael?'

'No.' And I didn't care either. Oxo wriggled in my lap.

'It's a care order.'

'I don't care what it is.'

'It's from the courts. It says you have to come with me.'

I shook my head. 'No. No way.'

'You don't have a choice, lad. Don't make this hard on yourself. Don't make this hard for the lady who's been good enough to give you a home.'

I looked at Rachel. 'Please. I don't want to go. I want to stay here. I don't care if I have to sleep in the coal shed. Please don't make me go.'

'I'm sorry, Mikey. We just don't have room for you.'

A sudden flash of inspiration. A rescue plan. 'What about Aunt Jean?' I liked it there. She was pretty cool once you got through the fag smoke.

Bloomsbury extinguished my last flicker of hope. 'She doesn't want you, lad. She's made that quite clear.'

'But, why?'

He didn't answer for a moment. When he did, I saw the first faint hint of emotion in his eyes. 'She's taken your father's side.'

'What's that supposed to mean?'

'What I say, lad. She wants nothing more to do with you.'

The words cut through my heart like a saw. How could she side with my dad after what he'd done? Bloomsbury had to be lying, trying to turn me against Aunt Jean. I'd gone to stay with her the night before my mum died. 'That's not true. Aunt Jean wouldn't—'

'She would, lad. It's a fact. The sooner you get used to it, the better. You don't want to walk around your whole life deluded, do you?'

'I don't want to go to no kids' home. I know that.'

'Like I said, I have a court order in my hand that says you have no choice. I also have a policeman waiting in the car. Do you want me to call him?'

Oxo jumped off my lap and trotted over to the window. He jumped up, and rested his paws on the sill, as if he'd known what Bloomsbury had just said. 'What for?'

'There's no need for the police,' Rachel said.

A sudden surge of hope. She'd changed her mind. Come to her senses. She wanted to let me stay. She would send this Bloomsbury idiot packing, back to his stupid children's home, with his stupid bowler hat and his stupid piece of paper from the courts.

Rachel sat on the sofa next to me. She reached out and took one of my hands. She gave it a small squeeze. 'It's nothing to worry about, Mikey. You'll see. Within a week or two, you'll be glad you're not still cramped up here. And there's visiting, isn't there, Mr. Bloomsbury?'

'Every Saturday,' he confirmed. 'Subject to good behaviour.'

She smiled. It looked more like a grimace. 'I'll come and visit you every week. I promise. Keep you up to speed with Oxo and stuff.'

Oh, God, I hadn't even thought about Oxo, about being separated from my best pal in the whole world. That sealed it for me. There was no way I was leaving Whitehead Street. No way I was leaving my only real friend behind. 'I'm not going.'

She squeezed my hand harder. 'Please, Michael. Just for me. Give it a try.'

'No.'

She looked at Bloomsbury. He put his hat down on the pine coffee table and tucked the court order back inside his jacket pocket. 'For goodness sake, lad, see sense. Anyone would think I'd come to cart you off to war. I'm offering you a place at a very reputable establishment. You'll get bed and board, and everything you need. You'll still go to school.'

'I don't care.'

He changed tack. 'Do you think I'm to blame for your mother's death?'

I didn't even bother to answer that.

'Do you think the state can afford to keep the likes of you?' This time he didn't wait for an answer. 'Of course they can't. But, they try to give the likes of you a decent education, and a chance to grow up into responsible adults. I sometimes wonder why they even bother, for all the thanks they get.'

'Fuck off.'

Rachel dropped my hand like a hot potato. 'Michael Tate! Apologise!'

No way. I could see Oxo eying up Bloomsbury. Hackles up. A low growl grinding in his throat.

Bloomsbury took this as his cue. 'Okay. Have it your way. I'll fetch the police constable to deal with you.'

I watched him collect his hat and go into the hallway. Heard the front door open and bang shut. Oxo sat on the floor in front of me, head resting on my knee, eyes fixed on mine.

'Please don't make this hard on yourself,' Rachel said, her voice barely above a whisper.

'Then don't make me go.'

'I've got no choice, Mikey.'

'Don't call me that.'

'What?'

'Mikey. It's babyish. My name's Michael.' Mikey was my mum's pet name for me. As far as I was concerned, she was the only person allowed to call me that, apart from one or two close friends. But, not this woman, who'd betrayed me, and let a fucking twat in a bowler hat take me away from my dog.

'I'm sorry. If I could make it any different, I would. Believe me.'

'Liar.'

'Give it a go. You might be surprised.'

I didn't want to "give it a go". I had known a kid at junior school, who went to a kids' home. A right loner, always looked lost, clothes worn to threads. Norman something or other. Kids picked on him. Said he stank, pissed his pants, and shitty stuff like that. I didn't want to be like Norman, lost and abandoned. He had a huge, red blotch on the side of his face. A birthmark? Or something worse. Kids asked, but Norman never told. He used to hold his hands over his ears and run away when the questions got too much for him.

Oxo looked up at me as if to say, hey, it's me, what's going on?

'Michael?'

'What?'

'What do you say? Give it a go?'

'And if I don't like it?'

She didn't answer that. 'Why don't you take Oxo into the kitchen and give him one of his treats.'

What she really meant was go and say goodbye to him. I reluctantly agreed. Oxo followed me, a couple of inches from my heels, all the way. It was a mystery how that dog never got himself trampled.

I closed the kitchen door and went under the sink where his packet of Choco Drops was stored. Oxo sat, straight backed, ready to beg. I fished out a few and held them in the palm of my hand. 'There. You have them.'

He looked at me, as if to say, don't you want me to beg? Seemed to realise in half a second I didn't, and swiped them from my hand with a single slurp of his tongue. Into his mouth, straight down, no need to chew.

I crouched in front of him. 'You silly old dumb dog.'

Oxo didn't seem to mind being called names. Not when goodies were on offer. I gave him a couple more and folded the packet up. Enough. They were treats, not dinner. I stuffed them back under the sink. Now what did I say? Don't worry, Oxo, they're taking me off to one of those crappy children's homes. I probably won't see you again. Ever. I won't see you grow old. You won't see me grow up.

A tear spilled onto my cheek, hot and burning. 'You know I love you, don't you?'

Oxo sniffed my hand and licked it.

'I don't want to leave you. Don't ever forget that.'

He barked. A single yap. And then, he studied me intently.

'They made me go,' I blurted. 'Adults and their stupid, fucking ideas.'

He licked the back of my hand. A single lick which said more than any words ever could.

I sat on the floor, wrapped my arms around his neck, and cried my eyes out until the policeman walked into the kitchen and took me away. He looked like a fuzzy blob through the mist of my tears. I wanted to fight them all. Zap them and turn them to dust. Stay here forever with Oxo. But, I didn't. I let that copper lead me out of Rachel's house, and put me into the big, green car waiting by the kerb. I sat in the back with Mr. Bloomsbury, and didn't look back once, as we drove out of Whitehead Street towards North Oxford.

I could still hear Oxo whining in my head when we arrived at Woodside Children's Home. See his pitiful eyes looking up at me. Feel the warmth of his tongue on my hand. I'd failed him. Like I'd failed my mum. Michael Tate was the biggest failure the world had ever seen. Things didn't get any worse than this.

But, they did. A lot worse. A whole Grand Canyon worse. Just when you thought you'd hit the bottom, a trapdoor opened, and threw you down a load more steps.

Aunt Mary returned with a bowl of chicken soup and a slice of bread, balanced on a dirty white tray. 'You must sit up, mind. Don't want to spill it.'

I did as she asked. She balanced the tray on my lap. 'Would you like anything else? Some milk?'

Perhaps I'd died running around that playing field. Died and gone to heaven. Aunt Mary was an angel. 'Can I?'

She smiled and fussed with her bun. 'Course.'

Why couldn't all adults be like her? Surely, they were meant to look after kids, not beat the crap out of them for no reason. Why did they have to be such vicious pigs? No, not pigs, that was an insult to pigs. No pig would ever behave like Selwyn Davies or Kalvin Kraft; they had much better morals than that.

CHAPTER 20

I picked up my new set of clothes the following morning from Aunt Mary's stockroom. Two pairs of black trousers, one with a patch on the knee, the other with one leg shorter than the other, two black jumpers, one with a hole in the right elbow, two off-white shirts, and a pair of black shoes.

'I know they're threadbare. Bring the jumper back when you get a chance, and I'll stitch the elbow,' Aunt Mary said.

I nodded, shivering in my thin blue pyjamas. I still hadn't recovered from my ordeal running around the playing field, but whether I liked it or not, my days of skiving in the sick bay were over – Kalvin Kraft's orders.

Aunt Mary smiled at me. 'Go on. You'd better go and get a shower before breakfast.'

I thanked her and hurried back to the senior block. To say the place was a bit depressing was like saying death was a bit scary. It was as miserable as sin as my mother used to say. Grey-painted walls, blistered and peeling. Polished wooden floor. Half a dozen iron beds lined up either side of the room, a single metal locker for all belongings dividing them. Clothes had to be folded to the size of an eight-inch square rule book. God help any kid who failed inspection. One speck of dust under the bed could result in a punishment more befitting of murder.

I folded my new clothes and put them away, grabbed a hand towel from the same locker, and rushed along the corridor in my pyjamas to the shower room. The other kids had finished in the shower and were scrubbing their teeth at chipped white hand basins dotted along the bathroom.

'Where have you been, Tate?' The soft-spoken tones of Thomas Reader, the deputy superintendent. I'd learned from my first time around not to be fooled by his manner of speaking. He was every bit as vicious as the shouters and bawlers. More so.

'I had to get my stuff from the clothes store, sir.'

'Ah, "stuff." Such an ambiguous word, wouldn't you say?'

I had no idea what "ambiguous" meant. I agreed all the same. To be honest, as far as questions from staff were concerned, you were damned if you did, and damned if you didn't.

'Would you care to elaborate?'

'What do you mean, sir?' Something nasty stirred in my stomach. Dozens of eyes on me. An uneasy silence in the air.

'Elaborate on what you mean by "stuff"?'

'My clothes, sir.'

'There. That wasn't so bad, was it?'

'No, sir.'

He walked up to me, glasses steamed up. His precision-parted, black hair glistened. I smelled garlic and tobacco on his breath. 'You are aware that shower time is 6am, aren't you?'

Shit. 'I've not been well, sir.'

He grinned, revealing tobacco-stained teeth. 'Oh, dear. Poor you. Did you hear that, boys? Tate hasn't been well.'

A few snickers echoed around the bathroom. I heard a tap dripping somewhere, ticking like a hollow clock.

'Tell me, Tate, what caused you to languish in bed while the rest of the boys were all up, bright eyed and bushy tailed?'

'I had the flu.' I knew this was a mistake the instant the words left my mouth. I wanted to suck them out of the air and right back down my throat.

'You had the flu?'

'Yes, sir.'

'That's not what Aunt Mary said when I asked her why you missed assembly yesterday. She said, and I quote – "the boy has a chill".'

'Yes, sir.'

'Not flu.'

I looked at the beige tiled floor. 'Sorry, sir.'

'Since when has a chill been called the flu?'

I shrugged. Fuck it. I knew I had it coming. I might as well do something to deserve it. Act as if I didn't care. Disrespect him.

'Well?'

'Well, what?'

A few more snickers. Reader asked the other boys to leave, never once raising his voice. My bladder felt like a swollen river. Reader closed the door. I imagined some of the boys standing outside, ears pressed to the door, waiting for my punishment.

'Do you think you're clever, Tate?'

'No, sir.'

'Do you think you can just come swanning back here, without a care in the world, after the way you've treated Mr. and Mrs. Davies?'

How I treated that pair of fucking psychopaths? 'No, sir.'

'You were trouble before you went, and you're trouble now, Tate. Is that a fair assessment?'

My initial burst of bravado, my act of defiance, had now turned to jelly. 'I don't want to cause trouble, sir.'

'Your sort never do, do they? Trouble just seems to follow you around, like a bad smell, doesn't it?'

Like your breath. 'I don't know, sir.'

'How long did you spend in the sick bay?'

'Three days, sir.'

'Three days for a chill? I think that says a lot about your character, doesn't it?'

Maybe you ought to try running around a field naked in the freezing cold. See how you get on with it. 'Yes, sir.'

'We had to dig trenches in the war. Over six feet deep, on bone hard ground. Live in them for months on end. What do you think

144

would have happened to the war effort if we'd said, Please, sir, I've caught a chill, fly me home to Blighty, let me snuggle up in a nice warm bed?'

'I don't know, sir.'

'No? Then, let me tell you. You'd have been talking German and living under Hitler's house rules by now. Would you have preferred that, Tate?'

'No, sir.'

'Damned right you wouldn't. Where do you think this country would have been if we'd just given in at the first sign of a chill? But, are you grateful?'

This conversation was starting to have a familiar theme. It was as if they were all reading from the same script. 'Yes—'

'Don't lie to me. You lot wouldn't know grateful if it leapt up and bit you on the nose. You're all take, Tate. I've seen men, with fifty times your backbone, go to their graves to make sure this country stayed free from Nazi Germany. Young men leaving behind their loved ones to fight. Ensure your future. But, you don't care about that, do you?'

'Yes—'

'Don't care about all those poor lads, who laid down their lives for a spineless generation, like you.'

How was I supposed to feel grateful for something which happened before I was even born?

'No. You don't care. And, frankly, I sometimes wonder why the hell we bothered at all.'

What did I say to that? Fall to my knees and thank him for saving me from Hitler? 'I'm sorry, sir.'

'You're not sorry, Tate. You're not grateful, either. But, I've got better things to do than discuss the merits of great men with the son of a whore.'

My heart stopped. 'What did you say?'

'I said I've got better things to do than stand here chinwagging with the son of a whore.'

145

'My mum wasn't a whore.'

'Really? I have it on good authority she was screwing the local chip shop owner.'

Heat crept into my cheeks. 'That's a lie.'

'Liked to batter his sausage.'

'Shut up!'

He grinned. 'Some say the only reason the Tates didn't starve was because your mother went horizontal for a bag of chips and a pickled egg.'

Something fell through the bottom of my stomach. My heart pumped like a piston. 'You take that back.'

He stepped back, the grin slipping from his chops. One of his hands balled into a fist. 'What did you say, Tate? Are you disputing your mother was a whore?'

'Yes.'

'Yes, what?'

'Yes, I fucking am.'

He looked uncertain. 'I can see you're a chip off your father's block, Tate. You've got his arrogance. His swagger.'

I didn't care what he said about my dad. But, my mother…

'But, let me tell you, we don't tolerate any of that nonsense here. Do you understand me, Tate?'

I shook my head. Fuck off.

'I want you to repeat after me: my mother was a whore.'

'No.'

'My mother was a whore who sold herself for a bag of chips.'

'No.'

'A wishing well for drunks.'

I don't remember what happened next. I didn't make a conscious decision to attack him. I was vaguely aware of being in a struggle with him, my feet trying to get a grip on the slippery bathroom floor. The next thing I knew, Mr. Malloy, the senior block supervisor, was pulling us apart like a pair of fighting dogs.

146

I stood panting, holding onto one of the hand basins for support. My nose dripped blood. My head throbbed. Reader dabbed his face with a handkerchief and said something to Malloy. Precision parting no longer quite so precise.

Malloy ordered me to Kraft's study and told me to wait there.

'Do I get dressed first?'

'Get there. Now.'

I did. Mercifully, Kraft wasn't in his study. I saw an open fire burning in the study through a small side window. Apart from the reception and the staff quarters, Kraft's office was the only heated room in the building. The junior block had hot-water pipes running through it, but the senior block had nothing. No heating whatsoever.

I stood there in my pyjamas and bare feet, shivering from head to toe, more nerves than cold. I considered legging it to the bogs and having a piss before Malloy came to do his worst, but I didn't dare move. I was in enough trouble already.

The clock in Kraft's office said six-twenty. Breakfast was at six-thirty, assembly at seven, then out front to catch the school bus. I didn't think I would be getting any breakfast today. Ten minutes passed. Twenty. No Malloy. I wondered if he'd forgotten about me. But, he wouldn't do that. My imagination filled in the blanks and designed its own brand of punishments; things that would make running naked around the field seem like a happy memory.

Once, during my first time at Woodside, Kraft made me crouch in the corner of his office for over an hour, hands held out in front of me. Every time I looked as if I was sagging, he whacked me across the back of my hand with his cane. One, single swipe. That hour had seemed like a month.

Now what are you going to do?

I took another peek at the clock. Six-thirty-five. Perhaps he was busy with breakfast.

Or he's trying to make you suffer.

Fuck him. Reader had insulted my mother. If I ever got the chance, I would kill him.

Yeah, right, Mikey. You and whose army?

Malloy turned up at just past seven. He was tall, thin and stooped. His hooked nose was speckled red, like his cheeks. He opened the study door, walked in, and banged it shut without looking at me. I needed a piss. Why couldn't he have just done his worst in the shower room? Left me to get on with it?

Because he enjoys watching you suffer.

They were all sick in the head. Reader, Malloy, and Kraft all had staff quarters on the first floor above the reception. Although I'd never been up there, Craig McCree, the head boy, who also had a room on the first floor, boasted about what they had. Proper showers, with hot water. A massive bath. A bar, with a full-sized cinema screen. A games room. McCree was every bit as bad as the staff. A snitch. A two-faced piece of slime, and as dangerous as a rattlesnake.

'Get in here, boy,' Malloy's voice boomed.

I opened the door and walked in. Malloy was sitting at Kraft's desk. He was writing something on a notepad, one arm resting on the huge walnut desk. He didn't acknowledge me. I stood just inside the door, shifting weight from one foot to the other.

'Were you born in a barn?'

'No, sir.'

'Then shut the door, before I knock your head against it.'

I did as I was told. I wanted to see his eyes. Gauge his mood. But, he carried on writing, occasionally breaking off to check something on a calendar pinned to the wall above the desk. I watched the clock tick past seven-fifteen. I felt lightheaded. Nauseated. The need to pee nagged at me.

Malloy finished writing and put the pen on the desk. He swivelled around to face me. His eyes bore into mine as if he could see right inside my head and read my thoughts. I tried to make my mind go blank. No chance. It hopped from hatred to remorse and back again, like a scared rabbit.

He rested his hands in his lap. 'Well?'

'I'm sorry, sir.'

'You attack a dedicated member of staff, and all you can say is you're sorry?'

'Yes, sir.'

'I dread to think what might have happened if I hadn't come along, Tate.'

I looked at the floor. His eyes were on the verge of hypnotising me, like the snake in Jungle Book.

'What were you thinking?'

Was he asking me, or was this leading somewhere terrible? 'He called my mother a name.'

He pursed his lips. 'Enlighten me.'

I felt anger bubbling just beneath the surface. 'He called her a prostitute.'

'So?'

'She's not.'

'And you know this, do you?'

'Yes.'

'You think your mother would keep you informed of her sexual activity?'

I looked away, and bit down on my tongue.

'Well?'

'I know she's not a prostitute.'

'No, Tate, you don't. I have it on good authority she was a common prostitute. That's why your father killed her. That's why we've all been left to pick up the pieces of your wretched life.'

The only reason she's dead is because my old man is a bastard and a bully. 'Yes, sir.'

Malloy unfolded his bony frame from the chair and towered above me. There were half a dozen wooden canes mounted on the wall, each with varying degrees of thickness. He selected one from the middle and swished it through the air like a sword.

'Pull down your pyjama trousers and bend over the desk, hands on the top where I can see them. You need to learn respect, Tate. Respect and honesty.'

I did as he asked. What else could I do? I promised myself I wouldn't cry. Wouldn't piss myself. Wouldn't even give him the satisfaction of knowing he hurt me. I failed on all three counts. By the time he'd finished lashing my bare backside, I was standing in a puddle of my own piss.

'What was your mother, Tate?'

'A… whore.'

'A whore, what?'

'Sir.'

'That's right. And don't you forget it. A cheap whore who dropped her knickers once too often, and dropped her whole family in the shit. Now, get out of this office before I really lose my temper with you.'

CHAPTER 21

I made the school bus with about two minutes to spare. I didn't get anything to eat. I'd dressed alone in the senior block, tears spilling down my cheeks, hot and full of shame. I'd called my mother a whore. I'd never forgive myself for that. My dear, sweet mother a whore. I would be damned to eternal hell for saying that. And rightly so. Just as I'd stood by and let Billy the Bully murder her, I'd now allowed Malloy to put an indelible stain on her name.

North Oxford Secondary School was about a half-hour drive from Woodside. I stood up all the way; my backside hurt way too much to sit down, even on the cushioned seat. I would have no choice once I got to school, but wherever I could, I would stand up. My bum alternated between throbbing and stinging.

'Why don't you sit down?'

I turned around to see a grinning kid, with a mop of dark frizzy hair and black National Health glasses looking up at me. I'd seen him in the shower room, but he hadn't been at Woodside the first time around. Part of me wanted to wipe that daft grin off his chops, but I'd had enough arguments for one day, and I was still weak from my time in the sick bay. So, I just ignored him.

A few minutes later, he spoke again. 'What's the matter? Cat got your tongue?'

'What's it to you?'

He shrugged. 'Just saying.'

I turned away again and fiddled with the togs on my duffel coat. Some kids still had their hoods up. They looked like starving monks, faces white, hollow cheeks. In all my time at Woodside, I'd never seen a healthy kid. Except for McCree, but that slime ball didn't count.

The bus dropped us off about half a mile away from school. I stepped into a freezing January wind, and fastened my top toggle. I didn't put up my hood; I wanted the wind in my hair, to blow away the shame.

Kids split off into groups of twos and threes, messing about, pushing and shoving and letting off steam. Although I recognised a few of the faces, I hadn't got to know any of them from my first time at Woodside. I was only there for five months, and I hadn't been in any mood to make friends.

The lad who'd spoken to me on the bus fell in alongside me at the back of the group. He grinned at me again, revealing one crooked front tooth which seemed as if it might be hanging onto his gums by sheer luck. His sunken cheeks and dark eyes reminded me of a ghost, which in some ways he was. We all were.

'What did Reader do?'

'Nothing.'

'He keeps you behind in the showers and does nothing?'

'I don't want to talk about it.'

We walked in silence for a while. There was a constant pain behind my eyes as if someone was drumming their fingers inside my head. I also had a sore throat and a nasty burning sensation in my lungs.

'My name's Liam. Liam Truman.'

'Good for you.'

He laughed. 'A right regular tough guy, aren't you?'

'I don't feel well.'

He asked me again what Reader had done to me.

'What difference does it make?'

'I've been in Woodside just over a year. I started off like you, trying to tough it out. But, it sometimes helps to talk.'

'I've been here before, too.'

'When?'

'Eighteen months ago.'

'So, where you been? On holiday?'

I hacked up phlegm, and spat it onto the frosty ground. 'They fostered me out.'

'Why did you come back?'

I didn't want to talk about it. Not even to God. 'Because…'

He stopped and grabbed my elbow. 'We've got twenty minutes until assembly. You want to have a smoke?'

'You've got fags?'

He laughed, that wobbly tooth jiggling in front of his tongue. 'Well, I'm not suggesting we go and set ourselves on fire, am I?'

In spite of my mood, I smiled. 'Okay.'

We sat in the wooden bus shelter on a rock-hard bench; a stark reminder to my backside it had just been caned. He pulled out a pack of Woodbines, handed one to me.

'Where did you get these?'

'Hodges.'

Surely not the groundsman?

It was. 'He sometimes gives us smokes when he tells stories.'

'Stories?'

'About the war. Boring shit, really. I doubt if he was even in the war, but he likes to make out he was at Dunkirk and stuff like that. There's a few of us go down to his shed when we're on gardening duty. He's all right, though. He doesn't mean any harm.'

That was the first time I'd ever heard anyone compliment a member of staff at Woodside. Surely the kids had to do favours to get free cigarettes. 'I don't trust adults.'

He offered me a light, cupping his hand around his Zippo lighter. I sucked for all I was worth until the end glowed red. I took a deep drag. My lungs and throat erupted in a ball of flame. I nearly dropped the cigarette as I was seized by a coughing fit.

'Whoa, there. Steady on.'

Tears leaked from my eyes. 'I've been sick,' I offered by way of explanation. I didn't want to appear weak.

'I heard Kraft made you run around the field in the buff.'

I took another drag of my cigarette, this time careful not to take it back. 'He's a cunt.'

Liam looked at the ground. 'That's one word for him.'

We smoked our cigarettes in silence and then stamped out the butts. I asked Liam how he ended up at Woodside.

'My parents died in a car crash.'

'I'm sorry.'

He looked away. 'Shit happens.'

Wasn't that the truth? 'Couldn't anyone take you in?'

'No.' Short and snappy, as if I'd hit a raw nerve. 'So, what happened to you?'

I told him my parents had died, too. I skipped the bit about how. Said maybe another time. I told him how Aunt Jean had refused to take me in. Again, I omitted the reason. 'I used to think she was nice. Always happy to see me and let me stay over. Just goes to show you don't ever really know someone.'

'Blood's supposed to be thicker than water.'

I wasn't sure what that meant. I nodded anyway.

'You find out who the arseholes are when the shit comes down.'

I laughed at this. It sounded poetic, in a crude sort of way. 'True.'

'You still haven't told me your name.'

'It's—'

'Let me guess? Michael Tate.'

'How do you know?'

'Your reputation precedes you.'

I liked his way with words. 'Is that so?'

'It's so. How old are you, Michael?'

'Fourteen.'

'A year younger than me.'

My heart sank. I was hoping we'd be in the same class. 'Oh.'

'We can meet up at lunchtime, if you want.'

'I'd like that.'

He grinned. 'And Michael?'

'What?'

'Don't let the bastards grind you down.'

I thought about Reader and Malloy. Perhaps it was too late for that, but at least Liam seemed all right. 'I'll try.'

He punched me lightly on the arm. Then, he stood up, and headed off towards North Oxford Comprehensive School with all the swagger of a seasoned student. I followed him along the icy footpath. By the time we reached the school gates, I was puffing and blowing, like someone who'd trekked across the North Pole. There was a short, bald man standing just inside the gate with a clipboard, barking orders, telling kids to go straight to assembly.

'All right. All right, keep your hair on,' Liam said.

I laughed.

The bald man didn't. 'You find something funny, lad?'

I shook my head. 'No, sir.'

'Get to assembly. One more word out of you, and you'll be in detention.'

I wanted to tell him I hadn't said anything, just laughed, but my throbbing backside warned me against it.

As we reached the main entrance, Liam turned to me and held out his hand. 'Friends?'

I shook it, and something warm passed through me. 'Yeah. Friends.'

Maybe my time at Woodside wouldn't be so bad if I had someone I could count on. Someone to help me through the darkest days, pick me up when I fell down, share my innermost thoughts with. Like stuff that happened at the Davieses' house, and the real reason I had no parents. How I'd had to leave Oxo behind. Malloy calling my mother a whore. Thrashing me, because I refused to do the same. Someone who wasn't on their side, waiting to beat you to a pulp, just because you were a kid whose luck had dried up like Corrigan's Brook. A kid with nothing but a set of threadbare clothes and a duffel coat. A kid that missed his mum, missed his dog, and missed his tiny box room at Whitehead Street, more than he would have ever believed possible.

Little did I realise that this smart older boy, with his clever way with words and wobbly front tooth, would need me much more than I would ever need him. So much more.

CHAPTER 22

School was, not to put too fine a point on it, shit. I sat through double maths, double English, and double history, believing my brain would curl up and die. I looked for Liam at break time and lunchtime, but he was nowhere to be seen. I won't pretend I wasn't disappointed, but I'd made it this far on my own. It was hardly the end of the world. At least the school wasn't new territory for me; it was the same place I'd been to during my stay with the Davieses. The same freezing cold, drab classrooms, same teachers cast from stone, same sense they were all doing you the biggest favour in the world by even bothering to teach you. Even the same board rubbers hurled at anyone who dared to not pay attention. Same old, same old.

I met Liam at the bus stop. He didn't look half as chirpy as he had this morning. I nodded at him, unsure.

He spat on the ground. 'Fucking school.'

'What's wrong?'

'That wanker, Worthington, kept me behind at break time and lunchtime for detention.'

'Why?'

'Reckons I wasn't paying attention.' He shook a cigarette out of his pack, but didn't offer me one. He cupped his hand around the lighter and lit up. 'I mean, how the fuck are you supposed to pay attention when he's rattling on about Queen Victoria?'

'Good point.'

'Who gives a tin-shit about royalty, anyway? Bunch of fucking scroungers.' He offered me his cigarette.

I shook my head. My throat felt as if it had been fire-bombed and doused with pepper. 'No. Thanks.'

'Suit yourself.' He took another deep drag and flicked ash. It caught in the wind and spilled down the front of his coat. 'We ought to run away.'

I looked at him, checking for signs that he was joking. He didn't appear to be. 'But, where would we go?'

'We could go to the coast.'

'In winter?'

'I've got an uncle in Bournemouth. He might put us up.'

And he might not. I imagined trying to sleep under the pier and shivered.

He stamped out his cigarette as the bus drew alongside the kerb. 'I've got to get out of Woodside, Michael. I've fucking got to.'

We said little all the way back. I could tell he was mulling over escaping, thinking about how to make it possible, convince me it was a good idea. But, I'd already had a beating, and been forced to run naked around a field in the middle of winter. I didn't want to risk having runaway tagged to my file, not to mention the punishment that would go along with it.

Malloy was waiting to greet the bus as it pulled into the gravel courtyard. I crossed my fingers and made a wish that the bus driver would lose control and run the bastard over, crush his bones, and turn him to mincemeat.

As usual, my wishes went unanswered. As I stepped off the bus, Malloy clamped a hand on my shoulder, and told me to stand to one side. He did the same with Liam. When all the other kids were inside, he ordered us both to the staff room.

'Perhaps he's going to give us tea and cakes,' Liam joked, as we fell in behind Malloy.

He ushered us both into the staff room. There was a heavy stench of cigar smoke in the air. Rank and acrid. It burned the back of my throat. He sat on the edge of a white Formica table and looked at each of us in turn. 'You two idiots think you're smart, don't you?'

Liam didn't answer. He stared at the floor, seemingly mesmerised by the red and white speckled linoleum.

Malloy thumped the edge of the desk. 'Well!'

'I don't know what you mean, sir,' I managed.

'You don't? What about you, Truman?'

'What?'

'Don't get insolent with me, you warped little twat. You know full well what.'

Liam didn't. Neither did I. I wished to Christ I did. At least I could admit to it and get it over and done with.

'All right. If you want to play dumb, play dumb. Let me help you. I've had it reported on good authority you two imbeciles were smoking at the bus stop.'

My heart stopped. I imagined smoke billowing out of my nostrils.

Malloy straightened a stack of papers on the table. 'Well?'

'Well, what?' Liam said.

Malloy stood up. 'Do you think you're clever, Truman?'

Liam didn't answer.

'What about you, Tate? What have you got to say?'

'Sorry.' The word was barely a croak; my mouth didn't have any spit left in it. I remembered, all too vividly, the half a dozen canes fixed to the wall in Kalvin Kraft's office. My backside had just about settled to a dull throb.

'You're "sorry" are you, Tate?'

'Yes, sir.'

He shook his head. 'We have standards at Woodside. Standards we try to maintain at all times. Why is that, Tate?'

I had no answer to that.

'You little bastards are the lowest of the low. The dregs of society. It is our job to turn you into useful members of society, and that starts by learning to behave properly when you are away from Woodside.'

What about you bastards acting properly when we're inside Woodside? I thought. 'Yes, sir.'

'You've only been back one day, Tate, and you've already proved what an unruly, little shit you are.'

'Yes, sir.'

'Truman?'

'Whatever.'

Malloy studied him with those dark, menacing eyes. 'You may go, Tate. Your behaviour is duly noted.'

I didn't want to go. I wanted to wait for Liam, but I knew better than to defy a member of staff twice in one day. As I closed the door behind me, Malloy ordered Liam to go to Kalvin Kraft's office, and wait outside for him.

By the time I got to the senior block, my stomach was churning, the same way it used to when I was waiting for my old man to come home from the pub. I tried to stop imagining what Malloy was doing to Liam, but it was like trying to stop the wind blowing.

My bed and locker were situated in the middle of the right-hand row of beds. The sprung base sagged in the middle, and the sheets and blankets reeked of damp. I sat on the bed, thoughts of Liam dominating my mind.

All the other kids would be doing chores allocated at morning assembly, which I'd missed, because of the incident in the shower room. The grey walls reminded me of a battleship, the polished wooden floor, the upper deck. Captain Tate at the helm. Ten degrees starboard. Aye, aye. Steady as she goes. Shark-infested waters.

'Welcome back, Michael.'

Craig McCree's voice jolted me out of my fantasy. He stood a few feet away, brushing a strand of blond hair out of his eyes. I tried not to look concerned.

'Missed the place too much, eh?'

'Something like that.'

He smiled. You could fry chips in that smile. His eyes reminded me of a bird of prey. An eagle, perhaps, only eagles were noble creatures, McCree wasn't.

'We missed you, Michael.' He took a pack of cigarettes out of his jeans. Shook one out and clamped it between his teeth. 'How was the foster home?'

What did he care? 'All right,' I lied.

He lit up. 'A little bird tells me you like giving blow jobs.'

'That's crap.'

He blew a plume of smoke in the air. 'Not what I heard.'

'I don't care what you heard.'

'Heard you got so excited, you nearly bit Selwyn Davies' dick off.'

I clammed up. I didn't want to argue with him because there would only be one winner if I tried. McCree was seventeen. Head boy. The Golden Boy of Woodside. He even had a room upstairs tagged onto the staff quarters. Had his own shower for fuck's sake.

'Still, Selwyn Davies' loss is our gain, I say. What do you reckon, Michael?'

I didn't reckon anything. I tried not to let him drag me into a conversation.

'Credit where credit's due. Attacking Reader in the shower room. Malloy having to drag you off.'

I nodded. Safer ground than the Davieses.

'You did good, Michael. What with Reader calling your mother a whore like that.'

How the hell did he even know that?

'Is that what Davies did?'

'What?'

'Call your mum a whore?'

'No.' The truth.

'Must have been something bad to try to bite his knob off.'

'If you say so.'

'There's been a few changes, since you were last here. Have you met Uncle Bernie yet?'

'No.'

McCree sucked on his cigarette. He let the smoke out between clenched teeth. 'You've got to meet him, Michael.'

'Who is he?'

'Close your eyes.'

'Why?'

'Just do it.'

I didn't want to give McCree any excuse to go running to the staff telling tales. I closed my eyes.

'Are you ready?'

I took a deep breath and nodded.

I felt a sudden burning pain on the back of my hand, then the smell of scorched skin, followed by McCree's hideous braying laughter. I opened my eyes as he withdrew the cigarette from the back of my hand. I spat on the burn and rubbed furiously. At least my backside no longer hurt.

'Uncle Bernie, get it?'

Oh, I got it, all right. I would have given anything to take that cigarette out of his hand and thrust it into one of his reptilian eyes.

'Welcome back to Woodside.' He threw the butt on the floor and stamped it out. 'I'm going to go and tell Malloy someone's been smoking in the senior block, Tate. But, first, I'm going for a wank. You've got ten minutes. I suggest you get a window open, and clean that floor, before he gets up here.'

Bastard, bastard, bastard, my mind screamed. Welcome back to fucking Woodside.

CHAPTER 23

Liam didn't go to supper. He staggered into the senior block at just after nine that evening. The room hushed, as if someone had twisted a volume knob. A few of the others tried to talk to him, but Liam headed straight for his bed, and sat down clutching his ribs. I didn't know whether to approach him, but as far as I was concerned, he was a mate, and mates looked out for one another.

The pain in my hand had now dulled to a stinging throb. I stopped a foot away from him, unsure of what to say, and then I asked him the dumbest question ever. 'Are you all right?'

He looked at me, eyes glazed. Blood bubbled in one of his nostrils. He opened his mouth to speak, but said nothing. His wobbly tooth no longer clung to his mouth.

'Liam?'

'Go away.' The words came out mashed together: Gway.

I took a gamble and sat on the bed next to him. I waited a few moments and then asked him what had happened.

'What's it to you?'

I looked at the wound on my hand. 'It might help to talk about it.'

He didn't answer. He straightened his back and winced. He struggled for breath. There was a nasty whining noise in the back of his nose.

'Malloy's a cunt,' I said, sticking to something we could both relate to.

He glanced sideways at me. 'Tell me something I don't know.'

Remembering my earlier thrashing, I asked if he'd been given the cane.

Liam hacked a small laugh. 'I fucking wish.'

Now what did I say? It was obvious Malloy had done something terrible to him. But, what?

'You know the funny thing?'

I didn't. I couldn't see anything funny about Woodside and its psychopathic staff.

'All that bullshit about smoking, and he never took my fags off me. I've got one left. You want to go to the bogs and share it?'

I nearly spilled tears at that. In spite of his suffering, he was still willing to share his last cigarette with me. 'I'd like that.' And then, on consideration, 'What if someone comes?'

He grinned; a gummy affair mixed with blood. 'Fuck 'em.'

Fuck 'em, indeed. We hobbled out of the senior block and along the corridor to the shower block, like two wartime veterans returning from the battlefield.

He walked into a cubicle. 'Come on, squeeze in.'

I followed him in and locked the door behind me. I stood on the rim of the toilet and opened a small window to vent the smoke. We had about half an hour left before lights out. Before Malloy or Reader came around to send us to sleep on a bed of threats.

Liam sat on the toilet and lit his cigarette. He took a drag and blew a stream of smoke towards the window. He spotted the burn mark on my hand, red and inflamed. 'What happened to your hand?'

I didn't know whether to tell him. It seemed such small change compared to what had happened to him. I shrugged. 'No big deal.'

'McCree, right?'

'How do you know?'

He spat on the floor and wiped it into the tile with the tip of his shoe. 'I'm surprised he never caught you with that Uncle Bernie shit the first time you were here.'

I shook my head. I hadn't had much contact with McCree then.

'McCree will get what's coming to him,' Liam promised. 'Cocksucking little twat.'

I almost told Liam what McCree had said about me nearly biting Davies' dick off, but decided not to. Too close to the truth for comfort. It would open up a whole load of stuff best left unsaid.

'If it's any consolation. McCree gets passed around.'

'Passed around?'

'Do you have any idea what really goes on here?'

Apparently, I didn't. 'Like what?'

He passed me the half-finished smoke. 'Sex.'

'Sex?'

He laughed. 'Fuck me, Michael, do you always repeat things like a parrot?'

I took a drag and blew it out without taking it back. 'Sorry.'

He looked at the locked door, as if someone might be standing outside listening to our conversation, and then whispered, almost too low to hear, 'Sex for queers. Arse shaggers. Bum bandits. Shit prodders.'

I remembered Davies and almost threw up. 'McCree has sex with men?'

Liam clapped. 'Give the boy a medal, he catches on quick. The dirty pigs pay for it. McCree takes it up the arse in return for money and privileges. Why else do you suppose he lives upstairs? Lords it over the rest of us? He's like one of them, only he's not. Not really. He's nothing but a stupid, slimy kid, who's got no choice, just like the rest of us.'

'That's disgusting,' I said, thinking more of Davies than Craig McCree.

'It ain't the half of it.'

'What do you mean?'

'They're all fucking bent.'

'Who?'

He shot me a look as if to say I had the intelligence of a daffodil bulb. 'Malloy, Kraft, Reader. The fucking lot of them.'

I didn't know what to say. I finished the cigarette and dropped the butt into the toilet. It hit the water with a little Ksss sound.

Liam took a deep breath and winced. 'I reckon Malloy's cracked one of my ribs. I can't breathe properly. I'll break every bone in his fucking body one day, Michael. I swear to God.'

'No more than the cunt deserves.'

'If you want to know what he did to me, I'll tell you. But, you gotta promise you never say a word to anyone else about it.'

'I swear.'

'On your life?'

'On my life.'

When he spoke, his eyes looked dead. 'He took me into Kraft's office, study, shit-tip, whatever you want to call it. I thought he was going to cane me. Give me a few whacks and leave it at that. But, he didn't....'

I waited a few seconds, and then said, 'Don't bother if it's too painful to talk about.'

'It's all right. It's just the pain. Anyway, Malloy went over to a sideboard and took out a bottle of brandy and two glasses. He poured me a drink. A fucking good slug, too. Posh glass. Crystal.'

'He let you have a drink?'

Liam nodded. 'Then, he pulled out a huge cigar and sparked that up. Babbled on about how cold the weather was, and how much nicer it would be when the spring came. Asked me if I liked the spring or the summer best.'

'He's fucking mad.'

'Mad doesn't even come close to what he is. Trust me. He offered me a go on the cigar. I told him I didn't like cigars. Guess what he said?'

'What?'

'Said it was an acquired taste. But, he wouldn't force me, if I didn't want to.'

'So, he gives us a bollocking for smoking and then offers you a bloody cigar?'

Liam nodded. 'Anyway, I drank half of the brandy. My head felt all fuzzy. I wasn't drunk or nothing, but I wasn't bothered about what might happen, either. After he finished his cigar and drink, he looked at me funny. It's hard to explain. I asked him if he was all right. He said, "You tell me, Liam." I mean, what sort of fucking answer is that. He's never ever called me Liam before. That's when I realised he had me there for something else.'

'Something else?'

'Sex.'

'Malloy?' I squawked, unable to hide my astonishment. A vision of Mr. Davies popped into my mind.

'Well, I say sex. It wasn't sex. Not even the perverted sort of sex McCree has when he sells his arse for posh nosh and a trip out in a Bentley. It was Malloy's filthy version of sex.'

Once, when I was about seven or eight, I'd been in town with my mum. An old lady had been hit by a bus. Knocked over in the road. Dead as roadkill. My mum had warned me to look away. Drawn me in close to her. But, me being me, took a peek, anyway. Saw that old woman missing half her face, her eyes wide open, and staring in two different directions at once. This felt something like that, only I was looking at Liam's horrific injuries instead of the old woman's.

'He told me I had two choices,' Liam continued. 'The easy way or the hard way. He leered at me when he said "hard," as if it was our little joke, the fucking creep.'

'Maybe you didn't ought to tell me,' I said, as a tear trickled down his cheek. 'If it's too painful.'

He wiped the tear away with a swipe of his hand. 'It's all right. I want to tell you. I want you to understand what those bastards are capable of.'

'Okay. But we'd better get back soon. It's getting close to lights out.'

Liam nodded and winced. 'He made me strip. Like the fucking pervert always does when he's about to give you the cane. The dirty bastard gets off on it. Then, he left the office.'

167

'Just fucked off?'

Liam nodded. 'I thought at first he was just playing mind games with me. Going to leave me standing naked in the study for ages. Maybe all night.'

'Sick bastard.'

Liam wiped a fresh tear from his cheek. 'He came back about ten minutes later with Reader. I'll never forget the way those two took the piss out of my body. Then, they forced me to bend over the desk. Reader held my head down, pressed it right into the wood. I could smell Malloy's cigar mixed with the brandy. Then, he raped me.'

'Shit.'

'Not with his dick, Michael. He raped me with a billiard cue.' His mouth was twisted in an ugly grimace. 'And when he was finished, Reader held my hands behind my back, while Malloy smashed the cue into my mouth. That's what those bastards did to me, Michael.'

I had no words to comfort him. We walked back to the senior block in silence and went to bed without another word. I didn't sleep that night. I kept imagining what had happened to Liam, over and over, running around my head like a hamster's treadmill. I didn't think I would ever sleep again.

CHAPTER 24

We planned our escape for the last weekend of February, Friday 27th, the last day of school. Well, I say planned, but it wasn't much of a plan. We stole as much food as we could from Woodside, added some from kids' packed lunches at school, and didn't bother catching the bus back to Woodside.

Liam's physical injuries had healed reasonably well, and he'd even glued his lost tooth back in place with chewing gum. It looked comical, but the circumstance in which he'd lost it killed any humour. I was the only one he'd told, but other kids had some idea. A kid with injuries was a kid who'd been caught on the wrong side of Woodside's special brand of punishment. Injuries were worn like a macabre badge of honour, and no one, other than McCree, would taunt another kid carrying fresh wounds.

Birth defects didn't escape the merciless mickey taking. But, no one ever mentioned Liam's wonky tooth. Not once. But, my bucked front teeth? Fair game. Anything from Bugs Bunny to Ratty. I didn't mind. It was a way of letting off steam, and God knew we had to have some way of doing so.

My escape technique from the everyday horrors of Woodside was to lose myself in imaginary worlds. Worlds where I was King. Even the superintendent of Woodside. I would give all the boys special privileges, choice of the best cuts of meat, any toy they wanted, any game, roast beef on Sunday.

I'd got to know one or two other boys by now. One that me and Liam were particularly friendly with was Reggie. I don't think that was his real name. He was from London, reckoned he was related to the Kray twins. I very much doubted that, but he used to spin us some stories, and act like he was this big deal gangster called Reggie.

Quite a weedy looking kid, but no pushover. What he lacked in physique he made up for in stubbornness. I never once saw any kid beat him at arm wrestling. Good with his fists, too. Fast. Bam, bam, bam. Few kids took the piss out of him. Me and Liam had a row over whether Reggie should come with us. I wanted him to. Reckoned he'd be handy to have around, if we got any bother from anyone, but Liam thought we'd be better on our own.

'Three's a crowd, Mikey.' Yes, he was calling me Mikey by then. Like I said, all right for my mother and close friends. 'It'll mean having three different ideas on everything. Three mouths to feed. I like Reggie, but I don't want to sleep with him.'

I roared with laughter. Discussion over. Me and Liam would go it alone. My overactive imagination conjured up a picture of me and Liam coming back to Woodside one day, and rescuing Reggie and all the kids from that prison. We would be like the Three Musketeers, with Reggie on the inside, and me and Liam storming the outer walls.

There was also another lad, called Chris. Nearly six feet tall, and still only fifteen. Strong as an ox. Even McCree didn't bother with him. Me, Liam, Reggie, and Chris would sometimes go to the groundsman's shed, which was almost as big as one of Finley's barns. We would sit with Hodges and listen to his wartime tales. Chris had this nasty habit of spitting on the ground. Everywhere he went, a puddle of spit was sure to follow. Hodges once told him not to do it, it was bad manners, but Chris just looked at him with his dopey brown eyes, spat on the ground, and said it was better out than in.

The hardest thing for me at Woodside was seeing the young children from the junior block. There were about fifteen of them, ages ranging from four to eleven. The young ones always looked so lost, so abandoned, as if they'd been ripped away from their mothers at birth and thrown to lions.

Kraft made a big deal of public punishments. Bible readings were a part of every assembly. Even the big kids struggled with some of the words, so it was virtually impossible for the juniors to read the more difficult text. I always used to think it ironic children were forced to read from a book supposedly dedicated to righteousness, and then, they were publicly humiliated for getting something wrong.

I once heard a kid of about six mispronounce the word bosom. He called it bossom, like blossom. Kraft made that boy come onto the stage. He asked him to read the word again. I could see the boy's lower lip trembling. 'Bossom, sir.'

Kraft laughed, cane held stiff and straight by his side. 'Tell the assembly what a bossom is, Coates.'

The boy seemed confused by Kraft's laughter. He grinned.

'What's funny, boy?'

The smile slipped away, like grease off a griddle. 'Nothing, sir.'

Kraft swished the cane in the air. 'What's a bossom?'

'Nothing, sir.'

'Really, Coates? Are you standing there telling me a word printed in the Holy Bible is nothing?'

'No, sir.'

'Read it again.'

The kid held his Bible with shaking hands. 'She held him close to her bossom.'

Kraft whacked the kid's hands with his cane. The Bible clattered to the floor. 'It's bosom, you stupid, illiterate spawn of the devil. "She held him close to her bosom." Say it.'

Coates tried to, but his words were gobbled up by sobs.

Kraft whacked him once on the back of his knees. 'Say it.'

Coates never said it. He stood on that stage, in front of about thirty other children, and pissed his pants. A puddle formed at his feet, frothy and steaming in the freezing cold hall.

If I ever got the chance, I'd let Coates take a cane to Kraft, and hit the bastard as many times as he liked. Make him piss his pants.

Me and Liam had managed to steer clear of trouble since the barbaric rape with the billiard cue, but that hadn't diminished our hatred of Woodside. If anything, it had increased. Festered. We stood in the playground after school and watched the other kids hurry off to catch the bus.

'What if someone sees us?'

Liam laughed, but he sounded nervous. 'Like who? The teachers don't give a toss about us. They don't care if we catch the bus or jump in front of it.'

I wished I felt reassured by that.

He opened his rucksack. 'I've got some goodies.'

I peered inside. Sandwiches, two bottles of coke, three Bounty bars, four or five squashed cakes, and a purse.

'Whose purse is it?'

He grinned. 'Miss Parsons left her bag in the classroom at lunchtime, so I helped myself. God helps those who help themselves, so they say.'

I grinned, even though I wasn't very comfortable with him stealing a purse, even if it was a teacher's.

'There's over a fiver in there. Plus, I got about thirty pence out of Martin Makins.'

'How?'

'I told him we were going on an expedition for the BBC. Said if he made a donation, we'd make sure we gave him a mention.'

'And he swallowed that?'

'He'd believe I was his own brother, if I kept a straight face. What did you manage?'

'Not a lot. I've got a pound. And some Weetabix.'

'Weetabix? What the fuck are we supposed to do with Weetabix? Ask someone for some milk and a bowl?'

'I risked my neck going into the kitchen for those.'

'I don't even like Weetabix. It's like eating dried grass.'

'That's Shredded Wheat.'

'Same fucking thing, ain't it?'

We walked out of school and headed towards Oxford city centre. A sign said five miles. No way I could walk that far in my worn-out shoes. My feet were already frozen.

'So, where are we going?' I asked, as we walked along a tree-lined street, with neat, semi-detached houses set back from the road. 'Did you get hold of your uncle in Bournemouth?'

Liam looked momentarily confused, and then it seemed to register. 'Nah. He's moved.'

'Where?'

'Don't know. When I phoned, they said he didn't leave a forwarding address.'

'Why not?'

His good mood seemed to slide. 'How should I know? No one ever tells me anything.'

I dropped it. We walked on. Past a pub called the Jolly Miller. More houses. Such neat suburban lives. I wondered what went on behind all those closed doors, if there were kids just like me and Liam, living in fear every night, in case the likes of Mr. Davies came sneaking into their bedrooms with dirty hands and dirty thoughts.

I tried again. 'Do you still fancy the coast?'

'Too far, Mikey. We'll spend all our money just getting there. I reckon we ought to find a derelict house and set up home.'

'Where?'

'How the fuck should I know? I haven't got a map of derelict homes.'

He grinned, revealing that lone tooth hanging by its chewing gum thread. I didn't have the heart to tell him the tooth would rot with no gums to sustain it. It was his little victory. His two fingers up to Malloy. You might be able to smash me in the mouth with a billiard cue, but I've still got my tooth, so fuck you.

We rested on a bench about a mile out of Oxford city centre. Liam pulled out a pack of cigarettes. A full pack, filched from the staff quarters at Woodside. That kid was braver than I'd ever be. Marlboros. Filter tips. Absolute luxury after Hodges' Woodbines.

We lit up. The smoke felt harsh, but at least my throat was no longer inflamed. To be honest, I was starting to lose my enthusiasm for this adventure already. Darkness was erasing what little colour remained in the sky, my feet throbbed, and the hideous duffel coat barely kept out the cold.

But, that wasn't the main reason why my spirits felt as damp as the weather. We still didn't have a clue where we were heading. Every time we'd talked about it before leaving, Liam had said we were going to his uncle's. Now, that just seemed like a fanciful idea. The colder I got, the more I doubted he even had an uncle in Bournemouth.

To make matters worse, I was hungry, and, apart from my useless pack of dried Weetabix, Liam had all the food. I would have to stay hungry, or ask him to share. We finished our cigarettes, and ground them out on the floor.

'We could get a room,' I suggested. 'Have a bath and a proper bed for the night.'

Liam looked at me as if I'd just suggested hijacking a witch's broomstick. 'And then what?'

'What do you mean?'

'What do we do tomorrow?'

I seriously wished we'd worked this out better. We'd only been gone a few hours, and it was already beginning to look like the biggest mistake ever. We had nowhere to stay, no proper clothes, crap shoes, not to mention the shit we'd be in if we ever got caught and had to go back to Woodside.

Liam broke into my thoughts. 'Do you see what I see?'

'What?'

He pointed across the road at a white rendered building.

'A pub?'

He nodded like a cat that had just discovered a dairy. 'Not just a pub, Mikey. It's boarded up.'

'So?'

174

'So, no one's living there. We can break in and set up camp.'

'How we gonna get in?'

He stood up. 'I don't know. Come on, let's get over there before it gets too dark.'

We crossed the road. A rusty sign read: The Dolphin. Names and symbols were sprayed on the boards. Declarations of love. Declarations of hate. And other shit that meant zip to me. I followed Liam around the back. Rubbish filled the garden. A huge white bath, rotting kitchen cupboards, two dark red, leather sofas, a fridge, a cooker, tyres, wooden crates. The windows and the glass in the back door were also boarded up. There was an outbuilding, but I wasn't sleeping in there. No way. Apart from being freezing cold, there would be spiders, and I had a pathological hatred of spiders.

'We're in luck,' Liam said.

I could think of better words to describe the place. Shithole, sprang to mind. 'What?'

He pointed at a small plastic square set in the bottom of the door. 'It's got a cat-flap.'

I was about to remind him we weren't cats, when he unhooked his rucksack, dropped onto his knees, and tugged at the flap. Within a few seconds, it came free. He held up a hand triumphantly, and then pushed his way inside.

I wouldn't say it was a tight squeeze, but it had probably been easier for his mother to give birth to him. He pushed and grunted, shoes scrabbling on the ground for a foothold. Eventually, he popped through the hole.

A few seconds later, he poked his head back through the hole. 'Come on, Mikey. Pass your bag and my rucksack through. Then, come in.'

He looked so happy, as if, for the first time in his life, he'd played a game and won. I didn't fancy my chances of getting through there. I was slightly bulkier than him, and a damn sight less enthusiastic. But, it was better than nothing, and nothing was all we had right now. I passed the rucksack and my small canvas bag through.

'Careful. You'll squish the cakes,' he said, grinning like a clown.

I suppose it was inevitable. I got stuck halfway through. To tell the truth and shame the devil, as my Aunt Jean used to say before she got her loyalties all muddled up, my arse got stuck. And then one of my shoes fell off.

It's hard to explain the panic that sets in when you can't move. I couldn't breathe. I felt dizzy. Liam grew two grinning heads. He tried to pull me through the flap, but the harder he pulled, the more I flapped (no pun intended). To make matters worse, I caught my knackers on the metal rim of the blasted thing. Searing pain ripped up into my belly.

'Can't you push with your feet at the same time as I pull?'

'I'm trying.'

'Well try harder.'

'You pull harder.'

He did. And virtually castrated me. 'YOW! My nuts. My fucking nuts.'

He stopped pulling. 'How am I supposed to help you if you keep squealing like a girl about your bollocks?'

'Girls haven't got bollocks,' I shouted.

'I doubt they'd make as much fuss as you if they did.'

'Seriously, Liam. They feel as if they're in my guts.'

He laughed. 'Watch you don't get yourself pregnant.'

'Ha, ha, very—'

Without warning, he yanked again. Harder. Short sharp jerks, like Oxo on his lead when he saw a cat. And then I was through. Lying on a filthy kitchen floor, with my chin resting on a large coconut mat.

'What a girl.'

I was off that mat and up in an instant. I think Liam thought I was going to hit him. I never told him the real reason for my sudden burst of energy: a spider. More related to a money-spider than a tarantula, but a spider all the same.

CHAPTER 25

To say that the place was a bit creepy was like saying the Second World War was a bit dangerous. That pub held court to three of my worst fears: spiders, the dark, and ghosts. Yes, you heard me right. Ghosts.

After rescuing my shoe from outside, we went into the lounge bar. Liam was hopeful of finding booze. Broken glass crunched beneath our feet. I stayed a good way behind him, the coward in me letting him test the water first.

He flipped his Zippo into life, found a light switch, tested it. Dead. 'We need to light a fire.'

Now, I was getting worried. Even a dumb idiot like me knew the dangers of lighting fires in derelict buildings. I didn't fancy trying to get back through that cat-flap in a hurry, with flames licking my arse.

'What are we going to use to make a fire?'

He shrugged. 'Don't know. We could use some of that crap in the garden.'

Who's going to go back outside to get it? 'Oh.'

'Hey, we're in luck.'

'What?'

He pointed to one side of the room. 'There's a fireplace over there.'

I brightened. At least that wouldn't be as dangerous as lighting a fire on the floor.

'And it's got logs and newspapers in it, as if it was about to be lit.'

Before the deadly plague wiped everyone out, I thought, scaring myself a little more than I'd intended. Or before the landlord poisoned all his customers. This really creeped me out. I moved closer to Liam and the relative safety of the light from his Zippo.

Within half an hour, we had a decent fire going in the grate. We crouched in front of it like two cowboys around a campfire. It was the best I'd felt in ages. Getting warm, having a smoke, as far away from Woodside as two boys could get with only feet for transport.

I flicked my butt into the flames. 'What if someone sees the smoke coming out of the chimney?'

Liam shrugged. 'So what? That's what smoke's supposed to do.'

'But, the place is derelict. What if the cops see it?'

'Relax, Mikey. No copper will be suspicious of a bit of smoke coming out of a chimney in the winter, will he?'

I sincerely hoped not. I didn't want anyone, or anything, to spoil this. I knew it sounded daft, because we didn't have the means to stay there forever, but I wanted that moment to stretch on for the rest of my life.

We had no idea of the time. A clock on the wall behind the bar was as dead as the pub itself. Forever stuck at half past nine. Liam found two crates to use as makeshift stools. We sat in front of the fire, basking in our newfound freedom.

'At least there won't be any lights out tonight,' Liam said.

'Ain't no lights to put out.'

He laughed. And then, his face straightened almost instantly. 'I hate that fucking place.'

'Try not to think about it.'

He spat into the fire. 'Easier said than done.'

True enough. I half-expected Malloy to bang on the front door any minute, demanding we get back to Woodside. 'What are we going to sleep on?'

'There's bound to be beds or something upstairs.'

'You reckon?'

'Only one way to find out.' He stood up.

'Do you want me to come with you?'

'Nah. You stay here and keep an eye on the fire.' He flicked his lighter on and ambled across the room towards the door.

I watched his shadow disappear from view, leaving me on my own, with just the fire and an overactive imagination for company. I had a nasty tingling sensation in my stomach.

Don't be stupid. It's no different to when Liam was here.

But, it was. It was quieter. Deathly quiet, you might say. Broken glass littered the floor. The light from the fire gave it the appearance of hot coals. Something moved behind the bar; a shadow among the dripping shards of glass. My heart thudded in my chest. I tried not to look, but it was as if my eyes were hell-bent on disobeying the last dregs of good sense still left in my head.

My mother stood behind the bar, a duster in one skeletal hand, a tin of polish in the other. Her mouth hung open, exposing broken tombstone teeth. One eye stared at the wall, the other squinted at me through a mound of purple rotting flesh. Strands of hair sprouted from her mostly bald scalp.

I closed my eyes. Rubbed them hard enough to bring tears, and looked again.

'You can't make shit shine, Mikey,' she said, spraying the rotting wood with a burst of Mr. Sheen.

'Mum?' The word came out barely formed. More of a sob.

She shook her head. A clump of hair fell onto the bar with a portion of her scalp. 'I worked my fingers to the bone, Mikey. Looking after him. Making excuses for him.' She banged the polish down on the counter and ran those bony fingers through what was left of her hair. Several detached from her hand and knotted themselves in the matted strands like witch's curlers.

I stared at her the same way you might look at an accident. I stuffed my fingers into my mouth and bit down.

'Make sure you follow your heart, Mikey. Do the right thing and follow your heart.'

I gripped the sides of the crate and squeezed my eyes shut again. I shook my head, trying to dislodge that awful image of her decomposing corpse. I wanted to run, scoot through that cat flap, and never look back.

After a few minutes, marked only by the throbbing pulse of my heart in my ears, I finally found the courage to look again. She was gone. I let out my breath, unaware until now that I'd been holding it.

'There ain't no beds, but there's a double mattress on the floor in one of the bedrooms.'

I screamed at the sudden sound of Liam's voice. I fell sideways off the crate, landing on broken glass and gashing my hand.

'What's the matter with you, jumpy-drawers?'

I climbed slowly to my feet, nursing my injured hand, eyes fixed on the bar. Thankfully, my mother's rotting corpse was still no longer there.

'Mikey?'

I sat back on the crate. My knees were knocking together so badly I thought he would hear them. Now what did I say? My mother just paid a flying visit straight from the grave? I made a snap decision not to tell him about her. And another to go and check the bar for signs of finger bones, pieces of scalp, and hair. 'Jesus Christ, you scared the shit out of me.'

Liam sat down. 'You look like you've just seen a fucking ghost.'

I almost laughed out loud at the irony of his words. 'I'm just a bit jumpy. I keep thinking Kraft or Malloy will come out of nowhere and drag us back to Woodside.'

'If that wanker turns up here, I'll kill him, and burn his body on the fire.'

Something in Liam's voice told me he meant every word. 'Me, too,' I said, with less conviction.

'I'd chop him up into tiny pieces and grind his bones to powder.'

'No more than he deserves.' I glanced nervously over my shoulder at the bar for signs of corpses.

'Anyway, I thought we could go top to tail on the mattress. Use our bags as pillows.'

'What about blankets? It'll be freezing in the night.'

'I'll cuddle you, sweetie-pie.'

I hoped he was joking. 'But, seriously, what are we going to do?'

'Have a rummage. See if we can find something. If we can't, we'll drag the mattress down here in front of the fire.'

'Okay.'

'And make sure you have a piss first. I don't want you waking me up in the middle of the night to take you to the toilet.'

'I'm not a baby,' I said, thinking I was exactly that. I sucked blood off my hand. It tasted bitter and coppery and strangely comforting. We sat in silence for ages, just staring into the fire. 'Do you miss your parents, Mikey?'

'I miss my mum. My old man can go to fucking hell, for all I care.'

'Why?'

I told him. Everything. Spilled my guts, like a stuffed bear might spill its filling. Told him about the murder. Rachel and Oxo. How me and Tommy Preston had rescued Oxo from Finley's Farm. How the authorities had carted me off to Woodside.

When I was finished, Liam did a strange thing. He reached out and rubbed my arm the same way my mother used to when I was sick or afraid of something. Gently, up and down. 'That's fucking shit, Mikey. Really shit.'

I couldn't argue with that.

'Your mum should have called the cops on your old man. Got the bastard arrested.'

'She was scared of him, Liam. Scared of what he'd do when the cops went away, back to their nice, cosy lives. I mean, they would hardly lock him up forever just for beating her up, would they?'

He shook his head. 'They might have locked him up long enough for you to get away from him.'

I wished with all my heart I could rewind my life and do one thing different. Stop what had happened that night. But, I couldn't. It was done. Over. My mum was dead forever, and my old man was rotting away in jail somewhere. I hoped with all my heart he was suffering. Guilt. Illness. Anything.

'Maybe we could go and see your dog,' Liam suggested. 'Did this Rachel woman definitely keep him?'

I perked up. 'Said she would. Do you really want to go to see him?'

'I wouldn't say it, if I didn't mean it, Mikey. Oxo sounds like a great dog.'

Just the thought of seeing him again brought a lump to my throat. 'I'd really like that.'

'Then, we'll do it.'

I glanced at him. He looked like a cartoon character. His frizzy hair made him look as if he'd been plugged into a main's socket. His wonky tooth hung on for dear life to his mouth by its chewing gum roots. 'Do you want to talk about what happened to you? How you wound up at Woodside?'

He didn't answer for a while. Part of me wondered if he would clam up. Finally, he said, 'You sure you want to hear it?'

I was.

And so, he told me. 'My parents didn't die in a car crash like I told you. Well, not exactly. More metaphorically.'

'What the fuck's that when it's at home?'

He looked at me as if I was the dumbest thing to walk the Earth since the dinosaurs. 'It means not literally, dough-brain.' He paused. When he spoke again, his voice barely rose above a whisper, as if telling me the greatest secret ever told. 'I don't want you to think for one minute I didn't love my mother, Mikey, because I did. She was all right, mostly, but she had a weakness.'

'Weakness?'

He paused again. 'She was a tart.'

'Your mum?' I said, shocked.

'No, my Uncle Tom.'

'Sorry.'

'I only know what I heard when they argued. He accused her of having an affair with some teacher at school.'

'A teacher? Bloody hell.' If the teachers at my school were anything to go by, I couldn't believe such a thing was even possible.

Liam fiddled with his lone tooth, stretching the chewing gum like elastic. 'Yeah. Mr. Finnegan. A math teacher at the school where she taught. Some posh-knob's place in Slough. She was an English teacher, but she taught art as well. She was really pretty, Mikey. I'm not surprised men fancied her.'

I wondered what went wrong with Liam. Perhaps he'd inherited his dad's looks.

'I felt sorry for my dad,' Liam said. 'He was a builder. Good with his hands, but useless with his mouth. She used to win every argument they had. He'd go around banging doors, throwing his weight about, stuff like that, but it didn't seem to bother her.'

I wondered if this would end up the same way as my parents had.

'By the end, she was sleeping in the spare room. I heard my dad crying one night. It was fucking horrible, Mikey. Dad's aren't supposed to cry, are they? They're meant to be your hero. I put my head under the pillow to drown it out.'

'I know how that is.'

'Shit happens, right? But, sometimes that shit stinks so bad, you can't ever get rid of it. It's there forever. Right inside your brain. Anyway, we had a last Christmas together. Turkey and all the trimmings. Opened our presents. All the excitement, followed by the disappointment. All those brightly coloured parcels never turn out to be what you hoped for, do they?'

'No.'

'Like life.'

Even though he was only a year older than me, it was as if he had an adult's head on a boy's shoulders. To be honest, I never expected much from Christmas when I'd lived at home; not with my old man drinking most of the money down the pub.

'She left on Boxing Day. Just like that, Mikey. Gone like a puff of smoke. A letter explaining how we would be better off without her. That she loved me. Crap like that.'

'I'm sorry, mate.'

'Don't be. Her choice. My dad or Mr. Finnegan, with hairs on his fucking chin-ne-gan, or whatever the stupid song is. She chose Finnegan. Perhaps he had a bigger dick.'

I said nothing.

'What do you reckon, Mikey? Is it better to stay with someone you don't love, or run off into the arms of someone you do?'

'I don't know.' A genuine answer. I just wished my mother had found someone to run off with. Someone to start again with. A Mr. Finnegan to begin again.

'I've thought about this a lot. I reckon it's only all right to do it if you're not going to break someone else's heart. Because that's what she did, Mikey. She broke my dad's heart. Smashed into a thousand pieces. Left him like poor old Humpty-Dumpty at the bottom of that fucking wall.'

I couldn't help thinking it was equally bad to stay with someone you didn't love.

'He carried on as best he could. Going to work, coming home, burning my tea, drinking, getting up late, looking like shit, crying…'

I waited for him to carry on. He seemed mesmerised by the fire, and then he turned to me, tears glistening in his eyes. 'I want you to promise me you won't tell no one what I'm about to tell you. Do you promise?'

'You don't have to tell me if you don't—'

'I want to tell you. I trust you. But, you've gotta promise.'

'I promise.'

'Swear on your life.'

'I swear on my life.'

'It was January thirty-first. Two years ago. I walked home from school. freezing cold, wishing to Christ there was one teacher at school who would take an interest in what I wanted to do, instead of filling my head with a load of crap. But, something else was nagging me all the way home. A horrible feeling in my guts something was wrong. Really wrong. Do you believe in instinct, Mikey?'

I wasn't sure, but said I did.

'I had a front door key. My dad was never home from work much before six. Sometimes later, when he was working away on a job. I didn't mind. I thought it was cool having my own key. Grown up. Making myself a sandwich and sitting in front of the telly. He'd mostly go to the chippy when he got home, or cook something simple, like egg and chips and beans. Mum would have had a fit if she'd seen how we were living, but it was none of her business anymore. She sent me a card with some money in it the week after she left. I threw the card and the money on the fire. I was still so angry with her.'

'I can see why.'

Liam didn't seem to hear me. 'Anyway, like I said, I knew something was wrong all the way home. Then I saw my dad's builder's van in the drive. At first, I thought he'd come home early, but that couldn't be right, because he had a massive job on in Hazlechurch. That's when I saw smoke coming out the bottom of the garage door.'

At first, I thought he meant the house was on fire. 'Shit.'

'I already knew, Mikey. Even before I legged it through the house to the garage. He'd gassed himself. Stupid fucker only went and ran a hosepipe from the exhaust and fed it into the front of the car.'

'Oh, fuck.'

'He took the easy way out. The coward's way out. I don't know how long he'd been in the car. It was my mum's old run-around. He looked fucking weird. All red, like a lobster. Smoke filled the garage. I turned the engine off, and phoned an ambulance, but I knew he was already dead, Mikey. Knew it.'

'Shit...'

He pulled the lone tooth out of his mouth and fiddled with the chewing gum. 'It was worse for your mum, Mikey. She had no choice.'

Was there such a thing as worse when it came to tragedy? We sat in silence for a while, the log spitting and throwing sparks onto the floor. And then, I asked how come he'd ended up at Woodside.

He studied his tooth as if it might be an ancient artefact. 'I ended up in borstal.'

'How?'

'I lost it, Mikey. Lost the plot. Went fucking nuts. Out of control. I point blank refused to live with my mum and that fancy teacher friend of hers. I went to stay with dad's business partner and his wife for a while. But, I was a fucking nightmare. They had this drinks' cabinet in the corner of their living room. More like a bar. Optics, everything. Brandy and Scotch in decanters. Crystal tumblers. I smashed the lot up one afternoon after getting sent home from school for smoking.'

'No one could blame you for—'

'It was a shitty thing to do. They were only trying to help. But, I didn't want help. I wanted my old man back. I wanted my mum back. I wanted to go back to before she buggered off. Colin and Margaret were really good about me smashing up their bar. They didn't call the cops. Said they understood, but they didn't. How could they? I wanted revenge. I wanted someone to pay. Someone to take notice of me. Be sorry for what had happened.'

I knew better than most how that felt. I also understood no one could ever take away the pain. Make you feel better. You just had to swallow it, digest it, and if you were really lucky, crap it right out of your system one day.

Liam threw his tooth into the fire. 'There was this teacher at school. Mr. Hartson. As far as teachers went, he was one of the better ones. Let you get on with it. Talked to you properly. But, I started to believe he was my mum's new boyfriend, Mr. Fancy Finnegan. I know it sounds stupid, Mikey, but I really believed it. The day I attacked him, I could feel it building up all morning, swelling inside me. I had double chemistry with him straight after lunch. All I could think about was attacking him, getting revenge. Sounds fucking crazy, doesn't it?'

'It sounds as if you just got messed up by what happened.'

'He was writing something on the blackboard. Some chemical equation crap. It might as well have been Japanese for all I cared. I stood up and walked up behind him, got to within a few feet of him before he twigged and turned around. It was as if I was encased in a bubble, just me and him. The rest of the classroom faded to nothing. He dropped the chalk. His mouth hung open; it reminded me of a polo mint. Then, I went for him. Hit him again and again. He eventually got me in a headlock. He was shouting for someone to get a teacher. Every time he spoke, he squeezed my neck harder. I couldn't breathe. Then the world went black. I came around in the medical room.'

'Jesus.'

'I got expelled for that. You know what, Mikey? No one ever asked me how I felt. I got sent to borstal for six months. Just like that. Bam. It's as if they're doing their best to make sure you get completely fucked up. And, believe me, borstal fucks you up. You're not allowed to walk anywhere. It's like being in the army, only ten times worse. The short sharp shock. That's what they call it. It's just fucking legalised assault. The same as Woodside. No one wants to help you. All they want to do is make you feel like a worthless bag of shit. The police, the politicians, the cunts at Woodside. They get off on it, Mikey. They fucking well get off on it.'

I thought of Mr. Davies. Malloy. Reader. Kraft. Liam was right. They didn't just do what they did to discipline you; they did it because they enjoyed watching you suffer.

We sat in silence for a while. Everything we had said seemed to cement our friendship. Moved it on to another level. He reached down and picked up a piece of broken glass. 'Are you still bleeding?'

I looked at my hand, touched it. Wet and sticky. 'Yes.'

He drew the glass across the palm of his hand, deep enough to cut. He dropped the makeshift weapon and held out his hand. 'Blood-brothers?'

I pressed my wound against his. Hard. 'Blood-brothers.'

After a few seconds, he withdrew his hand. 'I promise to look out for you. Always be on your side, no matter what. Do you promise back, Mikey?'

I promised.

'We'll take the world on. We'll take the fucking lot of them on.'

Right then, in the glow of that fire, I truly believed that me and Liam Truman were invincible.

But we weren't.

He jumped up. 'Come on. We'll drag the mattress down here for the night. I can't be bothered looking for bedding.'

We ate the sandwiches out of his bag. A hearty meal of stale cheese and tomato, but they tasted grand. I imagined I was a cowboy, John Wayne, sitting in front of a campfire eating beef jerky, Indians waiting beyond the hills to attack.

Ready for anything those darned Indians had to throw at us.

We spent our first night of freedom on that filthy pub floor.

Liam fell asleep more or less straight away, his breathing heavy, a strange gurgling noise in the back of his throat.

I slept fitfully, terrified we would catch the place on fire and end up getting sent to borstal.

CHAPTER 26

The fire was out by the time I woke up. The pub was in darkness, thanks to the boarded-up windows. I crawled off the mattress and fumbled my way to the back door. I needed to pee. I stood by the cat flap, hopping from one foot to the other, remembering the struggle I'd had squeezing through the damned thing yesterday. I considered waking Liam, in case I got stuck again. In the end, I balanced on an upturned crate and pissed in the sink. It felt so good to empty my bladder.

I zipped up my fly, knelt down, and peered through the cat flap. The day looked charcoal grey. A fine mist of rain hosed down the rubbish in the back garden. It was disorientating not knowing the time after living such a regimented life at the Davieses' house and at Woodside.

With my bladder emptied, hunger gnawed at my stomach. I imagined my mother standing at the cooker, frying bacon, fried bread and mushrooms to go with it. Huge dollops of brown sauce on the bacon.

I made my way back to the lounge bar. I didn't fancy Weetabix without milk and sugar; my throat was as dry as a cornfield as it was. But Liam had goodies in his bag. Bounty bars. Cakes. Coke. I knelt down and opened his bag.

I swear he must have had the damned thing wired up to an alarm. 'Whayadoin?'

I almost toppled backwards. 'It's morning,' I said, as if that somehow explained why I was rummaging about in his bag.

'Huh?'

'It's morning,' I repeated. 'You need to get up.'

He propped himself up on one elbow, only a silhouette in the near darkness. 'I reckon we ought to take down the board at that window, let some light in. I'm going to waste all my gas messing about in the dark.'

'What if someone notices?'

'It's a back window. No one will see.'

I wasn't so sure, but he was right about the light. We couldn't set up camp in the dark. 'Okay, but I need something to eat first.'

He laughed. 'So, that's what you were up to. About to raid my bag.'

'I'm starving.'

He grabbed his rucksack and groped inside. He pulled out a bounty bar and a bottle of coke and handed them to me. 'We'll get breakfast on the way to Rachel's house. A cheese toasty and a cup of tea.'

Right now, I didn't care about proper food. I ate the chocolate in much the same way as Oxo used to wolf down his treats. I washed it down with half the coke and belched. Gas bubbles exploded from my eyes and nose. The initial buzz was quickly replaced by queasiness.

Liam ate half a cake and finished my coke. 'Fucking disgusting. Who puts ginger in a cake?'

'Where did you get it from?'

'Karen Savage.'

'Perhaps it's to ward off vampires.'

'That's garlic, you dodo.'

'Same thing, isn't it?'

Liam laughed. 'Let's hope I'm not with you if Vincent Price comes knocking on the door.'

'Who's he?'

'A blood sucking vampire, who bites people's necks.'

I shuddered. 'That's just made up shit.'

'It's not. There really are vampires. They start out as bats, but get stronger and stronger, and turn into vampires by sucking blood.'

'For real?'

'For real. Now, give me a hand to find something to pry the board off that window. I like to see who I'm sleeping with at night.'

'Ha, ha.'

'No offence, Tate, but I'd rather sleep with Karen Savage's mum than sleep with you.'

'No offence taken.'

'Karen Savage's mum looks like a fish. She's got big, fishy eyes and fat, puckered up lips.'

'All the better to snog you with.'

He made a gagging noise in the back of his throat. 'I'd rather eat cat sick.'

'Lumps as well?'

'You can have them.'

After searching for the best part of an hour, we finally found a long metal bar, with a two-pronged tip, lying behind the bar. Liam examined it in the flame from his lighter. 'Bingo.'

'What is it?'

'It's for pulling nails and stuff out of boards. I reckon they must have used it to open beer crates.'

I followed him to the window. I still wasn't sure about this. I didn't want anyone to find us. Ever. I wanted this pub to be our desert island. Do it up, get a few bits and pieces, a proper bed, clean the floors, some coal for the fire. It was scary how clueless you were at that age.

The thick plywood was only held in place with nails. Liam had it off the window in about five minutes flat. I closed my eyes against the sudden flood of light. Forgetting the lighter was on full flame, I burned my thumb and forefinger, and dropped it onto the bare floorboards.

Liam pounced on it as if it was a wounded pet. 'Watch it, Mikey. That lighter was my dad's.'

I apologised and watched him test the mechanism. Satisfied it was still in working order, he put it in his coat pocket, and looked at me, as if inspecting a soldier on parade. 'You look rough.'

I didn't think he looked that clever himself, what with his missing teeth and hair spraying out in all directions.

He patted me on the shoulder. 'We can go to the public bogs and get a wash. It's Saturday, so no one will pay any attention to us. Then, we'll get some breakfast and find Rachel. Where exactly does she live?'

'It's called Whitehead Street.'

'Do you reckon she'll be all right with us?'

'I don't know. I haven't seen her since my first spell at Woodside. To be honest, I'm more worried about seeing Oxo and leaving him again.'

'Yeah, but we can go and visit him anytime we like. We're not at Woodside now. We don't have to play by their stupid rules anymore, do we? The pub's our home. We ain't never going back to that shithole.'

'Unless we get caught.'

'We won't.'

'You promise?'

'We're blood brothers, Mikey. You don't even need to ask that.'

Getting back through the cat flap was fun. I got stuck again and had to be rescued by Liam. He nearly gave up after I farted. I thought he would never stop laughing. Even though I was stuck in that damned hole again, I liked the sound of his laughter. It was like birds singing on a winter's day.

We had bacon butties at a little café. A pot of tea. A proper pot. I felt as if I'd won the football pools. We also finished off the chocolate and coke on the way to Rachel's. Liam threw the rest of Karen Savage's cakes in the bin.

Whitehead Street ended up being about three or four miles away from the pub. Possibly more, because some old codger sent us the wrong way, and we had to double back on ourselves. Walking back into that street was a really strange experience. Seeing those two rows of terraced houses, split by the road, facing each other like opposing armies, stirred something inside me. Not quite nostalgia, but close. Brightly painted rendering lending individuality. Yellows, pinks, reds, purples, creams, blues. Net curtains hanging in the windows. St. George's flags dangling from windows like battle cries. Smoke billowing from chimneys. A funeral procession of black clouds marching across the sky.

'Are you all right, Mikey?'

I hadn't even realised I'd stopped walking until he spoke. Part of me wanted to turn around and run, keep going until I was back inside the pub. Safe. Just me and Liam, no adults to ruin everything with their wicked minds and wicked ways. But, a bigger part of me wanted to see Oxo again. 'Just a bit nervous.'

Rachel opened the door after what seemed like forever. At one point, I was convinced she'd seen us on the doorstep and called Woodside. She looked at me and Liam as if we'd just hopped off the ghost train. 'Michael?'

I nodded, trying to look past her and see where Oxo was.

'What the devil are you doing here?'

It was at that point I realised me and Liam had made one fatal mistake. We hadn't got a story ready. 'I've come to see Oxo.' And then, stupidly, 'My dog.'

Relief. She smiled. 'I do know who Oxo is.'

I stared at the floor.

'How did you get here?'

Liam treated her to his best toothless grin. 'We walked. A right long way. We'd appreciate coming in, if you don't mind.'

'Oh, you would, would you?'

My heart sank for a moment.

'You'd better step inside, then.'

We followed her along the narrow hallway and into the front room. Memories of the night my mother had died came flooding back, held in the fabric of the sofa, the colour of the bare cream walls, the dark blue carpet that didn't quite reach the edges of the room.

'Would you like a cup of tea?'

Liam thanked her. I sat there as dumb as the rope which had tied Oxo up at Finley's Farm. When she returned a few minutes later, and set down a tray on a small pine coffee table, I asked her the question which had been burning a hole in my brain. 'Where is he?'

'He's gone for a walk along the river with Don and the kids. They should be back soon.'

The mention of her husband took a swipe at my fragile confidence. I didn't want him to grill us. Or, worse, call the cops. 'Maybe we ought to go.'

Rachel frowned. 'You've only just got here.'

I decided to come clean. 'We've run away from—'

'We've left Woodside,' Liam interrupted. He looked at me as if I'd just confessed to murder. 'We're staying with my Aunt Cathy. But, we don't want anyone from Woodside trying to take us back.'

'But, you can't just leave... can you?'

'Strictly speaking, no,' Liam said. 'But, that place is a nightmare. We had to get out.'

Rachel poured the tea. 'It seemed all right to me.'

Liam shook his head and tried to whistle through his non-existent teeth. He managed a rather long drawn out lisp. 'You don't know the half of it. Anyway, I'm nearly sixteen.'

'What about school?'

'Don't worry about that,' Liam said. 'We still go to school. We just have to catch the bus from a different place.'

I didn't think Rachel believed him, but, she did seem happy enough to see us. We drank tea, ate bourbon biscuits, and chatted for about half an hour, as we waited for Oxo to come home. Every time Rachel broached the subject of Woodside or school, Liam steered her onto another topic with all the skill of a seasoned politician.

It's hard to describe how it felt seeing Oxo again after so long. He flew at me in a flurry of paws, yelps and dog spit, landing on my lap and knocking the wind out of me. He licked my face and performed his own version of doggy tap-dancing on my groin. He took a good ten minutes to settle down to mere excitement. I rubbed his ears, kissed the top of his head and closed my eyes as his tail whipped my face. And then I cried. Buried my head in his soft brown fur and blubbed like a baby.

After a few minutes' awkward silence, Rachel's husband buggered off to his shed with his oldest boy, Jamie. He didn't seem comfortable with us in his house. One of Rachel's daughters, Chloe, went upstairs to tend to the baby, who was really no longer a baby.

'She's two,' Chloe said, 'and a right bloody handful.'

Rachel wagged a finger at her. 'Less of the language, miss. You're not too old for a clip around the ear.' Her voice was soft and teasing rather than threatening.

'You'd have to catch me first.' She darted from the room, giggling.

Rachel's other daughter, Beth, stood by the dining table, thumb plugged into her mouth, staring at Liam with wide blue eyes. She must have been about six or seven by now. I thought it funny how quickly kids grow, how time shapes and changes them almost beyond recognition.

'Are you hungry?' Rachel asked.

I shook my head. 'No. We've had some breakfa—'

'Starving,' Liam interrupted. 'We had a sandwich earlier, but we had to walk miles.'

'Where does your aunt live?'

Liam nearly dislodged his glasses. He looked at me for support. When he realised he wasn't going to get any, he said, 'Eynsham.'

'But, that's miles away.'

Liam looked pleased with himself. 'That's why we're so hungry.'

And so, we ate jacket potatoes, with grated cheese and beans. It was one of the best meals I'd ever eaten. Normally, I would have saved some for Oxo, but I ate every last morsel and mopped up the bean juice with a hunk of bread. Oxo sat under the table the whole time, head resting on my knee.

When it was time to say goodbye, I kept it simple. I didn't want to get upset. I didn't want Oxo to remember me that way. I promised myself I would be back. No big deal. Maybe next weekend, even. I'd go to the butcher's and get him a lamb bone. I kissed him on the top of his head and hugged him around the neck. I don't think I'd have been half as ready to leave if I'd known I would never set eyes on him again.

CHAPTER 27

Rachel was still waving to us halfway along the street. Liam waved back, treating the world to his toothless grin, readjusting his glasses. 'She seems nice.'

'Yeah. Do you really have an Aunt Cathy?'

'Nope.'

'How do you just make stuff up like that?'

He shrugged. 'Needs must, Mikey. Needs must.'

We plodded on in silence. At least we'd had something to eat. Something more substantial than Bounty bars and shitty stale sandwiches. I could now understand why Rachel hadn't wanted me to stay with them. Only two bedrooms, and four kids. God knows where she put them all. She reminded me of the old woman who lived in a shoe.

We reached the pub, knackered and hungry again. By the time we'd crawled through the cat flap and lit a fire (only two logs left in the wicker basket by the hearth), I was about ready to collapse. My feet were blistered. Both big toes and both heels. The cut on my hand stung, even though it had long since stopped bleeding. I'd washed it in a public toilet on the way to Rachel's, but I was worried it might get infected if I left the wound open. I'd considered asking Rachel for a plaster, but she'd have only wanted to know what I'd done to my hand, and I was crap at lying off the cuff, unlike Liam, who seemed to have a natural born talent for it.

We spent the rest of the day gathering wood from the garden. Breaking up the shed was fun, even though it was mined with splinters. Liam found a sledgehammer in the cellar. I didn't go down there with him; too much likelihood of spiders. He also found an old broom with a wonky head. We swept the floor and threw all the broken glass down into the cellar. Anything flammable went on the fire.

Liam leant on the broom, shunted his glasses up his nose. 'You don't reckon Rachel would loan us some money, do you?'

'I don't know. And before you ask, I'm not asking her.'

'Why not? We could offer to do jobs for her, or something. Walk Oxo.'

'Now, you're being stupid.'

'Am I? There's about three quid left in the purse. That won't keep us in food for long.'

'I'm still not asking her. Her husband might call the cops on us if we start asking for money. He's a miserable bugger at the best of times.'

'So, what are we going to do, then?'

'We could get a paper round.'

Liam laughed. 'No newsagent's going to let a pair of scruffy unwashed urchins deliver papers for them. Anyway, you need parents' permission for that.'

'Really?'

'Yep.' He rummaged in his rucksack and pulled out a large green bottle. 'Maybe this will help us to think.'

'What is it?'

'Wine. Good stuff. French I think. I got it from the cellar. There's a massive wine rack down there. Only about four or five bottles left, but a shame to let them go to waste.'

By the time we were halfway down the bottle, my blistered feet no longer throbbed. My fear of spiders was also gone. I didn't care about what might happen tomorrow, I was just happy to be sitting in front of the fire in our very own private space, smoking fags and drinking wine. I wanted that moment to last forever.

Unfortunately, it didn't. Liam started talking about his time at Woodside. A subject certain to dampen the best of spirits.

'They ought to be hanged for what they've done, Mikey. Public gallows, like in Victorian times.'

I nodded. My head felt light enough to float. I didn't want to talk about Woodside. I wanted to talk about my dog. Or girls.

'You haven't met the Doberman yet?'

'Who's that?'

Liam took another swig of wine, wiped his mouth with the back of his hand, adjusted his glasses and spat into the fire. 'He's the biggest cunt who ever walked the Earth.'

'Worse than Kraft?'

'He makes Kraft look like a kitten.'

'I've never seen him.' Which was confusing, considering I'd spent five months there the first time around, and two months this time.

'He doesn't work at Woodside, Mikey. He's one of the outsiders.'

The wine was doing a good job of scrambling my brain. 'Outsiders?'

'The Doberman's one of the bastards who pays to abuse the kids. He's a copper. Tall fucker. Horrible, lopsided grin.'

He still meant zip. 'I ain't ever seen him.'

'You don't want to. He's evil. His name's John Carver. He likes torturing kids. Taking them down into the boiler room and handcuffing them to the railings.'

I sobered slightly as a picture of a medieval torture chamber sprang to mind. 'Sick fucker.'

'Tell me about it. He took me down there once. About six months ago. Arrested me when I came out of Hodges' shed.'

'What for?'

'Nothing. Told me to put my hands behind my back and slapped a set of cuffs on me. Marched me down to the boiler room. It was the tail end of August. Hot as hell. No windows. He told me to sit on a wooden chair. Just the sight of him made me want to puke. I asked him why he'd brought me down there. He didn't answer, just forced my hands over the back of a chair, and started pacing about the room like a wild animal.'

'What a cunt.'

'After a while, he bent down so as his face was right up close to mine. He asked what I was doing in Hodges' hut. I didn't understand. I'd done all my chores. Cleaned the windows on the senior block. Emptied the rubbish. Helped Hodges with raking grass. I told him I'd been doing nothing.'

'What sort of weirdo is he?'

'The worst kind, Mikey. The fucking worst kind. I'd been smoking, but I didn't tell him that. I just said I'd been helping Hodges tidy up. But he wasn't having any of it. Threatened to chain me to the railings and beat me with a truncheon if I didn't tell the truth. So, I opted for a half-truth, and told him Hodges had been telling me stories. Then he started going on about Hodges being full of shit. Talking a load of bollocks about being in the war. Evacuating the beaches at Dunkirk single-handedly.'

'What the fuck would he know about it?'

Liam nodded. 'Exactly. Then he started babbling on about no one having respect for the law. He slapped me across the front of my face with the back of his hand. He was wearing a ring with diamonds in it or something. It gouged a chunk out of my cheek. The chair almost toppled over. My face felt as if it had been ripped in two. I wanted to stand up, free my hands, relieve the stress on my shoulders, protect my face.'

'Cunt.'

'He fiddled with the ring for a while. Probably cleaning my skin from it. Then he crouched down, so as he was at eye level, and accused me of sucking Hodges' dick. I had no answer to that. It was as if my head just emptied. Flushed all my thoughts down the drain. He asked me if Hodges payed me to perform oral sex. Of course, I denied it. Then he kicked me, hard in the left shin. Pain roared up my leg and into my groin.'

'I would have told him what he wanted to hear,' I said. 'Just to shut him up.'

Liam shook his head. 'I wouldn't give him the satisfaction, Mikey. He asked me my name, my age, a load of other bollocks he knew the answer to, then he asked me if I knew about the laws governing homosexuality. I mean, what sort of fucking question is that?'

'What did you say?'

'I didn't get a chance to say anything. He started spouting a load of shit about it being illegal to perform sexual acts with a groundsman in his place of work. It would have been almost funny if it wasn't so fucking serious. Then he took the cuffs off and ordered me to strip. He handcuffed me to the railings by the boiler. He walked out of the room and left me standing there, naked, for what seemed like hours. When he returned, he had a truncheon. He beat me with the fucking thing until I passed out.'

I don't know if it was the wine or Liam's story that made me throw up. Probably a bit of both. I just made it to the grate before spilling my guts.

When I was finished, Liam said, 'Take it you don't want another bottle, then?'

I shook my head and plonked myself back down on the crate. I never wanted to touch alcohol again. 'How the fuck do they get away with it?'

'Because they have all the power.' He rummaged in his rucksack and pulled out a large notebook. He opened, it and flicked through several pages.

I swallowed a lump of something unsavoury. 'What's that?'

'My book of poems, Mikey. If anything happens to me, I want you to have it.'

'Nothing's going to happen to you.'

'You want to hear one of my poems? It's about Woodside.'

'Okay.'

He opened the book, cleared his throat, and read:

'How I wish I could feel,

The hot sun on my back,
Fresh cut grass,
Beneath my feet,
My father's hand,
Strong upon mine,
His aftershave,
Bottled nostalgia,
Promises of tomorrow,
Safe within his smile,
But the night stalker comes,
Cloaked in shadows,
The sound of his heels,
Marking time on the floor,
His stinking breath,
Whispering threats,
You'd better not tell,
You'd better not scream,
No one can hear you,
In the Abattoir of Dreams.'
I didn't know what to say.
'What do you reckon?'
'It's really good.'
He looked pleased. 'Do you think?'
'Fucking right. It's great.'

He closed the book and put it back in his rucksack. 'You've got to promise me you won't go sneaking a look at my poems while I'm asleep or nothing.'

'I promise.'

'Don't you forget. We swore blood brothers.'

'I know.' I'd be lying if I said I didn't wonder what else was in that book, but a promise was a promise. 'How do you even think of that stuff?'

He shrugged. 'It just comes out that way.'

'What is "The Abattoir of Dreams"?'

He shunted his glasses back up his nose for the umpteenth time. 'Woodside. Like a fucking slaughterhouse for every kid's dreams.'

We said little else that night. We bedded down in front of the fire, and fell asleep to the sounds of the wood spitting in the grate, and the rain lashing against the window.

CHAPTER 28

We woke up late on Sunday morning. Perhaps it was the long walk to Rachel's, or the booze, or both, but late it was. For once, I wasn't hungry. Sunlight poured through the window. My stomach cramped and gurgled. I made my way to the toilet just in time. To make matters worse, there wasn't any toilet roll. I had to use my underpants as a makeshift bog roll.

Liam didn't seem very impressed. 'That's fucking gross.'

'What else was I supposed to do? Go into the garden and wipe my arse on the grass?'

'Yes.'

'We need bog roll.'

Liam rolled his eyes. 'But, the toilets don't flush, do they? We'll still need to go outside to take a dump.'

'I can't crap in the garden.'

'Why?'

'What if something bites my arse?'

'What the fuck would go anywhere near your arse?'

'I still ain't doing it outside.'

'Then, you'll just have to go to the public bogs. But, you still need to fish your pants out of the pan.'

'What shall I do with them?'

'Throw them in the garden, or something. Anyway, I've had enough of talking about your pants. We need money, Mikey. If you don't want to ask Rachel, we'll have to pinch it.'

I wasn't too keen on the idea of stealing. That would likely get us nicked. We'd be back at Woodside, standing in Kraft's office, before you could say shitty pants. 'And where exactly are we going to nick this money from?'

He didn't hesitate. 'The church.'

My heart loop–the–looped. 'We can't steal from a church.' And then, relieved, 'They don't even have any money.'

Liam grinned. 'That's where you're wrong, Mikey-boy. They've got plenty of money on a Sunday morning, when they pass that collection plate thing around.'

'It doesn't seem right.'

'What?'

'Stealing from a church.'

'Why? They don't give a toss about the likes of us. Why should we care about them?'

Suddenly, I needed the toilet again.

'Besides, it's only like God helping us out. Making amends for all the shit we've been through.'

'What if we get caught?'

'We won't. We'll stay at the back. When the collection plate comes to us, we'll grab the money, and leg it straight out the door. We'll be gone before the vicar can say hallelujah.'

And so, the plan was set. St Mary's Church was a small stone building, about a mile away from the pub. By the time we got there, a large clock on the facing wall read: 11:30am. But, something wasn't right. The place didn't even look as if it was open, which was odd, considering Sunday was supposed to be their best day for business.

I tried to tell myself it didn't matter about stealing from the church; I wasn't really religious or anything. It wasn't as if I would need to explain myself to God. But, it still felt wrong.

Liam walked up to the door and peered inside. 'There's no one here.'

Good. 'I wonder why?'

He shot me an impatient look. 'How should I know? Let's go have a mooch.'

Shit. 'But, if there's no one...'

Liam disappeared inside. Reluctantly, I followed. The place smelled of damp. Pews lined either side of the aisle, leading to an altar and a pulpit. The stained-glass windows looked beautiful. Jesus, nailed to his wooden cross, took pride of place on the wall behind the altar.

Liam walked to a pew and picked up a Bible. 'You know what all this rubbish is, don't you?'

'No.'

'It's to keep people in their place by scaring them. If you're afraid of God, then you won't do anything to upset Him. But it's crap. God's a fairy story, just like Father Christmas and the Tooth Fairy.'

A man's deep voice rolled along the aisle. 'Is that so?'

Liam dropped the Bible. It clattered to the floor like a guilty secret.

The vicar smiled. 'You're a bit late for morning service. It finished at eleven. But, we have some refreshments out the back, if you're interested.'

'What sort of refreshments?' Liam asked.

'Tea and homemade cakes.'

I tugged Liam's arm. 'Let's go.'

The vicar stopped a few feet away from us. 'Everyone's welcome in God's house. We're only a small church, but we've got a big heart.'

We could get a lump of cake and a cup of tea at Rachel's. We didn't need to go hobnobbing with vicars.

'Would you like to say a prayer?'

I shook my head. The vicar's eyes seemed to shine behind his gold-rimmed spectacles. He had a kind face. His lips were curled in a permanent half-smile. There was a huge dimple in the middle of his chin. But, none of this made me want to eat cake with him. Or say stupid prayers.

He looked at Liam. 'What about you, son? It's good for the spirit to give thanks to the Lord for what he provides.'

Liam shrugged. 'What happens when you pray?'

'God listens.'

I groaned and looked at the floor. Why couldn't Liam just leave this alone? He didn't even believe in God.

'But, how can He hear you?' Liam persisted.

'I don't follow you, son.'

Liam seemed thoughtful for a moment, and then said, 'Well, it stands to reason, don't it? All those people praying, how's he going to hear them all?'

The vicar smiled. 'God hears everyone. We need not question how.'

Liam wasn't deterred. 'What about all the bad things that happen? All the kids that get killed? Wars? Diseases? Poor people?'

'God loves them all.'

'But, what's He doing to help them?'

'He's always there for them.'

'Horseshit.'

'I'd thank you not to swear in God's house.'

Liam didn't seem about to repent. 'All sorts of shit happens to good people. Where's God then? On holiday?'

'Please don't take the Lord's name in vain. It's—'

'What about the kids who are abused, just because they're kids?'

'I'm sure—'

'Or get a billiard cue rammed up their arse?'

'I'll have to ask you to leave, if you can't control your tone.'

'Bet you lot think you can come here on a Sunday, say a few prayers to your precious God, and then get on with your cosy lives.'

The vicar's hands flapped in front of his black gown like two birds trying to take flight. 'We do nothing of the sort. I care very deeply about what—'

'We've got a priest who comes to Woodside. He's—'

It was my turn to interrupt. 'Liam, for God's sake.'

Liam didn't seem put off. 'He comes in about once a month.'

'Woodside? The children's home?'

'I hear he likes the young boys from the junior block.'

'I don't have the faintest idea what you're talking about.'

Liam laughed. The sound echoed around the church. 'Don't you? I thought you had a personal hotline to God.'

'I'm afraid—'

'What do you think about a priest who likes young boys?'

The vicar didn't answer. He clasped his hands in front of him.

'Dirty old fucker. What do you think about that?'

If Liam had intended to get a reaction, this seemed to do the trick. 'Get out of here, you wicked boy. Get out of here, now.'

'How does that fit in with your fucking God?'

'Get out.' This time, his voice boomed around the building, and bounced off the walls like cannon fire.

Someone appeared from a side door. A short, fat man in a blue suit. My heart froze. Kraft. 'Liam?'

'Don't like the fucking truth, do you?'

'Liam! We've got to go.'

Liam sneered at the vicar. 'I'll bet you're even good friends with the twat.'

'You boys,' Kraft shouted. 'Hey, you boys.'

I moved towards the door and tried to warn Liam again.

Liam didn't seem to see Kraft. It seemed as if he was blinded by his anger. 'You're all the fucking same. God this, and God that.'

Kraft marched towards us, arms swinging back and forth like a soldier on parade. 'Truman? Tate? You stay right where you are.'

'LIAM! For fuck's sake. It's Kraft!'

Liam suddenly twigged. 'Shit.'

'I'll give you Kraft, you insolent little swine.'

Liam backed away towards the door. 'Come on, then. Try to catch me, you fat little fucker.'

The vicar's hands took flight again. Kraft broke into a trot.

Liam held up his middle finger. 'Swivel on this, you ugly bastard.'

We were out that door, and along the street, like a pair of greyhounds out of a trap. We didn't stop running until we were within yards of the pub. We stumbled into the back garden, panting and laughing, like the biggest jokers on the planet.

'Did you see his face when I flicked him the bird?'

Dread stirred in my stomach. 'Priceless.'

Liam rested on an upturned fridge. 'I'm going to go back to Woodside one day and kill him. I swear on my mother's life.'

'He deserves to die.'

Liam nudged his glasses up on his nose. 'Kill him slowly and feed him to the pigs down at Southgate's Farm.'

'Too right.'

'I'll bet that fucking vicar's a pervert, too.'

I wanted to crawl through the cat flap and get out of sight. I felt too vulnerable standing in that back garden. Too on show. I wanted to light another fire and have a smoke, laugh about Kraft and the vicar, make it seem less serious than it was.

Liam walked over to me. He balled his right hand into a fist and held it out. 'Blood brothers.'

I pressed my knuckles into his. 'Blood brothers.'

We were both unaware of the massive mistake we'd just made by going to that church.

CHAPTER 29

We spent our last night in front of the fire, drinking wine, and working our way through a packet of cigarettes Liam had bought from a machine outside a shop half a mile up the road. He'd also bought two chicken and mushroom pies, a big bottle of lemonade, and two bars of Cadburys Fruit and Nut with the last of our money.

I hadn't gone with him to get the goodies. I'd made out I had a bad belly, which was partly true, but it was mostly because I hadn't wanted to risk getting seen again. Paranoia was a funny thing. It crept up on you until you were convinced everyone was watching you. Even a helicopter going overhead made you think the cops were out looking for you.

With the fire lit, and another bottle of wine open – well, the cork pushed in because we didn't have a corkscrew – Liam turned to me and grinned. 'I've had an idea.'

After the church collection plate, I didn't think I was ready for any more of his ideas right now. 'What?'

He puffed on his fag as if it was feeding his brain ideas. 'Next Sunday, we could go out really early and nick all the paper money. My old man used to leave it out on a Saturday night so as the paper boy wouldn't disturb him in the morning. Loads of people do.'

As far as ideas went, it was better than trying to rob the church. 'It's worth a try.'

'Too right, it is. I reckon we'll get at least a tenner.'

I didn't contradict him. 'Great.'

He blew smoke rings in the air, looked at me and grinned. 'Did you see the look on Kraft's face?'

How could I ever forget it? I kept glancing at the window, half-expecting to see his face pressed up against the glass. 'We'd better hope he never gets his hands on us.'

Liam shrugged. 'He won't.'

I wished I shared his optimism. How were we supposed to survive in a derelict pub, with no money or clothes, other than the rags we stood up in? And, to make matters worse, Kraft would have surely set the cops onto us by now. He wouldn't just let it go.

'Next time Kraft sees me, I'll put a rope around his neck. I'll kill him slowly, Mikey. Throttle him so he's nearly dead, then throw cold water in his face, and bring him back round. Stick pins in his eyes.'

I didn't feel like joining in with Liam's fantasy; mostly because I thought it would probably happen the other way around.

'I'll make him run naked around the field, like he did to you, Mikey. Run until he has a heart attack.'

I smiled. 'Good.'

'Do you know what they did to Reggie?'

'No.'

'Kraft and his cronies tied the poor bastard to a bed out the back of the storeroom.'

'The sick bay?' I said, remembering my brief time in the care of Aunt Mary.

'They use it for whatever suits them. They had it all decked out with black curtains and medieval stuff when they took Reggie there. Tied him to the bed. Performed some sort of satanic ritual. Carved an upside down cross from his nipples down to his naval with a knife. Then, McCree raped him.'

'Jesus.'

'They're sick, Mikey. Sick in the fucking head. They belong in hell, and I'm going to make sure they go there.'

I didn't know what to say. I felt sick inside. Sorry for Reggie. Angry at Kraft and the others. How could they do this to a kid? A defenceless kid. It was too horrific to take in. A picture of Reggie flashed into my mind. In Hodges' shed, puffing away on a Woodbine, telling us his gangster stories. Bullshit about how he was a runner for Ronnie Kray. How Ronnie had told him he was the brightest kid on the block, and how he would give Reggie a proper job in the firm when he got old enough.

'They left him face down on the bed, crying and screaming for his mother. He hasn't even got a mother. He told me she died giving birth to him. I wonder what that poxy vicar would have to say about that?'

We sat in silence for a few moments. Liam took several gulps of wine and then handed the bottle to me. 'Reggie said Aunt Mary came into him the next morning. Untied him and treated his wounds as best she could. Bathed them with warm water and Dettol, as if that would make him better.'

I remembered Aunt Mary bringing me chicken soup and talking to me as if she actually cared. The only person, other than Rachel, who'd done that since my mother's death. 'At least she—'

'She's as bad as the rest of them, Mikey. Worse, even. She goes home to a nice warm house at night, knowing full well what's going on inside Woodside. Might even have kids of her own. But, she says nothing. Turns a blind eye. Brings out the warm water and the Dettol and thinks she can just wash it all away. She could go to the cops and tell them what's going on.'

'Maybe it's not as easy as that.'

A look crept into Liam's eyes that made my heart stall. 'What's that supposed to mean?'

'Going to the cops. Carver's a cop, isn't he?'

'I don't care. That bitch is as bad as the rest of them. If I ever get a chance, I'll do her in as well.'

I tried to stop myself imagining that upside down cross carved onto Reggie's body. How scared he must have been.

'We'll get them, Mikey. Once we're sorted out, we'll go back and get them.'

'Maybe we could meet Reggie from school one day, bring him back here.'

'As long as he doesn't rattle on every night about all that gangster crap.'

'Yeah. Like how he got stuck in that open window when they were burgling a house. How Ronnie Kray had to pull him through.'

Liam laughed. 'Reminds me of you and the cat flap.'

'I hope Reggie didn't fart in Ronnie Kray's face.'

'Gassed a fucking gangster. Only Reggie could do that.'

We laughed long and hard about that. A little close to hysteria. Maybe our only way of dealing with the horrors of Woodside Children's Home.

After a while, Liam turned to me, all traces of humour gone. 'This family they fostered you out to? What was it like?'

I looked into the fire. 'Absolute shit.'

'Wanna talk about it?'

I shrugged. 'I'm not sure.'

'Blood brothers need to know everything, Mikey. That's how we help each other.'

'I suppose…'

'Is it any worse than what happened to your mum?'

I lit a cigarette and told Liam how five months after I had arrived at Woodside, a car pulled up in the turnaround.

'A big dark-blue thing. Kraft had already told me I was going to be placed with a family. Rattled on about how important it was that I behaved myself. How I would only get one chance with a decent family. If I messed up, I would be back at Woodside with a permanent black mark against my name. No one would ever want me again.

'Kraft stood there, threatening me, mopping sweat off his face with a cotton hanky. There was a copper driving the car. A middle-aged bloke got out of the passenger seat and walked up to me. He was about six feet tall, thin, grey hair parted to one side, thin moustache, and watery eyes. Kraft shook his hand and then introduced him to me as Mr. Davies. He asked my name, and then invited me to get in the car. I didn't see Woodside again for another eighteen months.

'We drove right out into the sticks. They lived in a nice detached house, set right back from the road. It wasn't very far from Woodside, no more than half an hour away, which meant I still went to the same school. Davies dropped me off in the mornings on his way to work.

'I slept pretty well that first night. Had my own room. It was much bigger than the boxroom at Whitehead Street. Comfy bed and matching pine furniture. Like paradise after Woodside. His wife made me a packed lunch. A proper one. Sandwiches, an apple, one of those small, fancy cake things and a can of coke. For the first time ever, I had clothes that fit. Shoes with no holes in the bottoms. When I got home, I had a proper cooked meal. Lamb chops, roast potatoes, green beans, and gravy. The best dinner I'd had since my mum died.

'I was even offered a bath. Imagine that after the showers at Woodside? Those bloody things only had two settings; cold and freezing cold. I soaked in that bath, barely able to believe my luck. I even put bubble bath in it. Dared to close my eyes, and enjoy something for once. Surely too good to be true? And it was. Davies came in and started asking me all these questions. Told me to call him Selwyn. Asked how school was. If there was enough hot water. If it was nice being away from Woodside. I felt so exposed. I just wanted him to go away and leave me alone.

'Then he started rattling on about how sorry he was to hear of the terrible way my mother had died. He had a strange, misty look in his eyes. The steam in the bathroom had pasted his hair to his scalp. And then he asked me what I wanted for supper. If I wanted sandwiches and milk. I told him I didn't want anything. Just to be left alone.

'As he was about to leave, he offered to wash my back. Just like that, as if it was fucking normal for a grown man to wash a kid's back. It made every inch of my skin crawl. I drew my knees up in an effort to cover myself, wishing to Christ I'd put more bubbles in the bath. I shook my head. I couldn't speak. He let himself out of the bathroom without another word. A part of me wondered if I'd imagined what he'd just said. Fell asleep in the bath and dreamed the whole thing.

'Nothing else happened for weeks. Life with the Davieses seemed pretty good. I had enough to eat. Good grub, too, not like the shit at Woodside. I smelled a lot better, too. Girls even talked to me. I felt almost normal. No one to cane my arse. No more freezing cold block at Woodside. But, I should have known better. Good things don't happen to people like me.

'They bought me presents at Christmas. Books. Two comic annuals. Topper and Whizzer and Chips. Turkish Delight in a tub. Some gooey shit that ended up getting spilled all over my bed. A neat toy called a Slinky; a giant spring which walked down the stairs. Some Corgi cars. An Aston Martin, with real opening doors and lights that actually worked. We had turkey for dinner. All the trimmings. Stuffing, vegetables, gravy, and Christmas pudding, which Mrs. Davies set fire to.

'Christmas Day was the last good day I ever had. Early the next morning, Davies came into my room. I must have sensed him in my sleep or something, because I woke up when he sat down at the foot of the bed. He asked me if I'd had a good Christmas. Something crawled across the inside of my stomach.

'I switched on my bedside lamp, and waited for my eyes to adjust to the light. My alarm clock did its job for once and alarmed me. Just gone five. Mr. Davies was wearing his pyjamas. Baggy flannelette things, with green and pink squares all over them. I asked him what he wanted. He ignored me, and asked me again if I'd had a good Christmas. I nodded, gripping the blankets. Then he asked me if I liked living there with him and his wife, Dolly.

Again, I nodded. It was if all my words were stuck in the back of my throat, threatening to throttle me. He moved further up the bed, pinning me down with the sheets and blankets. He asked me if I wanted to go back to Woodside. I shook my head. I'd rather die. He seemed happy with that. He then told me he wasn't married to Mrs. Davies. Not in the proper sense of the word. Said they went to a registry office and got a marriage license, but they weren't married in the proper sense of the word. Dolly Davies was really his housekeeper. She'd only agreed to marry him so as the people where he worked didn't know he was a homosexual.

'I moved as far away from him as I could get. Which wasn't very far considering there was a pine headboard in the way. My brain felt like scrambled eggs. He started going on about how he had needs that only men could satisfy. I felt a tiny glimmer of hope. I wasn't a man; I was a boy. He destroyed that by putting his hand on my leg and asking me if I knew what sex was. I shook my head so hard my brain rattled. I thought about calling Mrs. Davies. Screaming her name at the top of my lungs. Begging her to come and help me.

'He seemed to read my thoughts. He told me Mrs. Davies knew all about his ways. She was the sole beneficiary of his will, and was more than happy with their little arrangement. I was shaking all over. I told him I wanted to go back to sleep. He reminded me that one word from him and I'd be back at Woodside.

'The rest happened in a blur. It was almost as if it was happening to someone else, or that I was dreaming the whole thing and watching myself from up on the ceiling. After that he came into my room about once or twice a month.

'Did he rape you?' Liam asked.

'No. It was always just my hand or my mouth. If I refused, he would stop feeding me. Make me do shitty chores for scraps of food, stuff like that. I've lost count of how many times I've had to scavenge in rubbish bins for food, or steal from kids' lunch boxes at school.'

'Bastard.'

I flicked my cigarette butt in the fire. 'Then, out of the blue, he went away for two weeks. London. It was then that I made up my mind he wasn't ever going to touch me again. I was either going back to Woodside, or to prison, but I didn't care anymore.

'On the night it happened, Friday, we'd had a fish and chip supper. By the time he appeared just before midnight, I was losing my bottle. What if I couldn't do it? What if I froze? He asked if I'd been a good boy whilst he'd been away. I was beginning to wish I'd taken a knife from the kitchen drawer and hidden it under the bed for protection.

'He told me he'd bought me a present in London. I didn't want his fucking present. I wanted nothing from him. Even kindness came with conditions. He reached into his dressing gown pocket and pulled out an oblong blue case. He handed it to me, that horrible glazed look in his eyes. He told me to open it. I fumbled with the catch, fingers shaking. He took the case off me, undid it, handed it back. There was a beautiful, gold watch, lying on a red, velvet backing. I'd seen nothing like it in all my life. He told me to take it out.

'I wanted to throw it across the room. Smash it into a thousand pieces. He asked me to take it out and turn it over. I did. Engraved on the back in fancy lettering: To Michael, with love. The words made me feel sick. I didn't want his disgusting love. I wanted my mum's love. Oxo's love. He told me he'd bought it at Allerton's in Bond Street. I put it back in the case, and laid it on my bedside table. I knew what was coming next. What I was going to do. My guts were churning over. I kept thinking, this is the last time you're ever going to put that disgusting prick of yours anywhere near me.

'I waited for him to get into position at the side of the bed, close his eyes, grab hold of my hair. Then, I bit down as hard as I could. He screamed loud enough to shatter glass. He gripped my head so tight I thought he was going to crush my skull. I didn't think he was ever going to stop. He sounded like a tomcat wailing in an alley.

'Mrs. Davies came waddling into the room. I don't remember much after that. It happened in chunks. Davies staggering out. The two of them arguing. An ambulance arriving. Mrs. Davies shouting and bawling at me, telling me I was in the deepest shit possible. I wanted to scream in her face. Ask her how she'd like it if he made her put his disgusting thing in her mouth.

'But I was just a kid, wasn't I? And kids matter about as much as midges on a hot day, don't they?'

CHAPTER 30

Me and Liam said little after that. Just sat before the fire, finishing the wine, smoking, taking in the day's events, our near miss at the church with Kraft, my story of what had happened at the Davieses' house. I didn't tell Liam everything. Some things were better left unsaid. And some things were plainly bizarre. Like how Davies used make me brush his hair and cut his toenails. Or get me to read poetry to him. Stuff I didn't understand. Flowery words wrapped up in riddles. Liam's poem was far better than anything in one of the crappy poetry books Davies sometimes read to me.

I didn't think I would sleep at all that night. My head kept fizzing and popping with unwanted thoughts. Images of Davies. That stupid little moustache sitting on his top lip, like a furry caterpillar. His greasy eyes – if there's such a thing as greasy eyes – roaming all over my body. But, I eventually drifted off to the sound of Liam's snoring.

At first, I thought the banging was in my dream. I was flying a kite, but the damned thing kept trying to drag me up in the air. There was a huge bird, like a vulture, only with wings the size of an airplane's. I opened one eye. My head felt as if someone had been tap-dancing on it.

Liam was already up off the mattress. 'Mikey? Get up. Get the fuck up. It's Carver.'

Carver was standing at the window, hands cupped against the glass. 'Get out here!'

Liam gawked at me. His hair looked as if it was trying to flee his scalp. 'Get up, Mikey.'

I tried to work spit into my mouth. 'What are we gonna do?'

'I don't know. I need to think.' And then, slightly less panicked, 'As long as he hasn't got a key to the door, he can't get in. He ain't never going to get through the cat flap.'

My brain tried to think. Tried to shake off images of giant vultures, and kites that wanted to fly kids. I rolled off the mattress and struggled to my feet.

Carver banged on the window again.

Liam flipped him the bird. 'Let's go to the other bar. I can't think straight with his ugly mush gawping at me.'

We walked into the public bar. Liam sparked his Zippo. The room looked as if a bomb had hit it. There was rubbish everywhere. Broken stools, upturned tables, a pool table missing two legs, empty crisp packets, broken glass.

He snapped the lighter shut and plunged the room back into darkness. 'It's only a matter of time before he gets in, Mikey. Coppers have skeleton keys.'

'Maybe we ought to just give ourselves up.'

'No fucking way. I ain't going to give up and walk out of here like a wet fart.'

'But, the only way out is through the cat flap.'

'How do you reckon he found us?'

That was one question too many for my throbbing head. 'How should I know? If you hadn't rowed with that vicar at the church...'

He was quiet for a moment, and then said, 'Don't blame me for giving that wanker a piece of my mind. They all swan around, as if they're as pure as angels, and we all know they ain't. All that well-meaning bollocks. The twat even knows Kraft, for fuck's sake.'

'I didn't mean—'

'I'm not surrendering.'

The darkness closed in around me and seemed to envelop my heart. 'All right. I'm sorry.'

'We have to fight until the end, Mikey. That's what blood brothers do, right?'

'Yeah.'

'We don't roll over in front of them, like a pair of soppy puppies.'

'Okay.'

'We owe it to everyone at Woodside to go out with a bang. Give them something to cheer about.'

'So, what are we going to do?'

He didn't answer for a while. I honestly believed we were about to die, never mind go out with a bang.

'We need a distraction. One of us could go back into the lounge bar, wind him up, while the other one gets out the cat flap. Then, while he's chasing the first one, the other one can escape.'

'What if he's not on his own? What if he's got someone else waiting around the corner?'

Liam surprised me by agreeing. 'You're right… maybe we could get out of a bedroom window instead. Out the front. I could pry the board off.'

Better than going through the cat flap, but still buggered if Carver had back up. There was a series of loud crashes. Liam flipped the Zippo to life and walked towards the other bar. I followed him. It wasn't good news. The window was now broken, and two uniformed coppers were knocking out the glass.

Carver shouted through the rapidly vanishing barrier, 'You stay right where you are, you little toe rags. Don't move an inch.'

I froze. Carver's contorted face peered through the last fragments of shattered glass. He ordered the two coppers to arrest us. 'Use as much force as necessary.'

Liam looked at me and pushed his glasses up his nose. 'We need to get out of here.'

'Where? For fuck's sake, Liam, where?'

'Don't you even think about moving,' Carver shouted.

One of the bobbies was nearly through the window, truncheon in his hand.

'Come on, Mikey.'

I followed Liam through to the other bar again, hanging onto his jumper. Liam flipped his Zippo and revealed a door with a large brass key protruding from its lock. He pulled it out and opened the door. 'We'll lock ourselves in the cellar and get pissed, Mikey. Go out with a fucking bang.'

Go out with a headache, more like, I thought. I heard the copper's boots treading on the broken glass. For some weird reason, I imagined the Giant in Jack and the Beanstalk. Fee-fi-fo-fum, I smell the blood of Woodside scum.

We made it through the door. Liam banged it shut. It took several attempts to lock the damned thing. Safe. For now.

A loud thump, probably a truncheon, followed by a man's deep voice. 'Do yourselves a favour, boys, open the door.'

Liam whispered, 'Ignore him.'

How the fuck was I supposed to do that? I followed him down into the bowels of the cellar, only the Zippo to light the way.

Another thud. 'Don't make me break down this door.'

We stopped by the wine rack. Liam shut the lighter off. 'Better save the gas.'

Great. Now, we were locked in a pitch-dark filthy cellar. Crawling with spiders and God knew what else. Not to mention coppers waiting outside to break down the door and kill us. I wished I could rewind my life, take it back to before we'd walked into that stupid church.

'Someone must have followed us when we left the church,' Liam said.

I wanted to remind him again whose stupid idea it was to go in there, but we already had enough shit to contend with without getting into a fight. 'Maybe.'

'I wonder how come it's taken them so long to come and get us?'

I didn't have an answer to that. I just wanted to get out of there. My imagination conjured up an image of rats, huge yellow teeth dripping with saliva, waiting to sink their teeth into my leg. 'We can't stay down here.'

'Why not?'

'Because we've got no food. Or water. Or light.'

'There's wine.'

'I don't want wine.'

Liam flipped his Zippo on. 'I'm going to have some.'

'Tate? Truman?' Carver's voice this time, as menacing as that lopsided grin of his.

Liam took a bottle of wine from the rack.

'Can you two toe rags hear me?'

'Don't answer him,' Liam whispered. 'He's only trying to scare us.'

Carver didn't need to bother on that front; I was already terrified enough to puke.

Liam told me to hold the lighter while he pushed the cork through. He took a long swig, grabbed the lighter back, and plunged the cellar into darkness again.

'If you open this door now, I'll put in a good word for you at Woodside.'

I heard Liam chugging the wine. And then, against his own good advice, he shouted back, 'Fuck off, pervert.'

My heart sank to the bottom of my feet, and right through the cellar floor.

'How brave of you, Truman. A right regular little tough guy.'

'That's me.'

I grabbed his arm. 'Winding him up will only make things ten times worse.'

'How can it? They're going to kill us, anyway. We might as well have some fun.'

'Fun?'

'Yeah, fun, Mikey. I only wish I could see the look on his ugly chops right now.'

'Can you hear me, Tate?'

I didn't answer him. I was too busy trying not to throw up.

'You've only been back at Woodside for a short while, boy. I don't think Mr. Kraft will look upon this too severely, if you give yourself up now.'

And pigs might fly.

'I promise.'

'Your promise isn't worth a wank, Carver,' Liam shouted. 'You can stick your promises up your arse.'

This response was followed by a series of heavy blows to the door. So loud in the silence. And then: 'All right, if that's the way you pair of clever Dicks want it.'

Liam slugged more wine. He smashed the bottle against the rack. 'I'll stab the fucker in the face the minute he comes through that door.'

I waited for the door to burst open, Carver and the bobbies to rush in and beat us to death with their truncheons, but nothing happened; just long rolling silence, broken only by mine and Liam's heavy breathing.

I sat down on the floor with my back against the wine rack. 'We're fucked.'

Liam sat down beside me. 'He must have gone.'

'He wouldn't just go.'

'I can't hear anyone.'

That was somehow more threatening. 'He's up to something.'

'But, what? It's not like he's going to tunnel beneath the pub and surprise us. He has to come through the door.'

'Unless…'

'What?'

'Maybe he's going to just leave us down here. Wait until we're starving, or dying of thirst.'

Liam didn't seem to care too much. 'Maybe.'

'We can't stay down here forever.'

'No surrender, Mikey. No fucking surrender.'

Time passed in vast black blocks. No activity outside the door. No banging. Just that awful empty silence. I thought a lot about how my life had turned out since my mother's death. Rachel, Oxo, Woodside,

Davies. One massive spiral leading down into this filthy stinking basement.

I heard a rustling noise outside the door. Something scraping.

'What's that?' Liam asked.

As if I knew. 'Maybe they've got one of those skeleton keys.'

'I left the key in the lock. They won't be able to…'

'What?'

'Listen…'

And then, I heard it. Water running. I scrambled to my feet, convinced he was going to drown us.

Liam hauled himself up, using my leg as a post. 'What the fuck's he doing?'

I strained my ears, trying to listen. Then, I smelled something. Faint at first, then stronger.

'Petrol!' Liam shouted. 'He's pouring petrol underneath the door.'

'What are we going to do?'

He threw his broken bottle on the ground. 'We're fucked.'

The stench was overbearing. Nauseating. Creeping under my skin.

'Can you pair of shitheads hear me?' Carver shouted.

'Don't answer him,' Liam said.

Carver continued: 'I've poured two gallons of petrol under the door. Can you smell it?' He didn't wait for an answer. 'So, here's the deal, boys. You've got one minute to open the door. If you still want to play silly buggers, I'll get the constable to light a rag, and put it under the door. Barbeque you alive. How does that sound?'

'He's bluffing.'

I grabbed Liam's arm. 'I don't think he is.'

'It's no skin off my nose,' Carver said. 'No one will shed any tears over a pair of runaways lighting a fire in a derelict pub cellar. They'll just say you got what you deserved.'

I was about to piss my pants. 'Liam?'

'Everyone knows what a nasty pair of scum you two are. The vicar at the church. Mr. Kraft. The shopkeeper you stole from. The witness who saw you walking around the back of the pub.'

'Fuck off,' Liam shouted. 'Fuck off and suck your own dick.'

'You've got thirty seconds.'

I couldn't stand it any longer. I stumbled across the cellar and staggered up the steps. The stench of petrol made me feel sick and dizzy. I twisted the key in the lock. As I did so, the door flew open, hitting me in the face, and knocking me back down the steps. And then, the world went black.

CHAPTER 31

I regained consciousness in the back of the police car. My head throbbed. Liam was sitting beside me, and we were handcuffed to each other. Two police constables sat in the front. At first, I couldn't quite understand what was wrong with Liam's face, but as my eyes grew accustomed to the light, I realised that one side of his head was swollen to almost twice its size. His right eye was completely closed. Blood dribbled out of his nose and leaked onto his upper lip. His lower lip was swollen and cut.

The copper in the passenger seat said, 'I see you're back with us, then?'

I didn't answer him. I looked at my best friend, beaten to a pulp, breath rattling in his throat. This was all my fault. But what choice did I have? I had no doubt Carver would have set fire to that cellar and let us burn to death. Enjoyed it, even.

Liam looked at me with his good eye. 'No... surrender.'

I nodded. 'Blood brothers.'

He managed a weak smile, closed his eye and slumped sideways.

'Why didn't you just give yourselves up?' the driver asked.

I ignored him and looked out the side window. Fuck him.

As we pulled up at Woodside, Kraft came lurching out of the building. In spite of the cold weather, he was sweating. His hands were swinging by his sides, balled into fists.

The driver switched off the engine and yanked on the handbrake. He wound down the window. 'We have the fugitives, Mr. Kraft.'

Kraft peered through the back window, licked his lips, and returned his attention to the driver. 'Where's Mr. Carver?'

'He's on his way.'

'We'll wait until he gets here.'

And so, we did. About half an hour. Kraft pacing up and down like a sergeant major, waiting for recruits on a parade ground. Carver pulled up in a small green car, with a blue light fixed to the roof.

Kraft asked Carver where he'd been.

'Gathering evidence.'

'What for?'

'In case this goes to court.'

'Court? Have you addled your brain? It will be dealt with in-house.'

Carver treated him to a lopsided grin. 'Just doing my job, Mr. Kraft. Just doing my job.'

'Never mind all that. Get these two down into the boiler room.'

Carver opened the back door. 'Out!'

We clambered out of the car like punch-drunk Siamese twins. At one point, Liam yanked on the cuffs and nearly broke my wrist. The two bobbies hovered around us, waiting for trouble, no doubt, but we were all out of fight. They escorted us through the reception room, along the dank, grey corridor, and down the steps to the boiler room. One cellar to another. At least this one had a light.

One of the bobbies asked Kraft if Liam ought to be looked at.

Kraft smiled. 'Don't worry about him. He'll be looked at, constable. Very closely indeed.'

Locked in the boiler room, sitting on the cold concrete floor, still handcuffed together, Liam turned to me, blood dribbling from his broken nose. 'Another fine mess you've gotten me into, Stanley.'

I tried to laugh. I mean, it was funny. Funny enough to split sides. But, I didn't laugh. I cried. Sobbed until there were no more tears left inside me. And then, I slept. Had that weird dream about the kite trying to drag me up in the air with it again.

Carver woke me up some time later. He kicked me in the side hard enough to knock the wind out of me. 'Wakey-wakey, Tate. I need to ask you some questions.'

'Huh?'

'Sharpen up, you little shit.'

I realised Liam was no longer next to me. And then, I saw him, handcuffed to a metal railing, hands pulled behind his back, forced to stand. If he so much as tried to crouch, his arms would be wrenched from their sockets.

Carver pointed to a wooden chair in the middle of the room and told me to sit in it. I shuffled across the room, legs and backside as numb as a builder's plank. I plonked myself down on the hard wooden seat.

Carver made me put my hands behind my back, and then, he handcuffed them. He stood in front of me, running his fingers through his hair, studying me as if I was a bug in the science lab at school. 'So, Tate, let's hear what you've got to say for yourself.'

What was I supposed to say? We ran away because we were sick of being treated like shit?

'Well?'

I shrugged. Pain scorched my shoulders and neck.

'I want you to explain why you and that sorry sack of shit over there thought it was a good idea to go into a church and insult a vicar?'

'I don't know.'

'Do you think you're clever?'

'No.' The truth. I was just about the dumbest kid on the Earth.

'Don't you have one shred of intelligence?'

Obviously not.

'Let's recap what you've done, Tate. You've absconded from Woodside. Broken into a pub. Stolen from a shop. Disrespected a vicar. Started a fire in a pub. Is there anything I've missed?'

I shrugged. A mistake. He slapped me on the side of my head. The sound echoed around the walls like gunfire. 'I said, is there anything I've missed?'

'No.'

Another slap. This time on the other side. Something cracked in my neck. 'You do know that you pair of imbeciles have burned that pub down, don't you?'

That stupid grin seemed to slip across his face in oil. I wanted to scream at him, tell him he was the one who'd burned down the pub. The one who'd set me and Liam up. But, what was the use? We were just two kids from a children's home. The lowest of the low. Lower than a dog turd on the bottom of a shoe.

'That pub is beyond repair, Tate. Where did you and Truman get the petrol from?'

'We didn't.'

'No? I suppose it just turned up at the pub all by itself, did it? Came waltzing through the door and said, Hey, bozos, want to have some fun?'

'No.'

'Damned right it didn't, you lying turd. So, tell me where you got it from?'

I didn't answer him.

'Which petrol station sold it to you?' He didn't wait for an answer. 'You do know it's an offence to buy petrol under the age of sixteen, don't you?'

'Yes.'

'What were you planning to do?'

'Nothing.'

'Make Molotov Cocktails?'

'No.'

'Throw them at the police when they came to arrest you?'

'No.'

This time he punched me, right in the middle of my forehead. My brain felt as if it had been shoved through the back of my skull. The chair tipped back, wobbled, and then fell forward.

'You're in such deep shit, Tate.'

Tears leaked from my eyes. Carver appeared like smoked glass. He paced back and forth in front of me, glancing at me, stroking his chin, running a hand through his hair.

He stopped and faced me. 'Understand this, Tate; we'll find out the truth, and you will be punished accordingly. So, whose idea was it to run away?'

'Mine.'

'Not Truman's?'

'No.'

'Are you sure about that, Tate? You don't look much like a leader to me.'

I squeezed my eyes shut, trying to get my vision back.

'Do you hear that, Truman? Tate's trying to protect you.'

Liam didn't answer. He hung off those railings, with his arms pinned behind him. He looked like a trapeze artist frozen in time.

'I don't think it will help you, though. I reckon that particular horse has bolted, don't you?'

Liam spat on the floor. An answer, of sorts. A tiny victory in this unwinnable battle.

Carver turned his attention back to me. 'You've also stolen from the school, haven't you?'

'No.'

'Don't you dare sit there and tell me barefaced lies, Tate. We found a teacher's purse in Truman's rucksack. Five pounds missing. Guess where that's being paid back from?'

I didn't know. I just wanted him to go away and leave me alone. There was a terrible, high-pitched ringing in my ears.

'From the coffers at Woodside. Kids will go hungry because of you. Do you hear me?'

Barely. The ringing in my ears was getting louder. 'Yes.'

'So, what sort of selfish shit does that make you, Tate?'

'I'm sorry.'

'It's a bit late for apologies, isn't it? The damage has already been done.'

I looked at the floor, away from those hypnotic eyes.

'Your sort never learn, do they? Just carry on making the same mistakes over and over again. You're nothing but a drain on society, Tate. A dirty, useless drain on this country's resources.'

'Fuck knows what that makes you, then,' Liam said.

Carver laughed. 'Don't worry, Truman. Your turn is coming. You keep it up and see what you get for your troubles.'

Liam spat a glob of blood and snot onto the floor. 'Fuck you.'

Carver turned his attention back to me. 'At least you had the good sense to open the door, Tate. Unlike that idiot over there, who reckons he's some kind of hero. You might just get to live because of that.'

I didn't want to live. I wanted to die. Be free of this place forever.

'Do you admit all the charges against you, Tate?'

'Yes.' There was no point denying anything.

Carver nodded. 'I'm going to leave you two love birds to it. Things to do. I'll be back later. Any funny business, Tate, and I'll cuff you to the railings like that clown over there, is that clear?'

'Yes.'

He walked up the steps and banged the door shut behind him. The lock clicked, leaving me and Liam alone in our new prison.

'Fuck him,' Liam said.

'I'm sorry.'

'Don't be. Do you know where my rucksack is?'

'It's down near the steps.'

'Do me a favour. Go in it and take my book of poems out. Hide it somewhere. I don't care about the rest of the stuff in there, but I want you to keep my book of poems.'

'But—'

'But, nothing. I ain't going to come out of here alive. I want you to take the poems, look after them.'

I walked over to his rucksack, hands cuffed behind my back, tears streaming down my face.

CHAPTER 32

I pulled the notebook out of his rucksack with my teeth. I hid it behind the boiler. I can't tell you how difficult that was with my hands pinned behind my back. To make matters worse, I burnt my right ear on the boiler.

Liam kept moaning about the pain in his shoulders, the numbness in his hands and arms. Then, I had one of my better ideas. I crawled between his legs and hoisted him into the air on my shoulders. Bolts of pain shot through my body, but just being able to help him in some small way was worth every minute.

After a short while, he asked me where I'd put the notebook.

'Behind the boiler. There's a metal flap. A vent or something. I've hidden it behind there.'

'You sure no one will find it?'

I wasn't. 'Yeah.'

'How will you get it back out? This place is always locked up.'

'Maybe I can ask Hodges to get it for me, when he comes down to check the boiler.'

'Do you reckon he would do that?'

'I don't see why not. Hodges is all right.'

Liam was quiet for a moment as if weighing up the pros and cons of asking favours from a member of staff. 'Yeah. Do that, Mikey. It's a good idea.'

I felt a slight flush of pride. At least I could do something right.

'I wonder if any of those stories about the war are true?'

I tried to shrug, and then realised I had about eight stones of dead weight on my shoulders. My neck made a nasty crunching sound. 'I don't believe all that stuff about storming German positions on his own.'

'Not with his limp.'

I laughed. 'Maybe that's how he got it.'

'He told me he was born with one leg longer than the other one.'

We fell silent for a while. I didn't know how long I could hold him up. My head was banging like a drum, and either Liam was putting on weight, or I was getting weaker.

When Liam spoke again, he took me by surprise. 'Do you believe in ghosts, Mikey?'

I made the mistake of trying to shrug again. 'I haven't really thought about it.'

He surprised me again. 'I do.'

'Really?'

'I don't see why not. We've all got spirits, haven't we? That's what makes us all different.'

'True.'

'Do you ever think about dying?'

Every day since coming to Woodside. 'Sometimes.'

'I wonder if there's really such a place as heaven. Or hell? If you believe in one, you've got to believe in the other.'

'Carver and Kraft are going to hell.'

'Too fucking right. And that vicar. And Reader and Malloy. The fucking lot of them.'

'I hope they all get burned alive.'

Liam was quiet for a moment, and then said, 'They can't be burned alive, if they're already dead.'

I laughed.

'I wonder what happens to people who kill themselves? I mean, it ain't right killing yourself, is it, Mikey?'

'It depends.'

'On what?'

'If you've got a good reason.'

'Maybe. If you're in loads of pain. Or dying anyway. But, not just because your wife has left you. That ain't no excuse, is it?'

I didn't want to disrespect his dad. 'It's hard to say. I've never been an adult.'

'Your mum had a lot more shit to deal with than my old man did.'

'Some people are just stronger than others.'

'I fucking hate him for killing himself. I wouldn't be in this mess if it wasn't for him. If he hadn't been such a—'

'Try not to think about it. It's done, Liam.'

He didn't seem to hear me. 'I used to think he was really tough when I was a kid. He used to walk about with his top off in the summer. Tanned, big muscles, hairy as a gorilla. Pick me up and put me on his shoulders, walk me to school. I used to feel ten feet tall. Nothing could ever hurt me. Not when I was with him.'

'He sounds like he was a better dad than mine.'

'I used to think he was made of stone. But, he wasn't, was he? He was as soft as a cowpat when it came down to it. Couldn't even be bothered to stick around to watch me grow up.'

My knees were buckling under his weight. I would need to put him down soon. Perhaps I could hold him for half an hour, rest for a while, and then, pick him up again. 'I'm sure he loved you.'

Liam snorted. 'Fat lot of good that is.' And then, after a few seconds, 'I wish he was here now, Mikey. Here to smash Carver's head against a wall.'

I managed another five minutes before giving in to the pain and putting him down. I straightened up, feeling guilty as he sucked in air through clenched teeth. Pain scrawled its signature across his forehead, giving him the appearance of an old man.

'I'll pick you up again in a bit. I just need to rest my shoulders a minute.'

'It's... all... right...'

I crouched down, relieving the pressure on my knees. The boiler hissed in the corner of the room as if trying to imitate Liam. The dirty concrete floor looked so inviting to my battered body. Just to lay down and go to sleep forever.

'Mikey?'

'Yeah?'

'You gotta promise me you'll make it out of here.'

'We'll—'

He shook his head so violently I thought he was having a seizure. 'No. Forget about me. They're going to kill me. I'm done. Finished. But, you'll be all right if you do what they say.'

'I don't want to—'

'Just fucking listen, Mikey. I haven't got the strength to keep shutting you up.'

So, I listened.

'One day, you'll get out of here. You won't be a kid forever. First chance you get, go. Don't let them get under your skin. Don't let them turn you into a robot who's got no feelings left. You understand what I'm saying?'

So tired now. 'Yeah.'

'There's four ways you can end up, Mikey: dead, destroyed, a turncoat like McCree, or stronger. Someone who's determined to make the bastards pay for what they've done. Do you get me?'

I couldn't see how Kraft and his sort would ever pay. They had all the power. But, I didn't want to disagree with Liam. 'I get it.'

'Promise me you'll make them pay.'

'I promise.'

'Find someone who will listen. Someone who isn't fucking evil like them. And you tell them what happened here, Mikey. How they raped and murdered kids. How they tortured us, and put us through hell, because we didn't have no one else to look out for us. You promise?'

I promised.

He spat on the floor. 'Blood brothers, right?'

I spat on the floor, too. 'Blood brothers.' I had an overwhelming urge to reach out and touch Liam's face, brush his hair back, and push his glasses back up his nose. But, my hands were cuffed.

'Don't let them get away with it. Go to the fucking newspapers if you have to. Someone will believe you.'

To be honest, I didn't think I would make it out of Woodside alive, either. 'I'm so sorry.'

'What for?'

'Letting Carver into the cellar.'

'Don't be stupid. It was either open the door, or get burned alive. At least this way, one of us lives to fight another day.'

'Why do you keep saying "one of us"? You might—'

'We both know I'm dead meat, Mikey.'

I didn't answer.

'You've got to do it.'

'I'll try. I promise.'

'Good. Because, otherwise, all this ain't worth a toss. They win. They get away with it. And it just goes on and on.'

My head was in danger of exploding. 'What a fucking mess.'

'Do it for everyone who's suffered in this shithole. Do it for me.'

I nodded.

'And don't you ever forget, I'll be up there watching you. Every fucking day.'

I wanted to tell him how much I would miss him.

How much I loved him, but the words were bogged down in a massive lump in my throat.

Instead, I crouched down between his legs, hoisted him back onto my shoulders, and relieved the pressure on his body as best I could for a while.

CHAPTER 33

They came during the night. I had no way of knowing what the time was, but there was no activity above us. No stomping on floors. No shouts. No screams. Just an eerie silence, broken only by Liam's breathing and the hiss-clunk of the boiler.

Kraft and Malloy were both wearing white wigs and black gowns. They looked ridiculous. McCree and Carver struggled down the steps with a desk. After positioning it along one wall, they both walked back up the steps, and returned a few minutes later with two chairs. Kraft sat behind the desk with Malloy seated to his right. Carver and McCree remained standing.

Kraft produced a small, wooden mallet and banged on the desk. 'Court is now in session.'

Carver ordered me to stand before the judge. 'And stand up straight, you spineless runt.'

I tried my best. My legs were shaking so badly my knees knocked together.

Kraft studied me for a few moments. When he spoke, his voice was calm and clear. 'State your name for the court.'

'Michael Tate.'

He turned to Carver. 'What is the charge?'

'Theft, criminal damage, going AWOL, arson, and resisting arrest, your honour.'

'And the other prisoner?'

Carver referred to his notebook. 'Truman is charged with theft, criminal damage, unauthorised absence, wilful neglect, assault, arson, carrying a weapon with intent to endanger life, resisting arrest, abusing a man of the cloth, blasphemy, and dereliction of duty.'

Kraft nodded, as each of the trumped-up charges was read out. He shouted across the room to Liam. 'Do you understand the charges, Mr. Truman?'

Liam hung from the railing, like an animal in a butcher's shop window. 'Fuck you.'

Kraft shook his head. 'I see the prisoner has lost none of his appetite for insolence. Have you anything to say in your defence, Mr. Truman?'

Liam didn't answer. He made a hacking noise in the back of his throat and spat on the floor.

Kraft turned to Malloy. 'Can defence offer any mitigation for the prisoner?'

Malloy shook his head. 'Unfortunately not, your honour. Truman has always been an awkward character. He has consistently shown a flagrant disregard for authority. On reflection, he might have benefited from a stricter approach regarding discipline, but, as I'm sure you're aware, your honour, hindsight is a wonderful thing.'

'Indeed. But, it is not the duty of this court to rake over the ashes of a prisoner's past. What's done is done. I understand the prisoner's father committed suicide?'

Malloy preened himself like a strutting peacock. 'That is the case, your honour.'

Kraft looked at Liam. 'The apple never falls far from the tree, does it, young man?'

Liam held his head as high as he could and looked Kraft in the eye. 'No. And sometimes people end up swinging from that same tree.'

Kraft banged his mallet down hard enough to split the wood. 'I see that tongue of yours makes a very effective noose. I would like to remind you that you're in a court of law. Everything you say can and will be used as evidence against you.'

Liam turned away, his face crushed by pain.

Kraft addressed Carver again. 'You say the prisoner resisted arrest?'

'Yes, your honour. We pleaded with both defendants to see sense, but Truman seemed to take some sort of perverse pleasure in taunting us. He said he'd poured petrol down the cellar steps, and he would set fire to it if anyone came through the door. We didn't have a key, your honour. The best we could do was try to appeal to their better nature.'

Kraft adjusted his wig and dabbed at his forehead with a handkerchief. 'It might be fair to surmise characters such as these don't possess a better nature.'

'I fear you're right, your honour,' Carver said. 'That has already been made apparent by the prisoners' behaviour in the church.'

'As I can unfortunately bear witness to. His language was both foul and abhorrent.' He turned to me. 'Why did you go to the church, Tate?'

To rob the place. 'I don't know.'

'If I might offer a suggestion, your honour,' Carver intervened. 'They went there to steal.'

'Steal what, Mr. Carver?'

'Perhaps the gold candlesticks?'

Kraft wrote something down on a jotter. 'Is that true, Tate?'

'No.'

Kraft turned to Carver. 'I'd be interested to know why they went to the church, Detective Inspector. The vicar is a personal friend of mine. I'm sure he would appreciate an answer. It might be prudent to see if you can elicit one from Truman.'

'Certainly, your honour.' He walked over to Liam and stood a few feet in front of him. 'You heard the judge. He wants to know the real reason why you went to the church.'

Liam tried to straighten his head and look Carver in the eye. His breath rattled in the back of his throat. His glasses were perched precariously on the end of his nose. 'We... went... there... to... pray...'

'Pray for what, boy?' Kraft said. 'Salvation?'

'To... pray... you... lot... die... a... slow... and... painful... death...'

Kraft banged the desk with the mallet. 'Silence in court. Detective Inspector Carver? You may elicit an answer by whatever means you see fit.'

Carver drew back his arm and punched Liam in the stomach. The force knocked Liam back. His arms were almost wrenched from their sockets. He was left panting and gasping for breath.

Carver paced up and down in front of him. 'Why did you go to the church, Truman?'

Liam stared at the floor.

'Did you go there to steal?'

Nothing. Just an awful rattling sound as he struggled for breath. Carver drew back his arm to hit him again.

'We went there to steal the collection plate,' I shouted.

Carver paused, arm suspended in mid-air. He leered at me, a glazed look in his pale-blue eyes. 'What did you say?'

I repeated it.

He turned back to Liam. 'Is this true?'

Liam twisted his head to one side and ignored him.

'Well, well,' Kraft said. 'Your depravity knows no bounds.'

'I can offer no defence,' Malloy said. 'The boy is beyond redemption.'

Carver grabbed hold of Liam's chin and tipped his head back. 'You despicable piece of shit.'

Liam tried to move his head. Carver headbutted him. I watched in horror as Liam's nose exploded in a spurt of thick, red blood. His glasses fell to the floor. One of the lenses shattered and fell out of the frame. He gurgled and spat blood.

'Mr. Carver?' Kraft said. 'Would you like to take a moment?'

Carver rubbed his forehead. 'I'm fine, your honour.'

'You may continue.'

'Thank you, your honour.' He studied Liam for a moment, and then said, 'Do you think it's a good idea to steal from the church?'

Liam squinted at Carver. I knew he couldn't see a thing without his glasses. I wished with all my heart I could stop the bastard assaulting him. The only thing I could think of doing was telling Carver it was all my idea. So I did.

Kraft looked at me as if I'd just spat in his face. 'What did you just say, boy?'

'It was all my idea. I talked Liam into it.'

Carver put his hand on the desk. 'The boy's a habitual liar. I would pay scant attention to what comes out of his mouth.'

Kraft nodded. 'Quite. I'd advise you to keep quiet, Tate. Is that clear?'

'But, it's true.'

I didn't see Malloy come up behind me. 'Shut up, Tate. No one's interested in your lies. One more word out of you, and I'll have you chained to the railing like Truman. Do I make myself plain?' I didn't get a chance to answer. I felt a blow to the back of my head, and then the world turned black.

When I came to, Carver was addressing Kraft. 'Truman obviously has no remorse, your honour. It's clear to me he has psychopathic tendencies.'

Kraft rested his hands on the desk. 'It's clear to this court the boy has no moral compass. A tainted upbringing. Parents who completely abdicated their duties. But, that does not excuse his behaviour. The list of charges against him reads like something out of a gangster novel. We can safely assume the prisoner displays a lack of empathy; that was clearly illustrated by his behaviour at the school and at the church. Theft can never be condoned. He has been given ample opportunity to mend his ways. We've bent over backwards to try to rehabilitate him.'

Malloy coughed. 'Indeed we have. Many times. A thankless and fruitless task.'

Kraft thanked him. 'McCree?'

241

'Yes, sir.'

'Have you anything to add?'

McCree stepped forward and brushed a thick strand of hair out of his eyes. 'Yes, sir.'

'Then speak now, lad.'

'I caught him in the junior block one night, sir.'

'What was he doing?'

'He was in bed with one of the young kids.'

'That's a fucking lie,' I shouted, unable to listen to any more of this crap. 'He wouldn't do something like that.'

Kraft whacked the desk with his mallet. 'Silence in court, or I'll have you removed into the care of Mr. Reader. And I, for one, know he won't appreciate having to nursemaid you, Tate. Not at this time of night. Do you understand?'

'But, Liam wouldn't—'

'One more word, and you'll wish your mother had cut your tongue out at birth.' He turned back to McCree. 'Please carry on.'

McCree shuffled awkwardly. 'I had to remove him, sir. He got all nasty. Accusing me of all sorts of stuff.'

'Like what?'

'Interfering. Spoiling his fun. That sort of thing.'

'Thank you, McCree.'

McCree stepped back a couple of paces and bowed his head.

Kraft put down his mallet, formed a steeple with his fingers, and looked at Liam. 'Words rarely fail me, Truman, but your actions sicken me to the core. I have taken all the evidence into consideration, and I'm afraid you leave me with no alternative but to pass a sentence of death upon you. May God have mercy on your soul.'

Liam laughed. He sounded like a hissing cat. 'Good.'

Carver stepped close to Liam, and spat in his face. 'I'm going to enjoy killing you.'

I shouted, 'You can't do—'

'Shut up,' Kraft snapped. 'And stand up straight.' He turned to Carver. 'Have you any further questions for Tate?'

'Yes, your honour.' He walked over to me, that dreadful, lopsided grin hitching up one side of his face. 'So, Tate, do you admit accompanying Truman on his rampage of destruction and thievery?'

The stupidest question I'd ever heard. 'Yes.'

'Do you admit stealing from the school?'

'Yes.'

'The church?'

'Yes.'

'Burning the Dolphin Public House to the ground?'

'Yes.'

'Abusing a police officer and resisting arrest?'

'Yes.'

Carver turned to Kraft. 'No more questions, your honour.'

Kraft thanked him. He then addressed me. 'Well, Tate, at least you've had the good sense to admit to your crimes, and I will take this into consideration when passing sentence. However, that does not excuse or condone your behaviour in any way whatsoever. You have proved every bit as devious, every bit as conniving, and every bit as willing to undermine authority as Truman. A proper little double act.'

Fuck you.

Kraft adjusted his wig. 'I don't think Morecambe and Wise have too much to worry about, though.'

Dutiful laughter from Malloy and Carver. McCree combed his hair with his fingers.

'Having taken into consideration your willingness to admit to your folly, and that you opened the door after setting fire to the cellar, I am prepared to show some leniency in your case. You are to spend one month in the boiler room in solitary confinement. You will be afforded two bowls of porridge and a glass of water a day. And Tate?'

'What?'

'I'd use the time wisely, if I were you. Consider your actions. Do you understand?'

Oh, I understood, all right. The bastards held all the cards. But, Liam was right. The only way I could ever get revenge was by staying alive.

Kraft banged the table with his mallet. 'Court is dismissed.' He stood up and turned to Carver. 'McCree and Tate can assist you with the body.'

'Yes, your honour.'

'Thank you, gentlemen. Goodnight.'

CHAPTER 34

Carver turned to McCree. 'I'll be back in a minute. You keep an eye on these two.'

'Okay.'

McCree looked at me and grinned. 'Better hope no one gobs in your porridge, eh, Tate?'

I wanted to rush at him, headbutt him, break his nose, smash his face into a thousand pieces, and poke out his eyes.

'Perhaps Uncle Bernie might come and pay you a visit one night. You'd like that, wouldn't you?'

'Piss off.'

When Carver was out of sight, McCree walked over to Liam. 'I'm going to enjoy watching you die.'

Liam didn't answer. He could barely breathe. He reminded me of Jesus nailed to the cross. Blood covered most of his face, and one of his shoulders was out of line. All he needed was a crown of thorns.

'Look at you,' McCree said. 'A fucking coward, just like your daddy.'

'Fuck… you…'

McCree punched Liam in the side of his head. There was a loud popping noise. Liam cried out.

'Leave him alone,' I shouted. 'Just leave him alone, you fucking bully.'

'You want some as well, Tate?'

Carver rescued us, if you could call it that. 'Dearie me, I've only been gone ten seconds, and the peasants are already revolting.'

McCree brushed hair out of his face. 'Truman was getting lippy.'

Carver held a truncheon in his right hand. He told me to get in the corner of the room by the boiler.

'Why?'

'Just do it, Tate. McCree, you stand guard over Little Jack Horner.'

McCree made a big deal of shoving me as I walked. He was probably hoping I would trip up and smash my face on the concrete floor. He shoved me against the wall. I hit my head for about the fiftieth time that day. He then kicked my legs out from underneath me. I hit the ground and cracked my elbow on the floor.

Carver walked over to Liam. What happened next is too painful to describe in detail. In a nutshell, he beat Liam to death with the truncheon. Broke every bone in his body by the sound of it. When he was finished, he dropped the truncheon on the floor, panting and wheezing.

I heard the plink-hiss of the boiler. McCree was silent. Carver unlocked Liam's handcuffs and let his body fall to the floor. His head hit the concrete with a loud smack. I tried to tell myself it was all over for Liam. They couldn't hurt him anymore. He was in a better place. But, all I could think about was the terrible sound of his bones snapping like twigs.

Carver retrieved the truncheon and walked over to me and McCree. He banged the blood-soaked thing against the wall above my head. 'Get up, fuck wit.'

I struggled to my feet.

'Here's what we're going to do,' Carver said. 'We'll go to Hodges' shed and get a wheelbarrow and two shovels. Then, we'll take that worthless pile of poop down to the bottom of the field, and bury him. Clear?'

'Won't the ground be too hard to dig at this time of year?' McCree asked. 'It's bloody freezing outside.'

'Did they postpone the war in the winter, because the ground was too hard to dig trenches?'

McCree shrugged. 'I don't know. I wasn't there.'

'And thank fuck you weren't. All the best men died in that war.'

'Don't say much for you, then, does it?'

'Don't get smart with me, you little ponce. You can disappear as easily as anyone else.'

'I was only kidding.'

'Well, don't. You're not big enough or ugly enough to pull jokes with me. You stick to bullying the little kids. Understand?'

McCree nodded, his cheeks flushed red.

Carver turned to me. 'Are you ready, Tate?'

Don't let them bastards get away with it. Go to the fucking newspapers if you have to. Someone will believe you. I nodded.

He ordered me to turn around. 'I'm going to unlock your handcuffs, but be warned, one false move, and you'll be going in the grave with that useless idiot.'

'Maybe we ought to kill him anyway,' McCree said.

Carver was silent for a while. My legs turned to custard. It was amazing how you could still be terrified of death, even when you didn't have anything to live for.

'Kraft wants him alive.'

'Why?'

'I don't know. You just keep it buttoned and do as you're told.'

Carver unlocked my handcuffs. 'Just for the record, Tate, I have a 9mm handgun in the waistband of my trousers. I'm sure Kraft would have no objection to me shooting an escaping prisoner, so I'd think very carefully about every single move you make. Capiche?'

I owed it to Liam to do my best to stay alive. 'Yes.'

Carver picked Liam's glasses up off the floor. He held them up in his blood-soaked hand for inspection. He walked over to the discarded rucksack, dropped them inside, and zipped up the bag. He handed it to McCree. 'It can go down the hole with him.'

Just as I thought it couldn't get any worse, Carver took a polaroid instamatic camera out of the desk drawer, and started taking pictures of Liam's battered body. At least a dozen snaps. The whirr of the camera's mechanism like the final nails being hammered into Liam's coffin.

Carver studied the pictures for a while, then put them in the drawer along with the camera. He grinned. 'Evidence for the judge, in case you're wondering. Right, let's get the gear. We haven't got all night.'

About halfway up the steps, Carver turned around, and pointed his truncheon at Liam's lifeless body. 'You stay right there, Truman. We won't be long.'

By the time we'd loaded Liam's body into the wheelbarrow and taken it to the bottom of the field, I was about ready to collapse from exhaustion. Carver had a powerful torch. He kept shining it in my eyes every time he spoke to me. I tried not to think about what we were doing. To pretend I was somewhere else. Out for a walk with Oxo. Anything other than the awful truth.

Carver ordered me and McCree to dig a hole in the corner of the field.

'What about Hodges?' McCree asked.

Carver shone the torch in McCree's face. 'What about him?'

'What if he finds the grave?'

'I'm not planning to put a headstone on it and lay a wreath, am I? As long as we trample the earth back down, he will be none the wiser.'

And so we set to digging. Carver kept making me jump into the hole to check its depth. A marker for my best friend's grave. McCree huffed and puffed and moaned. Said he didn't understand why Carver didn't make me dig the grave on my own.

'Because, it will be light soon. It'll take that idiot too long on his own, now shut up, and get on with it.'

Carver eventually called a halt. 'Right, that should be deep enough. Put him in.'

McCree wheeled Liam to the edge of the grave and tipped his corpse into the hole. Carver dropped the rucksack in after him and ordered us to fill it in.

When it was done, Carver made us replace the turf on top, and trample down the earth. He fussed with it, getting McCree to hold the torch while he did so.

Satisfied, Carver said, 'That'll do. I'll come back when it's light and take a proper look. Let's get this stuff back to the shed.'

With the garden equipment returned, Carver and McCree took me back down into the boiler room. He told McCree to go to bed, and then turned to me. 'You can have this one of two ways, Tate. The easy way or the hard way. Which would you prefer?'

'I don't care.'

'You'll care when I smash your teeth down your throat.'

'The easy way.'

'Good choice. I'm going to leave the cuffs off. First sign of trouble, they go back on, understand?'

You're all heart. 'Yes.'

He took the camera and the pictures out of the drawer and walked up the steps. 'Don't do anything I wouldn't do.'

I paced around the room. There was blood all over the floor by the railings. I massaged my throbbing wrists. 'I'll get them for this, Liam. I swear.'

The boiler hissed and clunked as if answering me. I retrieved Liam's book of poems. Would it really be safe to give it to Hodges? I mean, there was a whole raft of difference between listening to war stories, and trusting him with something as important as Liam's poems.

I clutched the book to my chest and closed my eyes. I felt the rhythm of my heart beating against the words; the rhythm of the words beating against my heart.

You'd better not tell, boy

You'd better not scream

No one can hear you

In the abattoir of dreams.

The concrete floor suddenly seemed soft beneath my feet. The stale air in the basement was replaced by cool fresh air. Wind ruffled my hair. Then, the tears came, rolling down my cheeks, hot and fresh. I cried for my mother. I cried for Liam. And I cried for every kid who had ever suffered at the hands of evil cowards hiding behind positions of power.

Spent, I opened my eyes. I was no longer in the boiler room at Woodside. I was sitting in my wheelchair at the gates, a fully grown, crippled adult once more. I saw lights in two of the downstairs windows. A young kid cleaning a window. Another sweeping the path in front of the building. A delivery van pulling up at the kerb.

Kalvin Kraft appeared and marched along the front of the building. He stopped next to the kid, punched him in the back, and walked inside, without missing a beat. The kid dropped the cleaning cloth and fell to his knees.

Don't let them bastards get away with it. Go to the fucking newspapers if you have to. Someone will believe you.

The wheelchair turned around and headed into the dark obscurity of the tunnel. The journey back to the hospital flashed by in a few seconds. No more voices, no stop-offs, just straight back through the emergency door and back into bed.

I watched the wheelchair take its customary place next to the emergency door, tyres screeching on the tiles. The brake snapped on. The bolt slid back into place. The magazine with the photos inside was still on the bedside locker. I heard the faint chatter of nurses at the night station.

How long had I been gone? It felt like months, yet...

I watched, transfixed, as fresh writing appeared on the door. The Abattoir of Dreams.

'Liam?'

No answer, just the faint whirr of the fan sitting on top of the chest of drawers. But I now knew, with near certainty, my mother had been murdered by my father, and Liam Truman had been murdered by Detective Inspector Carver.

But none of this altered the fact I had killed my girlfriend and jumped from the top of a block of flats, did it?

Or that I was lying in a hospital bed, paralysed from the waist down.

I tucked Liam's book of poems under my pillow.

I was fucked whatever way you looked at it, and soon, I would be in prison, at the mercy of Carver and anyone else who wanted to abuse me.

CHAPTER 35

Sharon, the nurse with all the personality of a disturbed rhinoceros, announced I had a visitor. It was mid-morning. I'd slept quite well after being returned to my bed. Probably exhaustion.

Jimmy walked in and sat down. 'How's it going?'

'What day is it?' I hadn't been in any mood to ask Sharon when she'd emptied my catheter.

'Friday.'

So, the whole experience at Woodside had been condensed into one night? 'Are you sure?'

He looked uneasy. 'Course I am. It's Friday morning. I'm on shift at midday. Why? What's happened?'

I told him everything, right up to holding the book of poems in the boiler room. The way I'd suddenly been transported back to the wheelchair, and along the tunnel to the hospital.

At first, he said nothing. He stared at the wall, where the emergency door now displayed its fresh message. When he spoke, something seemed to be affecting his speech. 'Jesus Christ. Carver killed Liam?'

'Yep.'

He rubbed the top of his head as if stimulating thought.

'But, what can we do?' I said. 'He's the one with all the power, isn't he?'

'He can't be allowed to get away with it.'

'Don't you think I know that, Jimmy? But, what can we do? Ask a nice policeman to come and take a statement? Who's going to believe a load of guff about being pushed in a wheelchair by an invisible pusher? It will just sound as if I've lost my mind... which is exactly how I feel.'

'You're not losing your mind.'

'I think it's Liam pushing me along the tunnel.'

'What if I look for this Children's Home?'

I wanted to sound enthusiastic, grateful, but it was virtually impossible. 'It's still not going to prove anything, is it?'

'It might, if I can find Liam's grave.'

'How? You can hardly ask Kraft if you can borrow a shovel and dig up the field.'

'I don't have to ask him.'

We fell into an uneasy silence. And then, I remembered I'd brought Liam's book of poems back with me. I fished it out from under my pillow. 'This is the book he asked me to look after.'

Jimmy's eyebrows almost reached his non-existent hairline. 'Really?'

'Yeah. There's one called The Abattoir of Dreams. It's about Woodside.'

'Can I read it?'

'I'll read it to you, if you want?'

'I'd like that.'

I flicked through the pages until I found it. I thought I might cry again, but my voice remained strong, right through until the end.

Jimmy shook his head slowly. 'Jesus. How old was he?'

'Fifteen.'

'He sounds so much older.'

I felt proud to have known Liam Truman. Someone who wasn't afraid to say, fuck you, you can take my body, but you'll never take my mind. Someone who had the balls to stick two fingers up at Woodside. Someone who deserved justice.

Jimmy wiped a tear from his cheek. 'I still think it's got to be worth looking for his grave.'

'I don't know, Jimmy. Kraft and Malloy rule that place with an iron fist.'

'What if I went at night?'

'But, you'll need torches, shovels. Someone will see you.' And then, I had an idea; one that made me stop in my tracks. 'But...'

'What is it, Michael?'

'There's a groundsman at Woodside. His name's Hodges. Decent bloke. Some of the lads used to go to his shed and have a smoke, listen to boring stories about the war. It's a long shot, but if you could talk to him, he might help. He's got a little cottage in the grounds, near the perimeter fence.'

'Are you sure he's all right?'

I wanted to say yes, one hundred percent, but I couldn't. For all I knew, Hodges had his own dark secrets. 'I haven't got a clue, but he's our only chance. No one will pay any notice if they see him working in the field.'

Jimmy was almost wearing out his bald patch with frantic, circular movements of his hand. 'I might get Terry to go with me.'

'Terry?'

'He's got your old job. But, he's solid. You'd like him.'

That was good enough for me. 'Okay.'

'Where exactly is the grave?'

'At the bottom of the field. In the right-hand corner, next to the fence.'

'We'll find it.'

I closed the book of poems and handed it to Jimmy. 'I want you to take care of this for me. Keep it safe. Do you promise?'

'On my life, Michael. On my life.'

We sat in silence. Everything still felt stacked in Carver's favour. Even finding Liam wouldn't be enough. There would still be too many blanks, too many horrors, too many innocent kids suffering. It seemed as if God had left the planet in the care of the Devil.

Eventually, Jimmy said, 'I'll go tonight. I get off shift at nine.'

'Be careful.'

'I think I'll just see how the land lies at first. Find the cottage, and work out the best way to approach this Hodges bloke.'

'Taking him forty Woodbines would be a good start,' I said, remembering how much the man liked a smoke. 'And he likes a nip of brandy. He always keeps a bottle in the work shed. Liam said he gave Reggie a drop one time after he'd had a really bad beating.' I didn't tell Jimmy how Reggie had been subjected to rape and torture.

'I've got some left over from Christmas. It's only cheap stuff, though.'

'I don't think Hodges is the sort of bloke who's too bothered about that.'

'Right, I'd better crack on.'

'By the way, I'm being transferred out of here on Monday.'

'Where?'

'They're putting me on remand somewhere.'

'Shit.'

'Carver will be able to do exactly what he likes, once I'm out of here.'

'Don't worry about him, Michael. We'll get him. We'll get the bastard.'

I wished I could believe that. 'I'm really grateful for what you're doing, Jimmy.'

He shrugged. 'It's nothing.'

'Liam would have loved you.'

Jimmy hugged the book of poems. 'I reckon the feeling's mutual.' With that, he walked out of the room without a backward glance.

CHAPTER 36

Carver came to the hospital later that day, a large, black book tucked under his arm, lopsided grin fixed on his chops. My insides froze as I remembered him beating Liam to death with the truncheon. Blow after blow, shattering his bones, smashing him to a bloody, unrecognisable pulp. Carrying him to the bottom of the field in that wheelbarrow, like a piece of garden rubbish.

'Good morning, Michael. I trust you are well?'

I ignored him.

'What's the matter? You look as if you've seen a ghost.'

'I've got nothing else to say to you. You've already charged me and told me I'm going to remand on Monday.'

Carver sat in the chair and put the book on the bed. 'I know. It's a cut and dried case. You're guilty as charged, blah, blah, blah. But, I'm away for the weekend. Taking Angie to Paris. Ever been?'

I stared at the writing on the emergency door. Wished to Christ the wheelchair would move over to the bed and whisk me away from this grotesque excuse for a human being.

'They say it's the most romantic city in the world. I doubt that's true; it's full of Frogs.' He laughed. 'But, it ought to put Angie in the mood, if you know what I mean.'

I didn't. And I didn't want to, either.

'She's a sucker for all that romantic slush. Give her a bottle of wine and a plate of oysters, and she's as good as ready to spread her wings.' He winked. 'It's important to keep a woman satisfied,

Michael, if you want your wheels to run smoothly, dodge the potholes.'

'It's a bit late for me to worry about that.'

He patted the top of my leg. 'I fear you might be right there. Right as Rudolph, as my dear, old daddy used to say, before his tongue got slippery in the ale house. Anyway, suffice to say, I should be refreshed and raring to go by Monday morning. In a better frame of mind to deal with a piece of shit like you.'

I felt like screaming in his face, calling him a murderer, telling him that I would make sure he got life for what he'd done to Liam. And then, I had a terrifying thought. What if Liam wasn't the only one? What if he'd killed others? Kids that just vanished. Maybe the field at Woodside was littered with unmarked graves.

'Michael?'

I stared at the message from my mother scrawled on the door: Be true to yourself, love-bug.

'Look at me when I'm speaking to you.'

I forced myself to look into those pale blue eyes; they reminded me of milky ponds. I had to keep it together. Not let on what I knew about him and about Woodside.

He seemed to stare right through me. 'Do you know, Michael, I'm sure I know you from somewhere.'

'You don't.' A little too abrupt.

He sucked the tip of his thumb. 'Have you ever been in trouble before?'

'I don't know, I—'

'Don't remember? Yes, I know, you've been trotting that one out, since I first interviewed you. But, it's been bugging me like a nasty itch in the middle of my back. I said to Angie only yesterday, "I'm bloody sure I know Michael Tate from somewhere." Course, Angie couldn't help me out, because she doesn't understand the first thing about my work.'

Lucky for her, I thought.

'I know it's too late for you, Michael, but it's far better not to let women get too close. Keep them out of your personal stuff. They only end up making a fuss. They like to be in control. It pays dividends to make them think they are.'

'I wouldn't—'

'Did I ever tell you about my first wife?'

'No.'

'I didn't tell you about Missy? Where are my manners? Missy was a nice enough girl. Her real name was Melissa, but her family called her Missy, so I wasn't about to argue with the wishes of family, blood being thicker than water and all that. Now, I'll let you into a little secret, Michael. Can you keep a secret?'

I didn't respond.

'I don't like screwing women. Does nothing for my libido. Angie understands that. She knows what's what. That's why I'm taking her to Paris for the weekend. It's what we call a compromise. All that romantic guff, and then, I let her find a man to entertain the business end of things, if you get my drift.'

Jesus Christ, was this really happening?

'So, I spend a few bob, Angie gets her fill, and everyone's happy. It's an arrangement we've had right back from day one. Like a contract. I learned from my mistakes with Missy, thinking I could smooth her out as we went along. But, here's a little tip for you, Michael. Women have bumps like braille, and you'd better learn to read them right, else you're in the deepest shit imaginable. Last piece of advice: never underestimate a woman.'

I tried to load my voice with sarcasm. 'Thanks.'

'Beyond all that lipstick and blusher, there beats a brain to match any man's. I got out of my wedding night obligations by getting blind drunk. I mean, by the end of the night, I could barely raise a smile, let alone the bed snake. In the morning, I blamed a hangover. And so it went on. Every time Missy wanted to get kissy, I had to make up an excuse. I even told her once I had some disease which made me impotent. What Missy failed to understand was I had other needs. She was just arm decoration. Someone to take to the policeman's ball and the Lord Mayor's banquet. Someone to come home to, have a meal with, keep the lines of enquiry from straying too close to home. To put it bluntly, Michael, the police force doesn't like homosexuals. They like them even less if they have a liking for underage boys. Am I making myself plain, Michael?'

'Yes.'

'As much as it pains me to say it, Missy was missing the point. She blamed me for everything. Her unhappiness, the weather, the price of a bottle of milk, the government. Which was all fine and dandy. If she kept rattling my cage, I'd just divorce her on the grounds of unreasonable behaviour and having a face like a pug. Move on to someone who was more appreciative of my attributes.'

Sharon popped her head around the door. 'Would you like a cup of tea or coffee, Detective Inspector?'

Carver treated her to his trademark grin. 'That's very kind of you, Nurse. Very kind, indeed. Perhaps later. I'm at a delicate moment with the suspect. I'd appreciate it if we aren't disturbed in the next half an hour or so.'

'Of course.' She shut the door.

'What a nice girl.'

I could think of other names for her.

'Where was I? Oh, yes, Missy. Turned out bad in the end, Michael. Beyond repair, you might say. She caught me in bed with a fourteen-year-old boy. She was meant to be at work, but came home early, because she had a migraine. At least that's what she was claiming. Bloody thing soon vanished when she walked into that bedroom, I can tell you. The woman was beyond reason. I tried to tell her it was only a kid from the children's home. No one would ever find out. We'd work through this. Just a glitch. But, she was having none of it. Do you know what she threatened to do, Michael?'

I couldn't speak.

'She threatened to go to the police. Can you believe that?' He didn't wait for an answer. 'There was a look in her eyes I didn't much care for. I've seen it in criminals when they get caught. Like a cornered rat. I had little choice, Michael. I beat her to death with the truncheon I keep in the wardrobe. Had to. I didn't want that tongue of hers upsetting the apple cart and spilling all the apples. Then, I had a genius idea. A once in a lifetime one. Ever had one of those?'

I shut my eyes and pleaded with God to make Carver go away.

'I got the kid blamed for Missy's murder. Said I came home and caught him red-handed. Arrested him on the spot and slapped the cuffs on him. I had to work the scene a bit, tie up a few loose ends, so-to-speak, but it wasn't too hard to lick the place into shape. After all, who was going to believe a worthless turd from a children's home?'

I felt nausea swirling around my head like thick fog. How long ago had this happened? Before my time at Woodside? After? Did I know the kid?

'Little bastard went to a young offenders' institute, until he was old enough for prison. He slit his wrists with a razor blade and bled to death. Good riddance to bad rubbish, I say. So, that was Missy. Far too prudish for her own good. I steered clear of women for a while after that. Once bitten, twice shy. Not worth the hassle. And then, I met Angie. A good woman. An honest woman. The sort of woman you can pin your colours to, and they won't fade in the wash. Bit like your mum, I should imagine, Michael.'

I almost bit my tongue in two.

'I knew her well. A tart with a heart.'

'My mother was not a tart.'

'How do you know that? I thought you had no memory?'

'I don't.'

'So, why say it?'

'I just don't like her being talked about that way.'

'Stick to the facts. She was a tart. Half the street had her at one time, or another.'

You filthy, disgusting liar.

'Might have had a go myself once.' He laughed. 'You never know, Michael, I could even be your daddy.'

My head felt about ready to explode.

'But, you don't remember me either, right?'

'No.'

'Are you sure about that?'

'Yes.'

'You don't remember Woodside Children's Home?'

'No.'

'What about a boy called Liam Truman?'

I shook my head; in case my voice gave me away.

He studied me for a moment, and then grinned. 'Perhaps we ought to take you to the top floor at Oxford nick and drop you on your head. See if that helps to jog your memory.'

Good idea. At least it would put an end to this nightmare.

Carver opened the book. 'How's your eyesight, Michael?'

'Why?'

'I've got some pictures to show you. It might help to give your memory a wiggle.' He leafed through the pages, stopped, smiled to himself. He turned the book to me. 'This is Missy's page. I took these before the cops came to arrest that boy for the murder.'

I tried not to look. Tried to shut my mind off and make it go blank, but looked anyway. Spread across two pages, about two dozen polaroid snaps of his wife's battered and bruised body lying on the bed. Her face resembled minced meat. Her mousy brown hair stained red. The photos showed the same scene at many different angles.

'Had trouble explaining the truncheon away. Said it was my grandfather's. I kept it stashed in the wardrobe. Kid must have found it in there.'

How fucking clever of you.

'I bought it at an auction. Lovely piece. Dates right back to Victorian times. Made of traditional Lignum vitae hardwood. Brass band at the tip. Engraved, too. VR. You know what that stands for, Michael?'

'No.'

261

'Your generation have no respect for history and heritage. No eye for craftsmanship. It stands for Victoria Regina. That truncheon was too good for Missy's narrow mind. A frying pan would have been far more appropriate, but done is done, as they say.'

He pulled the book away, leafed through a few more pages, and stopped again. He thrust the book under my nose again. I stared in disbelief at a young man's body, lying on a bed in a tiny room. The white sheet was stained crimson with blood.

'That's David. Missy's murderer. I really like the contrast of the blood on the white sheet. It makes the picture seem rather artistic, wouldn't you agree?'

My mind was racing, trying to imagine what else was in that book.

'That's Westcombe Young Offenders' Institute, in case you're wondering. It took two guards to hold him while I slit his wrists. I don't mind telling you it was messy, Michael. Messier than Missy. Bugger was as slippery as an eel once he started pumping blood. Still, needs must, as they say.'

'You're sick.'

Carver raised his eyebrows. 'Michael! Wash your mouth out with soap. You can be so hurtful sometimes. I can see you're shocked by the truth, so I'll excuse you this time. Those polaroid snaps are really good quality, don't you think?' He didn't wait for an answer. 'And you don't have to take them to Boots to get them developed. No prying, disapproving eyes. Instamatic cameras, eh, Michael? An invention right up there with sliced bread.'

He leafed through the book again. He stopped, sighed, and turned the book back to me. 'This one might help to jog your memory.'

I closed my eyes. I knew it was Liam. The pictures he'd taken in the boiler room.

'Open your eyes, Michael.'

'No.'

'Open them.'

'No.'

'Don't make me hurt you.'

'I don't care what you do.'

A long silence, marked only by the thumping of my heart.

And then, another man's voice. 'I need to speak to Mr. Tate.'

I opened my eyes to see the short stocky frame of Dr. Redstone standing by the bed. Thank God for small mercies.

Carver whipped the book away and snapped it shut. He stood up and tucked it under his arm. 'I did request we weren't to be disturbed.'

Redstone flapped a hand. 'I'm afraid this is a hospital, Detective Inspector, not a police station.'

Carver looked at me as if he was trying to unravel me with his eyes. 'I'll see you Monday morning, Michael. Bright and early. We can carry on our little conversation then.' He strode to the door and vanished into the corridor.

Redstone plucked the board holding my notes from the foot of the bed. 'How are you today, Mr. Tate?'

How the hell did I answer that?

CHAPTER 37

By lights out, all I could think about was Jimmy, and how Hodges might react to him turning up out of the blue with Terry. Even though Hodges seemed decent enough, it didn't mean that he was. If the whole thing backfired, they could end up down the nick, being interrogated by Carver and his cronies.

My mind took a brief rest from Jimmy and Terry, and wandered over everything else that had happened. My mother's murder. My time at Woodside. Liam's murder. The disgusting, grisly book Carver had brought to the hospital. His threats.

Try to think positive.

Good advice, under normal circumstances. But, this was like trying to think of solid ground while you were sinking in a bog, deeper and deeper with every passing moment.

'We're all fucked,' I told the empty room.

I looked at the emergency door. Closed and bolted. The Abattoir of Dreams scrawled at the bottom. Liam's poem. A haunting reminder of the impossible task we faced to bring those bastards to justice.

The bolt suddenly slid along its rusty sheath. The bar was pushed down, and the door opened, revealing the black abyss beyond. The wheelchair moved slowly towards the bed. 'Liam?'

As usual, there was no answer; just those gentle hands helping me into the wheelchair. And then, the wheelchair moved across the room and into the pitch-dark tunnel, wheels squeaking rhythmically.

A hand ruffled my hair, like my mother used to when I was really little. Laughing at her little love-bug. Teeth still intact, still able to deliver a pretty, white smile.

After what seemed like an eternity, I was finally delivered to a parking bay at one end of Woodside. I was once again dressed in scruffy clothes reeking of piss and damp. Black trousers, with a hole in one knee. A baggy black jumper. Black scuffed shoes.

There was a large white van backed up to a side door; the laundry van which came every Tuesday to take the dirty washing away. I climbed out of the wheelchair and walked over to van. I heard Mrs. Clarke, one of the kitchen staff, talking to the driver. They were both puffing away on cigarettes.

'I wouldn't mind, Ted. What time?'

'Seven thirty at the Hound and Hare?'

'All right. I'll look forward to it.'

'How about a quick one now?'

A bray of nervous laughter. 'No. God, what are you like?'

'We could go in the back of the van.'

'You save it for later, you dirty bugger, I've got work to do.'

Yeah, you save it for later, I thought. I've been planning this for weeks.

I sneaked along the side of the van and peered around the corner. I only had one chance to get in the back of the van while Ted was busy chatting up Mrs. Clarke. Flirting with his darling hippopotamus. I'd learned quite a bit about Ted and Mrs. Clarke during my numerous dummy runs. Both married. Both hated their jobs. Couldn't wait to run away together. She wanted to go to Ireland, Ted wanted to go to Norfolk. I didn't give a fuck as long as they didn't go in the back of the van.

I had enough food and money stashed in my small backpack to last about a week. This was my time, my chance to escape, start a new life.

A cigarette butt, with a coating of dark red lipstick, came whizzing my way. I ducked back behind the van.

'Come on, Sally. Ten minutes, tops.'

I called on God.

God answered. 'You're worse than a rutting stag, Ted Gribble. I told you, I've got work to do. I'm helping Aunt Mary mend clothes. I told her I'd only be a minute.'

'Give us a kiss.'

'Go on, then. Just a peck, mind.'

I prayed he would get to stick his tongue down her throat, choke the old bat, and have to resuscitate her. I took my chance, moved around the back of the van, and hopped inside. I buried myself beneath the canvas sacks holding the dirty laundry.

By the time Ted had finished with Mrs. Clarke, I was pretty well concealed. He closed the back doors and locked them. Phase one over. I had a strange tingling sensation in the pit of my stomach. I was out. Free.

I don't know how long we travelled for before Ted stopped the van. It seemed like hours, but I'd long since learned time was a strange thing; it moved at different speeds depending on what you were doing. School time ran like a backward snail; adventure time ran like a greyhound. This was somewhere in-between.

The doors opened, flooding the back of the van with lights. I held my breath, expecting Ted to spot something wrong at any minute. Perhaps a shoe poking out, or a finger. But, he didn't. I heard another woman's voice, younger than Mrs. Clarke's. 'You're early.'

Ted slipped into his easy patter. 'Rosie, darling, looking like a peach as always.'

Rosie might have looked like a peach, but she sounded as sour as a grapefruit. 'You can pack that nonsense up, Ted Gribble. You'd better come in and wait. The laundry isn't ready yet.'

Ted didn't offer her a good time in the back of his van. 'A cup of tea wouldn't go amiss, I'm parched.'

'You can have a glass of water.' And with that, they went inside.

I lost one of my shoes as I scrambled free of the sacks. Cursing, I untangled the laces from the sack cord. I was on backward snail time again. I jumped out of the van. The place looked like a guest house, much smaller than Woodside. I legged it out of there as fast as my legs could carry me, took a snap decision to turn right at the end of the gravel driveway, and then sprinted about two hundred yards along the road.

I stopped at a bus stop, and pretended to tie my laces. I needed to calm down. People would notice me if I kept running up the street like a kid possessed. They'd think I'd robbed somewhere, or worse. The last thing I needed right now was to get nabbed and end up at the local nick.

I sat down in the bus shelter and looked along the road. I'd spent so much time planning my escape in the laundry van, I hadn't stopped to think about where I might actually end up, or what would happen when the food and the money ran out.

Maybe I could go to Rachel's. She might offer to put me up for a couple of nights. And I'd see Oxo again.

You could take Oxo with you.

This idea excited me. Made me imagine walking along rivers towards London; me and my faithful dog, camping out beneath the stars, best buddies off to make a new life in the capital. As with most bright ideas, reality soon turned it black. I'd have to constantly think about him. Feed him. Take care of him.

A red, double-decker bus pulled up at the stop. I got ready to run in case anyone connected to Woodside got off. The way my luck had a habit of running out, it wouldn't have surprised me to see Carver get off the bus. Fortunately, he didn't, just an old lady, and a middle-aged man helping her down the step.

I needed to find somewhere to bed down for the night. I stood up and walked towards a signpost. Maybe it would give me some idea of where I was. It didn't. Feelham Town Centre 1 mile. It might as well have said Rome. There was a pub on one side of the road and a hat shop on the other. I saw several other shops in the distance, but I didn't want to risk going right into the town so soon after running away from Woodside.

I took a snap decision and turned left at the pub. It would turn out to be one of the best decisions I've ever made. St Leonard's lane was a narrow, cobbled street, with terraced houses on one side, and a high stone wall on the other. Near the end of the lane, I saw a beautiful stone church, and a small wooden bridge leading down to a marina.

Several boats were moored alongside the river. One looked about to disintegrate and float away like driftwood. I walked down to the jetty and sat by the river, legs dangling over the side. I slipped my backpack off and dug out some dried biscuits and a bottle of orange pilfered from Woodside. Army ration biscuits. Disgusting. Like eating tree bark. Not that I ever had!

I was tempted to kick off my shoes and jump in the river, feel the cold water against my skin, even though it looked filthy enough to poison fish. My reflection swirled in the water. I know it sounds odd, but at that moment, I was jealous of that reflection. It was as if it was another me, but one who didn't have a headful of bad memories to carry around.

It was nearly six years since my mother had been murdered. Four years since Liam had died. I'd pretty much managed to stay out of trouble at Woodside since Carver had murdered him. Well, I say trouble, what I really mean is trouble of my own making. I'd seen plenty of trouble of their making. Beatings, rapes, abuse, and starvation punishments.

Many people visited Woodside. Important people. Mostly, they seemed more interested in the younger kids. I heard they would sometimes release younger kids into Bluebell Woods and hunt them with air rifles. I never saw this happen, but I knew for a fact kids were passed around like pieces of meat, and thrown out like pieces of rubbish.

On a brighter note, McCree met a nasty end. It was common knowledge he used to visit a well-known politician for sex. He used to like bragging about it when he'd had a drink. Claimed the guy looked after him. Wined and dined him at the top restaurants in Oxford, took him to the theatre, the works. But McCree was in the senior block one night, cribbing on about how this bigwig made him do unnatural stuff. Disgusting stuff. One of the older kids asked him to elaborate.

'He likes to strangle me.'

'What the fuck for?'

McCree had turned pasty just talking about it. 'I don't know. Fucking weirdo gets off on it. The other night, I passed out. He had me tied to a bed, and he throttled me with his bare hands. And then, boom, it all went black.'

I don't think anyone shed any tears for McCree that night. I know I didn't. I went to bed and prayed to all the Gods, in all the Heavens, this politician creep would finish McCree off. A week later, for the first time in my life, my prayers were answered. McCree vanished, never to return. Of course, I'll never know for sure what happened to him, but I can take a bloody good guess. Good riddance to bad rubbish.

I sat by the jetty, lost in thought, until the sun faded. The sky turned to ribbons of pinks and purples. I walked back the way I'd come. I briefly considered dossing down on the old boat, but it would be just my luck that the owner would find me and turn me in to the police.

I opted instead to kip in the doorway at the back of the church. I used my backpack as a pillow and bedded down for the night with cool July air on my face.

CHAPTER 38

I opened my eyes to a chorus of birdsong in the trees overhanging the churchyard, and a middle-aged man, with a swatch of grey curly hair standing over me. He was dressed in brown corduroy trousers and a matching tweed jacket. At first, I thought he was a tramp, and I'd nicked his spot.

'Are you all right?'

I sat up and pulled my backpack close.

He smiled. His green eyes danced in the morning sunlight. 'You don't look very comfortable.'

I wasn't. In more ways than one. 'I'm all right.'

'Where are you from?'

'Nowhere.'

'Ah, nowhere. I know it well. Right next to somewhere, isn't it?'

'Huh?' My back was stiff, and one of my ears was burning.

'Is this nowhere far from here?'

'Something like that.'

'I'm Paul. Paul Brady.'

I wasn't going to tell him who I was, not unless he took me to a torture chamber and forced it out of me.

'I'm the Vicar of St Leonard's Church.'

Good for you. 'Oh.'

'Are you homeless?'

'No.'

'Are you hungry?'

'No.'

'You look a little thin, if you don't mind me saying.'

'I'm all right.' I wanted to tell him he'd look a bit thin, if he'd lived at Woodside for the past six years. Every single kid in that place looked thinner than a broom handle. I couldn't remember one kid who appeared anywhere near healthy.

'Tell me to mind my own business, if you like, but you're welcome to come back to the vicarage and have a bath and a meal... if you want.'

I was about to resort to my stock answer, when my stomach growled, as if to say, don't you dare turn down a free meal. But, what was the catch? Was he another pervert? Was he going to turn me in to the cops? I'd been taught not to trust adults. From my father to Kraft, the message had always been clear: trust no one.

'No strings.'

'Why would you want to feed me?'

He looked thoughtful for a moment. 'Because it's my duty, son.'

'But why?'

'We live in wicked times. Someone has to watch out for the unfortunate ones. Even if they are heading for nowhere.'

I wanted to believe him. My tired and aching body wanted to believe him. My growling stomach already believed him.

'I run a summer camp at the end of the month. Nothing fancy, just a week away with tents and burnt sausages. Out of tune guitar. We take a mini bus out to Caulston Hill. You'd be more than welcome to come along, meet a few young people.'

I shrugged. 'I don't know.'

'Your choice. Have you got a name?'

I hesitated. Should I tell him? Go home with him? My mind didn't seem capable of making such big decisions. No one had asked me what I had wanted to do since my mother.

He laughed. A throaty laugh that seemed warm and comforting. 'You can make a name up, if you prefer.'

With all the lies I'd told, Pinocchio sprang to mind.

'What about James Dean?'

'Who's he?'

'A famous actor. One lad who comes to camp calls himself Charles Bronson. He's another actor, by the way.'

I felt my resistance slipping. I was starting to feel as if I'd known Paul Brady all my life. 'My name's Michael.'

'Does the horse have a cart?'

'Sorry?'

'Do you have a surname?'

'No.'

'Michael it is, then.' He offered me his hand and pulled me up. I asked him how far Feelham was from Oxford.

'About twelve miles. Are you from Oxford?'

'No.'

He didn't look as if he believed that. 'Have you been to Feelham before, Michael?'

'No.'

'It's nice here. We have the river, the town, nice walks. It's not too busy. A good balance. So, what will it be?'

'Huh?'

'A place called nowhere, or back to my humble abode for a wash and a bit of scran?'

'Scran?'

He smiled. 'Food.'

I was done resisting. 'Okay. But, I can't stop. I've got to—'

'Get to nowhere. You said.'

I followed Paul Brady around the church and into St Leonard's Lane. He stopped at a terraced house, right next to the church. 'Here we are, then, home sweet home.'

I looked at the white rendered building. It looked no bigger than a doll's house. I was expecting a huge, rambling country house. 'Is this the vicarage?'

He smiled. 'Yes, Michael, this is the vicarage.'

'But, it's—'

'Small?'

I nodded.

'It doesn't matter what size house you live in, Michael. The mind is always free to travel beyond the boundaries.' He unlocked the door and invited me into his home.

I stepped inside, and promised myself I'd be out of there quicker than you could say God, if he so much as looked at me the wrong way. I followed him along a narrow hallway, and into the front room. The bare cream walls and black beams were striking. The skirting and doorframes were also painted black. His worn grey sofa looked about as old as the house.

He invited me to sit down. 'Would you like some tea?'

'Yes. Please.'

'How about toast and marmalade? I've got lime and orange.'

'I don't mind.'

'Neither do I.'

'Orange.'

He disappeared through a doorway. 'Make yourself comfortable.'

The sofa felt great after the hard ground outside the church. Soft enough to sink right into. There was a beautiful, oak mantelpiece above the fire, and a gold-framed mirror above that. On the wall leading to the kitchen, a large wooden cross. The bare floorboards had been stained dark oak. A mahogany coffee table sat in front of the sofa. A matching bookcase, chock-full of books, took up the entire wall opposite the fireplace.

Paul returned about ten minutes later, with a tray of tea. He put it on the coffee table, and then hurried back to the kitchen to fetch the toast. I tried not to gulp my food. Give it time to get down the hatch and meet your stomach, as my mother used to say when I was still her little love-bug.

Paul sat next to me and spread butter on his toast. Real butter, not that foul-tasting margarine they served up at Woodside. He ate about half a slice, and then poured the tea. He offered milk and sugar.

'Yes, please.'

'How many sugars?'

I had a choice? 'Three, please.'

He smiled. 'You look as if you could do with it.'

We finished out tea and toast in silence – apart from my rumbling stomach, which was doing its best to embarrass me. Paul turned to me, a serious look on his face. I thought, Oh, Christ, here we go. He's going to do something stupid, like put his hand on my leg, then I'll have to thump him and leg it.

'I know it's none of my business, Michael, and I don't want you to feel you have to talk, but I can see you've had a hard time of it. I want you to know if you feel like talking, God gave me big enough ears to listen.'

Something wrapped itself around my heart and gave it a little squeeze. 'Okay.'

'The bathroom's at the top of the stairs, second door on the right. Make sure you don't run too much cold water; the hot water tank's smaller than my congregation.'

'I can have a bath?'

He smiled. 'Of course you can. And you can use some of my deodorant if you want to. There's a dressing gown hanging on the back of my bedroom door. That's the room right next to the bathroom. You can wear that until I get back. I'll nip along to Mrs. Wiggins, see if she's got any clothes that will fit you. She's in charge of the jumble sales. We get some pretty good stuff donated, I'll see what I can do.'

'Thanks.'

'I'd offer you some of my clothes, but I'm afraid I'm rather more rounded than you. I'll be about an hour. I've got to make a few calls.'

'Calls?'

He must have seen the worry in my eyes. 'Don't fret, Michael. I'm only visiting parishioners. I won't get you into trouble. That's the last thing I'd ever do.'

'Thank you.'

'No need to thank me, lad. I understand what it's like to be young and have the whole world stacked against you. I'll see you later.'

I waited for the front door to bang shut, and leaned back on the sofa. I thought how miraculous it was that the laundry van had dropped me in Feelham, and how I'd chosen to walk in the direction I had from that bus stop. It was almost as if someone was watching over me, guiding me.

God?

I wasn't ready to believe that. Not yet. But, seeing as I'd ended up at Paul Brady's house, it did make me wonder.

The bath was amazing. I spent ages relaxing, lying back, and sinking my head under the water, for once not having to worry about someone attacking me. Pure bliss.

I put my dirty pants and vest back on after the bath. I walked to Paul's bedroom, and took the dressing gown off the hook and put it on, fastening it around the middle with the cord. It was a patchwork of light and dark green checks. Scratchy against my skin, but it made such a nice change to be clean.

Now what did I do? Go back down to the front room? Wait up here? What if someone knocked on the door? My Woodside paranoia crept in. I walked over to the window, and peered through the heavy, brown curtains. The window looked out onto St Leonard's Lane. An elderly woman walked past, pulling a shopping trolley behind her. She was actually wearing a coat. In this heat. It was already hot in the bedroom, and not yet nine o'clock in the morning, according to Paul's alarm clock.

His double bed was neatly made, with a white cotton sheet folded down over a thin blue blanket. There was a bible near the clock, a pen resting on top of the bible, and a glass half-filled with what looked like water. I wanted to throw myself on top of that bed, stretch out and rest my aching limbs. Just for ten minutes. Experience what it was like to lay on a proper bed, instead of those bloody awful things at Woodside with their busted springs and piss-stained mattresses.

I hit a compromise and sat on the end of the bed. The mattress creaked beneath my weight. Part of me still didn't trust Paul. I hadn't met one adult since my mother had died, apart from Rachel, who didn't want to either beat me up or abuse me.

We'd studied Victorian times in history. How the kids were sent up chimneys, beaten, treated like shit, sent to the workhouses. We were constantly reminded by the teachers how lucky we were not to live in such times, but nothing had really changed. The abusers. The bent coppers. The sadistic pigs. All still running the show.

I walked over to the bedside table. I took the pen off the Bible and placed it by the glass. Then, I picked up the Bible and held it close to my chest. I sat back down on the bed and sobbed like a baby until Paul returned home from running his errands.

CHAPTER 39

Paul allowed me to stay inside the house. He didn't pressurise me into going out and doing anything. We had a lovely fish and chip supper on Friday night. He found me five T-shirts, two pairs of jeans, Levis if you can believe that, two pairs of trainers, both Adidas, a zip-up top, and a lined blue coat. He also went into town and bought me five pairs of socks and ten pairs of pants to go with my haul. I felt like royalty.

We ate cheese and tomato sandwiches for lunch early on Saturday afternoon. I had a glass of milk to wash it down with. By now, I felt almost human again. Paul had also trimmed my hair, after I flat refused his offer to pay for a proper cut at the barber's. I didn't want anyone seeing me and spoiling what I had.

'How would you feel about meeting someone?'

I looked at Paul as if he'd just suggested a visit to Woodside. 'I don't want to. I'm not ready to meet anyone.'

He smiled and tugged on the end of his bulbous red nose. 'This isn't just anyone. It's Becky.'

A girl? Even worse. I looked like Friar Tuck with my terrible haircut, and I had a spot on my chin. And I didn't have the first idea about girls. 'No, I don't—'

'She won't bite.'

I looked away. A blush crept up my neck.

'She was in the same position as you two years ago. Didn't have nowhere to go. Hardly dared to look anyone in the eye.'

'I don't want to meet anyone.'

Paul put his plate on the coffee table. 'You can't hide away forever, Michael.'

'I'm not hiding.'

'Becky helps me make sandwiches for the homeless. People donate cakes and crisps and stuff like that. We've got a collection box at the church, and we take them out every Saturday evening and drop them off with a guy called Finn. He sorts out who gets what. Acts as if it's a massive chore, but you can tell he enjoys bossing everyone about. Makes him feel as if he's doing something worthwhile. Which he is.'

'I don't want to go anywhere near Oxford.'

He sighed. 'Okay. I understand. But, at least say hello to Becky.'

I finished my milk and wiped away a creamy moustache. 'I'll think about it.'

Too late for that. The back door opened, and a girl's voice called, 'Hiya, Paul. We've got a jam sponge from Ida Carnegie. She says it's for you, not the handouts. Said she made it especially.'

Paul walked through to the kitchen. 'That's very thoughtful of her.'

'And John Westwood left a whole box of crisps. Said they've gone out of date, so he can't sell them on the market. He didn't want them to go to waste.'

My heart pounded in my chest. I wanted to run upstairs and lock myself in the bathroom.

'Wow. What a haul. Should keep them going for a while.'

'There's nine packets of biscuits as well. Lemon puffs and all sorts.'

To my horror, Paul said, 'Michael? Come on through, and meet Becky.'

For a moment, I considered legging it out the front door.

'Michael?'

I stood up and told myself it was only a girl; she was hardly going to bare her teeth and bite my head off, was she? And she was a friend of Paul's.

'Michael?'

I stood in the kitchen doorway, looking at the most beautiful girl I'd ever seen in my life. Her long blonde hair was fixed on top of her head with a bright red headband. Her blue eyes shone in the morning sunlight. She wore a white T-shirt with Save the Dolphins emblazoned across the front in purple writing.

She smiled, revealing a row of neat white teeth. One of the top ones jutted out slightly from the rest. 'I'm Becky.'

My heart caught the words. 'Hello.'

Her smile seemed to tease me. 'How are you settling in?'

Time stood still. It was as if no one else existed. 'All right.' Jesus Christ, is that the best you can do? The kitchen felt ten degrees hotter.

'I've got to go out,' Paul said. 'Can I leave you two to get on with it?'

I looked at the floor and shrugged.

Becky asked, 'Shall I make a start on the sandwiches?'

'That would be great. There's a bottle of lemonade in the fridge. Help yourself.'

And, with that, he left. Now what? I had no experience of girls, other than seeing them in the playground at school, clumped together in groups. A giggle of girls. Little aliens, whispering to one another in their own secret language.

Becky took a sliced loaf out of the bread bin. 'Do you want to butter, or cut the cheese?'

'I don't mind.' My throat was as dry as a sandpit.

'Okay. I'll butter, you cut the cheese. Cut it thin, though, we've got fifty to make, and there's only one block of cheese.'

I nodded. Now struck mute, apparently.

Becky laughed. 'Paul expects us to make things stretch as far as Jesus did with the five loaves of bread and two fish.'

I smiled.

'You have got a sense of humour, then?'

'Maybe.' We set about cutting the sandwiches. Becky wrapped them in foil and wedged them into the overstuffed fridge. When we were finished, she took the lemonade out, and plonked it on the side. 'Would you like some?'

'Yes, please.'

She took two glasses from a cupboard and poured our drinks. 'Why don't we sit in the front room. You can tell me all about yourself.'

Until this moment, I was only vaguely aware of the term love at first sight. I had no idea whether such a thing actually existed. How could you love someone if you didn't even know them? But now I understood; the proof was sitting in Father Paul's armchair opposite me.

She took a sip of lemonade. 'How did you meet Paul?'

'I was sleeping at the back of the church.'

'That's a funny place to sleep.'

I could think of a few words to describe it; funny wasn't one of them 'Yeah.'

'I couldn't do that. The graves would creep me out too much.'

Graves were the least of my worries after Woodside. Apart from ending up in one, of course.

'Paul told me you were living here.' And then, quicker, 'But, he said nothing else about you. He's not like that. He's straight down the line. If you tell him something, it stays with him.'

I felt comforted by that.

'Do you want to talk?'

My heart did. But, my head told me to keep it to myself. 'Not really.'

'It's hard, isn't it?'

'What?'

'Talking.'

'I suppose.'

'Where are you from?' And then, quickly, 'I won't say a word to anyone, Michael. Me and Paul don't let outsiders in.'

'I'm from Oxford.'

'Nice place.'

Not the parts I'd seen, but I agreed anyway.

'I love all the buildings. The architecture. The history.'

You ought to go to Woodside. 'Yeah.'

'We go to Redcastle Square to hand out the food. Do you know it?'

I didn't. Other than school and Woodside, my experience of Oxford was pretty limited.

She took another sip of lemonade and studied me with those clear blue eyes. 'Things can get better, Michael. It just takes time.'

I doubted that very much. My mother and my best friend had been murdered. No amount of time could ever mend that.

We finished our drinks, and then Becky said, 'How old are you, Michael?'

'Nearly eighteen.'

She smiled. My heart turned to wax and melted. 'I've just had my eighteenth. Two weeks ago.'

'Happy birthday.'

'Thanks. Time flies when you're having fun. It's nearly two years since Paul rescued me.'

'Rescued you?'

She seemed thoughtful for a moment. 'Yeah. Gave me my life back. Paul's a good bloke. The best.'

I had no argument with that. 'I know.'

'We're all friends here, Michael. Friends forever. Even the ones who never come back send postcards and letters. No one ever forgets Paul. Are you planning on sticking around?'

Woodside had taught me to take one day at a time. 'I'm not sure.'

'I ran away from home when I was fourteen. I couldn't handle it anymore. I met Paul when he came to Oxford one night handing out food. He was dressed in a pair of old jeans and a big baggy black coat. I thought he was a tramp, but then, he started handing out sandwiches and crisps. I was starving. I only ever got proper food when I'd begged enough money to go to the chippy.'

'Why did you run away from home?'

Becky studied her hands for a moment. 'Let's just say, I didn't get on with my stepdad. He was a bastard. He used to beat my mum up, and other stuff. I didn't have much choice.'

'That bad?'

She nodded. 'So, I ran away. Lived on the streets.'

'That must have been really difficult for you.'

'Tell me about it. I had to sharpen up my wits pretty quick. The winter was the worst. I could never get warm. The cold got right down inside me, down into my bones. Even when I cadged booze, it still made no difference. Paul told me alcohol lowers your body's temperature anyway, so drinking to stay warm is a really dumb idea.'

At least me and Liam had managed to light a fire in the derelict pub. I couldn't imagine what it must have been like for her, sleeping outside in the winter.

'I lost count of the number of men who propositioned me. Dirty sods, who didn't seem to care I was only fourteen.'

I knew that feeling well. 'That must have been really scary.'

'Worse than being at home, in some ways. So, when Paul came along that night, I was quite a hardened little bitch. After I'd figured out he wasn't a tramp, because no self-respecting tramp would go around handing out food, I thought he was going to proposition me. But, he didn't. He wasn't like anyone else I'd ever met before. He was kind and honest; a rare thing in this world.'

'I know what you mean.'

'He asked me if I wanted cheese and pickle, or cheese and tomato. I mean, come on, who gives you a choice when you're on the streets? Then, he told me not to take too long making up my mind, because he had to be home by midnight, or else he'd turn into a pumpkin. That made me laugh for the first time in ages. I took the cheese and pickle. And again, the next week, and the week after that. I reckon he brought me those same sandwiches for at least two months without fail. Just as winter kicked in, he asked me if I wanted to come home with him, and help out with the church. I didn't take much persuading. I knew Paul was a decent bloke. I went home with him on the third of October. The best decision I've ever made. Stayed in that little box room upstairs.'

'I know it well.' It was like a palace after Woodside.

'God's special room.'

Pretty good description. 'Yeah.'

'Paul got me on my feet. I got a job at the newsagent's, and helped Paul out at the church. Early this year, I got promoted to manager at work, got myself a little flat above the bookmaker's in town. It's not much to look at, but it's mine. My space. I get to choose who comes in there.'

'Well done,' I said, genuinely pleased for her.

'You stick around, and you can do the same.'

'I don't know about that. I haven't got any qualifications. I'm pretty useless.'

'You're not useless, Michael. Adults have a habit of making kids feel that way, but it's up to you to prove them wrong, show them that your life's worth something.'

'Maybe.'

'There's no maybe about it. I'll help you, if you want.'

Why was everyone being so kind? I had a brief flashback to my mother holding my hand when I was about seven or eight, telling me I could be anything I wanted to be, that dreams can come true. I saw something of my mother in Becky's eyes; it was something I would later come to recognise as belief. And with belief, even clipped wings can learn to fly.

'Well?'

'I'd like that.'

She grinned. 'Deal?'

I was in love, and it made me feel as if I could walk on the ceiling. 'Deal.'

CHAPTER 40

I loved my year staying at Paul's. He never made demands. He cared for me in a way I didn't think possible, and proved that men weren't all selfish, perverted pigs. He taught me, by his actions and his love, there were actually good people in the world.

Although I still wasn't convinced of the existence of God, I was coming around to the notion of something other than just life on Earth. If you put it into the context of lighting a fire, I'd gathered a few twigs and thought about finding a match.

Although Paul was obviously serious about religion, he never asked me if I wanted to go to church or read from the Bible. I once asked him why God didn't stop all the suffering in the world, all the wars, all the bad people doing terrible things. He told me it wasn't up to God; it was up to us.

He admitted questioning his own faith when he was a young man. Questioning the very boundaries set by the church. When I asked him why, he told me it was a delicate subject, complicated, perhaps one day. Sometime later, Becky told me that Paul was a homosexual. That he had to keep it hidden from the church. That I must never tell a soul. I would have rather died than betray Paul Brady's trust.

Summer Camp the following year was probably the best time of my life. We sang songs, ate food cooked over an open fire, and listened to Paul strumming his guitar. He blamed a sore throat on his tuneless singing!

I met Charles Bronson, two lads who were just called the Twins, and a sixteen-year-old kid called Pete, who rarely spoke. He didn't need to; his pain was written clearly enough in his eyes.

On the final night, Paul said a prayer. It was a magic moment, sitting around the dying embers of the fire, listening to Paul giving thanks for one of the best weeks ever. Then, he asked the group if anyone wanted to say a prayer.

Pete stared into the fire, poking the ground with a stick. The Twins had a minor disagreement about whether to say something for their dad.

'What about you?' Paul asked Charles Bronson.

'Does it have to be a person?'

'No.'

'I want to say one for my dog.'

One of the twins snickered. Paul silenced him. 'That's fine, Charles, we can say a prayer for your dog.'

Charles sniffed. 'My old man killed him. Took him down the knackers' yard at Gaskin's Field and had him shot with the horses. He made out the dog had run away, but Jed Crippen said he saw my old man with the dog when they were hiding out in the scrap cars. Said Gaskin took my dog down to the shed where they slaughter the horses. Shot him. Burned him on a bonfire.'

'That's terrible,' Becky said.

Charles nodded. 'He was a cunt... I mean, bastard. Sorry. I don't mean to swear Paul, but he knew how much the dog meant to me. How much I loved him.'

I remembered Oxo. Felt the kid's pain.

'What was his name?' Paul asked.

'Who, my old man?'

One of the twins thought that was really funny. 'No, your dog, numb nuts.'

'I called him Patch. He had a white patch over one eye. Like a pirate.'

'Pirates have black patches,' Twin said. 'Not white patches. That's more like a surrender flag.'

Paul held up a hand. 'Okay. That'll do. We'll say a prayer for Patch.' He then turned to me. 'Michael?'

'Can I say a prayer for Liam?'

'Of course.'

'Who's Liam?' Becky whispered.

'A friend.'

'Anyone else?' Paul asked. 'Pete?'

Pete shook his head.

'Becky?'

'Just anyone who's suffering.'

Paul clasped his hands in front of him and prayed for Liam, Patch, and the twins' father. He finished with words I'll never forget. 'Know that those we miss are always with us. In our hearts. Nothing can extinguish the gift of love; God's greatest gift to us all.'

Me and Becky stayed up long after the others had gone back to their tents. She looked so beautiful in the glow of the fire. She turned to me after a while, and asked, 'Did Liam die?'

I nodded.

'Do you want to talk about it?'

I didn't. It was too complicated. If I told her the truth, I would have to tell her everything, and I wasn't ready to do that.

After a short silence, she asked, 'Have you got any family?'

'No. My dad murdered my mum. He's in jail, and she's in a cemetery somewhere in Oxford.'

Becky gasped. 'Oh, God, I'm so sorry.'

'Don't be. That useless bastard's the one who ought to be sorry.' I, then, told her the whole story, right up until I'd found her dead at the bottom of the stairs.

We didn't talk for a long time after I'd finished. Finally, she said, 'That must have been so terrible for you.'

'You could say that.'

She reached out and pulled me close. I could smell her perfume, sweet and inviting. She stroked my hair softly; a tenderness I hadn't felt since I was still young enough to let my mother do that.

'Life's never how it's supposed to be, is it?' she said. 'When you're little, you have all these dreams. I wanted to be a ballerina before my dad ran off with another woman. Before my mum moved that rapist in. What happened after your dad... did what he did?'

I cleared my throat. 'I got taken into care. Put in a children's home.'

'Is that where you ran away from?'

'Yeah.'

'Did you meet Liam there?'

I nodded.

'If you ever want to talk about—'

'I don't.'

We sat in silence for ages. I could feel the rise and fall of her chest, feel her warmth, both physical and emotional.

Becky finally said, 'I didn't tell anyone about my stepdad. Not even my mum. I only told Paul about it last year. I know it's really hard to talk about things, Michael, but you do feel better when it's all out. It's as if this great weight is lifted off your shoulders. You're not even aware it's there until after it's gone.'

But, Liam was still so raw. Unfinished. It would take an absolute miracle to bring Carver to justice.

Without warning, she changed the subject. 'Do you like me, Michael?'

Like her? I loved her with all the flowers in my heart. 'Yeah.' Nonchalant. Reserved. Typical of me.

'Do you like me a pond, a river, or an ocean?'

I sat up. 'Huh?'

'Do you like me a bit, a lot, or loads?'

That was easy. 'Loads. Why?'

'Do you want to know a secret?'

'What?'

'I like you a lot, too.'

My heart grew wings and flew around the campfire. 'You do?'

'You're one of the nicest boys I've ever met.'

'I am?'

'Why do you look so surprised?'

'I didn't think—'

'You can kiss me, if you want.'

Now what are you going to do? my mind squawked. You've never kissed a girl before.

She leaned closer, wrapped one arm around the back of my neck, and closed her soft, warm mouth over mine. When we broke free, she smiled. 'You're a lovely kisser, Michael Tate.'

I swallowed my heart. 'I am?'

'Would you like to be my boyfriend?'

I grinned so wide, I almost split my face in two. 'I'd love to.'

CHAPTER 41

Things moved pretty fast after that final night at summer camp. I moved into Becky's flat just before Christmas and got a job washing pots at a local hotel in Feelham High Street. Nothing spectacular, but it helped to pay the bills. With our combined income, we found a better flat, and moved out to the edge of town.

We still helped Paul at the church, and lent a hand distributing food to the homeless in Oxford. I worked at the George Hotel one 'til nine. I'd made a friend at work, Jimmy Pearce. We'd sometimes go out for a drink together, shoot a few frames of pool, have a laugh. He had a girlfriend called Lucy, and the four of us would occasionally go to the cinema or ice skating in Oxford.

Life was good. Me and Becky got on well. If I said we never argued, I'd be stretching the truth a bit, but it was never anything serious. Just me leaving my socks on the bathroom floor, or leaving the toilet seat up. I can't tell you how much that pissed her off. I didn't get what all the fuss was about; I thought I was doing well to hit the target.

By the following summer, Woodside was no longer the first thing I thought of in the morning, or the last thing at night. Don't get me wrong, it was always somewhere close to the surface, especially my promise to Liam to make them pay for what they'd done, but I felt so powerless. Who was going to believe me? The likes of Carver and Kraft held all the power. I'd just be dismissed as someone with a grudge. An ungrateful wretch who was just full of sour grapes.

That all changed on June third, Liam's birthday. I always thought about him when the date rolled around, but this year was different. I felt overwhelmed by a terrible sadness. An aching loss. As if a piece of my heart had gone missing.

Becky seemed to sense this, in spite of my best efforts to hide it. 'What's wrong?'

'Nothing. Tired.' About as convincing as a cat claiming to like birds.

'Would you like a drink?'

'A beer would be good.'

She fetched me a cold one from the fridge, popped the tab, and handed it to me. I swallowed half the can without stopping, hoping the alcohol would blunt the edges of my feelings. It didn't.

Becky poured a glass of wine. 'Do you want to talk?'

I put the can on the coffee table. My chest felt as if it was swelling like bread in an oven. And then, I sobbed so hard I could barely breathe. On and on, like a burst dam.

Becky held me close, pulled my head onto her chest. 'Hey, hey, it's all right. You let it all out.'

When I was spent, I sat shaking in her arms like a helpless child.

'What sparked that off?' she asked.

I wiped snot from my top lip. 'It would have been Liam's birthday today.'

'How long's he been gone?'

'Seven years.'

'Do you want to talk about what happened?'

'I don't know.'

'Did he have an accident?'

That was probably the easiest question I'd ever had to answer. 'No.'

'What happened?'

'Carver killed him.'

'Carver?'

'A copper who used to come to the children's home. A sadistic bastard. He beat Liam to death with a truncheon.'

The colour drained from Becky's face. 'A policeman murdered him?'

'Yep. Detective Inspector John Carver.'

'Jesus, Michael, I don't know what to say. Why did he kill him?'

'Because he's a fucking psycho.' I spent the next hour recounting everything that had happened at Woodside, right up to my escape in the laundry van.

When I was finished, Becky brought fresh drinks. 'Does anyone else know what happened?'

'No. We buried him at the bottom of the field, like I said, and that was the end of it. One of the kids, Reggie, kept asking if I knew where Liam was, but I told him I didn't. I was just concerned with staying alive, getting the fuck out of there.'

'And you've been carrying this around with you ever since?'

'I didn't know what else to do. I made a promise to Liam I'd tell someone. But, who? I could hardly go to the cops. Not with Carver around. No one would believe me, anyway. They're all in it together.'

She drank half of her wine, and then said, 'But, you have to tell someone, Michael. You can't let them get away with it. Not all coppers are like Carver. They're not all evil.'

'And how, exactly, do we know which ones are which? They don't come with psychopath tattooed on their foreheads, do they?'

After several hours' deliberation, we decided the best thing to do was ask Paul's opinion.

Paul listened intently. He looked as if he was contemplating asking God Himself. Finally, he suggested I go to the police.

'But, what if they don't believe me?'

'You said you buried this poor boy at the bottom of the field at Woodside, right?'

'Yes.'

'So, tell the police where he's buried.'

'What about Carver?'

Paul looked uncertain. 'You'll just have to take a leap of faith, Michael. Go to Feelham Police Station. I know the desk sergeant down there. Donald Osbourne. He's a decent guy. I'll have a word with him if you like?'

I still wasn't sure. It seemed way too risky. Even if the desk sergeant was all right, it didn't mean Carver wouldn't get wind of it, and stomp all over it with his size tens. No one understood the hold Carver, Kraft, and all his cronies had over me. It was easy for Paul and Becky to say go to the cops; they hadn't been beaten and systematically abused by these people, had their soul stripped bare.

Paul said, 'All you can do is follow your heart, Michael. God will watch over you.'

We had tea and biscuits, and then headed back to the flat. I closed the front door and stood with my back to it. 'I can't do it, Becks.'

'You don't have to decide now. Think about it for a while. Maybe leave it until after we go down to Brighton with Jimmy and Lucy.'

'It's too risky.'

'Paul said he'd have a word with the desk sergeant.'

'How does Paul know he can trust him?'

'Sometimes, you have to just take a chance. You said he beat Liam to death with a truncheon?'

My stomach knotted. 'Yes.'

'There might still be evidence on it. Blood.'

I walked along the hallway, and into the tiny kitchen. 'You're a genius, Becks. Why didn't I think of that? Carver would have forgotten to clean the bloody thing off, what with him being a copper.'

'I'm only saying. No need to be sarcastic. I'm only trying to help.'

I poured a glass of water, drained it in one go, and banged the glass down on the side. 'I know. But, the odds are all stacked in their favour.'

'You're giving them too much credit.'

'You weren't the one who got tortured and abused by them.'

'I—'

'Watched their best mate get killed.'

'All the more reason to at least try, Michael.'

'I can't.'

'Why?'

I hesitated. I felt naked and exposed. Finally, I said, 'Because I'm scared I'll end up in prison. That I'll lose everything that's good in my life.'

'That won't happen.'

'You know that for sure, do you?'

'I'll help you.'

'That's not an answer.'

'I'll be there for you every step of the way.'

'You'll have a job, if they trump up a load of fake charges against me.'

'They won't do that.'

'You don't know what they're capable of.'

'You've got me as a witness. And Paul. It's not as if you're just going to walk into a police station on your own, is it?'

'They killed a fifteen-year-old boy, Becky. And others. The ones who disappeared. Even McCree was murdered. This isn't like telling tales at school. It's fucking dangerous.'

She put a hand on my arm. 'I know.'

'I couldn't stand it, if I lost you.'

'You won't lose me.'

I wanted to believe her, but every time I imagined walking into a police station, a picture of Carver popped into my mind, grinning that lopsided grin, and smacking his mighty truncheon against the palm of his hand.

'I'll think about it after Brighton.'

That was easier said than done. I thought about nothing else in the coming weeks.

CHAPTER 42

It had done us good to get away for the weekend with Jimmy and Lucy. The four of us had enjoyed a good time in Brighton, even though thoughts of Carver kept invading my mind like a nauseous fog. Back in the flat, things started to boil again. I wanted to go to the police, but I didn't trust them. How could I? Even those two bobbies who had turned up with Carver at the derelict pub had been willing to burn the place down, with me and Liam still locked in the cellar.

'I don't even know where to begin, if I do go to the cops,' I said. 'They won't believe me. The rapes. The murders. The satanic shit.'

Becky handed me a glass of orange juice. 'All the more reason to expose them. Get them locked away where they belong.'

I wanted to tip the juice away and replace it with whiskey. 'I might be the one who ends up getting locked away.'

'God will look out for you, Michael. It's time to tell the truth.'

'Liam said I ought to go to the newspapers.'

Becky didn't agree. 'What are they going to do? They can hardly go to Woodside and dig up the field, can they? They don't have the authority. But, the police do.'

In the end, after going around in circles for over an hour, I agreed to go to the cops. I had to do something; my head felt as if it would burst open and spill my thoughts all over the floor.

Paul arranged the meeting with Donald Osbourne, the station sergeant. He came with us and introduced me to a man massive enough to fill a door frame. His bushy beard looked as if it could house birds.

His long pock-marked nose vanished into his moustache, like a slide into a thorn bush.

Paul introduced us. 'This is Michael Tate, and his girlfriend, Becky.'

Osbourne nodded at me and Becky in turn. 'Pleased to meet you both. Would you like to come through to the interview room, Michael?'

My heart stuttered. 'What about Becky?'

'Was Becky present when the alleged incidents took place?'

'No.'

'Then I'm afraid she must wait with Father Paul in reception.' He rang a bell. A constable appeared as if summoned like a servant. 'Cover the desk for me, Weaver. Make these people a nice cup of tea.'

'Yes, Sarge.'

We disappeared along a narrow corridor and into a small room which was about ten feet square. It reeked of pipe tobacco. He invited me to sit at a desk.

He folded himself into a chair opposite me. 'Let's have an informal chat first, then we'll take it from there.'

'Okay.'

'Paul tells me you have some serious allegations concerning a children's home. Is that correct?'

I hesitated.

'Michael?'

I nodded.

'Can you tell me the name of this children's home?'

'Woodside.'

'And where is this home located?'

'Oxford.'

He opened a notebook and scribbled something down. He looked at me, stroked his beard, and invited me to tell him what had happened.

I didn't tell him about my time with the Davieses, only that I'd spent eighteen months in their care before being returned to Woodside.

Osbourne scribbled furiously as I spoke, occasionally looking up with alert blue eyes, asking me to slow down a bit.

When I was finished, he put his pencil on the desk. 'These are some serious allegations you are making, Michael.'

'It's the truth.'

'And you claim this Carver fellow locked you and Liam Truman in the boiler room at Woodside?'

'Yes.'

'And he beat Liam to death with a truncheon?'

'Yes.'

'And you buried Liam Truman at the bottom of the field at Woodside?'

'Yes.'

He referred to his notebook. 'With another boy called Craig McCree?'

'Yes. But, he's dead.'

'How did he die?'

'I don't know. I think a politician killed him.'

Osbourne raised his bushy eyebrows. 'Are you serious?'

I was. 'Apparently, he liked to throttle him when he had sex with him.'

'How do you know about this?'

'McCree told us. Then, he just vanished, like loads of other kids did at Woodside.'

'Do you know this politician's name?'

'No.'

He picked up his pencil and tapped it on the desk. 'Are you willing to make a formal statement with effect to what happened at Woodside Children's Home?'

'What does that mean?'

'I type up everything you've told me, get it all in order, then you sign and date it, if you're happy with it, and we take it from there.'

'Will you arrest Carver?'

He didn't answer at first. When he did, his words were measured. 'I can't say what will happen, but I have to warn you, it might not result in any arrests.'

'So, it might be a waste of time?'

'I can't answer that. I have to deal with the facts. I wish I could be more positive.'

'But, it happened. We buried Liam at the bottom of that field. Kids got raped and murdered in that fucking place.'

Osbourne held up a hand. 'And we will investigate.'

'Why can't you just go to the field and look for the grave?'

'It's not as simple as that, Michael. We have to follow the proper procedure. For what it's worth, we wouldn't even be having this conversation, if I wasn't willing to give you a fair hearing. You seem like a decent lad. Father Paul speaks highly of you, says you've got yourself a good life, and a good woman to keep you on the straight and narrow. Sings your praises. I'll do all I can to help you.'

'And if no one believes me?'

He didn't answer that. Instead, he said, 'I joined the police force to fight crime, Michael. I've always trusted the truth to prevail. If your allegations are true, these men need to be brought to justice.'

Justice? That was just about the dumbest word ever invented. I remembered Liam handcuffed to the railings in the boiler room, Carver whacking the truncheon into his body, over and over again, smashing his bones. Kraft sitting behind that desk, dressed in his black gown, ridiculous wig perched on his head, sweat dribbling down his face. Where was the justice in that pathetic kangaroo court? Where was the justice when Reggie was tied to a bed having an inverted cross carved on his body? When McCree sodomised him? Or when my mother was lying at the bottom of the stairs, battered and bruised beyond recognition? Or when Davies put his disgusting thing in my mouth, or forced me to beg for scraps of food when I wouldn't do what he wanted?

I didn't believe in justice. Justice wasn't for the likes of me and Liam. It was just a smokescreen for all those evil bastards who took everything and gave nothing.

'What happens when I sign the statement?'

'It will be handed to my superior officer, and a decision will be made from there.'

'A decision?'

'Whether there is sufficient cause or evidence to investigate.'

'Will it be done here in Feelham?'

Osbourne shook his head. 'No.'

'Where?'

'Oxford.'

'So, Carver could end up investigating himself?'

'It doesn't work like that.'

'But, he could lean on people, right?'

'I'm not prepared to speculate on what Mr. Carver might do.'

'I am. He's evil.'

'For what it's worth, most policemen try to do the right thing, Michael. Have their hearts in the right place. There might be a few rotten apples in the barrel, but the police are on your side.'

I wanted to believe him, but how could I? Even someone who seemed as honest and straightforward as Sergeant Osbourne couldn't really give me any reassurances.

'I'll type up your statement this evening. You go home and have a think about it. Have a chat to your girlfriend. To Paul. Come back tomorrow afternoon and let me know what you want to do.'

'Okay.'

We walked back to the main office. He opened the door to the reception area and showed me out.

Becky smiled, but it didn't lighten the worried look in her eyes. 'How did it go?'

'Not too bad.'

We walked out of the police station into a shaft of bright summer sunshine. It was the last time I ever saw Donald Osbourne.

CHAPTER 43

I didn't go back the following day. Or the day after. Every time I thought I'd made my mind up, I changed it back again. I chatted to Becky, argued with her, threatened to leave her, chatted to her some more. Round and round, like a bloody dog chasing its tail.

Paul told me to follow my conscience. He promised to pray for me. I wasn't even sure if I had a conscience anymore; it seemed to have got itself buried beneath an avalanche of doubt.

As it turned out, I didn't end up making a decision one way or another. Paul came to the flat on the Monday morning. Becky invited him into the front room, where I was working my way through another can of beer. His expression was sombre, as if in shock.

I plonked the can on the table. 'What's the matter, Paul?'

'I've got some bad news.'

My heart dropped into my stomach. It was Carver. Had to be. I knew this would happen as soon as he got wind of my statement. 'What?'

'It's Donald Osbourne. I'm afraid he's dead.'

I heard the words, but couldn't seem to attach meaning to them. 'What do you mean, dead?'

'He died this morning on his way to work.'

'How?' Becky asked.

'Knocked off his bicycle on the A473.'

Becky's hand flew up to her mouth. 'Oh my God. Poor man.'

'I'm afraid he was the victim of a hit and run.'

I picked up the can and chugged the rest of the beer. My head couldn't cope; it felt ready to explode.

Becky invited Paul to sit down. She offered him a cup of tea.

'Thank you.'

Carver, Carver, Carver, my mind screamed over and over. This had his name written all over it. But, would he really kill another police officer, just for taking a statement from me? It didn't seem logical. And then, it hit me. Carver had no reason to kill Osbourne. His sole purpose was to warn me. Let me know he was watching me. Waiting. Still in complete control.

We sat in stunned silence for a while. Becky brought Paul his tea. I asked for another can of beer. Becky spared me her usual really, at this time of day? look. I'd been drinking heavily lately, but it was the only thing that helped me get to sleep at night.

After a while, Paul said, 'Don's cycled that route nearly every day, for the best part of twenty years. It wasn't even dark when he was hit. It must have been a drunk driver.'

I swallowed more beer and kept my paranoid thoughts to myself.

'Have you decided anything regarding the statement yet, Michael?'

'No.' I finished my beer. 'I can't think straight.'

Becky scowled at me. 'Perhaps you ought to knock the drinking on the head.'

I walked to the fridge and grabbed another can. 'The drink's the only thing keeping me sane at the moment.'

'You think it is,' Becky said. 'There's a difference.'

I popped the tab, took a few sips, and banged the can down on the side. 'I'm going to work.'

'You might want to brush your teeth before you go, you stink of booze.'

I ignored her and stomped out of the flat. I walked the half mile to work with my feet on the floor, and my head somewhere above the clouds. I must have changed my mind about signing the statement at least a dozen times by the time I got to the George.

Somehow, throwing myself into work acted as therapy. At first break, I sat outside by the bins with Jimmy and had a smoke.

'You look rougher than a badger's armpit,' Jimmy said.

I lit up. 'Thanks.'

'Something on your mind?'

'It's nothing.' Perhaps the greatest understatement of the twentieth century. 'How's Lucy?'

Jimmy smiled. 'Still pregnant. Still moody.'

My mind slipped back to Paul's words. It's Donald Osbourne. I'm afraid he's dead. I knew Carver was responsible. Anyone capable of beating a boy to death with a truncheon was capable of anything.

'Are you and Becky all right?'

No, we're carrying around this dirty great big secret that's eating us both up on the inside. 'Not really.'

'Want to talk?'

I almost blurted it out. The lot of it. Woodside, Selwyn and Dolly Davies, Carver, Liam, the abuse, the torture. But, what good would it do?

'Mike?'

'No. It's all right.'

And that's how we left it. I left work at nine. I considered nipping into the Dog and Duck for a few beers before going back to the flat. Perhaps if I got home late enough, Becky would already be in bed, and we wouldn't have to get involved in another stupid argument. The only reason I decided not to go into the pub was because I looked like shit and smelled a damn sight worse.

I walked up the stairs to our third-floor flat. My workbag clunked on the metal rail all the way up. I was so knackered. I could barely put one foot in front of the other. I unlocked the front door and stepped into the flat.

Something was wrong. I couldn't put my finger on it at first. It just didn't feel right. Then, I realised what it was: the telly wasn't on. The flat was deathly silent.

'Becks?'

No answer. I could now smell something. Faint, but familiar. Aftershave? I hung my workbag on a row of brass hooks, kicked off my trainers. 'Becky? You home?'

Still no answer. Maybe she'd gone to bed, decided she didn't want to argue with me anymore. I checked both bedrooms. Nothing. Beds still made, sheets folded down two inches over the counterpane, pillows stacked on top.

I went to the kitchen and took a can of beer from the fridge. I popped the tab, walked into the front room, and stopped dead. I dropped the can. It deposited its contents in a frothy spurt all over the floor. Sitting in the armchair, gun resting in his lap, Detective Inspector Carver treated me to his sickening, lopsided grin. There was a length of orange rope coiled up on the arm of the chair.

Becky was on the sofa, hands cuffed behind her back, mouth gagged with a blue scarf her mother had bought her after they had mended their relationship on Becky's last birthday.

'Hello, Michael, so glad you could make it. We've been expecting you, haven't we, Becky love?'

I looked from one to the other, feet glued to the floor. 'What the fuck...?'

Carver stood up and waved the gun at me. 'You sit on the sofa next to you girlfriend, Michael. Take the weight off your feet.'

'What do you want?'

He pointed the gun at my face. 'Sit down, or I'll shoot you.'

I did as he asked. My hands were shaking so badly, I had to tuck them under my legs.

Carver paraded up and down in front of the sofa. 'Well, isn't this cosy?'

'What the fuck do you want?' I asked.

He ignored me and looked Becky up and down. 'God knows how you pulled such a pretty bird, Tate. Wonders will never cease.'

I glanced sideways at Becky. Her eyes were wide, terrified.

'Too slutty for my liking, but a looker all the same.' He glanced at his watch. 'We've got to know each other quite well in the short time I've been here, haven't we, Becky?'

Becky shook her head.

Carver returned his attention to me. 'You ever heard the saying, you don't realise what you've got until it's gone, Michael?'

My head was racing in a dozen different directions at once.

'From what I can gather, Tate, this girl pulled you out of the gutter. So, answer me this: why did you want to drag her down into your filthy mess?'

'I didn't—'

'Or, more to the point, why did you want to go spreading malicious lies about me?'

'They're not lies.'

'Yes, they are. Filthy dirty lies. Now there's a policeman lying dead in the morgue. His poor widow will struggle for the rest of her life to cope with her tragic loss, all because you couldn't keep your trap shut.'

'I—'

'It's a good job I've got a good man inside Feelham nick. Someone who knows how to clear up a potential mess. Get rid of statements from liars. Talking of mess, I had to reverse back over that poor sergeant to make sure he was dead. I hope you're proud of yourself, Tate.'

Becky made a moaning noise in the back of her throat. Carver smiled. 'Even Becky can see the error of your ways.'

'What do you want?' I asked again.

'Me? Nothing in particular. Just tying up a few loose ends. Giving you a chance to say sorry to your girlfriend for getting her killed.'

'Do whatever you want to me, but let her go. Please.'

'Too late, Tate. That horse bolted when you walked into the cop shop, telling a pack of lies and half-truths.'

'I'm sorry.'

Carver frowned. 'What for, Michael?'

'Talking to the police.'

'But, you're talking to the police now.'

'I meant—'

'If you'd just kept your mouth shut and let bygones be bygones, I'd pretty much forgotten all about you, and that scumbag friend of yours. What was his name?'

I didn't answer.

'Mouthy little shit, if I remember.'

I felt heat bubbling up inside me. 'I wasn't going to sign that statement.'

'Really?'

'Really.'

'So why did you tell Donald Osbourne all that rubbish in the first place?'

Because it's fucking true. 'I don't know.'

Carver shook his head. 'You knew full well what you were doing, Tate. Trouble is, you picked a day when Constable Weaver was on duty. He's a good friend of mine. Do you know what a friend is, Tate?'

I shook my head.

'Friends look out for one another. Watch their backs. Weaver told me you came into the cop shop with a vicar in tow.'

I was about to deny it when Carver continued, 'Quite a nice bloke, for a vicar. I had a nice long chat with him. I'll give credit where it's due, Michael; that man didn't say a bad word about you. Clammed up and refused to say anything other than his name, rank, and number. But, silence is its own worst enemy sometimes. Just in case you're interested, Father Brady committed suicide. Hanged himself from a rafter in his cosy little cottage down by the river.'

My mind tried to process what Carver was saying. I stared at the muzzle of the gun. 'You're lying.'

'I'm not in the habit of lying, Tate. I leave that up to scumbags like you. Anyway, I made him write a nice, long suicide note apologising to the church for his liking for young boys. Quite a heartfelt confession. Almost brought a tear to my eye.'

I tried to speak, but the words stuck in my throat. I wanted to grab the gun and shoot the bastard right between the eyes, but I just sat there, a useless, cowering wreck.

'Still, at least he's with his boss now. I'm sure the Lord will have a forgiving heart where the good vicar is concerned. Now, do you want to do this the easy way or the hard way?'

'What?'

'Didn't your mother teach you any manners? It's not what, it's pardon. I asked you if you want to do this the easy way or the hard way.'

'You're sick.'

Carver laughed. 'You're a right one to talk.'

'I've done nothing wrong.'

He made a sound like a hacking dog. 'You've done plenty wrong. Trouble is, you always think it's someone else's fault. You're never willing to take responsibility. Never willing to learn. Are you aware of the expression, history always repeats itself?'

I thought of Liam. Sergeant Osbourne. Paul. I was well aware of how history repeated itself. I didn't answer. I looked at Becky. Her eyes looked as if they were trying to scream.

'Right. Strip off completely, and then lay face down on the floor.'

Becky tried to say something through her gag. 'Umph, mumph, umph.'

Carver ignored her and waved the gun at me. 'You can do this with a bullet in your back, if you want, Tate. Your choice.'

I did as he asked. Carver yanked my arms behind my back and snapped handcuffs on my wrists. He ordered me to lay face down on the floor and bound my feet with rope. He looped the rope through the cuffs, trussing me up like a chicken.

'You do not have to say anything, Tate, but anything you do say will be written down and completely ignored. Is that clear to your limited brain?'

I closed my eyes. Tried to make everything go away. Convince myself that this was all just a terrible nightmare. Any minute now, I would wake up, and realise I'd drank myself into a stupor again, crashed out on the living room floor.

'Because I'm a compassionate man, I will let you say goodbye to your girlfriend before I take her into the bedroom.'

'Leave her al—'

'Save the theatrical attempt to act like a man. You're no more a man than a dog turd. Do you want to say goodbye to her, or not?'

I shook my head, rubbing my chin on the worn carpet. I wasn't going to give him the satisfaction of watching me break down.

'Are you sure? We don't want any regrets festering in that head of yours.'

I bit down hard on my tongue. Hard enough to make it bleed.

'All right. Have it your way.'

Carver dragged Becky out of the living room. One of her sandals fell off as he pulled her around the corner. Her muffled screams rolled around my head like echoes from hell.

A few minutes later, Carver returned. 'Are you comfortable down there, Michael?'

I ignored him.

'Becky's as well as can be expected. I was going to shoot her, but then I got to thinking. A scumbag like you would hardly have access to a firearm, would you? So I thought a kitchen knife was in order.'

I tried to free myself. I only succeeded in burning my chin on the carpet.

'And then, I had another idea. A good one, this. You'll like it. I asked Becky how old she was while we were waiting for you to come home from pots and pans duty. Twenty-one. I thought it might be a nice touch to stab her twenty-one times. It will certainly give the psychiatrists something to consider when they write their reports, won't it? They love to overanalyse and work hidden meanings into murders.'

'You won't get away with this, you cunt.'

'Michael! Calm yourself. Sticks and stones. You have a little rest and leave the dirty work to me. I'll be back soon. Then we can talk about what to do next, okay?'

I experienced the same complete helplessness I'd felt when my mother died. When Liam died. Carver was right, history had a way of repeating itself. All too often.

He took one of my discarded socks off the floor and stuffed it in my mouth, pushing it back as far as he could. 'Don't move.'

I lay trussed up on that floor for what seemed like hours. I heard thumps and muffled screams coming from the bedroom. Something crashed to the floor. More thuds. I banged my head against the floor as hard as I could, trying to knock myself unconscious.

I didn't notice Carver return to the front room. He grabbed my hair and yanked my head back. He brandished a blood-stained knife in front of my eyes. 'Pack that in right now, unless you want me to slit your throat.'

I could barely breathe. He let go of my hair. My head thumped against the floor. He pressed his shoe against the back of my neck. I could smell shoe polish. 'I want you to listen carefully, Tate. Your girlfriend is dead. She put up a valiant fight. Still alive when I stabbed her in the eye. Credit where credit's due, she had spunk, which is more than I can say about you.'

I tried to move my head, but he pressed down harder with his foot. 'I'm going to untie the rope in a minute, but I promise you, one wrong move, and I'll make sure you die a long and lingering death. If you behave, I'll make it quick for you. Do you understand?'

I don't know how the hell he expected me to answer.

He stepped off my neck and rolled me onto my side with his foot. I noticed that he was dressed in my white T-shirt, jeans and trainers. All soaked in blood.

'I'm just going to get cleaned up and changed back into my suit. Don't move.'

Time ticked by in unrelated chunks. I briefly wondered if I might be able to get up, throw myself through the window before he came back, but my limbs were too numb to move, my mind too numb to think.

Carver returned about fifteen minutes later, untied the rope, and released the handcuffs. 'Your water isn't very hot, Michael. Almost cold. Don't you switch the water heater on?'

Did he seriously expect an answer?

He rolled me over onto my back. He was back in his charcoal suit. Spotless black loafers. Hair combed. Pale blue eyes showing no signs of humanity. He ordered me to dress.

I took the sock out of my mouth and forced myself to put on my blood-soaked soiled clothes and trainers.

'This gun has a silencer fitted. I will have no hesitation in shooting you if you so much as move a muscle without my permission. Am I making myself clear?'

I tried to focus on praying. Begging God to take me away from this shit.

Carver grinned. 'Come on. We're going for a little walk.'

I was past caring. I wanted to die. Everyone I loved was dead. No, not just dead – murdered. The world was full of evil bastards. It wasn't survival of the fittest; it was survival of the greediest and the cruellest.

Carver walked me to the fire escape, gun pressed into my back, close enough to feel his hot breath on my neck. 'For the first time in your life, Tate, you're going right to the top.'

And so, we did. To the top of Evenlode flats. The cars parked on the street looked like Matchbox models. A cool breeze blew across the roof space, like God's whisper.

'You can jump, or be pushed. Your choice.'

'Fuck you.'

'Tut, tut, Michael. That's no way to speak to an officer of the law.'

'You're nothing but a murderer.'

He laughed. 'Sticks and stones, Michael. Any last requests?'

I glanced sideways at him. 'Yeah. Go to hell and burn for all eternity.'

'You've been listening to that silly old vicar too much. I don't want to burst your bubble, but there's no such thing as heaven and hell; that's just a load of made up babble. Life's for enjoyment, Michael, taking what you want, fulfilling your wishes. Of course, there's always a price to pay. I've been cleaning up the mess at Woodside for ages. There must be a good twenty kids buried in that field; that's why we moved out into Bluebell Woods with the last one. Kraft and Malloy have an insatiable appetite for sadism.'

'They're—'

I didn't feel him push me. I was suddenly hurtling towards the ground, wind whooshing through my ears, sucking at my skin. Ten seconds? Twenty? Every ounce of air was knocked out of my body. There was a brief roar of pain, and then blackness. Sweet, unending blackness.

CHAPTER 44

No wheelchair. No trip along the tunnel. No hands helping me back into bed. It was as if I'd fallen from the top of those flats and landed right back in bed. I looked over at the wheelchair sitting dormant against the wall, illuminated by the first light of dawn spilling through the window behind me.

The emergency door was gone. No trace of it. No writing, no rusty bolt and no release bar, just a blank wall with its cracked and peeling paint. I suddenly felt very alone. Vulnerable. Almost as if my only lifeline had just been snatched away from me. The only thing linking me to my past.

In many ways, I wished I'd never come back to the hospital, that I'd been allowed to stay in my past. Perhaps even change it. Prevent the murders of all those people, or at the very least, avenge them. I would have given anything to just have an hour in a locked room with Carver, see how he faired handcuffed to a chair, whilst I smashed every bone in his body with a truncheon.

How long had I been away? Had all those years been condensed into a matter of hours? Minutes? I looked down at my body, half-expecting to see the blood-soaked clothes I'd been wearing when I'd fallen from the top of the flats. Thankfully, just my pyjamas, but my wrists still carried the marks from the handcuffs. Red and angry. I ran a finger over the broken skin, tangible evidence of my latest experience.

My thoughts turned to Paul Brady. Dear sweet Paul, the kindest man I'd ever known. Murdered by Carver and painted as a child molester by that sick bastard's lies and actions. I wanted to shout out, demand to see someone, tell them the truth. I was innocent. Carver was the one who'd murdered my girlfriend. Taken me to the top of the flats and shoved me off. Murdered Paul and Sergeant Osbourne, too, but I needed evidence, something solid.

It was hard to believe any of this had really happened. But, it had. My mother's earring, the book of Liam's poems, and the red marks on my wrists were all proof of this. I thought about the constable at Feelham nick, who'd told Carver about my visit. It seemed as if the bastards were everywhere. Prison would be a living hell. It was better in some ways when I'd known nothing; the truth only made everything seem ten times worse.

The teachers at school had taught us how great England was, how we'd won the war and conquered the world, how everyone should be grateful for the British Empire, but all that stuff was a crock of shit, wasn't it? What hope was there for society when children were being used to satisfy the depraved needs of their so-called carers? None. Rotten to the core.

I don't know how I managed to drift off to sleep with so many terrible things running around inside my head, but I must have, because the next thing I knew, Emily was standing beside the bed in her starched, blue uniform. 'Good morning, Michael.'

I kept my wrists hidden beneath the bedsheet. 'What time is it?'

She checked a silver watch pinned to her uniform. 'Eight forty-five. I'm surprised you're awake, you're usually zonked out until mid-morning.'

'I had a nightmare.' A massive understatement.

'Poor you.'

'What day is it?'

She smiled. 'I thought your short-term memory was in good order?'

'I need to know.'

'It's Saturday morning. Why?'

I tried to come to terms with the fact I'd just relived three years in a few hours.

'How are you feeling?'

'Better for seeing you.'

'How's the pain?'

'My head hurts.'

'I'll get you some aspirin.'

'Thanks.'

'I'm going to miss you when you go, Michael.'

I was taken aback. 'I'll miss you, too.'

'For what it's worth, I don't believe you're any more capable of murder than I am.'

I almost told her what had happened with the emergency door and the wheelchair, but I didn't want her to think I'd completely lost my mind. 'Thanks.'

'You can have my phone number… if you want to stay in touch.'

'Is that allowed?'

'I can talk to who I like outside of work. It's got nothing to do with anyone else. I'll visit you in prison, if you want.'

I did. More than anything. But, I didn't want Emily to see me reduced to ashes in a prison system which would make Woodside look like a holiday home. 'You don't want to get involved with me. I'm bad news.'

She studied me for a while. I felt my face getting hotter. A strand of hair was tickling my face. I wanted to reach up and brush it away, but I didn't want her to see my wrists.

'Do you remember anything at all about your past, Michael?'

'It's still all blank.'

'Perhaps it will come to you in time.'

I tried to smile. I think I managed a frown. 'Maybe.'

She touched my arm lightly. 'I want you to know I'm always here for you if you ever need me.'

'Thanks.'

'I mean it.' She turned, and left me alone without a backward glance.

I didn't know what I'd done to warrant Emily's faith; it was both touching and comforting, a tiny speck of light in an ever-darkening world, and a reminder that not everyone was rotten to the core.

And then, the tears came. Warm and welcome. I cried for all that was lost, but mostly for Liam, Becky, and Paul, taken so cruelly from this world by Carver's evil hand. Taken long before their time. I hoped with all my heart heaven existed; a place where all those who had suffered on this Earth got their final reward.

CHAPTER 45

I spent the next twenty-four hours in complete turmoil. Not one word from Jimmy. I don't know what I'd been expecting. A phone call to tell me they'd convinced Hodges to dig up Liam's grave? Or, worse, Carver to come and tell me that they'd arrested Jimmy. But, Carver was in Paris with his phony wife, so at least that wasn't possible. Thank heavens for small mercies. One thing I'd learned whilst lying in that hospital bed was that silence wasn't golden; it was as black and as empty as death itself.

Emily walked in and closed the door. 'There's some people here to see you.'

'Who?'

'Two detectives from Thames Valley police.' And then, quickly, as if she'd read my mind, 'Don't worry, it's not Carver.'

'Did they say what they want?'

'They said it's urgent.'

'You'd better show them in.'

'I could tell them you're sleeping, if you want?'

'No. It's all right.'

Emily showed the two detectives in. 'Michael is still suffering the after-effects of his trauma, so I'd appreciate it if you didn't upset him.'

One of the detectives removed a trilby hat and revealed a bald head. He had a small moustache and a hooked, beak-like nose. 'We won't, Nurse. Rest assured.'

Emily looked at me. 'Ring the bell if you need anything.'

I nodded.

Bald Guy said, 'I'm Detective Inspector Thomas Hart. This is Detective Constable Peter Guard. We have two gentlemen down at Oxford nick right now making statements, along with a Mr. Geoff Hodges, the groundsman at Woodside Children's Home.'

My heart leapt over a fence. 'You do?'

Hart nodded. He pulled a notebook out of his breast pocket, licked the tip of his pencil. 'In your own time, Michael, I want you to tell me everything you know with regard to the body which was exhumed from the playing field at Woodside Children's Home.'

I told them everything, right up to Carver beating Liam to death with his truncheon.

Hart looked at me for a few moments, and then said, 'That's quite a story, Michael.'

'It's the truth.'

'We believe you,' Guard said, 'but we still need to formally identify the deceased. We're hoping that dental records will determine who he is.'

'What about Carver?' I said.

'Don't worry about him. This is a murder investigation, and Detective Inspector Carver is now part of that investigation.'

'He didn't only kill Liam.'

Hart raised an eyebrow. 'No?'

I told him about how Carver had faked Paul's suicide and made him write a note confessing to being a child molester. How he'd knocked Osbourne off his bike and reversed back over the body. His visit to my flat. Stabbing Becky, and walking me to the top of the flats, and pushing me off.

'Where's Carver now?' Guard asked his superior.

'Weekend leave. He's gone to Paris with his wife.'

'Fake wife,' I said.

'What do you mean?' Hart asked.

I told him how Carver had killed his first wife. 'He doesn't like women. He likes boys. He's a sick bastard. He beat his first wife to death, with the same truncheon he killed Liam with. She came home and caught him in bed with a boy. Carver fitted the kid up with her murder. He took great pleasure in telling me all about it.'

Hart turned to Detective Guard. 'This just gets better.'

'Do you want me to get a warrant issued for Carver's arrest?'

'Not yet. I've got a better idea.'

'He's also got this photo album,' I said. 'It's got pictures of his victims in it.'

'Did he tell you this?'

'He showed me it.'

Guard let out a sigh between clenched teeth. 'Jesus.'

Hart snapped his notebook shut and addressed his constable. 'I want you to stay here. I'll go and have a word with the superintendent, put a few suggestions to him, see what he thinks is the best way to take this forward.'

Guard nodded.

When the Detective Inspector was gone, I asked Guard what would happen next.

'We need to just sit tight. Play it by ear.'

'I'm meant to be going to remand tomorrow.'

'That's not going to happen now, Michael.'

His words did little to reassure me. I didn't think they truly understood how dangerous and manipulative Carver was. Detective Guard sat next to the bed and flicked through my car magazine. The photos of our weekend in Brighton dropped out. He picked them up off the bed and studied the one of Becky sitting on the pier. 'Is this your girlfriend?'

'Yes.'

'I'm sorry.' He put the photos down, seemed thoughtful for a moment, and then said, 'We'll get him, Michael.'

I wished I shared his optimism. We sat in silence. Guard leafed through the car magazine. About half an hour later, Emily came into the room and told me Jimmy was here to see me. 'Shall I show him in?'

I looked at Guard for approval. He put the magazine down and stood up. 'I'll go grab a coffee.'

Jimmy looked haggard and unshaven. There were dark circles beneath his eyes. He nodded at Guard as they passed in the doorway. He flopped down in the chair and ran a hand across his bald head, seemingly smoothing out imaginary hair.

'What happened?'

He kept rubbing his eyes as if trying to erase what he'd seen. When he spoke, his voice was low and expressionless. Almost robotic. 'We got to Woodside around half nine. Walked along the edge of the building and found Hodges' cottage. I kept thinking someone would see us and call the cops. There were lights on in the main building. By the time we knocked on the door, I was having second thoughts, wondering what I'd do if two strangers came to my door telling tales of murder and a body buried in a field.'

'I really appreciate what you've—'

Jimmy held up a hand. 'It's nothing compared to what you've had to deal with, Michael. Nothing at all. Anyway, Hodges finally answered the door. I told him we were there on behalf of you and Liam Truman. Said it was a matter of life and death and asked if we could come in and talk.'

'What did he say?'

'He didn't look too keen at first, but he finally agreed. Between you, me, and the gatepost, he'd had a few drinks. There was a half-empty bottle of whiskey on the coffee table, which might have gone some way to lowering his guard. That and the fags we took him. Anyway, I didn't waste any time. I told him everything I knew. How you'd buried Liam at the bottom of the field. What Kraft, Malloy, and Carver had done. I didn't spare him any of the details.'

'Did he believe you?'

Jimmy nodded. 'When I was finished, he banged the mug down on the table, and fixed me with bloodshot eyes. He said he knew his wheelbarrow and shovels had been used that night, but he couldn't figure out why. It was hardly something kids would do for a prank.

Let off stink bombs, or squirt glue in the padlocks, maybe, but take his stuff and go gardening? No way. Anyway, we waited until it was pitch-dark, and then went to the bottom of the field. We took turns, two digging, one holding the torch. Hodges kept lighting up when it was his turn to hold the torch. I thought someone would spot us. It took us well over an hour. Terry found Liam's rucksack first. And then, well....'

I imagined Liam's body rotting away in that cold grave for all these years. An unknown boy in an unmarked grave. Treated like a piece of rubbish and discarded like a piece of rubbish.

'Hodges had a phone in the cottage. He called 999 and told the dispatcher what we'd found. We had to show the cops the place where we'd found the body. A few people were spilling out of the building by then. The police cordoned off the grave with tape. Me, Terry, and Hodges were taken to the police station. We had to go through our stories, answer all these questions, mostly about how we actually knew the body was buried there. I kept telling them how you'd got your memory back, remembered everything. In the end, my mind seemed to blank out. They let us go home yesterday afternoon, and took me back in for questioning again last night.'

'I can't thank you enough for this, Jimmy.'

He shrugged. 'It's nothing. The good thing is, I think they believed us.'

I told Jimmy about my last trip along the tunnel. How Carver had murdered Becky, Paul, and Sergeant Osbourne. I also told him what Carver said about killing his first wife. How he'd shown me his gruesome photograph album.

Jimmy took a deep breath and then let it out slowly. 'I'm not a religious man, Michael, but I'm going to church tonight. Pray the cops get enough evidence to send that bastard away for life. Throw away the fucking key.'

'Amen to that,' I said. 'Amen to that.'

CHAPTER 46

Detective Inspector Hart returned to the hospital just before lights out. He told Guard to go home and get a few hours' sleep. Guard didn't look in any condition to argue. He closed the door behind him.

Hart sat down next to the bed. 'How are you bearing up, Michael?'

Did he want the truth, or the stock answer you always give when someone asks that dumbest of questions? 'I'll tell you how I'm bearing up, Detective Inspector: like someone who's been dumped underneath a ton of shit, and asked if he can still smell the roses.'

'If it's any consolation, Michael, we'll do our level best to nail Carver.'

To be honest, it wasn't. Although I would take a lot of pleasure watching Carver get what he had coming to him, it could never make up for what he'd done. No punishment could fit the crime. Becky was still dead. Liam was still dead. Paul was still dead. And that bastard would get a nice comfortable cell for the rest of his life. Probably even get special privileges. And that was only assuming the cops got enough evidence to prove his guilt.

'And what happens if he gets away with it?'

'He won't.'

'And you know that for certain, do you?'

'We believe we've got enough evidence to nail him. There was a pair of glasses in a rucksack in your friend's grave. Luckily for us that rucksack was waterproof. There was a perfectly formed fingerprint in the blood on one lens. It matches Carver's.'

'Really?'

Hart nodded. 'We went to see Carver tonight when he got back from Paris. Told him to go straight to the hospital in the morning, and escort you to remand.'

'What if someone tips him off about Woodside?'

'Only myself and the superintendent know about the fingerprint. He's not going to know we're on to him. Even if he does, my guess is he'll just shrug it off, won't believe there's any evidence to point the finger at him. The superintendent's pulling the strings on this one, Michael.'

I didn't feel very reassured. Anything could go wrong. I reminded Hart of my trip to Feelham Police Station, and Sergeant Osbourne's death.

'I'm well aware of what he's capable of. Don't worry, we've got plain clothes officers watching his house. If he does anything other than go to bed tonight, we'll nick him.'

'Why don't you just arrest him, anyway?'

'Because I've got a better idea.' He fished a small black box out of his pocket. 'We want him to come to the hospital tomorrow morning as planned, then we want you to get him to talk about the murders, and record it on this.'

'What is it?'

'It's a dictaphone. It's got a mini-cassette inside which will run for ninety minutes. If we hide it somewhere, you can set it to record just before he shows up.'

'What if he finds it?'

'He won't be looking for it. As far as he's concerned, he's just coming here to take you away. He won't think he's being set up. I know John Carver. He's an arrogant bugger. He'll think it's business as usual. He won't be wondering if you've got a dictaphone stashed away somewhere.'

I wasn't so sure. Carver had terrorised me enough times to make me think he was capable of anything. 'Where am I supposed to hide it?'

Hart looked at the bedside locker. 'In the drawer. We'll make sure he gets here bang on nine o'clock. If you switch it on at five minutes to, and leave the drawer open about half an inch, that should be adequate to catch everything he has to say.'

'What if he doesn't want to talk?'

'Ask him why he murdered all those people. Draw it out of him. Tell him you accept you're going to prison. That he's won. Maybe even congratulate him. Stroke his ego. Lie. Cajole. But, always remember why you're doing it, Michael. You can gain a lot of strength from what he's put you through.'

'Okay.'

'You're not on your own anymore. We'll be right here in the hospital, waiting. Listening. As soon as you've got enough evidence on the tape, press the bell, and we'll be straight in.'

I wanted to feel reassured, believe Carver would get what he deserved, but I just felt empty and hollow. It was as if someone had taken a knife and gutted me like a fish.

Hart put the dictaphone on the bed. 'Okay, let's give it a test run. The four buttons along the top are easy enough. Play, rewind, fast-forward and record. Just press record and put it in the drawer.'

I did as he asked.

Hart nodded. 'Testing, one, two, three. This is Detective Inspector Hart from Thames Valley Police speaking. End of message. Okay, Michael. Take it out, rewind it, and play the tape.'

The message was loud and clear.

'Easy enough, right?'

'Right.'

'Rewind the tape and put it back in the drawer for the morning.'

As long as no one tips Carver off, I thought. And then, another thought born of paranoia. What if they're all in this together? Hart and Guard. The bobby outside the door? All part of an elaborate set- up to trap me? What if Carver's at the hospital right now, laughing his bollocks off?

Hart looked at his watch. 'Any questions, Michael?'

About a million. 'No.'

'I've posted a bobby outside the door for the night. Anything you want, just call him.'

'Okay.'

'Try to get some sleep.'

I had more chance of running a bloody marathon. I watched Hart leave. He closed the door, leaving me alone with just my thoughts. The wheelchair sat motionless against the wall, no visible trace left of the emergency door and its messages.

There was a funny feeling in the bottom of my stomach. Sick, yet at the same time exhilarating. My thoughts turned to Becky, Paul, and Liam. How could Carver just murder them in cold blood? What sort of monster was he? It was like a game to him, full of players he controlled. He hadn't joined the police force to uphold the law; he'd joined the police force because it had allowed him to stand above the law.

I picked up the photo of Becky sitting on the pier. So pretty. So innocent. It was a good job we didn't know what was coming our way. A blessing we can't see into the future. This time, the picture remained static. I did not join Becky on the pier, or talk about going to the police.

'I'm so sorry,' I whispered. 'So sorry it ended the way it did.'

Becky gazed into the distance, waiting for her boyfriend to come back from his latest sulk. I now remembered everything. Our plans to have children. Two girls and a boy. I would get a better job, maybe train as a chef, and we would buy a nice little house out in the country somewhere. Settle down. Have a black Labrador, go for walks in the summer, picking blackberries, the kids taking turns on my shoulders.

The children would want for nothing. They would be loved. Looked after. You didn't think for one minute someone like Carver was going to come back from the past and kill all your dreams. That bastard not only murdered Liam and the others, he murdered my future. Becky's future. Our unborn children's futures.

I felt a nervous tingling in my stomach just thinking about putting that swine behind bars for good. I didn't realise the significance of this at first, and then, it hit me: I could actually feel something below the level of my belly button for the first time since I'd come around from the coma.

CHAPTER 47

As predicted, I didn't sleep a wink that night. I might have dozed off once or twice, but nothing substantial. Emily came on shift at eight. She breezed into my room and treated me to a nervous smile. 'Big day, huh?'

I nodded. I wanted to tell her everything, but I didn't want to say anything that might jeopardise the plan to trap Carver.

'I understand Detective Inspector Carver's coming to take you to remand at nine.'

Just the mention of his name sickened me. 'Yeah.'

'We've been told not to interrupt you when he comes.'

'Right.'

'I just wanted to come and say goodbye before....'

I changed the subject. 'I had some sensation in my tummy last night.'

A smile stretched right across her face. 'That's fantastic news. I'm really pleased for you.'

'Is it normal?'

'It might just be water retention. I'll have a word with Dr Marston.'

I dredged a smile from somewhere deep inside me. 'Before you go, I wanted to say thank you for everything you've done for me.'

She looked away. 'I'm just doing my job.'

'Sharon's just doing her job. The doctors are just doing their jobs. You've been a true friend throughout my time here.'

'That's because I care about you, Michael.'

'Can I let you into a little secret?'

Her lovely green eyes sparkled in the early morning sunlight. 'Of course.'

'I care about you, too.'

She brushed a kite tail of hair behind one ear, and then leaned over and kissed the top of my head. 'My prayers will always be with you, Michael. If you ever want me to come and see you, well...' She fished a small piece of note paper out of her pocket and handed it to me. 'That's my home number. My private number.'

I took the paper and tucked it in my pyjama pocket. 'I might take you up on that.'

She smiled. She looked as if she was going to turn back as she walked out the door, but she merely paused, and then carried on about her business.

I switched the Dictaphone to record at ten minutes to nine. I left the drawer open about a quarter of an inch and spent the next ten minutes hovering somewhere between determination and pessimism. Something was bound to go wrong. Carver was a lot of things, but he wasn't stupid. Someone would tip him off. All his cronies were like a network of cancerous cells, ready and waiting to leak their poison into anything weak and vulnerable.

Carver strolled into the room and smiled at me. He closed the door and sat down next to the bed. 'That was a bloody good weekend, Michael. Ever been to Paris?'

'No.'

'You ought to go. Might do you good to recharge the old batteries.'

'I'll bear that in mind.'

'Angie found herself a gigolo, the dirty girl. Michel, or some poncey name like that. Had a ponytail. Can you believe that, Michael? A man with a fucking ponytail. I swear the world's gone mad. Or perhaps it's just the Frogs. Hopping mad.' He smirked at his own stupid joke. 'Still, it does a girl good to let her hair down. That's probably where you went wrong with Becky.'

My stomach flipped over at the mention of Becky's name. I tried to console myself. He would be the one going to prison, not me.

'If you'd kept her satisfied, she might not have looked elsewhere. You have to plug in now and again to get a spark.'

I stared at the wall. Tried to turn my mind as blank as the yellowing paint.

'A girl needs attention. Especially when she's hooked up to a loser like you.'

Don't let him goad you. Concentrate on getting him to talk about the murders. 'I don't know anything about Becky. Like I've told you a hundred times, I can't remember anything.'

'Oh, yes, I remember.' That disgusting, lopsided grin greased the side of his chops. 'That old chestnut. King of the cop outs. Second only to I didn't do it. The prisons are chock full of fools who swear they're innocent. But, let me tell you, Mikey, no one listens to the likes of you. Your kind always go where you belong and belong where you go.'

'Is that right?'

'Speaking of which, the hospital is going to provide you with your own private ambulance to take you to remand. How about that for first class treatment on the National Health? And you not even a tax payer. But, don't worry your head about that, Michael, there's always more than one way to pay your dues.'

And you're about to find out all about that.

'I'll be riding in the back with you, in case you get any clever ideas about trying to throw yourself out of the back.'

'I don't think I'm in any fit state to throw myself anywhere, am I? Much as I'd like to.'

'Don't get all sulky on me, Mikey. This is a momentous day. Let's not spoil it with petty whining.'

Say something. Don't let him keep putting you on the back foot. 'I suppose we're two of a kind really, aren't we?'

Carver's grin slipped away. 'What the hell do you mean by that?'

'I killed my girlfriend. You killed your first wife.'

'Are you trying to wind me up?'

'No. You told me you killed your first wife and set up a kid with the murder.'

Carver stood up and walked over to the wall. 'I killed Missy because she was a fucking liability, Tate.'

'You told me she caught you in bed with a fifteen-year-old boy.'

'Missy was a mistake. I'm nothing like you, Tate. I'm not a dirty piece of scum like you.'

'You still killed her.'

'For the greater good.'

'Beat her to death with a truncheon.'

'I'm warning you, Tate. Don't play games with me.'

'I'm not playing games. I'm only saying what you told me when you showed me that photo album with all those dead bodies in it.'

He stepped away from the wall. 'You'd do well to remember who you're talking to. The severity of your prison existence depends on my good nature.'

'I'm only saying.'

Carver took a few steps towards the bed. 'Talk isn't cheap, Mikey. It's costly. Very costly.'

Keep talking then. 'Don't you ever regret killing Missy? I mean, I regret killing Becky, even though I don't remember doing it.'

Carver sat back down next to the bed. 'I'll let you into a little secret, Tate. Life's too short to have regrets. What's the point in wasting time worrying about ifs and buts? My only regret, if you could call it that, is I married the bitch in the first place. The whiny, little mare should have found herself a Workhorse Joe. Someone with a nice little nine-till-five.'

'What about the boy?'

'What about him?'

'Don't you care he got put inside for something he didn't do?'

'Why should I? He was just another piece of scum like you, Tate.'

327

I felt like throwing up. I consoled myself with the fact he'd just confessed to his wife's murder. But, was it enough? What about all the others?

'Killing someone, and getting someone else blamed for it, is like killing two birds with one stone.'

'Like killing Becky and getting me blamed for it?'

For the first time since I'd met John Carver, he looked unsure. His mouth hung open. 'What did you say?'

'I remember what you did, Carver. You killed Becky and pushed me off the top of those flats. Just like you murdered your first wife and made sure that the poor kid got sent down for it. Cut his wrists in prison.'

A shadow passed before his eyes, turning them from pale blue to grey. 'You remember?'

'I went to Feelham nick to make a statement. You killed Sergeant Osbourne. You killed Paul. You killed Becky. And you tried to kill me.'

'Well, well, well, you have been a busy boy inside that empty head of yours, haven't you?'

'Just saying.'

He seemed to mull this over. When he answered, his words were cold and measured, like ice cubes popped from a tray. 'I did what I had to do, Tate.'

'Why didn't you just kill me?'

'If I'd just killed you, the vicar and your girlfriend would have been kicking up enough stink to drown a skunk's arse. I had no choice. Not once you'd opened your mouth.'

I wanted to tear his face apart with my bare hands. 'You killed them, because you enjoyed doing it. What sort of sick bastard makes a vicar commit suicide? Write a note confessing to liking young boys?'

'I had it on good authority Paul Brady was a queer. I simply lowered his age of consent.'

'I hope there is a God. I hope He's watching you.'

Carver laughed. 'There's no such thing as God.'

'I thought the police were supposed to protect people, not murder them.'

'If that's what you want to believe. My only regret is Osbourne. It's never pleasant when you have to do away with one of your own. At least it was quick once I'd reversed over him.'

'You're sick.'

'Me? Michael, you do surprise me. I thought by now you'd have realised throwing insults at me is a dangerous pastime.'

'I don't care.'

'Really? You should. No disrespect to your bird, but I'd let sleeping dogs lie, if I were you. By the way, I thought stabbing her twenty-one times was a nice touch. A work of art. The vicar, too. Bit more creative than getting rid of the usual rubbish at Woodside.'

'Creative my arse.'

'Nice to see you've lost none of your illiterate touches, Tate.'

I felt Carver had incriminated himself enough, but I wanted to say something about Liam, in case the bloody fingerprint wasn't enough. 'They've found Liam's body.'

His eyebrows joined the frown on his forehead. 'What did you say?'

'I said they've found Liam. The boy you handcuffed to the railings in the boiler room, and beat to death with your truncheon, remember?'

'Truman? That mouthy piece of shit got what he deserved.'

'You really believe that, don't you?'

'Absolutely. Nothing but scum. Another notch on the truncheon.'

I reached over and pressed the red button to summon assistance.

'What are you doing?'

Within a few seconds, Detective Inspector Hart walked into the room with a young bobby. 'Hello, John.'

Carver stood up. 'What are you doing here? I'm about to escort Tate to remand.'

Hart shook his head. 'No, you're not, John.'

'Has something happened. I heard they found a body at Woodside Children's Home. Do you need me out there?'

329

'John Edward Carver, I'm placing you under arrest on suspicion of the murder of Liam Winston Truman. You do not have to say anything, but anything you do say will be taken down and may be given in evidence. Do you understand the charge?'

'What the hell are you talking about? This scumbag murdered the Coombs girl. Killed her and tried to commit suicide. You know that. Is this some sort of joke?'

'It's no joke. Turn around and let the officer put on the handcuffs.'

'This has got to be a fucking joke.'

'So you keep saying. Now turn around. We can either do this peacefully, or by force. Your choice, John.'

'Someone tell me this isn't happening.'

I watched him turn to face the wall. The bobby cuffed him.

'You haven't got one shred of evidence. You're wasting police time, Hart. Valuable police time.'

Hart pulled the Dictaphone out of the drawer. 'There are police teams digging up the field at Woodside as we speak. To date, they've unearthed three bodies, including that of Liam Truman. We believe we have sufficient evidence to charge you with his murder. Who knows what else we'll find? We also have reason to believe you are responsible for the deaths of Becky Marie Coombs, Paul Brady, and Sergeant Donald Osbourne. Your car has been impounded, and officers have obtained a search warrant for your home.'

'On what fucking grounds?'

'On the grounds you beat Liam Truman and your first wife to death with a truncheon. I'd like to inform you we have located the truncheon and sent it to the lab for testing. We have also found a book in your property, containing photographs of numerous deceased people.'

'I want my brief.'

'As you wish.'

Carver glared at me. 'I should have made a better job of you.'

'Is that an admission to the attempted murder of Michael Tate, John?' Hart said.

Carver didn't answer. I watched him being led away by the bobby. Hart turned to me. 'You did remember to switch it on, right?'

I fucking hope so. 'Yeah.'

'Good man. We'll be in touch.'

I felt both triumphant and empty. I wanted to cry, but no tears would come. I wanted to run up the stairs and shout from the rooftops, but, well, for obvious reasons! I picked up the photo of Becky, and held it close to my heart, where she had always been and always would be.

CHAPTER 48

John Carver was eventually charged with the murders of Becky, Paul, Donald Osbourne, and Liam. Of the fifteen other bodies recovered from the playing field at Woodside, there was little or no evidence to tie him or anyone else directly to the murders. They found bone fragments on Carver's truncheon belonging to Liam, and a dozen notches carved into the wood, believed to be markings relating to other killings.

The fingerprint found on Liam's glasses, along with Carver's taped confession, were enough to seal his fate for my best friend's murder. Evidence relating to Sergeant Osbourne's murder was found on Carver's car. Fingerprints found at Paul's house, and at my flat, also served to bring charges against him for the murders of Paul and Becky, respectively.

The macabre photo album of his victims was shown to the jury. One woman had to leave the room. Most of the others were visibly shaken. The judge ordered a short break after that.

I felt many emotions watching Carver in the dock. Revulsion. Anger. Hatred. Joy he was finally getting to pay for some of his crimes. But, then, the case took an unexpected turn. Carver agreed to give evidence against the staff at Woodside, most notably Kraft, Reader, and Malloy.

I don't know if he managed to cut some sort of deal, or if he decided the rats could all sink on the ship with him, but Carver sang like a bird. He blew the lid off the whole thing. The abuse. The satanic rituals. The provision of children to paedophiles. Murder. Everything. It was such a sweet moment watching Kraft in the dock; the same man who'd condemned Liam to death in his kangaroo court in the boiler room. Kraft and Malloy both got life, Reader, fifteen years, and several of the other less prominent offenders, sentences ranging from one to five years.

The Judge summed Carver up perfectly. 'You are one of the most despicable men I've had the misfortune to come across. You have not only betrayed the trust of the state, you have betrayed the trust of innocent children, and anyone unfortunate enough to cross your path. I have no hesitation in passing a sentence of life imprisonment. It is my recommendation you shall serve a minimum term of thirty years before being eligible for parole. Take the prisoner down.'

I watched him being led away from the dock by two uniformed policemen. He stared straight ahead, not one flicker of emotion in those pale blue eyes on that gloomy, overcast February morning.

Me, Jimmy and Emily headed off in Jimmy's car to Feelham Cemetery after the trial. Although I had some degree of feeling back in my legs, I still couldn't walk, or put any weight on them. I was being pushed really hard in rehab, bordering on torture at times, but, as yet, my legs were about as useful as chicken wings.

Jimmy and Lucy had kindly offered to put me up indefinitely. I can't begin to express my gratitude to both of them. I truly believe in fate. My going to work at the George Hotel was no happy accident. Me and Jimmy were destined to meet. To finally bring Carver and his cronies to justice.

Emily asked how I was feeling.

'Glad it's over.'

Jimmy looked at me in the rear-view mirror. 'Did you see Carver's face when the Judge addressed him? Looked as if a vampire had drained his blood.'

'I hope he suffers every single minute he's inside. I hope they make his life a fucking misery.'

Emily squeezed my hand. 'At least he can't hurt anyone else now. None of them can.'

I couldn't help wondering how many more Krafts and Carvers were still out there preying on defenceless kids. We pulled up outside Feelham Cemetery. Jimmy got the folding wheelchair out of the boot. They helped me out of the car, and into the seat. The physical world was nowhere near as graceful as my spiritual encounters in the hospital.

Emily retrieved a bunch of chrysanthemums from the passenger seat and handed them to me. The gravel pathway leading to the cemetery was mined with potholes. A fine drizzle fell across the graveyard like mist.

We walked to the last row of graves and stopped at Becky's. It was marked by a simple wooden cross, with her name engraved on a small brass plaque. As soon as I had time, I would choose a proper headstone.

'Do you want to be alone?' Jimmy asked.

'Give me ten minutes.'

Emily reached down and touched my arm.

I couldn't believe Becky was lying in that cold wet earth. Twenty-one forever. The girl who had given my life meaning. I remembered the first time I'd seen her at Paul's house, making sandwiches, and smiling like sunshine. I felt blessed to have known her for the short time I did. She'd taught me so much about self-belief and working hard.

I wished Liam was here to express my feelings in a poem. Put every beat of my heart into words. I looked at that grave, wanting to tell her how she'd saved my life, how my heart had been ripped in two by what Carver had done to her. Done to all of us. That I'd swap places with her in a heartbeat.

The picture of Becky on Brighton Pier now sat in a frame on the sideboard in Jimmy's flat. I would sometimes stare at that picture, willing it to move, come to life, take me back to before everything had gone so wrong. For weeks, nothing happened. Not even a flicker. But,

I'd stopped, and picked that picture up on the way to court this morning. Held it close. I swear she looked right at me and smiled. As if to say, don't worry, it's almost over.

I rested the flowers in my lap and prepared to wheel myself closer to the grave. The wheelchair suddenly bucked and lurched as if engaging in a non-existent gear. At first, I thought it was the wind, but there was only a gentle breeze. And then, the wheelchair moved along the edge of the grave. Slowly, wheels sticking in the mud.

I looked behind me. Nothing. I heard the brake snap on. 'Liam?'

No answer. Invisible hands took the flowers out of my lap. Every hair on my body stood on end as they drifted slowly through the air. I watched, open-mouthed, as they were lowered to the grave. Taken one at a time from their wrapper and laid in front of the wooden cross to spell out two words: Sweet Dreams.

'We got them, Liam,' I said, through my tears. 'We got the bastards.'

There was a slight pause, and then, the wheelchair tipped back and bumped down on the muddy ground.

We got them, Mikey. We got them good.

EPILOGUE

It has now been over forty years since the events at Woodside Children's Home. A lot of water has passed under the bridge since then, you might say. John Carver committed suicide six months after the trial. For what it's worth, he hanged himself with a bedsheet. Part of me was pleased, part of me disappointed he wouldn't spend the rest of his life suffering in his cell, thinking about what he'd done.

Kraft died in prison five years later from a heart attack, and Malloy ten years after that from pancreatic cancer. Reader served twelve years and was released from prison in 1998. He hit a tree in his car two months after his release and died a week later from his injuries. Apparently, he said he'd swerved to miss a hitchhiker standing in the middle of the road. A hitchhiker, with a rucksack on his back, and a mop of frizzy hair. The police believed Reader was suffering from the aftereffects of his head smashing through the windscreen. Talking a load of mumbo-jumbo. Hallucinating.

I couldn't possibly comment!

After months of intensive rehabilitation, I walked again with sticks. No great distance, and I still relied on my wheelchair quite a bit, but at least I was mobile again, and able to lead a purposeful life.

Emily and I were married five years after the trial. No big fuss or fanfare, just a simple registry office wedding, with Jimmy as my best man and Lucy as a witness. We've remained good friends with them until this day.

We bought a small bungalow on the outskirts of Oxford, and have been blessed with two children, Martin and Keith. Martin's an engineer, and Keith is a chief petty officer in the Royal Navy. I retired last year after a career in social work. My job brought me into contact with abused kids. I can only say I did my level best to make sure I listened to every single one of them and acted upon all I could.

I still have Liam's book of poems. It is my most cherished possession. I read it occasionally. Flick through those yellowed pages with their faded words. I draw a lot of comfort from knowing Liam wasn't really killed by Carver. That was just his physical body. His spirit is forever free, soaring high above the mess and confusion of this world.

The flowers, which mysteriously glided out of my hands and onto the grave, stayed fresh for over two months. No water. No vase. Still spelling the words, Sweet Dreams. The greatest work of art I've ever seen.

I don't fear death anymore. For me, it's not final; it's simply the beginning of something better. Something more beautiful. The proof lies in that hospital room, past the emergency door, with its messages, and beyond the abattoir of dreams.

ALSO BY MARK TILBURY

The Revelation Room (Book 1)

The Eyes of The Accused (Book 2)

The Abattoir of Dreams

The Liar's Promise

The Key to Death's Door

You Belong to Me

Torment

The Last One to See Her

A Prayer for the Broken

Printed in Great Britain
by Amazon

87575301R00197